Dear Reader:  **S0-BSF-211**

The novels you've enjoyed over the past years by such authors as Kathleen Woodiwiss, Rosemary Rogers, Johanna Lindsey, Laurie McBain, and Shirlee Busbee are accountable to one thing above all others: Avon has never tried to force authors into any particular mold. Rather, Avon is a publisher that encourages individual talent and is always on the lookout for writers who will deliver *real* books, not packaged formulas.

In 1982, we started a program to help readers pick out authors of exceptional promise. Called "The Avon Romance," the books were distinguished by a ribbon motif in the upper left-hand corner of the cover. Although the titles were by new authors, they were quickly discovered and became known as "the ribbon books."

Now "The Avon Romance" is a regular feature on the Avon list. Each month, you will find historical novels with many different settings, each one by an author who is special. You will not find predictable characters, predictable plots, and predictable endings. The only predictable thing about "The Avon Romance" will be the superior quality that Avon has always delivered in the field of romance!

Sincerely,

WALTER MEADE
President & Publisher

DIANE WICKER DAVIS

CALL BACK THE DAWN

AVON
PUBLISHERS OF BARD, CAMELOT, DISCUS AND FLARE BOOKS

CALL BACK THE DAWN is an original publication of Avon Books.
This work has never before appeared in book form. This work is a
novel. Any similarity to actual persons or events is purely coincidental.

AVON BOOKS
A division of
The Hearst Corporation
1790 Broadway
New York, New York 10019

Copyright © 1985 by Diane Wicker Davis
Published by arrangement with the author
Library of Congress Catalog Card Number: 84-091783
ISBN: 0-380-89703-2

First Avon Printing, August 1985

AVON TRADEMARK REG. U. S. PAT. OFF. AND IN
OTHER COUNTRIES, MARCA REGISTRADA, HECHO EN
U. S. A.

Printed in the U. S. A.

WFH 10 9 8 7 6 5 4 3 2 1

To Patricia Maxwell

SEVEN PINES PLANTATION
Mansfield, Louisiana

February 1859

Chapter 1

DAMASK *hurried up the path from the quarters, closely followed* by Jims. Her small nose was raised, delicate nostrils spread to sniff the crisp air. It was a raw day. Pulsating drumrolls of thunder flowed across the wintry landscape. High above, black, lightning-streaked clouds tumbled across the sky, and the chill wind wailed a mournful dirge through the swaying boughs of the tall pines.

Nothing had happened to spur the joy that welled up inside her, but Damask's fragile, fine-boned face glowed. The tip of her pink tongue flicked out to lick the sharp metallic flavor of the air from her upper lip. So tame a motion as walking was unthinkable! Lifting her faded cotton skirt, she ran up the path, laughing aloud. Jims chuckled. He understood. Not like Lulu, who reminded her she was a lady and ladies did not run and ladies did not laugh for no reason and ladies—Oh! There were a thousand things ladies didn't do!

Damask was too ridden by duty to give in to her surges of pleasure very often, but when she did, it was with a wholehearted, childlike abandon. Graceful leaps carried her up the steps to the porch, where she whirled around, flinging her arms wide. "Isn't it a glorious day?"

Sparkling eyes the nut-brown hue of cinnamon lovingly swept the scene before her. The tongue of pine woods reaching down the hollow to hide the Gin Field. The neat row of cabins shaded beneath those swaying trees. The cookhouse, where Aunt Sarah sang and cooked and sang some more. The Old House, where Gramps lived. Seven Pines. She loved every stick and stone and clump of red earth. Gramps was always saying it wasn't natural the way she loved it. As though it breathed and had a life of its own. But that was exactly the way. Seven Pines. It was the very beat of her heart.

She looked down to see Jims, arms set akimbo to his stocky frame, grinning up at her. "Child, you see them black clouds and that lightning and the wind what about to blow us off? Well, that ain't my notion of no glorious day."

"Smell it, Jims!" Damask demanded eagerly. "Life! You can smell it in the air!"

"Sure enough, child. I can smell it. These wild days like this whips the blood to a fever, and life just boils up inside."

Damask jumped down a step, pressing a kiss atop Jims's shiny pate. "That's because you feel it, too."

While Damask and Jims were entering the house and arguing about whether she would or would not go to bed to rest after a night spent helping to birth a baby in the quarters, a stranger was halting his raw-boned nag in the weeds at the side of the road. Calculating eyes as cold and clear as ice moved within the narrowing thatch of shining black lashes.

Seven Pines. The wind banged the faded sign against the snake-rail fence that marched its zigzag course beside the Mansfield-Logansport Road: a grand name for that dusty wagon path winding through the hilly pine-forested uplands. There was little to impress the casual visitor; even less to impress this man. The grass was faded and dry, a dusty dun color. The wind-whipped fields were covered with the bare skeletal stalks of cotton and corn. Barn and stable and corn cribs sagged like weary old men.

The threatening clouds crashed and cracked with a booming roll that rippled away to the horizon. The nag pranced with fear, her tired brown eyes rolling until the man spoke, his voice soft and deep and calm.

His big hand was gentle, rubbing and patting her neck, and he continued to talk in a low rumble while his curious gaze climbed the easy slope rising from the road. The house rested on the crest, shaded by, he counted them, seven towering loblolly pines. It was a large house, broad and deep and unpretentious. Two stories high with a cypress-shingled roof broken by large red-brick chimneys and a pair of dormers that seemed to eye him with a cheerful benevolence. A set of deep porches encircled both stories with foot-square columns of hand-hewn cypress rising to the roof. A simple fence of upright bars with a horizontal railing filled the spaces between the columns around the second story. Wide doors and tall, broad windows led onto the porches.

The house needed paint. Patches of shingles were missing. A second-story shutter hung askew, and even from that distance, he could see the sag in the second tread of the broad center steps. Yet with all its imperfections and neglect, the house and land seemed to be waiting with an air of welcome.

A long-forgotten sense of peace and homecoming invaded him to attack the inner sanctuary of solitude that was his bulwark against a savage world. For the briefest of moments the hard line of his lips softened and the icy brilliance of his eyes warmed. It is only a place, he reminded himself firmly. Land. Buildings. People. A means to an end.

The parlor was empty. Surely Jims had said he left the stranger there. The creaking of a weak plank on the porch drew Damask's eyes to the side door. She smiled. Did he find the lure of the stormy weather as irresistible as she did? Crossing the room with her light, quick step, she paused to peek through the rectangular glass light.

He was out there. One lean brown hand was braced high on a weathered cypress column, the other drawn into a fist resting on his narrow waist, his feet, encased in black leather boots, were planted firmly on the foot-wide unpainted planks. A gust of wind lifted a gleaming wave of blue-black hair from the lean dark face framed by the roiling gloom of thunderclouds and the stark relief of a snowy ruffled shirtfront. His skin was smooth and ruddy, shadowed darker in the hollow between high cheekbones and forceful jaw. Arched black brows broke a classic profile. Thick sooty lashes cloaked his eyes. The ridging of a strange curving scar, beginning at the tip of his brow, crossing the temple and ending at the cheekbone, gleamed white against the darkness of his skin. There was a suggestion of strength and purpose in his stance, and a self-confident set to his shoulders.

What, Damask wondered, could he possibly want with her brother? The porcelain knob was cold beneath her hand as she swung the door open.

Only his head turned. Ice-blue eyes, outlined by a ring of dark sapphire, captured Damask's startled gaze. He stirred, the fist uncurling, his hand dropping from the column. The thicket of black lashes closed about his vivid eyes until nothing was left but glowing pinpricks of light.

Damask's polite smile of welcome trembled, and broadened to a smile of radiance that birthed a saucy dimple at the corner of her lips. He was a stranger to her, yet, there was something. Familiarity, as though she were meeting an old friend.

"Welcome to Seven Pines. I am Damask Downing."

For a heart-stopping moment, he stared, seemingly transfixed. Abruptly, the curious, compelling gleam in his eyes flickered and died while one brow lifted in a questioning arch. "Miss Downing, I am Bram Rafferty."

There was warmth and depth to the basso rumble with its hint of an Irish lilt. And something else. Challenge. He expected her to know his name. Not only that. He expected her to react unpleasantly to it.

The warm glow in Damask's eyes chilled. Jims had told her he was here to see Wade. But her brother was gone. He had risen with the morning sun, a remarkable occurrence in itself. He had been gay and laughing, almost frenzied in his desire to leave for Acadian Star. He had business to discuss with Uncle Harry and Cousin Garnett Lee, he told her. The business? Nothing a drab little country mouse would understand, he laughed—and rushed off without so much as a cup of coffee to see him through a full day's journey.

Damask's heart sank to her slippers. Wade knew this man

was coming. He knew and he left because he had never faced an unpleasant scene, whether of his own doing or not.

"Please, Mr. Rafferty, won't you come inside. I begin to feel the cool of the day."

He followed her into the parlor, declining her offer of a chair. As she seated herself, his eyes bored into her as though she were a curiosity or a puzzle he had to solve. A cheerful fire snapped and crackled, sharing its warmth and light, but it did not dispel the gloom beyond the hearth or the desolate moaning of the wind through the eaves. Thunder boomed overhead and Damask shivered. Winding her fingers tightly together, she waited for him to speak.

"You have no idea why I am here, do you, Miss Downing?"

"No, sir, I do not."

He said nothing, but his arched brows flattened, drawing down over his eyes. The scar on his temple began throbbing with life, and he turned upon her with an intensity that thrust her back into the soft plush upholstery.

"I am a gambler, Miss Downing," he cracked out harshly. "Known professionally as Black Irish Rafferty. Your brother's recent visit to the City was a long stint at the gaming tables."

Damask sighed with relief. A debt of honor. It must be. And a substantial one to bring this gambler up from the City. But Wade, himself, had told her he disliked gambling and went along only when his friends insisted. So it couldn't be too bad. Certainly no worse than those bad railroad and canal investments or the racehorse that had pulled up lame. She had found the money to pay for those. It wouldn't be easy, but she would pay this, too.

Her brittle gaze met the gambler's. "I assume my brother has lost a sum and you are here to collect?"

"Yes. Seven Pines. Lock, stock, and barrel."

Damask's expression congealed. Lock, stock . . . Seven Pines! An icy blade of fear stabbed through her. "I don't believe it!" she shouted, bolting upright. "My brother would never—"

"Damask! Damask! Jims, let me by! Damask!" A small girl with bouncing dusty gold ringlets and sad brown eyes burst through the shadowed archway hugging a cloth doll with a drooping china head. "Miss Pettigrew is bro-oke!"

Damask raised her bloodless face to her sister, wincing away from the screeching wail. "Tessa," she begged softly, fingertips pressing against her suddenly throbbing temples. "I have a guest. Could we wait to fix Miss Pettigrew?"

It was a futile request. She knew it. Oh, God! Seven Pines, lost!

"*No!*" Tessa screamed and stomped her foot before lurching across the room to fling herself to her knees beside Damask. "Look! She's bleeding!"

The doll was thrust into Damask's face. Her hands rose automatically to close around it while she stared dully at the cotton spilling from a gaping shoulder seam. "Tessa, please—"

"She's blee-eeding!! If you don't fix her, she'll die like Mama and Papa and I'll have to bury her in the dirt!" Huge tears rolled in a grief-stricken cascade across Tessa's cheeks, her small hands clasping together prayerfully. "I don't want Miss Pettigrew to die!"

"No, love," Damask said softly, clutching the doll to her breast as though it were her beloved Seven Pines she was protecting, "of course you don't."

"She's gonna die! She is!"

"No, Tessa, I promise . . ." Her voice cracked with strain and she felt a dewy sweat breaking across her forehead. "I promise, Miss Pettigrew will be fine. Hush now, love. You can help me. I will need—"

"I did it!" Tessa's eyes brightened as she dug into her grubby apron pocket, withdrawing needle, thread, and scissors. "Look!"

"Oh, Tessa." Damask stroked her cheek. "That was very smart. You knew just what Miss Pettigrew needed."

Tessa squirmed beneath the praise, rewarding Damask with an adoring look and an imperious, "Hurry!"

"I will, sweet." A glance promising a reckoning slid the gambler's way. "This will only take a moment."

Bram nodded his acquiescence. Kneading the knotted tendons on his neck, he watched Damask thread the needle and knot the thread with an ease that spoke of both practice and self-control. A hard-won effort, those steady hands and that cool facade. He was forced to admire it, but he didn't like it. He had expected . . . no, *wanted* her to be more like her brother. It would have made things . . . easier.

Her face had not regained its color. Pale ivory skin blended with the froth of wispy champagne-colored curls escaping the massive bun to form a halo around her heart-shaped face. Dark, finely arched brows and lush dark lashes framing her expressive cinnamon eyes were a startling contrast. Bram's expression hardened. She was as dainty and delicate as a Dresden figurine. Not at all the kind of woman he preferred. But what did it matter?

Jesus! he thought with roiling disgust. Why was he surprised that Downing had slipped away without preparing her? A moment's thought and he would have known to expect it. He had met men like Downing. Weak. Their very weakness a formidable strength.

"Damask," Tessa's stage whisper hissed, her eyes rolling around to touch the stranger, then leaping away, "who is that man?"

The needle hovered over the age-yellowed muslin. "Tessa, this is Mr. Rafferty, a . . . an acquaintance of Wade's. Mr. Rafferty, this is my sister, Tessa."

"How do you do, Miss Downing." Bram acknowledged the introduction with a courtly bow.

She giggled. "You can call me Tessa. Everyone does. Miss Pettigrew wore out. *People* wear out when they get old, too," she informed him. "That's what Gramps said. He wore out. Did you know that?"

"No, I didn't."

"C'mon." Tessa hopped up and caught Bram's hand, tugging him to the side door. "Look! That's Gramps under the green apple tree. Bif just took him out. See that? He's got a chair with *wheels* on it. He lets me ride sometimes. It's fun.''

"Tessa, Miss Pettigrew is all stitched."

Swooping on Damask with a glad cry, Tessa clutched her doll in a tight hug and examined the neat seam.

Damask's throat ached from the effort of holding in her fury while she cast about for some treat that would lure Tessa from the parlor. A growing desperation fed the chaos of her thoughts until she remembered. "Tessa, there is a surprise for you in my room. Have Jims take the red box from the top of my armoire. Then you can take it out to show Gramps."

Tessa squealed, "A 'prise!" and was gone in a flurry of dancing skirts.

Damask waited for the clattering rush of footsteps to die away. "I don't know what you expect to accomplish with this charade, Mr. Rafferty, but I know my brother would not gamble away Seven Pines!"

"I have his signed note, if you would care to see it."

The paper crackled a warning as she opened it and smoothed it out. It was true! The note was Wade's. No one else could have imitated his curiously unformed script: here, round, childishly formed letters; further along, crabbed and cramped; then a barely decipherable scrawl ending in the well-practiced swaggering signature.

The paper fluttered to her lap. Despair overrode even her burgeoning compassion for Wade. Seven Pines. Home and heart and soul. Gone. Everything. Her stunned gaze moved across the threadbare carpet, whose faded flower pattern had once been as vibrantly rich as her childhood in those golden years before her parents' death. Dismally, she tried to imagine a life removed from the land she loved. Where would they go? What would they do?

How could it all have been lost on the turn of a card? It was so unjust that the will to fight replaced her despair. Her eyes snapped open and her head jerked up, color rushing into her cheeks. That a gambler should now own Seven

Pines! A parasite sucking the sustenance of another man's toil!

"Wade would not have wagered Seven Pines unless he was pushed into it! I want to know why he did, Mr. Rafferty!"

"Greed, Miss Downing."

"His . . . or yours?"

Rage leapt into his eyes and as quickly died away. "Believe what you will."

The compulsion to tear the note to shreds and order Black Irish Rafferty off Seven Pines was so strong that Damask curled her hands into fists, crumpling the paper in defiance. Delicate bluish lids closed over her burning eyes and her head bowed beneath the weight of her rage.

Anything else! She could have found a way. She always had! Anything but this! To lose it all! It was . . .

No, it wasn't unbearable. She had survived worse with the death of her parents. She would survive this. And she would do it with dignity, if nothing else. It was done. It couldn't be undone, only . . . accepted. But it was hard. So hard. Her thudding pulse slowed, the ragged breathing eased.

Calmly, Damask smoothed the crumpled note before folding it into its formerly neat quarters and extending it toward the gambler. "When do you want us out of the house?"

"I do not."

"I . . . I don't understand."

"No doubt. Your brother was to have prepared you, but I'm not surprised he shirked that task."

Damask's eyes flickered, the pattern of gold forming an aureole around the black iris widening until her eyes were the bright hot color of molten gold. "I will not stand for any criticism of Wade!"

He appeared unaffected by her outburst. "You may not be so ready to defend him when we have concluded our business."

"Please! I would have this done as quickly as possible! I find your presence offensive, sir!"

"Do you?" he drawled. "That may prove difficult for you, Miss Downing. You see, your brother feels that the best solution to the problem you find yourselves in is that you and I be married."

"Married!" The word was a thread of horror trailing from Damask's blanched lips. "Wade would never suggest anything so outrageous!"

"I assure you, the thought was his."

Damask leaned forward, clenched fists upon her knees. "You do agree that it is out of the question."

"No, I do not."

The need to move, to escape those cold dispassionate eyes, propelled Damask from her seat. She jerked to a halt at the fireplace, holding out her icy hands to the flames. *Wade! Even you could not ask this much of me!* She breathed deeply, fighting a shudder of revulsion, sucking in the oak-scented heat while trying to bring some order to her turbulent thoughts.

Tessa. Gramps. Wade. They were all dependent on her. And her people? What would happen to them under the gambler's thumb? The oldest of them had served three generations of Downings. None had ever known another master. The gambler was unused to the responsibilities of running a plantation. Would he be too harsh? Even cruel? Could she walk away from her people, leaving them helpless in the clutches of a man who might be pitiless? If she stayed—Oh, God! Her stomach churned at the thought— would she be able to thwart his harshness? Or would she be forever caught by it, too?

Her eyes, muddied with misery, lifted to the daguerreotype of her parents, nestled among the family mementos on the heavy oak mantel. Guilt, the old aching guilt, settled about her like a shroud. *I had to prove it, didn't I, Papa? I had to show you I could do it, and I did. I did, Papa. Until now.*

Damask swallowed the bitter gall of defeat. Black Irish

Rafferty. That's what he said he was called. Black Irish Rafferty.

Her lips twisted as she jerked around. "A gambler! Battening off the fruits of another's labor!" Her voice was guttural with loathing. "I would starve before being chained to you for life! And what good would it do? How long would it be before you, too, lost Seven Pines at the tables?"

She beat against a stolid wall of outward indifference. His face remained calm, only the pale eyes darkening to blend with the ring of sapphire.

"You need not worry that Seven Pines will be wagered again," he said, his voice mild but threaded with steel. "I am finished with gambling professionally, and I am very much aware of the value of Seven Pines and what it represents. I will not jeopardize it in any way."

What it represents. Home and heart and soul. To her, it was life. To him? "What does Seven Pines represent to you, Mr. Rafferty?"

Disconcertingly, his steady gaze wavered. The scar writhed to life and his darkened gaze dulled to a lightless, flat sapphire. Had her question sliced across a raw nerve?

"Perhaps, Miss Downing," he began, his voice so calm that Damask was left to wonder if she had imagined that brief flash of pain, "you would be willing to starve, though I believe you would find life—even a life with a gambler—preferable to a death that is slow, painful, and degrading."

Damask's eyes raked him, her delicate nostrils quivering as though she smelled something inutterably foul.

"Are you willing to watch Tessa and your grandfather starve? Can you possibly believe your brother is capable of providing for all of you?" He pressed on inexorably. "And you? What would you do? Governess? Seamstress? Companion to a complaining old woman? The wages would barely keep you. They would not stretch to feed, clothe, and shelter your family.

"You need me, Miss Downing. And I need you. Were I to put you and your family off of Seven Pines, I would be forever ostracized in this community. Frankly, I care very little what people think of me, but it would make things needlessly . . . awkward.''

Awkward! Her fingers curved into claws. He was destroying her life to save himself from *awkward* moments!

"If you marry me, none need know that your brother lost Seven Pines. I don't think word of it will travel from the City to Mansfield. We can have a mock sale to spare him further humiliation.''

Humiliation. And it would be. Wade wasn't as strong as she was. He was . . . sensitive. So easily hurt. Not like her. He always said she was as tough as boot leather, and she supposed she must be. She could pick up the pieces and go on. He couldn't. The humiliation would kill him.

"If you decide to accept my offer," he continued, "your life will go on much as it does now. You will never need worry about your family. I give you my word you will know every comfort it is within my means to provide.''

"Your word!" she scoffed bitterly. "You ask me to take the word of a common—''

"You don't know me, Miss Downing," he cut in angrily. "You may find my word better than that of your brother!''

"Your promises are fragile things, Mr. Rafferty! If I accept this offer, and find your word worthless, it will be too late! You come here expecting—''

"I expect nothing!" he growled. "I offer you a . . . a business arrangement, if you will.''

A glimmer of hope brought an alert gleam to Damask's eyes. "A business arrangement? And what would you expect of me as a wife?''

"I would expect you to be a wife in every way.''

The uncompromising tone sent her hopes plummeting. *In every way.* The unwelcome vision of just what that meant sickened her. It could have been so different. It would have been so different with Hunt Marlowe, who had loved her since she was in short skirts and he was in short pants. Hunt Marlowe, who was even now establishing his law practice in the City in hopes she would join him—someday. Someday when Wade decided it was time he took his rightful place as the master of Seven Pines. Would that day ever have come? If it had, her gaze moved to the dark curtains covering a window while her mind's eye looked beyond to *her* land, could she have given it up?

"Miss Downing"—the persistent, steadfast voice with its trace of a lilt pulled her attention from her own thoughts— "many marriages are arranged between complete strangers, and most are able to reach . . . companionable arrangements. Our aims will be one: to see Seven Pines grow and prosper. Your family will be provided for, your brother will be protected. In return, I ask for only one thing: a son."

Damask stared at him in mute horror. The life he so calmly planned was too hideous to contemplate.

"Companionable arrangements!" Grief choked her voice and tightened her chest in a vise of pain. "You speak of my life! My life! A life that could be very long! I am twenty-one years old! Twenty-one, Mr. Rafferty! How many years will I have? How many barren, empty years spent to put food in the mouths of my family and a roof over their heads?"

"Damask! Damask!" Tessa's high sweet voice throbbed with happiness as she burst into the parlor waving her doll garbed in its new bright red frock. "Miss Pettigrew loves her—"

"Tessa! Not now!" Damask commanded angrily.

The laughter stopped midkey, joy fading from the innocent eyes, which filled with the rapid tears of a child. Tessa's cry climbed the scale as she retreated to the hall, closely followed by Damask.

"Tessa, I'm sorry. So sorry."

They sank together on the first tread of the stairs, hugging and weeping, their babbling apologies indistinguishable. Tessa's childish tears were soon ended, but Damask, grieving for the death of a long cherished dream, could not stop. She cried in great shuddering sobs that frightened Tessa who drew away from her with wide terrified eyes.

"Damask?" she whispered uncertainly.

Damask didn't know when Tessa moved, nor did she feel the steel-tendoned arms that lifted her gently from her crouch. "Where is her room? No, Tessa," Bram said sternly, "wait here. I'll return in a few minutes. Jims, her room!"

He climbed the stairs easily, the sobbing girl hardly more of a burden than thistledown in the cradle of his arms. Jims pointed to her door before hurrying away, and Bram entered Damask's spare, but daintily feminine bedchamber. He was pleasantly surprised at the simplicity of furniture and ornaments, being more accustomed to beruffled and bric-a-brac-cluttered boudoirs. Only one thing gave him a pang of displeasure—or perhaps it was a twinge of conscience.

Reclining against the pillow was Miss Pettigrew's twin, her round empty blue eyes reminding Bram that Damask was young and fresh and innocent. Frowning heavily, he carried her to the bed, throwing the doll facedown on the far side as he laid Damask on the crocheted coverlet.

He turned to leave, took a step toward the door, then halted. A muttered curse warmed the air, and he swung back to glare at her as though she clung to him, physically preventing his escape. His left hand balled into a fist pressing into the palm of his right hand, the fingers tracing the curving path of a puckered scar across the back of his left hand.

Huddled into a ball of misery, Damask's sobbing continued unabated. The sound shuddered through Bram until his steady gaze wavered, his expression of assurance faded. If only she were older! If only she were some pinch-faced, purse-lipped . . .

No, not that, he thought with a wry twist of his lips. Then he would have been the one shouting about how barren his life would be!

He turned to leave, knowing there was nothing he could say. As he descended the stairs, a tiny bird of a woman with wrinkled black skin and a blacker scowl rushed up them. A muttered "devil gambling man" drifted back to him, and Bram paused then continued down to Jims.

"Miss Tessa be waiting for you in the parlor, sir."

Tessa, small and forlorn, sat stiffly erect on the sofa, Miss Pettigrew clutched tightly in her arms. Brown eyes with that fathomless innocence of a child rose to Bram. "You made Damask cry," she said solemnly.

"Yes, Tessa, I did." He lowered himself to the sofa. "She is upset by something I told her, but she'll feel better soon."

Tessa rested her cheek atop Miss Pettigrew's china head to think this over. Beside her Bram waited patiently.

"Are you sorry you made her cry?"

"Yes."

"Damask never cries. It scares me," she whispered.

Bram took her hand and set his finger beneath her chin, raising her face. "You shouldn't be frightened. You cry sometimes, don't you?" She nodded. "It makes you feel better, doesn't it?" Again that solemn little nod. "It will be the same for Damask. There is nothing for you to fear because of her tears."

"She'll feel better?"

"Yes."

Tessa smiled, her small face beaming as she leaned toward Bram. "Miss Pettigrew likes you," she confided. "She says you talk to us and don't treat us like babies."

Bram gifted Tessa with one of his rare smiles. "Tell Miss Pettigrew that I like her, too. I'd be pleased if you'll both be my friends while I'm here at Seven Pines."

Chapter 2

BRAM waited for the next luminescent flash to read the face of his pocket watch. Just after midnight. He set it aside and swung out of bed, lighting a long thin cigar before pacing to the window. The promised storm had arrived with a roaring north wind hurling huge droplets of rain against the porch in a steady drumming beat.

It was over. The words belled in his mind with weary astonishment. Nineteen years of subordinating every need to the driving ambition that gave him no peace and no rest. Nineteen years of work, hunger, desperation. It had been raining that night, too. The night his ambition was born.

The memory was so acute that Bram's nape crawled with the sensation of icy sleet trickling down his neck. Goosebumps paraded across the ribs that once were poorly protected by a ragged woolen coat. The fear was alive again, as it had been when he had run through the deserted, night-blackened streets of New Orleans. He flinched at the re-membered echo of hoofbeats. The scars on his temple and hand throbbed as though they were freshly cut. Throbbed as they had when he vaulted a fence and shimmied across the muddy ground under the ice-burdened branches of a legustrum and discovered a new world, a hope, a dream. Looming out of the widow's veil of darkness was a mansion with tall white pillars and a deep portico. In every light-drenched window was a wreath of holly with a burning candle.

Christmas. Christmas wasn't for boys like him. It was for men like the one who alighted from a carriage before that broad door. A man with a fur-lined cloak of blue and shining boots. A man with a mellow, fluid laugh that pierced the shroud of darkness and struck deep within the soul of his secret audience. A man whose imperious knock commanded the opening of that door, magically spilling music and cheer into the night. Then it closed. The man was gone, unaware that a boy lay beneath the legustrum with his clothes freezing to the ground while he muttered, "Someday . . . Someday . . ."

That vision remained as crisp and clear, every detail as vivid to the man of twenty-nine as it had been to that boy of ten. Now, the dream born on that long ago night was realized. Not by his own work and sweat, but by chance.

Bram inhaled deeply of the cigar and listened to the drumming beat of the rain. It carried him back to a more recent time. Wade Downing's slender, elegant hand with long pale fingers drumming restlessly on the green baize cloth. Watch those fingers: the pause when the hand was good, the bland shallow blue eyes raised while the drumming increased; the slump when the hand was bad, the drumming slow, the eyes disappointed.

Jesus! Downing was a fool! Throwing away everything a man could work for a lifetime to achieve! A child would have known to call his bluff!

He wasn't sure who had been more stunned by the result of the game. Later, in his painfully neat room in Mrs. Murphy's boarding house, as he sat slumped in a chair reading and rereading the note that made him the owner of Seven Pines, Wade came with his offer of marriage to his sister. A perfect package. The land and a wife. Not just any wife, but a Downing with family ties to the wealthy and powerful Kinloch Scarborough and the French Tureauds. The poor, hungry Irish boyeen who had watched his parents' dreams wither in the fiery test of America would found a dynasty of Raffertys who would take this new land and mold their own destiny.

The dream seemed so real, its accomplishment so simple while he listened to Downing's hesitant voice and watched the furtive slide of his pale eyes. Suppressing a sharp sense of discomfort, Bram agreed. After all, it was the perfect solution for everyone.

Only, it didn't seem so perfect after he had met Damask. Or maybe it seemed too perfect. She was nothing like her brother. There was no nasal whine in the soft, musical voice that had greeted him. There was no spare angularity to her exquisite face. There was nothing vapid in her gentle smile with its surprising gift of a saucy dimple. Her luminous eyes were alive with intelligence, and he sensed in her a stubborn strength that might yield like a reed in the wind, but would forever rise up undamaged when the storm was over. She was the dream he refused to dream. Yet he could not deny the feelings she roused in him. Hungers he thought long dead.

At supper her grandfather had suggested that they delay any decision, letting it be known Bram was visiting with a view to buying Seven Pines. It would give them time to grow accustomed to their change in fortune, and would give Damask time to pursue an alternative to his offer. Any alternative. Bram could only hope she would fine one.

He stared out over the scene illuminated by the tongues of lightning licking the earth. He could see the cookhouse and, farther back, in a grove of sheltering pines near the foot of the gently rolling downslope, the quarter street lined by a twin row of slave cabins.

A clap of thunder broke directly overhead. The window panes rattled and a jagged bolt of lightning blazed a white-hot path to the heart of a tall pine. The tree exploded with a sound like a cannon shot . . .

Damask's eyes popped open to inky darkness. She lay rigidly still, listening to her racing heart. Something was wrong. She knew it. A sound. A sound had yanked her from her exhausted sleep.

Heavy layers of covers flew. Slender legs flashed and she was up, shaking hands exploring the bedside table. Her fingers encountered the icy-cold leaf-shaped silver saucer of the candlestick. She scrambled for matches in the drawer, and lit the wick. She pulled on her worn flannel wrapper, snatched up the candle, and rushed into the hall, protecting the flame with one hand.

"Miss Downing?"

"Mr. Rafferty! I heard a noise!"

"Lightning struck a tree at the quarters. It has fallen toward the cabins." ·

"The cabins!" A terrible fear struck her, and she whirled to rush for the stairs.

"Miss Downing! It's too dangerous for you to go out in this storm!" His thumping steps followed her. "I'll see to whatever needs to be done!"

Damask rounded the corner at the bottom of the stairs. Lulu was there, and Jims, struggling into an oiled canvas slicker. She shoved the candlestick into Lulu's hand and reached for a slicker hanging on a peg beside the back door. Bram Rafferty's tanned hand closed around hers, trapping it over the peg, and she threw him a glance of furious impatience. "I will be needed!"

His grip tightened. "I'll take care of it."

The flat statement brought Damask's head up with a snap. "These are still my people, Mr. Rafferty!"

"No, Miss Downing," he said, his voice as calm and implacable as the expression in the icy depths of his eyes, "they are my people now."

Damask heard Lulu's low mutter and Jims's restless movement, and her heart ached with the weight of the decision she was about to make. The gambler owned them now because he owned Seven Pines, but they belonged to her. The land and the people were hers because she loved them and had worked for them and had kept them safe for as long as she could. And she would never give them up—no matter what the price.

She drew herself up, shoulders thrown back in the worn

flannel wrapper, sleep-mussed braid swaying below her hips, all rigid pride and determination. "Not if I am your wife."

His hand convulsed around hers in a painful grip and his glittering eyes narrowed to meet her own. Did she imagine it, or did his dark skin pale a shade?

"And will you be?"

There was a frayed edge to the question. Why? Did he approach this marriage with the same distaste as she? If he did, what hope could they have for ever reaching those *companionable arrangements* he mentioned? Did it matter what was between them? She was doing this for Seven Pines as he was. That would be her happiness and her reward.

"Yes." She heaved an inward sigh of relief that her voice sounded more resolute than she felt.

"When?" he asked and frowned, as though angry with himself for asking.

A brief uncertainty shook her. When? She hadn't thought that far ahead. She only knew she wanted to delay as long as possible. "June." She swallowed hard. June. It seemed far, far away on this stormy winter night.

"June," he bit out with a brief nod of his head, and moved her hand aside to lift the slicker and pull it over his head. "Wait here. I'll let you know what has happened as soon as I can."

"I thought we just decided—"

"That these are still your people. That doesn't mean I will allow you out on a night like this!" he snapped impatiently, and nodded for Jims to open the door.

"Allow!" Damask shouted. "Who do you think has been going out on nights like this before you came along?"

"Then you should be glad to have a rest." His solemn gaze touched her briefly before he plunged out into the storm.

Jims shrugged his shoulders, giving her a sympathetic look before he followed.

"Did you hear that . . . that wretched man?" Damask blazed at Lulu as she charged for the door.

"What you doing, child?"

Hand on the knob, Damask swiveled back. "Mr. Rafferty may as well learn right now that I will do what is right, his wishes to the contrary!"

Battered by the solid wall of wind and rain, Damask slipped and slid down the mucky clay path to the quarters, moving ever slower as the breath was sucked from her lips. She almost wished . . .

But she would die before admitting it, even to herself. A cannonade of thunder rumbled around her. Brilliant flashes of lightning patterned the sky as she reached the quarter street at last, wet to the skin and shivering uncontrollably.

"Lord! Lord, help us! My baby! My Sim!"

Azaline's cries rent the night, sending a frisson of fear along Damask's spine. She froze.

The cabin, one side crushed beneath the outspread branches of the smouldering tree, was ablaze. Flames wavered through spraddled cracks in walls and roof.

She slogged through the mud to the men gathered at the opposite end of the cabin. "Jims! Jims, what's happened?"

"Miss Damask! Lord, help us! Sim be in there! Master Bram, he go in after him, and when he do, that fire just blaze up! Johnson and Dread done axe they way through this wall, and Dread gone in after 'em."

"*He* went in after Sim?" She pushed the wet strings of hair from her eyes and turned to the gaping hole in the wall. Why? Why would he do it? Sim meant nothing to him.

The rough soles of Dread's feet inched out. Johnson caught him around the ankles and pulled. They fell out in a tangle of arms and legs: Dread, Bram Rafferty, and Sim. Azaline brushed by Damask, lifted her son, and cradled him to her while Johnson wrapped them both in his massive arms.

"Dread, how is Mr. Rafferty?" Damask shouted above

the roar of wind and rain as she fell to her knees beside Bram, who lay motionless. Behind her, Sim choked and began to cry, and she breathed a sigh of relief.

"Dunno, Miss Damask, he don't look like he coming to."

"We be seeing about that!" Johnson boomed and released his wife and son. Bending over the prone man, he lifted him to a sitting position, and proceeded to pound on his back with the flat of his hand. "Gotta knock that smoke plumb outa him." Thwack. "Plumb out!" Thwack.

Damask saw Rafferty's lashes flutter and reached out to touch Johnson's arm. "That's enough. I think he's coming around."

Bram shuddered, choked, and began to cough in terrible racking spasms.

"That's good," Johnson rumbled. "Git shut of that smoke."

Waving clumps of black hair were plastered to his forehead as Bram raised his face to the icy rain as though he needed the needlelike sting to prove that he was alive. Why? she thought. Why did he risk his life for a slave child that meant nothing to him? Perhaps . . .

The pressure of a slit-eyed glare killed the quivering birth pangs of a tender thought.

"What are you doing here?"

His voice cracked on the last word and he began to cough again, a cough that gave Damask a sneaking satisfaction that shamed her. Still, she couldn't help thinking it served him right for bellowing like a wounded bull!

"I told you to wait at the house for your own good!"

"This is my good, Mr. Rafferty."

The yellow glow of the bedside lamp cast Lulu's shadow high on the wall where Bram watched it twitch in self-righteous disapproval. "Miss Damask say her be here after her git dry and change." Her piquant face frowned her dislike as she turned aside to set the tray with its bowl of oint-

ment and clean cotton wrappings on the table. She then
stretched to her full five feet and clasped her hands at her
waist. "Jims told me what you done in the quarters. That be
a fine thing," she said as though reciting a lesson learned by
rote.

Bram looked up from his steaming coffee, the suggestion
of a smile lurking around his mouth. Lulu was a tiny birdlike
woman with bright boot-button eyes and a shockingly deep
voice with full, ringing, authoritative tones. Obviously, she
begrudged the very breath that gave substance to her words.
The impulse to smile died. He had made an enemy of her,
and Bram suspected that Lulu's opinions, once formed,
were carved in granite.

"Don't praise me too highly. If I'd stopped to think about
it, I wouldn't have been such a damn fool."

She sniffed, as if to say that was what she thought all
along. "Let me see that leg."

He set the coffee aside and began rolling up his trouser
leg.

"No, sir!" she barked. "Shuck them things! Can't have
that wrapping git wet when we done. That's right. Now,
hop in that bed and cover yourself. Miss Damask be coming
directly. That's it. Now stick that leg out here."

Damask joined them as Lulu was tying the cloth bandage
around the burn on his calf. Bram, wincing as she roughly
jerked the knot tight, heartily hoped that Damask would
tend the burn on his arm. His gaze strayed to the corner of
her lips where a tiny indentation hinted at the dimple. Had
he imagined it? The warmth of her smile. What would it be
like . . .

"Lulu, go up to the attic and check the pots. We may
have some new leaks. I'll be along when I finish with Mr.
Rafferty."

Lulu's sparse eyebrows scaled the narrow expanse of her
forehead. "Ain't leaving you by yourself with this devil
gambling man!"

"Lulu!" Damask gasped and caught her arm, hauling her

out into the hall. "How could you?" The horrified hiss reached Bram clearly. "We know nothing about him! Don't you understand that he is your master now? He has the power of life and death over you! And you insult him! I swear, if you do such a thing again I won't wait for him to punish you! I'll do it!"

"Child, you know you wouldn't do no such thing!"

"Oh, yes I would. Do you think I could stand by while he gives you a beating? No! If you are insolent to him again, I'll send you to work in the cookhouse with Aunt Sarah! Now, go check the pots!"

Bram heard the sound of Lulu's footsteps recede, and Damask edged back into the room, her eyes everywhere except on him.

"Lulu was my father's mammy, Mr. Rafferty. She has raised us all and is very protective. Too much so sometimes, I'm afraid."

He noted the nervously twined hands drawn to her breast, then his eyes climbed to her face, drawn tight with a fear that seemed to settle in his own chest like a lump of lead. What was it about her? Her strength and loyalty? The gentleness a secret part of him yearned to know? What was it that tugged at his resisting heart?

"Her feelings are honest. I can respect that," he said more harshly than he intended. "You need not fear that she will be ill-used at my hands."

"Thank you." She said the words reluctantly, and Bram knew that it was hard for her to show him appreciation when Lulu was hers. Loved, respected, obeyed, but hers, nonetheless.

Her hands were deft and gentle, smoothing the greasy ointment over his seared skin. Bram relaxed, the warmth of the fire seeping into him, the fragile feminine scent of violets wafting about him. The sense of homecoming, of peace crept upon him. The controlled line of his mouth softened and the icy hue of his eyes warmed as they raised to meet her searching gaze.

"Why? Why did you do it?"

"Do what?" he asked, displeased at the husky roughness of his own voice. That was a tone saved for another kind of woman, not this one.

"You could have been killed, and Sim means nothing to you," she said, her forehead knitted thoughtfully.

The statement shattered his peaceful mood. The soft curve of his mouth thinned into a hard line. Simple humanity wouldn't be motive enough for a man like him. He wouldn't be expected to act to save a child from burning to death.

"Nothing, Miss Downing? Sim is a slave, an investment. Money, Miss Downing! Money!"

He expected her to turn and flee from him in horror. Instead, she stood her ground with that thoughtful expression unchanged.

"I don't believe that was your only reason, Mr. Rafferty. I don't believe it, and I don't know why."

And she still didn't know why the following afternoon. But, by then, she no longer cared. He had demanded to see the accounts, then refused her offer to explain them! He would ask if he needed help, he said. Perhaps she would like to remain nearby, *just in case,* he added, throwing a sop her way. She wanted to storm out, but gritted her teeth and settled down with her knitting, a tedious task at the best of times. Those accounts were hers. The lovingly kept visible proof of her work. She wouldn't leave them to him willingly.

The needles clicked a resentful rhythm as she flayed him with a dark look. There he sat. Master of the house! In Papa's chair! At Papa's desk! Scrawling with Papa's pen! Knit, purl, knit, purl . . . It was infuriating! Knit, knit . . . The fast-paced creaking of the rocker lurched to a halt.

Across the room Bram laid aside the pen and flexed the cramp between his shoulders, as he studied the neat columns spread before him. Seven Pines was a profitable plantation, yet it was indebted to the tune of fifteen thousand dollars. A small fact that Downing had failed to mention. And for good reason. No one would accept it as surety for a wager if they knew it was collateral for a prior loan.

What a mess! So what were his choices? Absently, he dug into the pocket of his frock coat draped across the arm of the chair. He could tear up Wade Downing's note. The act of a gentleman, perhaps, but he wasn't a gentleman—yet. And if he did? He had no illusions that Downing had learned his lesson. What would happen the next time he lost Seven Pines? Who would Damask be offered to then? No, he wouldn't tear it up.

The chased silver cigar case was cool to the touch. Bram slipped the tiny clippers from his waistcoat pocket while he sniffed an aromatic cigar. Dammit! His savings would be swallowed by the gaping maw of Wade Downing's debt!

He rolled the cigar to and fro between forefinger and thumb while he mentally calculated his assets. Four thousand in cash, once the debt was paid. Another thousand in shares in the New Orleans Gas and Light Company. The sugar cane land outside Baton Rouge. That could be sold.

What of Dublin, that tiny plantation—a grandiose name for those few acres—down Bayou Lafourche from Thibodaux? Bram's blue eyes hardened with the steely light of determination. No, he wouldn't sell that, no matter what sacrifice he had to make. His first, and only, honestly purchased land. Jesus! He thought he would burst with pride the first time he walked those acres. There had been little diminution in that swelling pride in the years since. It would be no drain on his resources, neither money nor time. A tiny profit was realized from it each year and his mulatto overseer, Karl von Hessemann, would look after it equally well with or without direction from him.

Bram nodded his satisfaction, clamped the cigar between his strong white teeth, and struck the match. His gaze wandered passed Damask, moved back, and stopped. He had forgotten she was there. Shaking the match out, he removed the cigar and lifted it with a questioning arch of his black brows.

The thick fringe of rich chestnut lashes dropped to shield her eyes. "Have your cigar, Mr. Rafferty. I have no objections." She bent to her knitting, waiting eagerly for the first whiff of tobacco, a smell that never failed to summon nostalgic memories of her father.

The treble chirr of the flaring match sounded and a whiff of acrid sulfur tickled her nose. She was rewarded with the fragrant scent of a fine Havana cigar, and memories. Back, back in time, to a small girl slipping into Papa's study, crawling into the big leather chair with her first reader and falling asleep, enveloped by the smells of tobacco and ink and books . . .

The rustling of a turning page sent time whirring to the present. Her gaze moved to the man leaning over the ledger, the cigar clamped between his teeth, one lean brown finger tracing a path down a column, pausing, then inching along. He reached out to pull the lamp closer, holding the ledger up to the light. Raven black curls fell across his forehead and Damask watched his impatient, long-fingered hand rake them back while he read. The clicking needles slowed. Something was odd.

A gambler—the word sent a delicate shudder of distaste rippling through her—a gambler should be a pale drawn man. The gaslight of a gambling house or a riverboat saloon would not give a man his healthy outdoorsman's color. Nor would days spent sleeping and nights hunched over a deck of cards give him the sinew of a man whose days are spent in heavy labor.

The creaking rocker slowed to a stop. His skin was bronzed by long hours in the sun, his broad back rippling with contoured strength. When she had touched his shoulder to spread the ointment across the burn, she had felt hard, well-defined muscle, swelling with quiescent power.

The knitting lay forgotten in her lap. Her eyes fastened upon him with a peculiar intensity. The circle of yellowish light burnished the lean planes of his face to a dull gold. His expression was thoughtful, his full attention on the figures before him. Even when quiet, he had an aura of energy and purpose about him.

Her husband. In four months this stranger would be her husband. The man who had all rights over her. The man who would save or destroy Seven Pines. Which would it be? Would that energy and purpose be used for good or ill?

"Is this correct, Miss Downing? You have not bought new clothing for your negroes in the past year?"

The needles clicked convulsively in Damask's hands. A hot flush of shame burned her cheeks. "That is true."

"They must be in rags. You don't think you owe them at least a change of clothes per year?" The words came clipped with a bright edge of contempt.

"There was no money . . ."

"No money, Miss Downing. Your own figures tell that you made a profit of nearly five thousand dollars last year. I see here you bought lumber in Mansfield. Why? I was given to understand that you have your own sawmill."

"The mill has been broken for more than two years."

"Jesus!" Bram threw aside the pen and stood abruptly. "Your brother has little regard for the truth, Miss Downing. You are indebted for fifteen thousand dollars. He said the plantation was free of debt. He described it in glowing terms: the house, the acreage, the sawmill, the cotton gin . . ." He jerked around to glare at her suspiciously. "The cotton gin does work?"

"Yes."

"Have you any idea what could have happened to him? There are those who would not condemn me for taking my money's worth out of his hide."

Terror spurred Damask to her feet. "You won't hurt Wade!"

His rapid pacing arrested, he turned back to look at her. "No," he said with an indifference that frightened Damask more than the implied threat, "that isn't my way."

"Master Bram?" They turned together, looking at Jims.

"Johnson be at the back door waiting for a word with you."

"Send him in here, Jims."

Damask sank into the rocker and dropped her head into her hands. Who was this man she had promised herself to? The man she would spend the rest of her life with? What was he capable of doing?

"Miss Downing." She raised her head at that imperious tone. "I did not mean to imply that your brother would suffer at my hands. There is no need for you to be frightened."

There was a shuffling footstep at the door and she watched him stride forward to greet Johnson, whose soft cornshuck hat was crushed in one huge hand. He ducked his head as he stepped through the door ushering Sim before him. The boy's only garment was a faded red flannel shirt that reached well below his knees. Raindrops sparkled like shining stars in the matting of midnight curls as he reared back his tiny head to stare up at the two men.

"Master Bram," Johnson began in a nervous basso rumble. "I just come to say thank you for saving my baby. And I want you to know . . ."

"Johnson, Sim is safe. Let's leave it at that."

Damask was surprised to see him stoop to Sim's level and chuck him beneath the chin, his own unguarded smile as wide as the gurgling toddler's. After searching through the pockets of his frockcoat, he pulled out a piece of hard candy and pressed it into Sim's tiny fist.

Johnson leaned over his son. "Say thank you to Master Bram."

Sim, attacked by a sudden fit of shyness, grabbed his father's leg and buried his face in the folds of the rough wet osnaburg pants.

"It's a poor day for him to be out without a coat and heavier clothing," Bram said as he touched the boy's arm with a strangely tender gesture.

"Azaline keeps him wrapped good and warm in a blanket in the cabin."

"I see."

Johnson lifted the child and left. Damask waited. The gambler turned to her with a dark look, his eyes bright with contempt beneath flattened brows. His scorn abraded her pride, but she vowed she would offer no reason, no excuse. She owed him nothing. Nothing.

Chapter 3

THAT *icy stare of condemnation followed* Damask *into her dreams* and pushed her from her bed with the first feeble light of dawn. Silence! Silence broken only by the cock's crow! The folds of her threadbare gown swayed about her bare feet as she rushed to the window, flinging wide the dark heavy drapes. The wintry gray prison bars of rain dripping from the eaves were gone! The day promised fair. She could be out and about and doing!

She flew to the armoire, eager hands reaching for her black wool riding habit. *He* had said he would ride out on the first clear day to inspect the land. She could hardly wait!

The habit jacket was years old and that much too small to be comfortable. Damask trailed her fingers across the buttons straining against the holes. It would do for another day, another year. Clothes meant little to her; she, too, had gone without so that Seven Pines might thrive.

She hurried out, noting the closed door to *his* room at the opposite end of the hall. A late sleeper. Her lip curled. He had a lot to learn. A slugabed wouldn't get the work done. Light, tripping steps carried her down the stairs.

She stopped suddenly at the foot, one fragile hand settling atop the round knob of the newel post. A gambler. A man used to late nights and late mornings and lazy days. He probably thought there was nothing more to do than issue orders, ride over the fields occasionally, and keep accounts.

Turning slowly, her speculative gaze climbed the stairwell. Would he consider the endless daily details drudgery?

A tiny hope blossomed. Would he leave the work to her? She knew and loved it. He didn't. Was it possible that nothing would change?

He had paid meticulous attention to every detail of the accounts during the rainy days, but that was money. Money. Why was she so convinced that money had nothing to do with his rescue of Sim? She hated her certainty even though it was better to have the hope, however ephemeral, that there was some good in him.

And he had tried to keep her out of the storm *for her own good.* He didn't know that she neither needed nor wanted to be protected. Like most men, he very likely thought all *ladies* were feather brained ninnies who swooned at the drop of an eyelash. Well, she wasn't, and she wouldn't be treated like one.

Why were there so few men like Papa? Even Hunt, who loved her, looked askance when she invaded masculine discussions of cotton prices and factorage costs. No one, since Papa, had understood. Not even Gramps, who looked forward to the day she would have a man to take some of the burden from her. What he and Wade could not understand was that it was not a burden. It was her life.

Only Papa understood and encouraged her, though there were times when she wondered if it might not have been different had Wade taken the same interest she did. Still, Papa didn't think it was unladylike for her to want to gather the reins of Seven Pines in her own hands.

Papa, she thought, and felt the old pang of grief and guilt. Sometimes she wondered whether Mama and Papa had forgiven her for sending them to their deaths.

She moved, feet dragging. The thick winter drapes in the parlor held in the warmth and blocked the morning sun, casting a pall of gloom that seemed appropriate to her sinking mood.

Damask's slender, tapered fingers touched the daguerreotype of her parents, tracing the stern face that stared out from the rusty-brown portrait with an expression of reproach. Papa had never looked so forbidding in life. Not her big brawny Papa with his curly golden hair and compassionate, twinkling blue eyes.

It still didn't seem possible that he and Mama could be gone. Every minute of her parents' last day at home was as clear and bright as a polished jewel. Wade woke with a fever that morning; somehow, he always had a fever when Mama planned to go away. Mama had fretted and Papa had set his jaw in that way he had and she . . .

Damask blinked away incipient tears. She wanted them to go. They were always planning that second honeymoon trip to the City, and for one reason or another it was always being canceled. She wanted them to go. She wanted Mama to go to the opera and the concerts she loved. She wanted Papa to see his brother and his factor and all the family and friends that wrote those wonderful long letters.

At least that was what she told herself. But what she really wanted was to be left in complete charge of Seven Pines. She wanted to prove to Papa how smart she was and how much she had learned. So she badgered Wade into supporting her when she insisted that they go.

It had been fun playing the lady of the house and the mistress of the plantation. Discussing meals with Aunt Sarah. Checking supplies with Jims. Riding through the fields every day. Taking Harford's report each evening and recording it in the plantation journal. She wanted everything to be perfect. Papa would be so proud of her.

Only he never came back. The steamer exploded. Her parents died in a rush of scalding steam and were buried in a bend of the Mississippi River south of Baton Rouge. Her Papa did not even rest in the soil he loved so much.

Wade said she shouldn't feel guilty. It wasn't her fault that the steamer exploded. She should remember what Papa always said. When a man's time comes, it doesn't matter where he is or what he's doing. She shouldn't feel guilty because she insisted they leave. She shouldn't feel guilty because she made him help her. He would learn to live with it, in time. She shouldn't blame herself, he said. No one else would. Even if they knew what she had done.

It was strange, but in her grief she had felt no guilt over their deaths, until then. And then, she could feel little else. It was her fault that her parents were dead and Seven Pines was masterless. She knew what to do for it, and Gramps was there to take most of the work until she was old enough for it. But what could she do for Wade? Rootless, restless Wade, whose place she had usurped, both in her father's heart and at Seven Pines.

She tried to interest him in taking his place as master. Remember how Papa talked about his seasons as a young man, he would ask wistfully. How could she forget? Papa had made his days as a carefree young dandy sound like an unending round of soirees and balls and gaiety. Wade, she determined, would have no less. It wasn't his fault that Papa was gone. He shouldn't have to suffer for it.

So, he went for one season, then another and another. It wasn't his fault that he was ill-starred. There were people that way, Papa used to say. They had a fat little rain cloud perched above their heads, and it followed wherever they went. With Wade it was bad investments, bad horses, bad luck. An endless drain on the wealth of the land, but what could she do? She owed Wade that and much more. She had to do everything she could for him, even when . . .

Her eyes squeezed shut over the memory of Bram Rafferty's contemptuous expression. It had hurt. She tried not to let it, but it did.

"Miss Downing?"

His voice, cool and contained, brought her swinging around. He stood in the archway, vigorous, even in repose. Fawn trousers were molded to his long muscular legs. A tangle of wiry black hair spilled from the plunging vee of a white cotton shirt whose full, flowing sleeves masked the breadth of his powerful arms. Knee-high black boots gleamed, and a broad belt, cinched tight around his waist, accentuated the fanning width of his shoulders.

She noted the leather coat folded across his forearm and the broad brim of the black felt hat pinched between his fingers. He was ready. Anticipation set her heart pounding.

She could almost feel the cold caress of the wind. It had been so many days and there was so much to do. She needed to see about . . .

"I wanted to let you know that I'll be riding the fields all morning," he said, turning away.

"Mr. Rafferty, would you like to have breakfast before we go?"

He swung back, brows arched over an inquiring gaze that raked a path from her frayed and patched hem, lingered on the all but popping buttons marching across the swell of her breast and rose mockingly to her eyes. "We?"

"Of course," she began resolutely while one hand with a will of its own drifted to a precariously situated button. Why was she now so uncomfortably aware of how small the jacket had become? She forced her hand to her side and raised her chin. "Who better to explain to you what you will see?"

He shifted, irritation pinching the corner of his mouth. "It's a raw, cold day, Miss Downing. There's no need for you to be out in it."

Anticipation changed to apprehension, and her heart began to race. "But I want to be, Mr. Rafferty. There are things—"

"I prefer to make this circuit of the fields with your head driver." A frown shadowed his face. "I can reach my own conclusions about what I see."

"And what will you see, Mr. Rafferty?" She hurled the question, rage pounding in her temples and flushing her face. "Dirt? Easy money? Well, it isn't easy! There are late frosts and too much rain and not enough rain and army worms! There are sick hands and broken implements and worn-out mules! What can you know about the work and the worry, day in and day out? You've never walked across your own rich red earth, knelt to it and felt it warm against your hand! You've never lifted it in your palm and sniffed it and watched it sift through your fingers! You've never felt your heart swell to bursting because it was yours and it was your work that made the cotton grow tall and green. I've done all of those things, Mr. Rafferty. The land has been my child and my husband and my life!''

Chest heaving with commingled fear that everything would be taken from her and rage that *he* who understood nothing would presume to do it, she stared at him and saw something perilously near empathy. ''Can the land ever mean all of those things to you, Mr. Rafferty?'' she cried out.

His sober gaze shifted to a parlor window, sharpening as though he was seeing the land beyond. ''It means more to me, Miss Downing. For you it is life; for me, it is the hope of the future.''

Hope. She had never been without it, Bram thought as he raised the collar of his leather coat against the cutting wind. She hadn't learned that there was no life without hope, and he was glad that she hadn't. It was a bitter lesson.

He nudged the mare in the flank, trotting toward the edge of the muddy field that glistened with shining streaks of sunlight. The lingering taste of the wet weather was in the chill wind rustling through the shriveled leaves on woody cotton stalks. Muted sounds traveled from all corners of Seven Pines, but no one was within sight. Bram reveled in the solitude. He had been alone too long to take much joy in the close, constant presence of family and servants. He thought of his ready-made family, Grandfather Barton and Tessa being another small thing Wade had failed to mention.

The tug of unwelcome emotion made him shift uncomfortably in the saddle. Tessa was the problem. Tessa, who brought to throbbing life the long-suppressed memories of another little girl that demanded attention. Tessa, who would not allow him to stand aloof. In the short space of days he found himself unable to deny her anything she asked.

His eyes softened to a misty blue, and a bittersweet smile arced along his mouth. She trusted him, utterly and simply. It was a heavy burden for a man who had spent years trusting few and loving no one.

It was that perfect trust that made him reluctantly agree to be hers and Miss Pettigrew's guest at a tea party one rainy Sunday afternoon while Damask napped upstairs. It had been awkward holding the dainty cup and saucer he could have swallowed in his fist. And Jims's extreme gravity, belied by a merry twinkle, hadn't helped. But he would have cut out his own tongue before laughing or showing any discomfort. In the end he had enjoyed it, and Tessa had cast off her newfound dignity to listen with vocal delight to stories of the riverboats and the City that a small girl would enjoy—things he, until then, did not realize he had noticed.

His response to Tessa was a painful wrench. She brought the long-ignored, but not forgotten, past crowding into the present. But there was much to give him pleasure, too. A child's love, once given, was all but unchangeable.

Not so the so-called love between adults. Fortunately, that had been easy to avoid, until . . .

Bram frowned, thrusting aside that disturbing fancy. Damask Downing was a woman like any other, even if she would be his wife.

He straightened in the saddle. Today he would see what he had won. He would see if the suspicions raised by the neat rows of figures in Damask's ledger were true.

"Master Bram."

He turned to watch Harford, the head driver, jolt up on a stiff-legged mule.

"Miss Damask say you want to see it all today."

Bram's eyes dropped to the horny, calloused hand nervously fingering the whip looped over the saddle horn and a frown darkened his expression. "Yes, I do. The fields first."

"Yes, sir," Harford said as they began a slow clop through the muddy field. "This here be the Gin Field and them woods over yonder be the Pig Woods. We call it that 'cause the hogs stay there through the year. Plenty of acorns and nuts to fatten 'em up. We usually rounds 'em up come September and drive 'em to the fattening sties at the barn. Persimmon Bayou . . . well, we call it that, but it ain't nothing but a slough what dry up in summer. It winds through there, and it's the line 'tween this place and the neighbor.''

Beyond the Gin Field, they passed through a wooded hollow and wound along the edge of the Persimmon Bayou Field, a hill with a flat crown sloping sharply away on the east and west. Bram studied the winter-killed stalks, short and scraggly on the crest and sloping sides, tall at the foot where the rich soil had washed down. He would have to explain the theory of contour plowing and bring in guano to build up the soil.

A wagon path winding through a broad band of woods brought them to the North Field, where a small group of hands fought the clinging mud to slog their way down the rows, pulling up the dead cotton stalks to pile for burning in the night.

And there Bram found the first confirmation of those suspicions raised by Damask's ledgers. The bitter wind fluttered tattered rags of coats and whipped at the women's skirts, which were drawn up between their legs like bloomers and tied at the waist to keep the hems clean.

"Git yourselves over here!" Harford shouted. "The new master want a look!"

Heads popped up and feet pumped as they hurried to form a line just out of range of the horse's steaming breath. Only one was slow.

Bram watched her thin hands press against her jutting belly as she tried to run. Pain, so old he thought it had been with him always, coiled in a nauseating knot in his belly, but was quickly burned away by a growing fury.

She reached the line gasping for breath, her face tinged gray, and Harford began enumerating the hands' names and the work they were assigned. The words buzzed in Bram's ears without comprehension.

The land! That was all *she* had talked about. The land and her work! But nothing about these who performed the labor! In rags! And not a penny spent to clothe them for more than a year!

"Master Bram?"

A muscle worked frantically in his jaw as he nodded to Harford and turned his horse north.

"Master Bram," Harford ventured cautiously, "that Airy be a good field hand. It's just now, with her time drawing on, her be a mite slow."

"She shouldn't be in the fields at all. Put her to lighter work—today!" He set his heel to the mare's flanks and galloped toward the distant trees.

A carpet of pine needles muffled the sounds of the horse's hooves. Bram, with Harford following, threaded his way through brambles and pine trees, exiting the cool shadows in a growing stump-studded clearing. Nearby, two mules lazily cropped dried weeds in a small circle around their tether. Further along, a muscular black with broad features and an unsmiling face drank thirstily from a gourd, watching the two men who arm-wrestled on a weathered stump.

Harford, jiggling with the jarring gate of his mule, passed Bram at a trot. Yanking back on the reins, he cursed and uncoiled the long, braided cowhide whip, sending it snaking through the air to snap within inches of the men's clasped hands. They went tumbling backward, then popped up and gaped in slack-jawed amazement, round eyes riveted to the whip as though they had never seen such a thing before.

"Dread! Fetch the boys for Master Bram," Harford grunted toward the black who was setting aside the gourd, then swiveled an irate glare on the culprits. "You two fool niggers having yourselves such a good time out here, I expect ya'll won't mind coming back to finish your work on Saturday morning!"

"But, Pappy Harford . . ."

Harford rose in the stirrups, shaking the butt of the whip in a brawny fist, still strong in spite of his years. "You looking to work the Lord's day, too!"

They subsided into silence while men came from all corners of the clearing, stretching out in a single line. Once again Harford gave their names and the work they were assigned, giving special mention to those who excelled at some task.

More of the same. Bram's passionless blue eyes moved from man to man. Some bootless and the others might as well have been. Most of their clothes were neatly patched, but little could be done for fabric worn thin. Nodding to Harford, he turned away without a word.

They followed the wagon path through the woods in silence, circling the western edge of the North Field, following the tumble-down fence to a corn field, where the bleached white stalks canted crazily in the direction of the storm's wind. But Bram had seen enough of the fields and the slaves. More than enough.

At the corn cribs he dismounted, picking up an ear from the pile that had tumbled onto the wet earth from a hole in one wall.

"They in powerful pore shape," Harford said mournfully. "Need to be tore down and built from scratch, but Master Wade say they ain't no use in wasting no time and money on such as that."

Bram prized a few moldy kernels from the cob with his thumb. "How bad is the corn you get from these cribs?"

"Well, sir, they's five cribs here and they ain't one without a leaky roof and holes in the walls. We lose a lot to the coons and the rest git mighty bad to the end of the season."

"I see." A five-thousand-dollar profit! Where in hell had it gone? The working muscle began ticking an angry beat in his jaw. He swung into the saddle, wordlessly setting off for the barn.

The door sagged off its upper hinge. Inside, the earth floor was swept clean and fresh hay was strewn in the empty stalls. The anvil in the corner was oiled and rustfree, and the bridles and mule-collars hanging from nails on the walls showed evidence of careful tending and numerous repairs. The stable had been the same. Well-kept, the equipages carefully tended, but worn and rotting from prolonged use.

If there was such a thing as sin in this world, Bram thought, it was this. The waste! The utter, futile waste of it all! And *she* said she loved it! How could she, and let it come to . . . this.

He stalked through the back door into the bright sunlight. A jaundiced eye fell on the mangy, splay-backed mules and he strode to the fence, propping his foot on the bottom rail. It gave with a splintering crack and the ticking muscle went wild. Hands curled into fists, he turned to Harford.

"Return my horse to the stables. I'll meet you after breakfast tomorrow to see the rest. And put that damn whip away! I won't have it used here!"

Mud squished away from the soles of his boots with every step as he rounded the mule pen, heading for the soft, grassy slope beyond the rickety bridge spanning the shallow hollow.

A grassy avenue separated it from the garden, and Bram stopped there. He was too angry. He would wait until he had cooled down before he confronted her.

He reached for his cigar case, glancing at the garden as he did. The gardener, Glasgow, was planting onion sets. Working with him were two children. The cigar snapped between Bram's fingers. They couldn't be more than five years old! Damn!

Glasgow began speaking and suddenly the children popped up and ran toward the grassy avenue where Bram stood, apparently oblivious to his presence.

The smaller one stumbled, the wet tail of his ragged red flannel shirt slapping against his short legs. Down the row he ran, falling flat in the mud, picking himself up and shrieking with excitement. He reached the grass with a flying leap and charged into Bram's leg, bounced off, and fell.

Bram, scowling, caught him beneath the arms and swung him up. The boy gave one frightened squeak as his bare rump came to rest on a leather-covered forearm. Angrily, Bram took off at a rapid pace, pausing to thump his boot on the slatted incline at the Old House, where Grandfather Barton lived. His face twisted into a blacker scowl, and a red haze of fury rose before his eyes.

The back door swung open in a rapid arc, slamming

against the outside wall with a crash that reverberated through the Big House. Lulu, crossing the dark tunnel of the center hall with an armload of neatly folded linens, stumbled and gaped.

"Tell your mistress that I want to see her! Now!"

Eyes like black marbles flicked over the boy's frightened face. "Miss Damask be in the parlor."

Bram's normally graceful long-limbed stride was jerky, his features were contorted, his face flushed ruddy with fury. He burst into the parlor.

"I want you to look at this!" he spit viciously. The startled boy was thumped down onto the floor before an equally startled Damask.

"What are you doing with Sandy?" she cried, her slender hand fluttering to his mud-streaked cheek in a protective gesture.

"Look at him, dammit!" Bram thundered. "He's in rags! It's freezing cold out there and he was working in the garden! Touch him! His skin is like ice! Jesus! He can't be more than five years old! Working in the garden!" A shaking hand raked his hair and he sucked in a long breath that did nothing to calm him. "Slave child he may be, but he's still a child and I won't have children worked here! By God!" His long fingers coiled into his palm and his brawny fist shook a threat beneath Damask's nose. "While I'm here, there will be no whips and no child labor! They aren't animals! This child feels cold and hunger just like you do . . ."

"Mister—"

"I'm not interested in your excuses! These people work in rags in the freezing cold while you sit in your fine warm house and your brother gambles with their safety! Do you have any idea what condition this place is in? I doubt there's a roof that doesn't leak! The corn and hay are mildewing! Fences are falling down! The bridge at the barn is a hazard! The mules are beyond a good day's plowing . . ."

"So! You've discovered Seven Pines is falling down around our ears and you're angered that your play of the cards has brought you so little ready profit!'' Damask's head was thrown back, cinnamon eyes aglow with raging temper.

Awareness sneaked into a vulnerable crack in Bram's own raging temper. "If I were seeking a ready profit, Miss Downing,'' he ground out hoarsely, the scar on his temple writhing, "I would not have agreed to marry a shrew and support her family—including her wastrel brother! I would simply have evicted you from Seven Pines and sold it for that ready profit!''

Damask's palm cracked across his cheek with a force that snapped his head. He captured her wrist in a bruising grip and leaned close to her flushed face, infuriatingly aware of the heaving breasts crushed against his forearm.

"I would advise you never to do that again.''

Defiantly, she gave him stare for stare. "You will never—*never*—speak of my brother that way again!''

"The sainted Wade Downing," Bram sneered, his grip on her wrist tightening. "Are you so great a fool that you cannot see him for what he is?''

"There is goodness in Wade!" Damask cried out. "He has only to find himself!''

"And I am the devil incarnate," he rumbled, "yet it was not I who foisted my own sister on a stranger to satisfy a gambling debt!''

"No, but you leapt at the chance to cloak your black heart in a veil of respectability!" Damask trembled, disgust stark in every feature.

"Remember, colleen, my black heart can still see you evicted from this place.'' He was shocked at the brutal threat that slipped from him. Was it the disgust he saw in her face that spurred him to it? Or was it the awareness of her as a woman? The softly curling sensual heat that settled in his loins like mist crawling through a forest glade?

"You would not dare! You need me to give the lie to your villainy! The Downings are respected in this community! Should you cast us out, you would not be able to hold your head up here!''

She was all hot cheeks, burning eyes, and righteous indignation as she glared up at him, and Bram felt the caustic deluge of desire. A desire so strong, he could feel sweat beading on his forehead. His hand convulsed around her wrist and she cried out. He flinched and loosened his grip, but was unable to let her go. How could he, when he wanted to pull her into his arms and drink from her lips, then brush a questing finger over the throbbing pulse in the vulnerable hollow of her throat. And he wanted to do more. Much more.

He had to conquer it, that desire. He didn't want to hurt her or frighten her, but it would be better if he did. Better for her. Safer for him.

His smouldering eyes locked with hers as he pulled her resisting wrist to his lips and brushed a moist kiss across the pulse. "I bend my head to no man," he said huskily. "You are proving quite reckless, Miss Downing. I promise, I could send you on your way without a moment's discomfort. You should remember that yours is the more acute need and act accordingly."

Chapter 4

BRAM *was up and out, taking the stairs in stockinged feet before* Damask even awoke. The waning moon rested on the ragged black lip of the horizon as he sat on the steps to tug on his boots. He leaned back, bracing himself against the column. The flare of a match threw red-tinged light across his frowning face. It had been a long time since he had done anything that shamed him, but he cringed now at the memory of threatening Damask with eviction. It was a sadistic act when she was helpless.

While Bram blew rings of smoke and pondered the raveling edges of his control, the indigo sky faded to steel gray. Bif came out to get wood from the cord stacked at the corner of the Old House. Aunt Sarah and Amarintha, followed by Airy, whose massive stomach preceded her, ascended the beaten path from the quarters to the cookhouse. Seven Pines was beginning a new day, her people fanning out from the quarters to attend to their early morning chores.

Minutes later, Bif appeared again and joined Bram. "Mr. Barton requests that you join him for breakfast, sir."

Bram nodded and flicked the butt of his cigar away with an inward sigh of irritation. He suspected it was too perfect an opportunity for the old man to let pass.

He stepped into the cabin, sweeping the single room with a swift glance. It was dark, and the shutters were closed against the cool of the early morning. A bed and cot were at one end, covered with bright patterned quilts. Three large trunks were ranged along the wall opposite the mud and stick fireplace that radiated heat. Basking before that warmth was the old man, crippled legs muffled in a heavy blanket, his head resting against the high back of his rolling chair. Beside him was a small table surrounded by ladder-back chairs with cowhide seats.

"Mr. Barton."

"Ah, Mr. Rafferty! You came. Excellent! Have a seat, please." He cocked his head as though listening for the scraping of the chair. "Would you pour our coffee? It will be a while before Tessa joins us. You've found conditions at Seven Pines little to your liking, I understand." He came directly to the point, as Bram had expected.

"Mr. Barton, I spent the weekend going over the records. Seven Pines is a profitable plantation, yet no money has been spent on improvements in three years. The negroes are in rags. The place is rotting to the ground."

Leo Barton's wizened head nodded, blind eyes staring toward the warmth of the fire. "Do you remember when the *Lucky Lady* went down in 'fifty-two? My daughter and her husband died in that explosion. Wade was seventeen. Old enough to assume the responsibility of Seven Pines. Old enough in years, but . . ." He shrugged. "You've met my grandson. I suspect you see his weaknesses very clearly."

So, Bram thought, not everyone here thinks Wade Downing will *find himself.* But she does. It was conviction he had heard in her voice and seen in her eyes.

The old man fell silent, the carved lines across his forehead deepening. "Wade always said he would not waste his time when an overseer could be hired, but Damask was passionately opposed. I agreed with her. She was fourteen and my eyesight was failing rapidly, but she had made every step her father made from the time she could walk. There was very little I needed to do to build upon what he had taught her. When my eyesight failed completely, Damask shouldered the burden of overseeing, record keeping, buying supplies, corresponding with the factor in Shreveport. Everything. She was seventeen, Mr. Rafferty. My Damask has never known what it is to be young and carefree. Her youth was another victim of that explosion.''

He fell silent, the lines of his face falling into sad folds and Bram waited patiently, knowing the old man was lost in his memories.

"Planning. Always planning. The sawmill was her idea, and she talked about importing cattle from Texas to improve our herd the way most girls talk about a new frock. That worried me! Her youth slipping away while her father's dream for Seven Pines absorbed her every thought. I was afraid she would wake up one day, look back, and regret all she missed. I was even more afraid she wouldn't.''

His head nodded, arthritic hands gripping the chair arms. "Wade reached his majority. On his twenty-first birthday he began court proceedings to remove Seven Pines and his sisters from my guardianship. He succeeded. I can't blame the courts. An old, crippled, blind man against a young man with every appearance of vigor and strength. I would have chosen the young man myself.

"The profits from Damask's management were gone in less than six months, along with her dreams.'' He frowned and turned his head toward Bram. "Have you looked at my granddaughter, Mr. Rafferty? Really looked at her? She has not had a new dress in three years. What little money is left after Wade's creditors are paid, Damask spends on food, clothing, medicine, shoes, and tobacco for the negroes. This year Wade's debts had mounted so high she was forced to make a choice between feeding or clothing them. Which would you have chosen?''

Bram swallowed hard, loathing for Wade Downing churning his stomach. "She didn't tell me. Why?''

"You didn't give her much of a chance, did you? Even if you had . . .'' He spread his hands with a shrug. "Would you fix my coffee? Two teaspoons of sugar and cream.'' He remained silent until Bram placed the cup in his hands. "If you are to understand Damask, you must realize that she is more mother than sister to Tessa and Wade. In spite of everything he does, she is fiercely protective of him.'' He sipped his coffee and looked up with a puzzled frown. "Damask told me that you kept raving about whips and child labor. Might I ask what you meant?"

Bram stiffened. "Isn't it obvious?"

"I'm afraid not."

"I don't believe in whipping slaves."

"Nor do we," the old man said firmly.

"Then why was Harford carrying a whip yesterday?"

"A whip? Harford was carrying a whip?" Stunned disbelief was quickly followed by a broad grin, then an outright laugh. He set his cup aside and slapped his knee, cackling with mirth. "That old devil! That wily old devil!"

"I fail to see the humor," Bram interjected drily.

"Sorry." Leo Barton caught his breath and rubbed his dry eyes. "I hope you won't hold this against Harford. He's a good man and the best driver I've ever seen. You must understand that none of us could know your attitude. It certainly isn't the usual one. I'm sure Harford thought if he carried the whip, he could use it lightly, where you might not. You see?"

"Yes, I do." Bram grinned. "You're right. He is a wily old devil. I approve of that. It shows he can think and act for himself. But where did he get the whip in the first place?"

All humor vanished from Leo Barton's wrinkled face. "Wade. He brought two here soon after he was given his inheritance, but Damask put an end to any notions he had about using them. It was the only time I've seen her really angry with him. John, Damask's father, wouldn't have one on the place. He was firmly convinced that love, not fear, was the way to rule his slaves."

"A wise man." Bram stirred his coffee idly, raising a thoughtful gaze to the old man. "The children working in the garden?"

"Getting in Glasgow's way. He's a Pied Piper when it comes to children." He turned his head toward Bram. "I think, Mr. Rafferty, you have as much to discover about us as we have to discover about you."

* * *

It was midmorning when Damask was *summoned* to the study. She entered, dust rag clenched in her hands, and paused for the pleasure of glaring at Bram Rafferty's bent head. The pen scratched rapidly across the sheet of paper and a warm wind whispered through the open drapes. But she felt cold. Icy cold. Hope, he had said. But what was life except hope? And he was stealing hers, just as surely as a thief steals a purse.

"Mr. Rafferty," she began in a voice that should have frozen him to his marrow, "Jims told me you need a pass for Samson to go into Mansfield."

His head rose and he lay aside the pen and raked a hand through his wayward black curls with an impatient gesture that appeared almost nervous. He stood, and the gaze that met hers held a note of pity that pushed her chin to a haughty angle. "Miss Downing, I would like to apologize for what I said—"

"Hypocrisy, Mr. Rafferty?" she rapped out. "We both know you meant every word!"

"At the time, but—"

"Please!"

A muscle jumped in his clenching jaw and his expression hardened. "Very well. I thought there might be less confusion if you wrote the pass, since I don't know what your slave patrols are like."

"Efficient," she answered shortly. "Sometimes too efficient."

"Do the planters hire patrollers or do it themselves?"

"Hire. Some of the most beastly, no-account wretches imaginable. They seem to take pleasure in beating the poor people who are about without their papers." She didn't look directly at him, but found a point over his shoulder. "Might I inquire what you are sending Samson to town to do?"

"Of course. Had you any idea of the condition of your grandfather's inclines on the porches?"

"No." She looked at him now, alarm in her eyes.

"The wood is rotten, Miss Downing. Since your sawmill

is inoperable, I'm sending Samson to town for lumber. I want new ones constructed immediately.''

"I see. I had no idea . . ." Damask bowed her head and steeled herself. "Thank you, Mr. Rafferty.''

Sliding into the chair he had vacated, she withdrew a sheet of paper from a slot in the desk. The pass was quickly written and the blotter rolled over the wet ink. She stood, extending the paper, and the edge of her sleeve slipped, revealing mottled purplish bruising around her wrist.

He hissed sharply. Dark fingers, warm with life, imprisoned her hand while he pushed the sleeve up her forearm. Damask stood quiescent for long minutes while he stared at the angry imprint of his hand on her flesh. She could see the sheen of blue at the base of his lashes and the tiny lines, white on bronze, radiating from the corners of his eyes. Leaping muscles ridged and tightened in his cheek and jaw and brow.

His thumb brushed across the livid bruise with a touch so soft she might have only imagined it. "You are too tender for such harsh handling," he murmured. Without another word, he took the pass from her hand and left.

Damask looked down at her wrist, rubbing it lightly with her fingers. What had he seen there to awaken the agony she saw coiling deep within those brooding eyes?

A wispy breeze slipping through cracks lifted tufts of dusty lint as Bram entered the Gin House. His steps sent lonely echoes bouncing off of the bare plank walls. He stopped to nudge a weak plank with his toe, and thumped a column with the heel of his hand. The cavernous second floor was open on one side and he stepped close to the edge, staring out in the direction of the Big House.

His nostrils flared with emotion, bitter gall rising in his throat. The pale color of his eyes darkened to sapphire and his big hands clenched into fists that left a rim of white across the knuckles.

He had bruised her! Her fair skin was marked with the clear outline of his hand! That vision blurred and re-formed.

His mother. Soft black hair falling across her face. Her shaking hand brushing it back. Blood trickling from the corner of her mouth. One eye swollen shut. Her wrist branded with the angry red imprint of his father's hand.

Why? Why were those memories reaching out to tear him to pieces now? They had been safely buried years ago!

He leaned against the wall, his eyes hot and burning. He felt the most ridiculous impulse to cry. The way he had cried as a child. Lying in the dark, so inured to the smell of human excrement and filth he no longer noticed it. Lying in the dark, listening to the skittering of rats, jerking violently when one climbed the wide board that served him for a bed. Lying in the dark, helplessly waiting for his father to come home. Waiting for the drunken anger. Waiting for the sounds of his heavy fist punching his mother. Crying bitter, lonely, frightened tears while his sister, Mary, held him, her tears trickling warm against his neck. Crying, until they realized it was quiet. Too quiet. Rising. His toes curling away from the cold floor. Reaching for the latch high above his head. Easing the door open a crack. Listening to his father's wrenching, hopeless sobs. Listening to his meaningless apologies. Listening to the promises that were forgotten with the next bottle. And all the while his mother—weeping, forgiving, consoling.

A breath shuddered into Bram's lungs. By God! He wouldn't remember! He would be careful. Work had served him well in the past and there was work aplenty here. He headed for the stairs, his dark face set in a mold of icy purpose.

On the ground level, strong square columns were spaced evenly around the edge of the building, only one side walled where a shed was attached to the Gin House. Bram fingered a crack in the cogwheel. Turning away, he stepped over the rutted circle carved in the hard-packed earth by plodding mules attached to the levers that turned the wheel. He stared up at the second wheel, then looked to the broad leather belts that engaged the gin works. All about him was evidence of repeated wear and repair. How many days and weeks were lost in the ginning season? Time lost was money lost. The earlier to market, the higher the price. New parts for the gin were a first priority.

Rastus, a rangy rawboned hound that had attached himself to Bram, followed his every step as he left the Gin House and poked his head into the shed. Rope and bundles of hemp sacking were piled in a corner with tools arranged neatly along the walls. Large split-oak baskets, used during the picking season, were stacked floor to ceiling.

Next door was the tall, cumbersome Screw Press, where the cotton was baled. Bram studied the massive wooden screw used to compress the bales and thought with longing of the modern steam-driven gin and press he had seen. That was out. At least for a few years. His money would stretch only so far, and he had no intention of falling into the trap of borrowing against the next year's crop. He would do what had to be done. The rest would have to wait.

It would take time and money to replace the rotting structures and worn-out tools. The mules were ancient beasts. Perhaps two new teams would see them through the year. Seven Pines was too rundown to show a clear profit soon, but a man with a will to see it thriving could have it at peak capacity in just a few years.

There was much to be done. But would he want it otherwise? If Seven Pines had been well-kept and prosperous, would he ever have felt it was really his? No. Nothing had ever been easy for him. Only his money, his work, and his worry would make Seven Pines his. When it prospered, as he knew it would, he would have earned the right to call it his own.

His thoughts drifted pleasantly, contemplating fat, sleek cows, a sturdy new stable and barn, new wagons and plows, shining equipment and plump bales of cotton with the marking *B. Rafferty, Mansfield, Louisiana,* being rolled onto the New Orleans docks.

Damask sighed and moved the envelope she used to mark the page of her book. Not a single word had penetrated the obscuring curtain of her thoughts. She closed the book and absently set it on her lap. It was obvious her mind was only concerned with what she had learned during her long visit with Gramps.

His explanations of why Bram Rafferty had acted as he had carried her through amusement at Harford's devious means of thwarting him, to anger that he could believe she would treat her people so harshly, to a relief so profound it left her limp. Now she knew he would not mistreat her people, nor see them go hungry or ill-clothed. And she could see the meticulous attention he was giving to Seven Pines. He would not leech the wealth of the land without thought for the future. Had Wade done them more good than ill?

How could she know for sure? She knew no one who might be acquainted with him.

The forgotten book inched down onto her thigh, and the envelope crackled. Picking it up, Damask slid it into the spine, then she started.

It was from Cousin Elize, in New Orleans, whose husband spent most of his time in the gaming halls of the City! Perfect! She could never ask Uncle James or Cousin Andy if they knew anything about a gambler called Black Irish Rafferty without giving a reason. Her pride would never permit that. Besides, the truth would send them flying to Bonne Volonte for Papa Kinloch, and up to Acadian Star for Uncle Harry. Then they would all descend on Seven Pines as they had after Mama and Papa died. She shuddered at the memory. That crisis had passed to her satisfaction and since then her every letter to her far-flung kin had oozed optimism with never a debt mentioned.

But this crisis was coming, and Elize could help. She would write first thing in the morning.

The promise of summer wafted on the warm breeze, and the deadness of winter had been vanquished by the heavy rain. Damask found it impossible to cherish her hurt when the healing sun warmed her and the gifts of spring thrust up in patches of fresh green and clumps of jewellike flowers. A split-oak basket swayed beneath her hand.

Tessa ran ahead with a happy shout to Bram while Damask studied the Big House, framed against the green and blue of trees and sky. A snatch of song, snappy and humorous, flitted through the open door of the cookhouse to lift Damask's spirits higher. It was all so precious to her. More precious than it had ever been since she'd come so close to losing it. Tears dimmed her vision and she resolved never to take her family and home for granted again.

Her innate optimism was sent winging by small hints of things to come. The more thought she gave to Rafferty's anger, the more her own dissipated. The more thought she gave to what he said, rather than how he said it, the less fault she could find. He shouldn't have spoken ill of Wade and he shouldn't have bruised her wrist, but she suspected he was so driven by rage he was unaware of his own strength. In her mind, that rage was assuming the rarified heights of a towering virtue.

What fault could she find with his anger that Seven Pines was falling down around their ears when she had suffered the same frustration and disgust? How could she blame him for his fury about "whips and child labor" when she shared his opinion? Why should she cling to her fear when every indication of Bram Rafferty's intentions was positive? No matter how she twisted and turned his words, she could not disagree with him. And his anger served only to prove the depth of his convictions.

Damask set the basket on the back steps. Tessa was chattering gaily while she held a board between two sawhorses. Bram was on the opposite end, sawing off a length, pausing occasionally to respond to Tessa's endless stream of questions. He had shed his shirt. The cotton cloth wrapped around the burns on his chest and arm was stark white against the bronze of his skin. Ridged muscles drew tight across his flat belly and bands of muscle swelled and rippled beneath his taut flesh. A rippling centered itself in the region of Damask's heart and spread downward in warm, sensual wavelets.

She couldn't seem to tear her eyes away from the thick curling mat of hair crawling from the band of his trousers to his collarbone, and the tips of her fingers tingled so that she dug them into her palms.

A bead of sweat dripped from a damp curl and sped across his forehead and she lifted her hand and swept the back across her own itching brow.

She should have been shocked, even outraged, to see him working alongside Samson and Dread and Johnson. Her father had never worked with his hands, he had stood back, directing the work of others. Somehow, she knew this man would never be content to do that. He was too forceful, too restless to stand by watching. Very likely he would come in most days as sweaty and dirty as any of his field hands. Why did she like that idea?

Samson, who had returned from town not an hour before, suddenly appeared. "Master Bram, you want I should get them tins?"

"Yes, Samson," he said and looked back at her. "Oh, thanks, Samson. Tessa, this is for you. Miss Downing . . ." He held out a tin of chocolates.

"Oh," Damask breathed. If she had a real weakness, it was for chocolates, and this was a rare treat for her.

"Bram! Thank you!" Tessa squealed and ran around the sawhorse, reaching up on tiptoe. He was still too tall. "Stoop down, Bram!" She caught him around the neck and planted a moist kiss on his cheek, and he started to rise. "No! No! Now it's Damask's turn."

Cinnamon eyes met icy-blue and skittered away.

"Damask! Thank Bram for your present!"

"Thank you," she whispered, then sneaked a peek at his face. Finding him looking every bit as uncomfortable as she felt, Damask could not contain a merry trill of laughter. "Tessa, you're impossible! I do thank you most sincerely, Mr. Rafferty."

He smiled, a slow, reluctant curving of his lips, as though

he was unaccustomed to smiling. A boyish smile that be-
guiled, even as it seduced Damask with thoughts that skirted
the pale of virginal innocence.

"Damask loves chocolates, and she hardly ever gets
any," Tessa informed him, then turned an arch look upon
her sister. "Well?"

The warm sensual wavelets licked with a voluptuous heat
that seared away reason. Her feet moved and her lips hovered a hair's breadth from the lean dark cheek roughly stub-
bled with a day's growth of beard. The tingling in her
fingertips was almost painful. She braced her hand against
his chest and felt that thick matting of hair. So soft. So surprisingly soft.

Her touch shaded his eyes to the hue of blue smoke, and
she felt a tiny rill of movement in the muscles beneath her
hand. Her lips touched his cheek and she smelled clean,
hard-working man.

Regretfully her heels sank and her hand moved from his
chest in a slow, lingering movement while her wide unsettled eyes gazed up into his.

"C'mon, Damask!"

Tessa was in a hurry to dig into her tin, but Damask hung
back, unable to look away while his burning gaze held hers
shackled.

Chapter 5

THE *fragrant scent of a fine Havana cigar wafting through her* open window wakened Damask from a dreamless sleep. She lay quiet, soaking in the warmth of the April morning and watching the metamorphosis of dawn in a patch of sky framed between the fringe of the pine trees and the eaves of the roof.

She had been wrong about Rafferty, at least partially. It was best for everyone—everyone, except herself—that he wasn't a slugabed who knew nothing about running Seven Pines. He was the first one up, sneaking down the stairs in stockinged feet every morning to have his first cigar of the day on the back steps. It was almost as though he reveled, as she once had, in those few minutes when the day and the land were his alone.

No, he wasn't lazy. It seemed to her that his aura of energy and purpose had seeped into the very walls and penetrated to every corner of Seven Pines. So much had been done, Damask was a little breathless just thinking about it. The shutters had been removed and repaired. The house painted a pristine white, the shutters holly green. The roof was still bald in spots, but cypress shingles were on order in Shreveport. New parts for cotton gin and sawmill were on their way up from New Orleans. Johnson and Azaline had moved into their new log cabin. Four new young and feisty mules were playing in the pens.

With all that, the plowing and planting were moving along at a pace never before achieved, and the quarters hummed with contentment, respect for the new master growing by the day.

Whatever else he was, he was a hard worker who asked nothing he was not capable of and willing to do. She was glad. She was, Damask insisted to herself when a pang of sorrow cut through her. The most important thing was to see Seven Pines reach its full potential. The most important thing was that the work get done, no matter who did it.

She climbed from the bed and went to the window, sinking to the floor beside the low casement. Crossing her forearms on the sill, she propped her chin on the back of her arm and stared through the bars of the porch railing.

She missed it. Calculating the number of bushels needed to seed an acre. Planning which fields were to be planted in corn, which in cotton, which in peas. Instead, she was relegated to the house and quarters.

Woman's work, when once she had done it all. At least she could take pride in doing it with the same energy that he gave to his work. Too much, if Lulu's and the housemaid's groaning was any measure.

She winced lightly when the tip of her third finger pressed against the sill. Raising her hand, she studied the rough scratched skin, so tender after more than two weeks of steady sewing. It would be a long time before she picked up her needle with any pleasure.

But it had been worth it. The long exhausting day of shopping in Mansfield. Samson loading the wagon with bolt after bolt of osnaburg, linsey, calico, gingham, and red flannel. There had been a wooden crate of wide-brimmed straw hats for the men, a stack of colorful kerchiefs for the women, and tall piles of woolen blankets.

Could she be so selfish as to complain when he was clothing her people and giving minute care to the land and crops and livestock? A sigh escaped her. No, not even when it hurt to realize that he was doing a better job than she might ever have done.

But how had he, a gambler removed from the land,

learned about guano and crop rotation and harness galls? And why was he so reticent about discussing himself?

Even Tessa could wheedle nothing about his past from him. And Gramps had become singularly obtuse when she questioned him. He would give her that aggravating, sweet, secretive smile and say: Yes, it was true they had coffee together every morning. No, the gambler never discussed himself. Oh, they talked about the crops, the negroes, politics. Yes, he was pleasantly surprised by him. No, he had no worries about Seven Pines in his capable hands. And then, that aggravating, sweet, secretive smile again. When she questioned him, a trifle tartly, he pressed her hand and said, "There is more to the gambler than meets the eye, child. Close your eyes and look to your heart. You will see him." Now what had Gramps meant by that!

When she looked to her heart she saw nothing but an intruder in her life. A man who had won her plantation, taken her place as its master, and would take her in marriage. She shivered, remembering the day he arrived.

"Wade would not have wagered Seven Pines unless he was pushed into it! I want to know why he did, Mr. Rafferty!"

"Greed, Miss Downing."

"His . . . or yours?"

Greed. But what she had seen was every evidence of honor and generosity. Still, she could not forget the look in his eyes when he had said: *For you it is life; for me, it is the hope of the future.* Would he have done anything to achieve the reality of that hope?

It was a question that could not be answered until she received a reply from Elize. Even then, there might be nothing to tell her. She might still be left with this strange attraction-repulsion, and no explanation for it.

It had grown with every day. She found herself watching him and warming to his rare smiles. She caught herself slicking her tongue across her lips as though she could lick away the tiny prickles of his beard-stubbled cheek. She caught herself scrubbing her palm as though she could rid herself of the sensation of that soft matting of hair and his warm, sweat-dampened chest. She found herself staring at his hands, long-fingered, capable, graceful hands, and wondering what it would be like to have them move across her flesh.

She would be his wife. She would sleep beside him every night. She would bear his children. She would tend him in sickness. She would marry this stranger for Wade and for Seven Pines.

But the thought of a life of private enmity and public accord was abhorrent to her. Was it possible that he might meet her halfway if she extended the hand of friendship?

They could have that, if nothing else. He had done so much for Seven Pines and her people. Couldn't she respect him for it, and try to forget what had brought him here?

Before she could change her mind, Damask grabbed her muslin dressing gown, and slipping it on, she rushed down the stairs, its voluminous folds whipping about her bare feet.

The back door creaked as she peeked out. He sat on the porch at the top of the steps, back braced against a column. He turned slowly, eyes widening with surprise.

She had not expected her reaction to seeing him. Not the flutter in her stomach. Not the lurch of her pulse. Not the constriction of her throat. What if he rejected her overture?

Staring at the unruly curls crowding across the crown of his head, she pasted on a spuriously confident smile. "Good morning."

"Morning," he answered and flicked away the stub of his cigar while she walked to the steps and sank onto the top one, the folds of her dressing gown fanning out and coming into intimate contact with his thigh. She quickly slanted an oblique look at him. He seemed unnaturally absorbed by her toes peeping from beneath her hem. They curled under, inching beneath the shelter of her gown. His gaze climbed to her chin and angled off, and aberrant emotion trailed a ticklish finger the length of her spine.

Rastus slunk up, one absurdly long ear lifting an inch at a basso murmur of encouragement. Settling his muzzle across

Rafferty's knee as if it were a weight too heavy to carry, he rolled his melancholy eyes and snuffled with pleasure while his back was stroked and scratched.

Was it only she who found the silence uncomfortable, she wondered, her attention glued to those big brown hands smoothing Rastus's rusty-red fur.

"Did you want something, Miss Downing?"

"Want something?" She straightened and sought the safer sight of a hawk spiraling into the sky. This wasn't going to be as easy as she thought. "No, it . . . it was just too nice a morning to stay inside."

"Morning, Miss Damask, Master Bram," Aunt Sarah sang out as she climbed the path from the cookhouse. "Thought ya'll might like these biscuits hot from the oven. Master Bram, that Bif done show me how you like your coffee. He say that Nawlins coffee be thick as molasses on a winter morning. And this sure enough is! Can't have no man starting the day without his coffee the way he like it."

"Here, Aunt Sarah." Damask, relieved at the interruption, reached for the tray and balanced it on her knees.

"Well!" Aunt Sarah's attitude was one of impatient waiting.

A smile nipped at Damask's mouth as Bram hurriedly stirred sugar and cream into his cup, and took a too-hasty sip of the scalding liquid.

"Well?" Aunt Sarah questioned. "I got to know if it be right, 'cause if it ain't, I'll be trying again."

"No need. It's fine. Just too hot." He ran his forefinger over the tip of his tongue, and Damask's smile widened.

"Good! Ya'll eat up 'fore it git cold." Aunt Sarah scowled and wagged a chubby finger at him. "Any man what work as hard as you, they needs plenty good eating to keep up they strength."

"You'll have me fat as a porker if you feed me any better."

"Humph!" Arms akimbo, she stalked back to the cookhouse with a satisfied twitch of her new calico skirts.

He chuckled, a rich, deep sound that brought Damask's

head swinging around. "I wouldn't have dared to wait for it to cool."

His confession startled a laugh from her. "Aunt Sarah is a termagent. Just wait until one of us gets sick. Her potions would kill a mule, and she comes to the Big House to stand over us until we've taken every drop."

"I'll try to stay healthy."

Damask smoothed butter over a steaming biscuit and drizzled it with honey. "That's no help. It's nearly time for her spring tonic, and *everyone* takes it—healthy or sick! I promise"—she sent a maliciously gleeful look his way— "you'll wish you had stayed in New Orleans, even before the first sip. The smell is awful. Here—" She held out the biscuit.

As fast as a striking snake, Rastus uncoiled and snatched the biscuit from her hand, swallowing it in one audible gulp and whining for more.

"Rastus!" she shrieked with laughter.

"Get on with you! Get!" Bram flicked his hand lightly across the hound's shoulder.

Rastus's slavering muzzle swung toward Damask, eloquent pleading in his sorrowful eyes.

"Don't look to me, you wretched hound! Go on! You've had all you'll get from us."

Rastus slunk a few feet away, collapsing in a cloud of dust, sad eyes following Damask's every move. The biscuits were eaten beneath his unblinking stare, his muzzle resting on his paws, watchful eyes rolling from one to the other and back again. Relenting at the end, Damask tossed him the last biscuit, laughing aloud when he perked up to wolf it down.

"A sorry beggar, isn't he?" Rafferty said with a smile that plumbed the depths of his eyes.

"He'd make a good hunter," she replied, "if anyone took the trouble to train him."

"I'll give it a try when I get back."

"Back? You . . . you are going away?" The thought of

him leaving filled her with an inexplicable, ridiculous sense of loss.

"Yes, I need to take care of some business in the City. I'll leave in a couple of weeks and get back just before the, uh . . ." His gaze touched her and danced away. ". . . the wedding."

The wedding. June. In the blink of an eye she would be his wife. Her hands squeezed about the cool edges of the silver tray in her lap. "Aren't you worried about leaving Seven Pines with the planting underway?"

"No, you can oversee it," he said, and reclined against the column with a quirking grin, "but if you expect me to admit you can do it better than I can, you'll have a long wait."

Damask's mouth rounded to a small *oh* of astonishment. He was teasing her! Teasing her about her *overseerish inclinations*, as Wade was prone to call them, thereafter clucking sympathetically and hugging her and mourning that so few men could appreciate a woman like her. Was it possible . . .

The question was seared away by a sudden realization. He was leaving. She would be in charge of Seven Pines. For a few weeks the dust could settle in the Big House, Lulu and the housemaids could get a well-earned rest, and she could ride the fields and check the mules at night and even sneak a hoe to the far corner of a field where Jims and Lulu and Harford couldn't see her while she scraped the grass away from the tender young cotton. It was her own version of the Pearly Gates opening wide to a blissful Heaven.

She set the tray aside and wrapped her arms around her updrawn knees, basking in the warmth of the rising sun. Joy curled along her lips and sparkled in her eyes. He trusted her with the land, and the step from trust to fully sharing its work was a small one. It was a beginning. Perhaps . . . perhaps they could live in harmony. It was a tiny hope, but one that produced a fresh awareness of the promised beauty of the day.

Spring had arrived with clouds of white blossoms topping the slender trunks of dogwoods. The azalea at the corner of the cookhouse was a solid mass of fuschia flowers and the orchard was abloom. She thrust her delicate nose in the air to breathe the fragrant fruit scents of apple, orange, and plum blending with bay and sassafras and the ever-present pine.

"What a glorious day," she declared.

"Glorious," he echoed huskily, but his eyes were not on the sights of spring around them.

His unfocused gaze lingered on her smile, and Damask's heart jumped like a rabbit startled from the shelter of a bush. As though he sensed her reaction, his gaze, now piercing and frighteningly brilliant, climbed and took her eyes unwilling captive. Every sense was painfully alive. The music of a freshening wind swishing through the treetops. The air perfumed by spring. The caress of muslin against acutely sensitive flesh.

"Glorious," he repeated in a low vibrato that resonated along Damask's nerves.

"Mr . . ." She swallowed hard. "Mr. Rafferty . . ."

The corner of his mouth quivered, but that meager evidence of humor did nothing to cool his ardent gaze. "Don't you think it's time you called me Bram?" he asked and leaned closer.

"I don't . . ." she quavered and discovered the pulse gone wild at the base of his throat.

It held her as captive as those brilliant eyes, pumping in a syncopated rhythm to the sweet, wild thunder of her own pulse.

"I don't—" she began and he leaned closer still. So close she could feel his breath, moist and hot against her mouth. Thought dissipated. Her lashes drifted down and she leaned toward him, lips parted . . .

Sweet quest and gentle test, his kiss teased an idling path to the corner where her dimple hid. A kiss that lingered to woo and tempt while his hand caressed shoulder and nape, his long fingers rising to bury themselves in the thickness of her hair. His mouth moved upon hers with an aching, searching tenderness that pulled Damask into the bewildering, uncharted region of passion.

His head lifted and she leaned toward him, mutely offering her forsaken lips, her dark lashes fluttering up. His head dipped hesitantly, his darkening sapphire eyes betraying an emotional skirmish. He groaned, a low thrumming sound of surrender, and crushed her to him.

Wildfire raced along Damask's veins. Her heart pounded against the hard planes of his chest, and her hands climbed to the glossy black satin of his hair. An exhilarating jumble of sensations assaulted her: the smell of bay rum and man; the fierce demand in his kiss—so different, so excitingly different from Hunt Marlowe's proper pecks; the throb deep inside her that grew and grew . . .

"Miss Damask! Master Bram! Come quick! Trouble's coming up the road!"

His arms convulsed around her, a painful pressure that was gone almost as soon as it began, and she was left alone and strangely bereft. Her face raised as though she longed for more, eyes glazed, lips swollen.

"Damask!"

Her name, in that deep smooth voice, now textured like the rough-hewn cypress columns. She blinked and wrenched back, eyes wide. Her hand fluttered to his arm, fingers digging into the rigid muscle.

"Bram," she breathed, still swirling in his sorcerer's spell.

"Miss Damask!" Jims burst through the door. "Samson done took that old pass you write for him last week. You know how anxious he is to get to Blackberry Hill every Saturday to see his woman and baby. Left 'fore daylight. Said he knew you wouldn't care and he didn't want to wait. Now them pattyrollers is bringing him up the road."

"Patrollers!" she cried out, the spell shattered.

Four men were riding up, the last one leading a mule. Damask craned her neck to look around the horses, then started running.

"Samson!" He was slumped across the mule's withers, one arm hanging down either side. "Samson?" He groaned, turning his head toward the sound of her voice and she gasped. His eyes were blackened and swollen shut. His nose was broken and his lower face so bloodied she could not assess the damage done to it.

"Damn nigger was trying ter run away." A stream of tobacco juice was aimed unerringly at Samson's bare foot, dripping in dark slimy strings to the ground.

"How dare you!" Damask choked out. Her eyes raked the men with scathing disgust. They were all the worse for dirt and filth and food-stained clothing, the dregs of indecent humanity.

The excuse of a man nearest her leaned from the saddle with a grin leering from his bewhiskered face and she flinched away. "You's a mighty purty little thing when you's all fired up."

Bram wrapped his hands around the greasy lapels of the man's checkered flannel shirt, snatching the startled ruffian from his saddle as though he weighed no more than little Sim. Before he could react to the unexpected attack, a hard bronze fist cracked against his jaw with such force it was jerked from the socket and the opposite side was snapped in two. Bram dropped his distasteful burden like a pile of dung. His eyes, as cold and relentless as death, touched first one man, then another, until all three had subsided into their saddles.

"Who might you be to be bringing my man here in this condition?" he demanded, the words thickened by rage.

The leader rested his forearm atop the saddle horn, reptilian eyes glittering from the shade of his slouch hat. "The name is Caswell. Jethro Caswell. Me and my brothers are the patrollers for this here road. We caught the nigger trying to skedaddle."

"And the poor creature was in this condition when you caught him?" Bram inquired in a deceptively calm voice.

The ill-suppressed violence in that question was apparent to Damask. She glanced down, spying the revolver in the holster of the fallen man, then up, sweeping his companions with a cautious look. They, too, recognized the menace underlying the softly spoken words. Bram had their undivided attention.

She eased down slowly, the drumming of her heart so loud she thought they must be able to hear it. The muslin hem of her dressing gown settled in the dust. One knee touched the ground, and she breathed a prayer of thanks that she was not encumbered with layers of petticoats and yards of skirt. The stench of unwashed man rose to gag her as she fought to free the revolver from the holster.

Caswell's laugh was ugly, a slick, oily sound that oozed through the quiet. His nostrils twitched like an animal scenting danger.

"He sassed me. Ain't no nigger sassing Jethro Caswell and walking away. What you asking all these here questions for?" he asked belligerently. "I know this here is the Downing place, and you ain't Downing! Tell him to come out with our ree-ward and we'll be on our way."

Reward! Damask could see the word slicing through the tether of restraint Bram maintained with increasing difficulty. Reaching out to drag two men from the saddle at once, he swung them together in a tangle, his muscles bunching with nearly inhuman strength. The first man staggered up and a fist like a pile driver sank deep into his belly. Air exploded from his lungs and he collapsed in a retching heap. Jethro Caswell charged Bram, roaring like a maddened bull.

The last of the group, a boy with the first growth of a downy beard struggling for its place alongside the dirt smearing his cheeks, reached for his shotgun.

"I wouldn't do that, if I were you," Damask warned.

"Now, ma'am"—he eyed her shaking revolver warily—"you know you ain't gonna shoot nobody, 'specially over no nigger."

"I suggest you sit very still," she said coldly. "There's no telling just what I might do."

"Miss Damask?"

"Johnson!" She went weak with relief, but dared not take her eyes from the boy. Thudding blows and rasping breathing spurred her fear that Bram might be hurt. "How is he doing, Johnson?"

"Don't know where he learn to fight, Miss Damask, but he sure whopping the tar outa that pattyroller."

"Good!" She could hardly believe that she was so bloodthirsty, but she had a strong desire to see Caswell's nose smeared across his face. "Now, mister," she addressed the boy, "drop your shotgun. That's right. Get down and walk over to that tree. My man here is going to watch you. If you hope to see the sun set today, you'll be very still."

The boy stumbled to the tree, hugging it as he looked over his shoulder to stare up at Johnson, a smutty-black avenging angel who scowled down from his six-foot seven-inch height.

Damask turned the revolver on the two men who were down, but saw there was nothing to fear from either of them. The first was unconscious, the second curled into a heaving, gasping ball. The heavy weapon swung down at the end of her limp arm and she found Dread at her side. "How did you know to come?"

"Jims come a-running to the quarters. He say he expect Master Bram wouldn't take kindly to this, and he might need some help."

Damask looked around. They were all there. Big Alf with a hoe, Custis with a machete, Harford with a timber axe clasped firmly in his hands. All her people. Bram's people, she thought with a thrill of pride. Her luminous gaze sought him just as the last pile-driving blow sank deep into Jethro Caswell's belly.

Bram leaned over, hands on his knees, and sucked in a deep breath, then leaned further, hooking a hand into Caswell's collar to drag him to the horses. He halted abruptly, eyebrows climbing at the sight of the revolver in her hand.

"There were too many. Even for you," she whispered, fighting the urge to run to him and fling herself into his strong arms. She waited. He wasn't done with the brothers

Caswell. It gave her keen satisfaction to watch him roughly haul the eldest to his feet.

"Can you understand me?" Bram barked, and was answered with a weak nod. "My name is Bram Rafferty! I want you to remember it! Bram Rafferty! I'm the new owner of Seven Pines. If you ever find a slave who tells you his master is Bram Rafferty, I suggest you let him go his own way. By God, if you, or any of your kind, cause one of my people to do so much as stub his toe, I will see that you regret it! Do I make myself clear?"

Jethro Caswell raked a sleeve across his bleeding nose and rolled his snake eyes up at Bram in malevolent hatred. "You gonna be the one to regret this, *Mister* Bram Rafferty!"

"I doubt it! Get on your horse and get out of here. Don't ever let me catch you on Seven Pines again. Dread, toss those two across their saddles. Johnson, let the pup go."

Bram's narrowed eyes followed their clattering progress onto the road. He turned around and stopped perfectly still, scanning the wide semicircle of weaponed men, noting the women and children crowding in behind them. A questioning look shifted to Damask and she hurried to him.

"Jims told them you might need help," she said, swallowing the lump of pride that threatened to choke her.

"Did he now?" Bram's eyes sought Jims, who was standing on the porch with a shotgun laid in the crook of his elbow. A twinkle starred the gaze that returned to rest on her. "He didn't know that a wisp of a colleen would be hefting a revolver almost as big as herself. What were you planning to do with it, if I might ask?"

Her small chin climbed, her expression resolute. "Use it, if I had to."

After a short, shocked stare, he grinned. "I suppose I should be glad you didn't decide to use it on me."

"I couldn't," she said softly. "Not now."

The grin vanished and his face grew serious. "Why not now?"

''Because I've seen that you will make a good master for Seven Pines.''

His face cleared, and something perilously near relief moved across his features.

Chapter 6

THE *weeks passed by more slowly than Damask could ever have* imagined. The tranquillity of the Big House was undisturbed by the firm, purposeful stride of his booted feet. Meals became interminable ordeals with Tessa picking at her food while she chanted the monotonous refrain: "Damask, when is Bram coming home?"

Even Gramps seemed subdued and often mentioned *the boy*, which made her smile. Gramps called every man under the half-century mark a boy.

Her busy days were filled with the evidence of his hard work, her nights were starred with dreams of that single kiss. As one day spun into the next, she, too, began to wonder when Bram Rafferty would come *home*.

Often, in the lengthening spring evenings, she would rock in tempo to her clicking knitting needles and try to decide how he had insinuated himself into the life at Seven Pines so thoroughly that it seemed incomplete without him. It was easy to enumerate the improvements he had made and the tasks he had performed. Those were a part of it, but not all. There was an intangible quality that eluded definition. Repeatedly, her thoughts returned to that first impression. The meeting of an old friend, a kindred soul.

Seven Pines for him, like her, was not just dirt and crops and people. The work was a labor of love for him too, a part of his heart and soul. Conviction grew that she had defined the intangible and with it, the reason for her eagerness.

He returned on a late May day. Tessa squealed and spread

the news through the house, then raced out to meet him while Damask . . . dithered, even though she felt there was nothing sillier than a dithering woman. But there she was darting to the door, jumping back into the house, turning to race up the stairs, pausing halfway to smooth a shaking hand over her worn frock, patting her hair and wondering how she looked.

Quelling those emotions with a stern command, she descended the stairs and walked out onto the porch by putting one foot carefully in front of the other.

He stood tall and dark and vibrant, framed in a shaft of sunlight pouring through the tops of the pines. One thick strong arm was wrapped about Tessa's waist, and his face tilted down to her, black curls spilling across his forehead.

As though he sensed Damask's presence, he looked up. Their eyes met and locked and questioned. Had she changed her mind? Had he? Did she regret the short time that was left? Did he? Did she hate him? Did he want her—want her as a true partner?

Tessa cut off the questioning looks abruptly by tugging on his arm and pulling him to the porch, where she informed Damask that he had brought presents for them both. He stood at the bottom of the steps, one boot propped on the second tread, and she stared down into the classic features of his face with its high cheekbones and perfectly arched brows and brilliant eyes and strange curving scar.

"Welcome home, Bram."

The soft, almost hesitant greeting eased beneath the guard Bram had consciously erected during his weeks away. He had spent the major part of his life needing no one. That wouldn't change just because he took a wife. There were practical reasons for it, he told himself. A wife was necessary in order to have the sons he craved, but she would never be necessary to him for herself alone.

He had tried to forget her laugh, a bell-like chime that sent chills chasing across his skin like a lover's sigh. He had tried to forget the saucy, tempting, teasing dimple. He had tried to forget her and the honeyed yielding of her kiss. He had tried to forget his barely acknowledged yearning for more, for tenderness and companionship and . . .

He had tried to forget and had almost . . . almost succeeded.

Welcome home, Bram. Sweet words to hear and sweeter lips to speak them, if they were meant. He probed her lustrous nut-brown eyes and longing settled in a painful lump in the back of his throat.

"Am I coming home?" he asked.

She hesitated. Disappointment lanced through him. Him, the man who told himself a wife—no, Damask Downing— would never be necessary to him for herself alone.

"I hope so. We've missed you, Bram," she murmured and her eyes dropped to the vicinity of his chin, "all of us."

He could not have spoken past the strangling vise of his throat if he wanted to, for her admission had stricken him with such a plethora of emotions he wasn't sure which was uppermost: the awesome gladness that weakened his knees or the terror that wrung his heart.

In the days that followed, the terror died away to an ache that settled at the base of his breastbone, announcing its presence with a throb whenever Damask laid a trusting hand upon his arm to ask a question, or when she smiled at him, or when her laugh rang with the crystal clarity of chimes.

She deserved so much, and he could give her so little. And never the one thing she deserved the most—a love that would shelter and protect and cherish. How could he when he didn't believe that love existed except in the minds of poets, impressionable women, and gullible men?

She was resigned . . . no, it was more than resignation, and that knowledge gave him more pain than pleasure—until she changed.

It was a perfect day for a wedding. The sky was a pale blue, bedecked with a lacing of gossamer clouds. A flirtatious breeze toyed with ribbons and feathered plumes and frolicked among full-skirted crinolines. The cheerful throng shifted across the grounds of Seven Pines like the bright colors of a kaleidoscope, groups joining, scattering, reforming.

Chatter and laughter flowed up to the brooding figure at a second-story window. Bram Rafferty's presence in the yard below acted like a magnet, drawing Damask to view him from the shelter of the curtains. A black broadcloth frock coat rode shoulders that were broad and thick. And his eyes, if she could see them, would be lit by a staunch integrity.

Was that integrity a lie? Her hand squeezed the curtain into a mass of wrinkles. If only she knew one way or the other, but Elize's letter, so long awaited and so recently come, had not answered a single question. It had only raised more, many more. She didn't need to have it in front of her. Every word was burned into her memory.

Cousin Damask, I cannot imagine how you have come to know a man like Black Irish Rafferty and it worries me. But I have gathered what information I could. He is a man of mystery here in the City. Andre says no one knows anything about him, beyond rumors. Apparently he immigrated here with his family as a child. They would seem to be gone or dead now. What he does when he is not traveling the riverboats during the season or gaming in the City during the rest of the year, no one knows. He has no friends, but no enemies either. The one thing that everyone is agreed upon, so Andre tells me, is that he has an obsession about owning land and becoming a wealthy planter. Rumors attach themselves to him like burrs. Most are too ridiculous to be repeated, but there is one that persists. Whether true or not, I cannot say, but it is said there was something strange about his father's death. The rumor is he murdered him.

Damask's dull gaze lifted, noting, but not touched by, the beauty of the scene. The orchard, where guests were strolling through the orderly rows, was thickly foliaged. The wisteria dripped grapelike clusters of lavender blossoms.

Her carefully tended flower bed, curving around the front corner of the porch, was abloom with geraniums, nasturtiums, violets, and daisies. Benches had been hastily constructed of split logs, facing the entrance to the center lane, which was shaded by apple and peach trees. Before that archway she would pledge herself to Bram Rafferty, the man who had an *obsession* about becoming a wealthy planter, the man who might have murdered his own father.

Her wedding day. It should have been so different. It should have been a happy day when the Downing and Marlowe families, so long friends, were joined in kinship. Instead, the Marlowes had refused to come, and the man who should have been her groom was not yet aware that she was marrying another man. She should have written him.

It would hurt him, and she didn't want to do that anymore than his family did. Not Hunt with his sober suits completely at odds with his cheerful personality. Not Hunt with his slate gray eyes and sandy sweep of flamboyant moustache he had affected when he began studying law—to add dignity to his youthful face, he told her with a mischevious grin.

Why had Hunt accepted her every delay of their marriage? Why hadn't he pressed harder, insisted that she set a date? Was Wade right? Did her ambition and ability to rule Seven Pines make Hunt uncomfortable? Would he be secretly glad she had married another? Was it only honor and habit that compelled Hunt to ask her to marry him?

"*Chérie,* you watch your young man, eh?" *Tante* Elodie Downing bustled in. "What a shame you go to bed so early last night. My Harry, he was very impressed. How they talk into the night to make my head spin. Garnett Lee, he find a man who have the same gloom as he. You would think the Yankee, he march on the doorstep tomorrow! La, these men, I do not understand!"

She paused for breath, her bright-eyed gaze roaming the room. "What have we here? You have not opened the trunk your young man have send? Have you no curiosity?"

Damask's eyes rested on the stylish pink-paneled trunk

with its dark rose-colored straps. It, along with Tessa's, had arrived on a steamer up from New Orleans at dawn and was delivered by wagon a short time before—a gift from Bram Rafferty. A gift from the man? Or a bribe from the gambler?

"Come, *chérie!* I must see what you have. Could you not hear Tessa's squeals of pleasure? It was like going through a treasure chest! Everything! From frocks and slippers to the doll with lace christening gown."

Tante Elodie stood before the trunk, frowning down at the expanse of her skirts. "Ah! To be *la jeune fille* again when *la mode* was more sensible! I see why the men complain of the crinoline. Your *Oncle* Harry, he call it a sign of the raving lunacy of women! So!" She planted her hands on her waist and gave Damask a despairing look. "How do I get close enough to see?"

Damask rather envied her aunt's gracefully billowing skirts, and would gladly have put up with the inconvenience to be so stylishly dressed. She wasn't so settled and sensible that she didn't have a young girl's hunger for beautiful things and it had taken a supreme effort of will to ignore the dainty taunting trunk. Had anyone, other than Bram Rafferty, sent it to her, she would have thrown the lid wide instantly.

"*Chérie*, hold my hand. If I get lost, come to find me, *s'il vous plaît.*" Her aunt laughed and began to kneel. The skirt billowed high around her shoulders and her plump beringed hand fought to crush it down.

"I think I have it." *Tante* Elodie edged toward the chest. "Closer than this I cannot go! *Très magnifique, chérie.* Quickly! I confess I am dying to see what you have!"

Obediently, Damask leaned over to unlock the trunk and lift the lid. A blur of white sprang out with a metallic twang. *Tante* Elodie shrieked and fell over backward while Damask leapt away with a startled cry.

"What was it?" *Tante* Elodie struggled up to peer over her ballooning skirt.

"A—" Laughter shook Damask. "A . . . A c-c-crinoline!"

"Sacre bleu! Your *Oncle* Harry, he always say the crinoline, it have the life of its own." *Tante* Elodie's dark dancing eyes met Damask's and they both dissolved into laughter.

At length, *Tante* Elodie dried her eyes and fluttered a lace-trimmed handkerchief toward the bulk of the crinoline. "Remove that thing before it attack us again, *chérie.*"

Still smiling, Damask stood it in a corner like a sentinel guarding the treasure chest. Her hand trembled slightly as she returned to lift the lid covering the tray.

"Tante Elodie," she breathed in stunned surprise. "So much!"

"Oui, chérie. Your young *galant,* he is very generous, I think."

Together they bent over the chest, removing and exclaiming over every carefully chosen item. There were soaps and perfumes scented of violets, Damask's favorite perfume. There was a large tin of bonbons with a silver bonbon dish, ribbons and silk stockings and frilly garters. There were wrist and half-length gloves in kid and silk: white, ecru, and black with daintily embroidered backs. Lace fans and a tiny footed bowl filled with hairpins. Shawls of paisley and cashmere and a Tunisian silk striped in shades of ecru and cinnamon. And a black lace mantilla with a black ebony comb.

"I'm almost afraid to move the tray," Damask said shakily.

"Ah, *chérie,"* *Tante* Elodie sighed, "your young *galant,* he know how to please a woman. Look at this." She plucked up the Tunisian silk shawl, draping it over her hands. "He have chosen the exact color of your eyes. And this, the cashmere. The color of your cheeks when you blush. He wish very much to please you, *chérie. Le bon Dieu,* he is very good to give you such a man as this *Monsieur* Rafferty."

Was God good to her? Who was Bram Rafferty? The man of kindness and integrity and strength who had won the hearts of everyone at Seven Pines? The man of generosity who had lavished her and Tessa and Gramps with gifts? The gambler surrounded by an aura of mystery? The man so obsessed with wealth and land that he might have done anything to get it and might do anything to keep it? The man who had murdered his own father?

The questions haunted her while she dressed in her mother's wedding gown from a time years before the rage for broader skirts. The white satin had aged to a creamy color. The skirt was slightly belled with row upon row of satin ruffles from the knee to the tops of the matching satin slippers. A wreath of pink roses crowned her head and a lace ruff at the neckline topped the form-fitting bodice with *gigot* sleeves, full at the shoulders and tapering to a close fit at the wrists.

If only Wade were home, she mourned silently as she placed her gloved hand atop the thickness of Uncle Harry's wrist and began a halting march to the melody pouring out through the parlor windows. It hadn't been easy to explain his absence, but she had managed. Sickness, she lied. He couldn't leave the City, but sent his regrets. Why hadn't she heard from him? Was he so humiliated by what he had done that he couldn't bring himself to face her? Didn't he know that she would forgive him anything? Had it really been his fault? Had Bram . . .

Did it matter? Seven Pines now belonged to Bram Rafferty and she would never give it up. Through a break in the rows of guests she could see the South Field with its neat rows of cotton, a foot tall and thickly garbed in green leaves. The reason for, the purpose of Seven Pines. Papa's dream. Her dream. No sacrifice was too great for it. Good man or bad, Bram Rafferty would be her husband.

She could not control the involuntary inward shrinking or force color into her blanched cheeks. But she could stiffen her spine and raise her chin and meet his sober stare with a steady, unflinching expression.

The gold band weighted her hand and heart like a shackle as the day wore on. Damask stood with her unsmiling groom and chatted with her neighbors. She picked at the food piled high on her plate. She danced with everyone, except Bram who seemed content to stand aside and watch.

The setting sun stained the western sky a hot pink, and lanterns twinkled in the trees like fireflies.

A shroud of light haze clung to the trees as the guests began drifting away, singly, in pairs, in groups, until only *Tante* Elodie and Uncle Harry and Cousin Garnett Lee were left.

Tessa, torn between the sorrow of leaving Damask and the excitement of spending a month visiting with her adored *Tante* Elodie, wept in Damask's arms and hugged Bram until he brushed the hair from her sweating forehead and promised a surprise from New Orleans.

The buggy rolled away into the night. The clopping hooves of the horses muted with distance and fell silent. The shrill song of crickets broke the silence. The frantic race of Damask's heart belied her outward calm.

Everything suddenly felt so unreal. Her noble motive seemed foolish next to the feeling that she had made the biggest mistake of her life. It was one thing in the light of day, when there was still a choice to be made, to say that no sacrifice was too great. It was another to stand alone in the hush of the night and know that the man who brooded beside her now had all rights over her.

"If you would like to go up, I'll follow in a few minutes."

Damask started violently at the sound of his voice. He would follow, he said. Follow and take her as his wife. Would he be patient or impatient? Kind or cruel? She tried to speak, but her heart was pummeling the breath from her lungs. Instead, she nodded and moved away on knees that threatened to wobble out of control.

Lulu, uncharacteristically silent, helped her change into a voluminous, beruffled lawn nightgown, then brushed her hair until it gleamed in the candlelight. Setting the brush aside, Lulu turned down the bed and plumped the pillows, then gave Damask a brief, hard hug fraught with unspoken commiseration and hurried out.

She was alone. Terrifyingly alone.

The distant sound of a fiddle drew her to the window. The glow of bonfires washed the indigo sky above the quarter street. Damask leaned against the sill, listening to the faint sounds of music and merriment. The minutes slipped by. She waited.

A sound shattered her trancelike state, bringing every sense to screaming life. A boot scuffed on the stairs and her heart felt as though it would burst. The stair treads creaked, and chills scampered over her skin in a madcap rush. Her trembling knees weakened. The doorknob rattled, a faint squeaking sound, and her heart leapt into her throat.

She could feel his presence in the room and the warm tendrils of vitality emanating from him awoke an unreasoning terror. The door clicked shut and a scream strangled in her throat. She froze and waited. Her nerves were stretched as taut as piano wire.

"Damask."

Imperious, harsh, gutteral: her name jangled discordantly. Like the lifeless wooden figure on her music box, she turned to face her future.

His rigidly set expression shifted into a frown that yanked the arch of his brows flat over his eyes. "You're . . . you're afraid of me." Accusation, statement, question all in one. "Did you think I would fall on you like a slavering animal?" he demanded, anger and disbelief mingling in the tone of his voice.

Her head snapped up. "I don't know what you will do!" she cried out. "I don't know you!"

He stared a moment, his eyes dimming. "No, you don't," he said heavily, weariness tugging his voice into its lowest range. He moved to the bedside table and began untying his cravat. "This won't get any easier for you if you put it off."

An icy hand of fear squeezed Damask's throat. She had made him angry. Would he exact his revenge on her? Whatever happened, he was right. It wouldn't get any easier. But if she could go back to the moment he walked into this room, she wasn't sure she could have changed anything.

The linen sheets were cool to the touch and the darkness that fell when he snuffed the candle was a blessing. She lay, ramrod stiff, listening to the swishing sounds of his clothes as he shed them. The feather mattress whooshed and sank with his weight, threatening to roll her toward him. He settled near, but not touching. She could feel the heat radiating from him and hear the soft even whisper of his breath above the music wafting through the open window.

She waited, her nerves stretched to snapping, her heart not daring to beat—and nothing happened. She was alert for the first warning of rustling sheets to herald his moving toward her. Instead, she heard:

"We'll need rain for the cotton soon."

"Wha . . . what?" she breathed, stunned, distrusting the evidence of her own ears.

"Rain. We'll need it soon."

"Yes, rain," she murmured in bewildered agreement.

A short, pungent silence settled.

"The house should be shingled when we get back." His smooth voice glided through the darkness.

"How . . . how nice." The tension began oozing away at his matter-of-fact tone discussing mundanities.

"I've left money with Jims to pay for them so the work can get done."

"G-Good," she said, biting her lip against the hysterical impulse to giggle. There she was waiting to be fallen on and ravished, and he was talking about rain and shingles!

The tension was gone, and the fear with it. But Damask wasn't sure whether she wanted to scream with laughter or weep with mortification. Was he trying to allay her fear, or did he find her eminently resistible? Worse, did he need to make no effort to resist her at all? Perversely, the prospect of being ravished didn't seem quite so bad.

Beside her, he stirred and rolled onto his side. Digging an elbow into the pillow, he propped his cheek on his knuckles.

"Am I going to have to talk about rain and shingles until one of us perishes from boredom?" he asked, a thread of laughter in his voice. "I've dreamed of doing many things on my wedding night, but that wasn't one of them."

"What have you dreamed of doing?" she asked in a throaty whisper that surprised her.

He leaned down, unhurriedly brushing her lips with his. "This," he murmured and cradled her cheek in the warm hollow of his palm and pressed gentle kisses along the line of her jaw to the lobe of her ear. "And this," he said, his breath hot against her temple. "Don't be afraid, colleen," his voice vibrated through her. "I can wait, if I must."

Damask's lashes drifted down and the weakness of relief sluiced through her. Whatever else he might be, the man of kindness had come to her tonight. He would not hurt her or force her.

His lips feathered down the curve of her neck and she arched to give him access to the thrumming pulse at her throat. "Would you?" she asked, a breathless sound of supplication.

He raised up and the cool touch of the breeze caressed the spot his lips had warmed. "Yes," he whispered, his thumb tracing the line of her mouth. "We will have a lifetime together. We can begin it when you are—"

"Bram—" She threaded her fingers through the short cropped curls at his temple. "You talk too much. Will we have to perish from boredom before we begin our life together?"

She heard the short huffing sound of his breath as it left him and then she was in his arms, molded to the length of him while his laughter rumbled in her ear. "If I've made a jackass of myself tonight, it was in a good cause. I won't ever hurt you, Damask. I swear it."

"I know," she murmured against his throat, "I know you won't." And she did. She believed it, heart and soul, with ever fiber of her being.

Fear was gone. There was only anticipation, then reality. The reality of lips that cherished, hearts that pounded in unison, and his hands ghosting across her flesh until she gasped with the pleasure of it. He touched her, searching out all of those secret feminine hollows and curves. Each touch sent a rush of wanton desire coursing through her. He courted and enchanted with his hard body and his gentle hands and his hungry lips. He brought her to the quivering peak of fulfillment. There could be no more, she thought wildly. She would die if her heart beat any faster or her breath rasped any quicker. She would die if he touched her again and this building tension exploded. Yet her knees yielded for the passage of his narrow hips and she yearned for more . . . for something more.

"Damask," he groaned against her ear, "this once . . . only this once . . ."

The pain was quick. A sharp tearing that made her arch against him with a cry that he muffled with his lips.

"Bram . . ."

"Rest," he whispered. "Rest. It won't hurt again."

"No pain." Wonder laced her voice as the tension climbed. "Bram!"

"Oh, God," he breathed and began to move in satin smooth strokes.

Passion, raw and wild, swept her away on its turbulent wings and spiraled into the star-studded night, where it burst in a blinding fusion of light and sound then showered back to earth in a glittering rain of stardust.

Above her, Bram shuddered and lay spent, braced upon the elbows that bracketed her head.

Damask had no way of knowing, but she thought what had happened must have been different, must have been unique to them. No woman who was treated this way at night could frown or carp at her husband during the day. It would be so easy to love Bram Rafferty. So very easy.

Bram rolled to the side and gathered her to him, holding her in the curve of his body as though he never intended to let her go. "Sweet dreams, colleen," he whispered and moments later she was wrapped in the comforting arms of contented sleep.

* * *

A movement woke her. Bram inching out of bed. She turned over and touched his arm. "Is something wrong?"

"Nothing. Go back to sleep. I'm going to find something to eat."

"Eat! At this hour?"

"Yes, eat," he chuckled as he leaned over the bed and trailed his finger the length of her nose. "Somehow I've worked up a powerful hunger."

"Oh!" A wave of heat crawled across her cheeks as she scrambled from the bed, snatching her nightgown on. "Wait here. I know where everything is. It will be easier for me to get it."

"It's too dark for you to be out alone."

She paused, fingers stilled around one button of her dressing gown. "There isn't anything I can't find here in pitch dark. All I need to know is, how hungry are you?"

"You may need me just to carry it," he laughed.

Damask resisted the urge to press her hands to her hot cheeks and rushed out. "I'll manage."

She tripped lightly down the stairs, her smile wide and happy. Swinging around the newel post as Tessa was wont to do, she paused and listened. A horse? Clopping up the drive in the middle of the night?

The front door swung open and Damask stepped onto the porch, watching the rider approach through a deep patch of shadow. He entered the silvery curtain of moonlight. It glinted off pale hair and she began to run.

"Wade! Wade!"

The figure was slumped unresponsively in the saddle. Damask ran with her hem snapping out behind her and met horse and rider in the gloom beneath the stand of loblolly pines.

"Wade! I'm so glad you've come home!" she cried, holding onto his knee while the horse ambled to the porch.

Her brother dismounted and slapped the reins about a column before turning to her. Damask resisted the urge to hug him. Unbridled displays of affection made Wade uncomfortable.

"Oh, Wade! Where have you been all this time?"

"Where I could have some peace, and people didn't question my every move," he sighed.

"But we needed you here. So much has happened."

"I know," he said glumly. "Let's go inside."

Damask trailed him into the parlor, biting back the questions he always hated while she lit the lamp. He sank into a chair and sat with slumping shoulders, the sharp contours of his face tugged down in an attitude of defeat so listless and overwhelmed it hurt her to look at him.

"Wade, you must have been so worried when you came back from the City. Why didn't you tell me? No worry is so bad when it can be shared."

"I couldn't! I couldn't tell you I had lost Seven Pines when I know how much you love it!"

She watched his thin delicate hands cover his face, and she went to him. Brushing the lank strands of pale, almost colorless hair from his forehead, she began to murmur soothingly, but he rejected her attempt to console him.

"I've lost it, Damask! Lost it all!" He raised his head and she could see the shining tracks of tears winding down his cheeks. "What will I do? How will I live?"

A flash of impatience hardened Damask's face momentarily. Not a thought for Tessa or Gramps or her, just himself.

"Oh," he moaned, "if only Mama were alive, she would know what to do."

If only Mama were alive. Impatience withered in a searing flame of guilt. If only Mama were alive. And Papa. And they would be, if it hadn't been for her. They would be here to help Wade. They would be here to see that he had everything he needed. Just as she tried to do. Just as she would always try to do.

"Sh, Wade. Everything will be all right. I promise. Bram and I were married today and—"

"Thank God! Thank God!" His tears dried abruptly, a

smile growing. "I knew you would do it! You'll see! Nothing has changed! And you'll make him give me all the money I need! I knew I could count on you!"

Damask evaded his clutching hands and stared at the leaping lights in his shallow blue eyes until his smile died and an ugly frown began to warp his features.

"What's wrong? You said you married him!"

"Yes, I did. But I cannot promise he will do anything more than give you a home."

"Why not?" Wade snarled. "He owes me that and much more!"

"He is paying whatever debt he owes you by supporting us all, Wade. Don't you understand—"

"You think so, do you?" The crest of his thin lips lifted in a sneer. "The man *cheated* us of Seven Pines!"

A band of pain squeezed Damask's heart in a relentless grip. "Wade! What are you saying?" Her voice shrilled in her own ears.

"I said he cheated me! Oh, I couldn't prove it. He's very good, and no one warned me he was a cardsharp. It was only afterwards that I learned, and then I would have challenged him to a duel . . ."

"No! No!" Damask gasped out. "Never do such a thing!"

A cheat! A cardsharp! It belied all of Damask's instincts about Bram Rafferty. Fragmented memories flashed through her mind. Bram's hand tenderly brushing straggling curls from Tessa's face. That look of agony in his eyes when he stared down at her bruised wrist. His smile, slow and reluctant, and the heart-stopping warmth that could grow in the depths of his eyes. His patience and kindness in allaying her fear. His hands, gently drifting across her flesh.

But there was also Elize's letter. The mystery. His obsession. Would he have cheated? A man as obsessed with his dream as she was with hers. What might she be capable of doing for Seven Pines? Lie, cheat, steal. She didn't like to think she could, but she had been raised by her honorable Papa. What of Bram Rafferty?

And Wade. There was no reason for him to lie. A lie could only hurt them all by making it impossible to accept what had happened. He loved her and Tessa and Gramps and Seven Pines. He wouldn't hurt them.

Wade stood and embraced her. "I know how hard this is for you. I'm sure he has been careful to insinuate himself into your affections, and you are too gentle and good to believe ill of him."

He *had* cheated them! Rage sprinted through her on hot winged feet. He had come here and befriended Tessa and Gramps. He had made her believe that he was kind and good. The sheer hypocrisy of it stunned her. Just hours ago she had lain in his arms and thought how easy it would be to love him! Her hand knotted into a fist, rising to scrape the taste of Bram Rafferty from her mouth with the bruising brush of her knuckles. She was married to him! Forever bound to a man without honor, without a conscience!

"Wade, knowing that he cheated you, how could you suggest that we be married?"

"You can't see it, Damask? What better way to be revenged on him? For the rest of his life he must live with our contempt, supporting us all the while!"

"Oh, Wade . . ."

"Damask?" Bram called out.

She froze, eyes wide as he rounded the archway and stopped.

"I was worried when you took so long, but I see I shouldn't have been. Downing," he said, a hint of distaste in the name.

"My brother has told me you cheated him out of Seven Pines!" she cried in a voice rough with scorn.

He stiffened, head snapping up as the furied blaze of his eyes cut toward Wade then sliced back to her. Cinnamon eyes and brilliant ice-blue locked in bitterness.

"Have you nothing to say? No denial?" she asked sharply.

"I expected it."

"You admit it?"

"I admit nothing."

"No, you wouldn't! A cheat! A cardsharp! A liar! Why would you admit you've stolen our land and tricked me into marriage! The union sickens me!"

"Damask!"

Was it threat or plea that rolled from his throat? She was beyond caring, too angry to be softened by a plea, too disillusioned to be affected by a threat.

"You've got your land and your house and the wealth it can bring you! And a wife, let's not forget that!" she sneered. "I'll give you respectability, however unwillingly, if a man like you can ever lay claim to it. But that's all you'll get from me! You can forget your fine strong Rafferty sons, because I will never allow you to lay your filthy hands on me again!"

His eyes burned, pinning her in place like a hapless butterfly. The scar on his temple throbbed and writhed, and his hands worked in convulsive fists. Damask could almost hear the hot words that wanted to pour through his clenched teeth, and she waited for his control to shatter and the words to come.

"I have explained myself to no man or woman for nineteen years," he said with a calm that was terrifying to watch. "I don't intend to start with you, unwilling wife or no. I told you once to believe what you will."

THE HONEYMOON

June 1859

Chapter 7

DAMASK *stood in the relative cool of the shadow cast by the texas* deck, a lonely figure in billowing skirts, the brim of her bonnet tugged back by the brisk breeze. Few passengers braved the heat of the day, so she remained alone.

She soon lost interest in the vast cane fields broken by the occasional planter's mansion set in pecan groves, and in the cascade of swirling muddy water slapping against the hull. Her hand tightened around the rail, pushing the loose, dull gold band away from her finger. She raised her eyes to the fluffy clouds sailing indolently across the light bright sky. Would this trip never end? It seemed as though she had been listening to the churning paddlewheel forever. Two days. Two eternities endured.

Why did he insist on this honeymoon trip? Insist. That made it sound as though there had been an argument, when there had been none. He simply stated flatly and unequivocally that they were going as planned, and that was that. Master of Seven Pines. Master of her people. Master of her.

A gambler. A liar. A cheat. A man capable of any foul deed. Her husband. She was yoked to him for life, a man she loathed.

How could she have been so easily deceived? Why hadn't she questioned his actions more? Of course he would spend money and time on improvements at Seven Pines. It held the promise of wealth. And Sim. What a fool she had been to doubt his own admission that it was money that had sent him

93

into the burning cabin! She could see everything so clearly now. He had played her like a fish on a line.

How right Wade was! She was nothing but a naive little country mouse too innocent for the world beyond the fences of Seven Pines. Only she wasn't quite so innocent anymore. She knew Bram Rafferty for what he was. He wouldn't find her so easy to dupe again.

''Damask.''

His use of her given name after two days of frigid formality sent a thrill of alarm through her, which was betrayed only by the ebbing color in her cheeks. She turned in a rush of bristling resentment, her gelid gaze settling on his intricately tied cravat.

''We are approaching the place where the *Lucky Lady* went down,'' he said. Her eyes widened, flying to meet his.

The cool remote gaze had kindled to warmth. She saw compassion in those eyes that spoke so eloquently of loss and sorrow and sadness. She tried to remember that he did nothing that would gain him nothing, but what could he get from this? And why did she feel that he, too, had suffered loss and guilt and grief? She yearned to accept the comfort he offered. She needed it, but not from a man like him. Before she could weaken, she whirled back to the rail.

''There, beyond the levee, is the plantation,'' he said. ''Do you see the grove of oaks? That is where the passengers are buried.''

''Papa? Mama and Papa are there?''

The river was high, lapping at the slope just below the crest of the levee, so that the steamer chugged along above the surrounding land. Damask looked down into the grove of oaks beyond the levee road: ancient trees with gray beards of moss trailing into the thick shadows, their arthritic limbs groping for the sky and twisting along just above the ground. She caught a faint glimmer of light reflecting from a headstone, and tears spread along the rim of her lashes.

If only . . .

Useless words. Nothing could be changed. But how could

she accept the fact that her parents were dead because of her? That Wade had lost his way because of her? That Seven Pines was now in the grip of the man who stood so silently at her side because of her?

Guilt tore at her as she watched the grove of oaks vanish into the distance and listened to the *sweet-sweet-sweet-sweet* call of a cardinal.

She stirred at last and raised a troubled gaze to Bram's face. He stood quietly, his long-lashed eyes sketching the outline of her features as though he were committing them to memory. He reached out, his fingers so close to her cheek she could feel the heat of his skin. She waited for that touch, a part of her aching for it, but his long fingers coiled into a fist and fell away to his side. His eyes closed as though he were steeling himself for something, then he swiveled on his heel and strode rapidly away.

Damask reached blindly for the rail. The gold band around her finger hit the wood with a dull thunk and she flinched. He was everything she despised, yet he had given her the comfort of silence, and his strength and warmth to ward off the bitterness of death. No one could have been more sensitive to her need for those things. If only this was the real man. If only . . .

Bitter words. As bitter as death.

Damask was not disappointed by her first view of the City. New Orleans, the *mecca* for all Louisianians, hugged a deep curve of the river, fanning out from the levee and stretching away to the cypress swamps far to the east. It was a stunning sight. As far as the eye could see were rooftops: slate, cypress, Spanish tile; hipped roofs, gabled roofs, flat roofs. Church spires pointed to the sky, and shining domes reflected the sun with a blinding brilliance.

Her wondering gaze followed the curving bend of the river to its intersection with the opposite bank. Rocking upon the cradle of the Mississippi were tall-masted sailing vessels flying the flags of a dozen or more nations. Interspersed among the graceful masts were the shorter, squat stacks of riverboats. A ferry trailed a white-foamed wake across the width of the river, heading for Algiers on the western shore. Vanishing around the far bend was a steam-driven towboat, pulling a sailing ship denuded of sails, its naked masts looking curiously vulnerable as it plowed through the roiling water.

Bram stood inside the salon, watching Damask through the window. Reason told him that she had little cause for blind trust, but illogical emotion hauled his spirits into the abyss. A muscle worked along the corded line of his jaw as he cursed himself for his stubborn pride. He should have denied Downing's accusation. Vehemently!

And if he had? a tiny voice asked. What would have happened? He would have humbled himself for nothing. She would never believe him over her brother, though how she could be fooled by that sorry excuse for a man was beyond him. No, his denial would never banish the doubt Downing's poison had instilled.

It was better this way. He wasn't looking for tenderness or companionship or, God forbid, love. He needed a partner, a mother for his sons. Though what she might do if he tried to put his *filthy* hands on her again, he didn't like to imagine. For now, the land was enough. The sons could wait for time to cool the heat of her anger and for Wade Downing to betray himself as he must eventually.

Meanwhile, he would continue this farce of a honeymoon trip. Why had he been so adamant that they come as though nothing had happened? It wasn't like him to fling himself at a brick wall at a headlong gallop.

There was business to conduct in New Orleans—which could easily have been handled by a letter. He wanted to make a last trip to Dublin—which was unnecessary. So, why? He stared at the heavy weight of the bun resting on Damask's nape and remembered the silken feel of her hair draped across his hand and her response to him, so unexpected, so passionate. Her every touch and moan and cry of pleasure had initiated him into a new world where passion was more than a bodily function; it was a realm of heart and soul and emotion.

A visceral response snapped his teeth together. He didn't want it, and yet, he knew, the frail hope of sharing that again had compelled him to insist on this trip. Away from Seven Pines, away from Wade Downing, she would see him as a different man. He would prove to her . . .

Damn! She was a woman like any other! And the proof of that was the fact that she had *sold* herself to him! Whatever her reasons, she had used her body to buy what she wanted. Vagrant memory struggled for life, and Bram smashed it into submission, sickness crawling through his belly.

With the same ruthless concentration he applied to a game of cards, he began sifting the faces of his past. It was maddening to find they had gone stale and flat. A mane of lush curls flickering like gold dust seemed brassy when compared to the bubbling champagne shimmer of Damask's silken tresses. The memory of smooth milky skin curdled beside the vision of Damask's honey-tinted glow and wild rose cheeks. Ripe, pouting lips appeared fleshy and overblown beside her sweet pure curve of delicate color. The sultry pout became distasteful when compared to the gentle smile with its flirtatious dimple. Voluptuous sensuality had palled. Bram stared at his wife with a frown, shifting restlessly.

He removed his broad-brimmed white straw hat to rake his hand through his hair. Replacing it, he tugged at the brim to shade the hot fury in his eyes. Nothing had changed! He was still the man he always was! He needed no one! Especially a woman who refused to believe anything but the worst about him!

"Master Bram?"

"What?" he ground out.

"You left your cigar case in the stateroom."

Bram took it. "Thank you, Nero. Is everything packed?"

"Yes, sir."

"Good. Meet us at the cabs with the baggage."

"Yes, sir."

Nero's voice was an uninflected monotone, barely rising above a whisper. It never failed to infect Bram with a vague uneasiness, and he turned now to watch Nero leave the salon. The boy didn't seem to have anything of his parents in him; not Aunt Sarah's gift of gab or Harford's cheerful outlook.

Bram suspected that Nero's years as Wade Downing's body servant might have something to do with that. Living under Downing's thumb must be hell. Dammit! He regretted signing Nero over to Downing. But after stripping him of all else, Bram felt he had to leave him with something. And for Damask's brother, all appearance and no substance, a body servant seemed to be the best thing. Still, Bram could not shake the feeling that it had been a mistake. He sensed a seething intensity behind the impassive expression that shielded Nero's skull-like face. Why had Downing insisted on making him a *gift* of his body servant for this trip?

Bram shifted his attention back to Damask. Who knew why Downing did anything, and what difference could the reason make? Nero was with him, whether he needed him or not.

Damask was wearing one of the gowns from her treasure chest. The skirt, draped artfully over the wire-cage crinoline, was a color the couturiere, Madame Blanchard, called *pensée*, a rich pansy purple. The overdress, in a rose color, had a broad gathered skirt falling to knee length, the hemline ornamented with a geometric design in pansy-colored cord. The simple bodice was form-fitting. A prim collar encircled her slender neck and the sleeves hugged the length of her arm. A small straw bonnet, adorned with silk pansies, perched atop her head. Bram caught a glimpse of a smile when she looked back to say a word to a fellow passenger.

She was not used to the strictures of a crinoline yet. Leaning too near the rail, she had belled out the skirt, giving

Bram a delightful view of lacy pantalettes and small black shoes. Lulu marched into view, tongue and finger wagging, and Bram's lean cheeks creased with amusement. A moment later the crinoline swayed drunkenly and Damask's cheeks stained with color as she swept an abashed look around to see if anyone had caught her undignified position.

The amusement vanished when her eyes met his and hardened with an expression that seemed to say: "You bought me, but little good will it do you."

Damask's first impression of the City was a disgusting stench that wrinkled her nose. The second, noise. She was both repelled and frightened by the bustle and filth of the docks that brought a vivid reminder of an anthill she had stirred with a stick as a child.

She stared out over row upon row of crates, barrels, and bales that stretched in all directions. And people. Everywhere! Stevedores with straining muscles wrestled bales of cotton with curved cotton hooks. Others rolled huge hogsheads or carried smaller quintels filled with sugar and molasses. Some wore gaudy handkerchiefs wrapped around their foreheads and all were bathed in sweat.

Nearby, a tallyman rubbed his bulbous nose while studying a small ledger sitting atop a barrel. Jerking a stub of pencil from behind his ear, he raised a raucous shout, pointing to a ship behind him before leaning over his jutting belly to add a note to the ledger.

Carts creaked across the wooden docks. Drays, pulled by teams of neighing horses or braying mules, laced their way around stacked bales, the draymen blistering Damask's ears as they cleared paths through a wayward throng of sailors and strumpets and top-hatted gentlemen. And there were children like none she had ever seen. Grime-encrusted ragamuffins with spindly limbs played hide and seek amidst a pile of stacked barrels. Everywhere she looked there seemed to be a thin-shanked hound whose jutting ribs could be counted, even from a distance. Except for one raggedly dressed old woman, sitting beside a basket of oranges, everyone seemed to be yelling at the top of their lungs.

Instinctively, she moved closer to Bram, unaware that he studied her face with a frown. "You look pale. Are you unwell?"

"No," she answered softly, disappointment stark in her voice. "It's so . . . so dirty and so . . . so noisy."

"It's New Orleans," he said shortly and led her toward the gangplank.

Why had he brought her here? Already she yearned for the peace and security of Seven Pines.

As they made their way across the docks to a waiting row of horse-drawn cabs, Damask sensed curious eyes and glanced toward four burly stevedores lounging on cotton bales. One of the men was short and swarthy, another was tall and exceedingly fair, the last two were sandy-colored with freckled skin and matching impudent grins. Their bold appraisal brought a flood of color to her cheeks and she quickly looked away.

Bram gave her a hand into the open carriage before directing Lulu and Nero to take the next one, with their luggage, directly to the St. Charles Hotel. She waited while he took Nero aside to give him a few private instructions, and saw him turn and stop and stare at the quartet of men.

His lips thinned and the thatch of black lashes narrowed beneath his lowering brows. Lean white-gloved fingers pinched the brim of his hat and flipped it back to Nero.

His gloves followed and Damask sat forward in stunned disbelief while he shrugged out of his coat and draped it across Nero's outstretched forearm. Bram's long brown fingers climbed the row of buttons on his waistcoat, and Nero, startled out of his usual passivity, shot a curious look her way as he stepped up to slide it down Bram's arms.

Damask watched in growing consternation as Bram loosened the white silk cravat at his throat. It simply was not possible! But his graceful fingers flicked several studs from their holes, loosening his shirt to midchest. His eyes never left the men who were standing now, their hard, grim faces alert.

Damask clutched at the side of the carriage, her eyes round with horror. Bram rolled his shoulders and laced his fingers, stretching his hands inside out, his lithe supple body assuming that loose, yet vigilant stance of a fighter. And all the while he stared at those men, ice-blue eyes glittering with defiance.

He moved forward and something flipped through the air in a long arc. Bram caught it, crouching just in time to meet the rush of his sandy-haired opponent. Sunlight reflected from the deadly curve of the cotton hooks, raised high with wicked intent. The hooks flashed out, the curving points entangled above Bram's head and Damask choked back a scream. She heard the breathless grunts and watched the muscles of Bram's neck cord and saw his opponent's face turn beet red. Their hands were clasped into a single frightful fist, the knotted muscles of their straining legs stretching white linen and rough worsted tight. Each tried to sway the other to no visible effect, until Bram managed to hook his boot behind the man's knee and send him tumbling. The three partners of the fallen man made a concerted rush for Bram.

"Dear God!" Damask groaned. Her eyes snapped shut while she waited for the sound of blows. But there were no blows. Only the hearty sound of masculine laughter. Her eyes opened wide on the sight of Bram pulling the downed man to his feet and the others crowding around to thump him on the back, their hard, grim faces smiling and friendly.

Weak with relief, she sank back into the seat with a shaky sigh and heard: "Saint's presarve us, Bram! Yer wife be a fine lady as any with one eye can see! She'll not be wanting to meet with the likes of us!"

"Well, now, Jerry Finn," Bram rumbled, "she wed the likes of me, didn't she now?"

Damask quickly pinched color into her ashen cheeks and tried to assume a friendly demeanor, though she could have cheerfully committed mayhem upon the person of one Bram Rafferty. She had just straightened the bow of her bonnet and smoothed the wrinkles in her skirt when she looked up to find Bram's eyes on her, overbright and as hard as steel.

"My dear," he said, and her nostrils flared with revulsion at the endearment. "I would like for you to meet some friends of mine. Jerry and Derry Finn, Horst Garald, and Salvatore Gianelli. Gentlemen, my wife, Mrs. Rafferty."

Jerry Finn snorted playfully and flashed an engaging grin at Damask. "Gentlemen! Begorra! He were always one for stretching the truth a wee bit, Missus Rafferty. How is it a purty colleen like yerself were picking this Irish blackguard o'er all the sons of Erin?"

Damask flicked a glance at Bram, and found his eyes colored with the hard light of challenge. Did he think she would snub his friends? Or worse, swoon away like a limp-kneed miss at an introduction to a stevedore? He'd have to learn she was made of sterner stuff.

As angry as she was at Bram, the fey spirits of Jerry Finn were irresistible. It wasn't hard to summon a dazzling smile for him, even as she was planning her needling dig for her husband. "He left me little choice, Mr. Finn," she said, dimple twinkling while an oblique look sought the rigid line of Bram's mouth.

"Och, sure now. He's the very divil once he sets his mind to a thing. But ye couldna done better for yerself than Bram Rafferty, missus, and it's Jerry Finn who's telling ye. 'Tis a fine man what don't forget his old friends when he's rich as a blooded gent!" He leaned forward, his voice lowering as he confided, "And the divil's own luck he had to be finding such a fine lady as yerself."

"Leave off, Jerry Finn." Bram thumped his arm. "I'll not have you courting my own woman beneath my very nose."

"Begad, man!" Jerry gave him a wounded look. "Ye've taken the finest colleen in all the land and do begrudge us a few words. I'll be speaking with ye about that, Bram Rafferty." He gave Damask a friendly nod and caught Bram's arm, leading him a few steps away. His three companions nodded shyly and quickly followed.

Damask soon discovered what was so important. A bottle was passed around the circle, each man giving a soft toast she suspected it was better she didn't hear.

Bram was once again the well-garbed gentleman when he climbed into the carriage, though there was a disreputable tilt to his straw hat and the bow of his quickly tied cravat was skewed just off center. Damask tamped down an irritating impulse to lean over and straighten it. The cab carrying Lulu and Nero pulled around them, and Lulu stabbed a fulminating look in Bram's direction.

Damask stared at her hands, chewing on her lip to keep from laughing. No doubt Lulu would not stint her harsh words when next they had a private moment. She knew a lady should condemn such uncouth behavior, and should certainly be offended by an introduction to common stevedores. But she, after her initial fright was over, had rather enjoyed it.

"Would you like to ride through the *Faubourg Ste. Marie* before we go to the hotel?"

"Yes, I would like that."

The lumpy dirt streets of the warehouse district were soon left behind. The carriage bumped over the slight hump where the slab granite paving began and rolled smoothly down Felicity Street. The *Faubourg Ste. Marie* was the oldest suburb in the City and many of its houses were of the old style, set high above the ground over an enclosed basement. Some were painted wooden structures, others pastel stucco, all set on huge wooded lots where tropical greenery abounded. It was quieter in the residential section, and Damask enjoyed the cool shade of overhanging trees and the quiet peace that reminded her of home.

Not so Bram. There were no new and interesting sights to divert him from his thoughts. The taste of raw whiskey burned his tongue and seared his pride. He might tell himself that he was his own man, that nothing had changed, but the time when he was answerable to no one but himself was passed. He had a wife now.

It had been sheer folly to indulge himself in that long-played game with Jerry Finn. That he had done without thinking. Introducing them to her was something else again. Neither they, nor Damask, would have thought anything of it if that introduction had not been made. The gulf between a woman of Damask's class and the men who worked on the docks was one that was rarely bridged—maybe never completely, Bram thought with a sinking sensation in his middle.

It had been a test, and one, he had to admit, she had passed with flying colors. If he hadn't known better, he would have thought she was plunged into awkward situations every day of her life. But then, she was a lady, and ladies . . .

"I cannot think," he heard Damask saying, "how a gambler could become so closely acquainted with stevedores."

One black brow quirked into an inverted vee. Here it came. The shrew's trick. Public hypocrisy, private snobbery. His thick lashes narrowed to slits, chips of glacial blue boring into Damask. "You disapprove?" he asked with icy displeasure.

She stared at him a moment as though puzzled by his reaction. "I don't disapprove at all. I rather like your Jerry Finn, and I admire you for recognizing your friends when your circumstances have changed, though theirs have not. That is the mark of a true gentleman."

Contempt faded from features that smoothed and flattened, becoming a bronze mask void of all expression. Suddenly his lips curled maliciously. "A true gentleman, is it now, Mrs. Rafferty?" he asked, his voice sharp and cutting. "But we both know a true gentleman never cheats at cards."

Damask's face went paper white. Bram suffered a painful pang of remorse for his hasty words and reached out, but she jerked away as though his hand were a loathsome viper striking at her.

"Nor does he force marriage on an unwilling victim," she hissed.

"Force?" he questioned with a gentleness that was at odds with the hot fury in his eyes. "You were free to say no at any time."

"Free! Free to do what? Leave my home and people and land to a double-dealing trickster . . ."

His hand snapped around her wrist. "Gently, my love, gently," he murmured. "Let's not forget that you sold yourself to that double-dealing trickster, and are now trying to renege on your deal."

"D-Deal?" she faltered, huge eyes starred with revulsion turned up to him.

"A son," he said with an unpleasant smile.

"Never!" she leaned toward him, her face flushed and eyes sparkling with defiance. "There are ways, no matter how many times you force yourself on me! I can promise you, you will never have a son from me!"

"Never is a long time," he said mildly, in spite of the rage that blurred his vision. "And who is to say whether I will need to use *force.*"

With that he released her arm and leaned back against the seat, staring blindly toward the rows of sycamores that glided passed.

"Why have you brought me here?" The question shuddered on the hard rim of desperation.

"Why else?" he said, not turning to look at her. "I'm now a *respectable* planter with a *respectable* wife. I want to show you off. The trophy of my ill-gotten gains."

Chapter 8

DAMASK *braced her hands on the recessed sill, leaning over to* look down on St. Charles Avenue. Their suite, a sitting room sandwiched between two bedrooms, was on the top floor of the hotel, a dizzying four stories from street level. The early morning sun cast long shadows across the street. Ladies and gentlemen strolled along the brick sidewalks. Urchins played. A row of horse-drawn cabs waited before the hotel, the cabbies gathered around a streetlight in what appeared to be a heated discussion. Heavy-laden drays rumbled over the slab granite paving stones, speckled with horse droppings and littered with refuse. Light carriages clattered as they wove rapid paths around the slower drays. A double-decker omnibus rolled to a stop before the colonnaded portico and the driver added his own hoarse cry to the cacophony of sounds climbing from the street.

"New Or-le-ans, Jack-son, Gre-eat North-ern Rail-way-ee Sta-tion! New Or-le-ans . . . Pi-ca-yune! Late-est Is-sue Pi-ca-yune! Pi-ca-yunnne! Flo-wers! Flo-wers! Ro-oses! Ca-me-li-as! Flo-wers! New Or-le-ans . . ."

Damask didn't like the City. She had her father's love for the unhurried pace, the clear fresh air and peace of the country. None of those things was to be found here. She sighed, moving away from the distressing sight of the street. A pensive gaze drifted toward the door leading off the sitting room. *His* room.

Damask curled up in a chair, raising her bare feet to the cushion and hugging her knees. Had she slept at all last night? She had stared into the dark with hot, dry eyes, listening to the strange sounds of a city asleep. Or did it sleep? She had heard church bells and barking dogs, shouts and rumbling drays all through the night. No crickets to hum her to sleep. No owls singing their question to the stars. No mooing of a solitary cow in the early morning hours.

The need for Seven Pines settled like a stone in her breast, and Damask rested her cheek on her knees. Nothing was forever. Soon. Soon she would be back home, where everything was comforting and familiar.

"You're not ready?"

Her head snapped up.

Bram's expressionless eyes dropped to her bare feet and followed the silken fall of her hair to the curling ends floating above the polished oak floor. He swallowed hard and looked away. "I have a cab waiting downstairs. If you wish to see the Vieux Carré, I would suggest some more appropriate attire."

Resentment knifed through her. Of course, he would suggest *some more appropriate attire*. He was going to parade his *trophy* for the world to see. As if respectability could be gained in such a way!

"I lost track of the time," she said without a hint of apology. "Lulu just went downstairs to press my gown."

His eyes, as flat and blank as a cloudless sky, moved to her. "Then you will have to endure my company for a time. I thought you might like these—in the way of a peace offering."

Damask buried her nose in the scented bouquet of violets, her cinnamon eyes staring over the ruffled curve of petals.

Bram sank onto the sofa, his gaze roaming the room until she began to wonder if they would sit forever and never speak another word. The tension grated on her nerves like a squeaky wheel and her fingers toyed nervously with the deep purple petals.

"A peace offering?" she asked. "Surely we are not at war."

Bright, bitter eyes swiveled from the marble mantel to her

face. A tinge of hot angry color fanned along his cheek-bones, and her mouth went powder dry. He said nothing, and she looked away.

An eternity of screaming silence passed.

"What did you want to see in the City?"

His voice sliced through the thickened atmosphere like a knife blade, and Damask's head swung toward him. "I . . . I thought you had made plans."

"Only for today and Tuesday night. Today we will see Madame Blanchard to complete yours and Tessa's ward-robe. Tuesday—"

"No!" she burst out, unable to endure either the gifts or the man. "That isn't necessary. Tessa and I are accustomed to much less." She moved so quickly her dressing gown slid wide, revealing a dainty length of honey-toned leg. Bram scowled and look away, and she grabbed the lace-trimmed edges and pushed them together.

"I'm sure you are, but you are my wife and Tessa is my charge. I would have you both garbed as befits that . . . honor," he emphasized with an ironical twist of his mouth.

Honor. The word made her cringe with disgust. As if he could understand the word after all he had done. The very thought of being dressed and perfumed and paraded, the "trophy of his ill-gotten gaines," made her light-headed with abhorrence.

"I won't be dressed up like a doll."

"But you will," he said flatly, the only evidence of anger in the ticking beat of the scar arching along his temple. "Do you think I would have gone to the trouble of cheating your brother of Seven Pines and marrying you, if I did not intend to make use of you to further my own interests?"

A chill slithered over Damask's skin. "You admit it?"

He stood abruptly, cramming his hands into his pockets and striding to the window to stare down into the street. "I'm asking you to carry your own logic to its proper con-clusion."

Her tongue slicked across her dry lips. "And that is?"

"That you will do what I require you to do, when I require you to do it, because if you don't . . ."

The threat hovered in the air between them and Damask's racing heart gave a sickening lurch. "If I don't?" she asked, fighting for air to breathe life into the words.

He shrugged, a negligent gesture that was at once terrifying and dismissing. "Everything you love is in my hands."

"You . . ." A dizzying rage swirled through her head, and she clutched at the brocaded arm of the chair. "You would use that as a whip to keep me in line?"

He turned slowly, an expression in his eyes that quivered on the precipice of pain. "If I am the man you think I am, yes, I would not hesitate."

Damask shivered uncontrollably, her eyes dark pools of despair. "You would hurt Tessa or Gramps?"

He sighed, a sound of angry frustration, and rocked back on his heels, throwing his head back to stare at the high ceiling. It seemed to Damask that he filled the room with a threatening, evil presence. In the hollow of those hands, knotted into fists and jammed deep in his pockets, rested everything she loved: her home, her family, her people. Her life would be spent yielding to his every whim in order to protect them. She must swallow her pride and self-respect to follow wherever he led.

He moved, his chin dropping to trap her in the glare of his eyes. "Do you think I could hurt either one of them?"

"Yes!" she cried, leaping up and leaning toward him, the nosegay of violets falling from her hand and scattering across the oak floor like livid bruises. "Yes! I think there is no low infamous deed you would not commit to get your way! How could I not think it? Look at what you have done already!"

His anger traveled the currents of tense air, reached her, and vibrated through her with the rhythmic cadence of a steamer's engine vibrating through the deck. His hands inched out of his pockets and balled into fists, and terror scrabbled at the back of her throat.

He took a step and she whirled, beyond any thought except flight. His hand latched around her arm and snatched her around, and she thumped into his chest with a force that knocked the breath from her. His fingers clamped over her shoulders and his face lowered to hers, his eyes lit by an unholy light.

"What have I done?" he grated out. "Have I hurt your grandfather or Tessa or your people? Did I hurt or force you on our wedding night?"

"No, why should you have?" she panted in heedless defiance. "I was doing my *duty* as a wife by submitting to you!"

"Duty." He grunted the word, as though she had balled up her small hand and landed an unexpected blow low on his abdomen.

"What else would I do but my duty?" she said scathingly, aware that she had found a chink in his armor, but unsure just what it was. Why should he care whether she came to him willingly or duty bound? Only she, so she thought, could know that she had taken illicit and joyful pleasure in her wedding night. The fact filled her with queasy disgust.

"Duty. What else?" he said, shaking off some indiscernible emotion. His hands loosened and his palms cupped the slender stem of her neck, his thumbs tipping her chin up.

She wanted to pull away, but found her treacherous feet frozen in place. She wanted to look away, but found herself mesmerized by the fiery blue of his eyes. A memory tiptoed into her consciousness and pirouetted like a forward child. A memory of his lips warm at her throat and his palm cupping her heaving breast and a tension that stretched and shattered and left her sated and replete.

His head lowered and his lips touched hers in a tender exploration. She struggled to resist, hardening her mind with thoughts of what he was, but a traitorous longing, a longing that seemed to have been with her always, leeched the resistance from her body. Her lips flowered and opened for the questing tongue that trailed a path from one sensitive corner of her mouth to the other.

Her sweet breath sighed and the tenderness became impassioned demand. One hand cupped her head, the other swept around her waist, sculpting her to his every contour. A thread of resistance remained in the tenuous fists that pressed against the muscular bulge of his shoulders.

Fevered kisses brushed across her cheek, and his teeth nipped the lobe of her ear. He buried his lips in the hollow of her throat, and the slender thread of resistance unraveled. Her hands spread across his shoulders, smoothed up to his nape, and fanned through his hair while desire spread its tempting spell.

"Damask," he groaned. "Damask, I need . . ."

His head raised, his hold upon her loosening so abruptly she was left leaning against him, her arms still twined around his neck. He caught them and pushed her away, his expression an accusation that vanished in the blink of an eye. Nothing was left but cool remote amusement.

"Duty, Mrs. Rafferty," he said with a quirk of a smile that was ugly to see. "And you do it so well."

Humiliation sluiced through her in a scalding flood. Careless of consequences, her hand snaked out. Her palm cracked across his cheek.

He stared down at her, the imprint of her hand flaming against his cheek. "If I'm the man you think I am, Damask, that was a very unwise thing to do."

They were delayed several hours in leaving the hotel. No sooner had Damask completed dressing in nervous haste than she discovered that her husband had disappeared. Nero found him in the vast ground floor barroom, staring into the dregs of a bottle of cognac.

They met at the foot of the broad, curving stairs. Like the ambassadors of warring nations, each was determined the other would not exceed him in civility. Neither mentioned the unhappy scene. Neither smiled. Solemnly, they stared across the vast breach of broken dreams and unnamed fears

and tacitly agreed to a fragile treaty. The rule for the day
was courtesy. Icy, soul-chilling courtesy.

As the cab crossed Canal Street into the Vieux Carré,
Bram called her attention to points of interest, as any good
tour guide would do. Damask responded with carefully
modulated enthusiasm, but her dislike for the City was
growing by the minute. The heat was oppressive, the hu-
midity stifling, and the air reeked of the open gutters, where
sewage and garbage rotted in stagnant pools alive with the
wriggling larvae of mosquitoes.

There was an alien quality to the old French Quarter with
its houses that turned inward, presenting a hostile back to
the world. The streets swarmed with everyone from beggars
to belles, and a babble of different languages. Damask's
sensation of being a stranger in a foreign land grew stronger.

Their first stop was the dark and cluttered shop of the couturiere, Madame Blanchard. Her small sitting room was littered with scraps of lace and swatches of cloth and elegant
drawings of the latest styles. Damask, chastened by the realization that she had so nearly brought disaster raining about
her head, submitted to what seemed to her an orgy of spending.

She fingered fabrics and studied sketches and thought at a
furious pace. If he was the man she thought he was . . .
Why did he keep saying that? As though he were in reality
something different.

The next stop was a small confectioner's shop for coffee
and pastry, eaten in a thunderous silence. If, she thought.
There was no if. They both knew what he was. A liar and a
cheat who would use anyone and anything to get what he
wanted.

At the milliner's he stood by in brooding solitude, his face
dark, his eyes shaded to sapphire as though anger still held
him in its inexorable grip. It was easy to believe that this
man was capable of murdering his own father. It was easy to
believe he was capable of anything. Anything, and she was
all that stood between him and her family.

He carried two hat boxes, and had ordered more with no

reference to her, when they left to stroll the narrow streets in strained silence. She flung a hollow gaze his way and wondered how she could have been so rash as to slap him. It had been an act of madness with a man like him. She would never again allow herself to strike out at whatever he said or did; but she had to admit, with the bitter scourge of honesty, that it was her own weakness she struck against. How could she have melted like hot wax in his arms? How could she have forgotten everything except the sensual thrill that sped along her nerves?

"Sir! Sir! I'll be carrying yer boxes for ye, for a price, of coorse."

Damask turned from the cobbler's window, noting the strange expression on Bram's face as he looked down at a scruffy child.

"Ye will, boy?" he said, surprisingly matching the Irish brogue with one of his own. "And what will ye be charging me for the task?"

Grimy thumbs hooked into the length of rope serving him for a belt, the boy looked up at Bram from a tangled mop of carroty red curls. Damask was shocked to see the expression in those dark indigo eyes was that of a cynical, world-weary man. Certainly not that of a scrawny child of no more than ten years.

"Two bits," he said firmly.

"Two bits! Ye've the gall of the Irish, boy," Bram said with a short laugh. "A man with a good trade makes but a dollar a day."

"Two bits, sir. 'Tis me final offer," he said stoutly, as though they were petitioning him rather than the other way around.

"What's your name, boy?"

"Michael O'Malley, sir. A fine Irish name."

Damask's incredulous gaze shifted between man and boy. Bram showed no sympathy for the child's pitiful plight. His face was as stern and unsmiling as Michael O'Malley's was resolute. And their attitude toward the simple task of hiring him to carry a few packages was bewildering. Each approached it as if it were a decision of momentous significance!

She studied the child curiously. Spindly legs and filthy bare feet jutted from torn and patched trousers inches too short for him. His pointed elbows pierced gaping holes in his sleeves. And his face! Damask had a strong urge to find the nearest dry goods store to buy lye soap and a stiff bristled brush to scrub the grimy dirt from his sunken cheeks and the beads from his neck.

"A fine Irish name, to be sure, Michael O'Malley. Ye'll be telling me what ye'll be doing to earn the grand sum of two bits?"

"There'll not be a scratch or a scuff on them fine hat boxes of yer lady's. And ye can load me down like a pack hoorse, sir. I be stronger than I look. I'll tote 'em where-someever ye please. 'Tis a fine day's work ye'll be getting from Michael O'Malley."

"Two bits it is then. Take my hand on it."

Gravely the small grubby hand was extended—after an ineffectual rubbing down the side of his filthy trousers—and they shook hands with all the solemnity of a factor and a planter concluding a deal concerning thousands of dollars. It was beyond Damask's comprehension.

The hat boxes were transferred to the boy's care, and a buxom negress appeared around the corner with a basket balanced on her head. *"Bels calas,"* she called out in a singsong. *"Bels calas, tout chauds, bels calas . . ."*

Bram stopped her. Money was exchanged for *calas* and he returned to Damask. "Try this. It's a rice fritter. Be careful, it's hot."

Damask glanced at the boy, who stood stiff as a poker, indigo eyes staring straight ahead. "Did you get one for the boy? He looks like he might be hungry."

Michael did not move a muscle. "Ain't needing no handouts. Jist pay me two bits when me work is done."

She would have said more, but Bram frowned and the words that trembled on her lips died. He took her elbow, guiding her into a cobbler's shop.

They roamed the shopping areas of the Vieux Carré, browsing through small shops selling everything from tobacco to fragile French crystal. Gifts were bought for Gramps and Tessa and Wade, a warm winter shawl for Lulu and a top hat for Jims. The larger purchases were to be delivered to the hotel, but there were numerous smaller ones that did, indeed, have Michael O'Malley loaded down like a pack *hoorse*.

When Damask suggested they could carry a few things, the young boy gave her a fierce look, declaring he would earn his two bits or leave them and their packages there. She looked to Bram for support, but he just shrugged his shoulders and arched his brows as if to say what could he do, then gave Michael a nod of—approval! She gave him a look as disapproving as any of Lulu's and marched off. Obviously, he condoned child labor on the streets of New Orleans!

By late afternoon, she felt there was no inch of the Vieux Carré left unexplored. At least that was what her feet were telling her. She gave Bram a brittle smile. "I cannot go another step."

"Around the corner is an excellent restaurant. Would you like to have dinner there before we return to the hotel?"

"If it means I can sit, I'll do anything!"

A glimmer of a smile answered her. "We've done too much today," he said, and tapped the end of her nose with a gloved finger. "You've got a sunburn."

"Oh, no!" Her hand flew to her nose, anxious fingers touching it. "Lulu will be giving me buttermilk facials for days!"

"The color becomes—"

Bram's gallantry was lost in pandemonium. Pounding footsteps. Michael cursing. Boxes and baskets scattering helter-skelter across the brick paved sidewalk. Damask gave a startled shriek and fell against Bram—with the aid of two rough hands. The cut strings of her reticule slid from her wrist and Michael tore past them in hot pursuit of a guttersnipe half again his size.

Damask clung to Bram's arm. "I was pushed! Who would do such a thing?"

"Your reticule was stolen. Are you hurt?"

"No, just surprised."

"Wait here. Our little Michael O'Malley might have the heart to tackle that ruffian, but I doubt he has the size."

A banshee screech sounded and Bram sprinted away. A burly bear of a man rounded the corner, with a kicking, spitting wildcat tucked securely in the crook of each brawny arm. Their caterwauling reached a deafening din, and he raised his arms, giving the boys a few shakes that left them panting for breath.

He saw Bram and a snaggle-toothed grin split his broad face, evidence that the work of a constable, or *Charley* as they were called by the citizenry, was no peaceful task. "Begorra!" he rolled. " 'Tis himself! Ye're a sight, sir, in yer fine clothes. 'Tis thinking I am ye were after these rapscallions?"

"That one," Bram pointed to Michael, "was carrying packages for me. He was after the other one who stole my wife's reticule. You can release him, Tim."

The thief had caught his breath and gathered his strength while eyeing the spontoon, a short pike carried by the Charleys in lieu of firearms. It was grasped in a massive, hairy fist drawn up under Michael's belly. The wily boy gave a flip of his legs, reaching across to grab the spontoon just below the pointed end. He tugged and jerked, then groaned in frustration before letting go with a yelp of pain when the grinning constable bounced the fight from him.

"Noo, sir," Tim said calmly. "He'd be off like a shot. Wouldn't ye, Michael O'Malley?"

Michael twisted around, giving him a baleful look. "To be sure! Ye can take me back as many times as there be steps to Ireland, but I'll not be staying! I'll be out before the day be done or me name ain't Michael O'Malley!"

"What has the boy done, Tim?"

" 'Tis the shame of it, sir. Michael be a good boy, but his mither and faither be dead of the Yellow Jack these two years and more. He's no one in the world to see to him now and was put in the House of Refuge, but he'll not be staying there.''

Damask came up to stand beside Bram and slipped her hand into the crook of his arm. His muscles tensed and she looked up to see his jaw rigid and the scar on his temple throbbing.

Michael skewed around. "I can take care of meself! There's work for any as looks! Don't need charity to make me way!''

"Put him down, Tim.''

The constable glanced doubtfully at the boy. "Sir, he be fast as a streak of lightning, and there'll be no catching him!''

"Michael O'Malley," Bram said sternly, "you'll be giving me your word you'll be staying. I've business to discuss with you. Will I have it?''

"What sort of business?'' the boy asked suspiciously.

"Work that will be keeping you out of the House of Refuge.''

"Ye've the word of Michael O'Malley, sir.'' The boy raised his reddened face to the constable. "Ye blithering ninny! I'll be standing on me own two feet now!''

Amusement crimped the Charley's snaggle-toothed grin as he set Michael on his feet. "What'll I be doing with this other one, sir?''

Bram spared a brief glance for the boy hanging from Tim's arm. "I'll come to City Hall later tonight to make a complaint. Michael O'Malley''—the boy jerked to attention—"do you know who I am?''

"N-Nooo, sir,'' he answered, obviously as startled as Damask was by that suddenly severe tone.

"My name is Bram Rafferty.''

Michael's eyes widened until the thick fringe of auburn lashes climbed to his brows. An expression of stunned recognition appeared. Almost as though he were gazing at last on a long-lost hero, Damask thought. His mouth snapped shut suddenly, thin shoulders squaring in a way that made her want to smile. Apparently, even a hero would not make Michael O'Malley stoop to maudlin sentiment.

"Ye were after offering me work, sir?"

"I have a plantation in the north of the state. I need a man I can trust."

Damask's head whipped around. "Bram . . ." His hand covered hers, giving it a warning squeeze.

"Ye've slaves, sir," the boy said with narrow-eyed suspicion. "What'll ye be needing Michael O'Malley for?"

"I have my own way of doing things, and I want someone I can train to follow my own high standards. I need a man to help me keep the records and to oversee the work, and keep things running smoothly if I should leave for any time."

A suggestion of a slump appeared in those rigidly squared shoulders. "Michael O'Malley's not the man for ye, sir. I have neither reading nor writing."

"You can be taught. I told you I want a man I can train. What I need is an honest man who isn't afraid of hard work."

Michael hitched up his pants, hooked his thumbs in his rope belt, and slanted a shrewd look at Bram. "And what are ye offering for this work?"

"You will have a room of your own and meals and clothes furnished. There will be a pony for you to ride the fields with me and, later when you've grown a bit, a horse of your own. Cash of four dollars a month, to be raised when you have learned enough to earn it."

"Four dollars a month, ye say?"

Bram laughed. "Ye've the gall of the Irish, boy," he said, slipping back into the brogue. " 'Tis me final offer."

"I know ye for a fair and honest man, sir. There's one thing I'd be asking of ye, were I to accept."

"You drive a hard bargain." Bram nodded for him to continue.

"Ye're well known for being a square player, sir. I've a notion to learn the cards, so it'll niver be said of Michael O'Malley that he cheated a man of his coin. I want the skill to beat him, and ye're the man to teach me. After that, I'll be trusting to me own luck.''

Damask stiffened, her fingers digging into Bram's arm. She raised an accusing gaze and saw him frown at her before he looked back to Michael.

''If you follow the cards, you follow a fickle master. I don't suggest it for your life's work.''

''To be sure,'' the boy scoffed. ''I'm no fool! 'Tis the land I'm after having, and the cards be a way to get it, as ye'll be knowing, sir.''

As ye'll be knowing, sir. Oh, he knew all right! Only he didn't trust to his own luck! Damask wrenched her hand from his arm and wheeled away, not trusting herself to keep from screaming.

''Sorry, sir,'' she heard Michael whisper. ''I could kick me own self for upsetting your lady. If ye're still wanting me, ye have the word of Michael O'Malley ye'll not regret it.''

''Tim, will you let them know that Michael will not be returning to the House of Refuge?''

''To be sure, sir. 'Tis me pleasure. I thought ye'd not like seeing the boy returned to that divilish place, seeing as how—''

''Thank you, Tim,'' Bram broke in. ''I'll be along later. Michael, catch that cab before it gets away.''

Damask listened to the heavy tread of the constable and Michael's fleet steps and choked back the impulse to call out to them and insist that Bram Rafferty was no model for a boy to follow.

''Damask, here's your reticule.'' She took it without looking at him. ''The boy didn't know . . .''

''He called you honest!'' She swiveled upon him. ''A square player! As if it were a commonly known fact. Tell me, Bram! Tell me the truth!''

''That I didn't cheat your brother!'' he lashed out. ''Would you believe me? I have everything to gain by telling you I won the land fairly; your brother has everything to lose by telling you I cheated. Tell me, Damask, what does he gain by lying? He drives a wedge of suspicion between us, destroying whatever chance you might have to accept this travesty of a marriage! By lying he assures your unhappiness . . ."

"And that is why I know he isn't! Wade loves me! He would never hurt me, and that is why I know he is telling the truth!"

Chapter 9

WADE *loves me. He would never hurt me, and that is why I know* he is telling the truth!

It was not her conviction that set Damask to tumbling and tossing through the night, but what came after it. The expression of blank surprise on Bram's face. The veiled look that followed as though he had whipped a curtain across his thoughts. However carefully he had managed to control his features, he had failed to shield the soft, sad expression in his eyes. A look of . . . pity!

How dare he look at her like that! He acted as though he knew something of which she was ignorant! He was trying to infect her with doubt about her brother! There was no vile, underhanded trick he would not use!

How could the Charley, Tim, and Michael O'Malley have looked upon him like he was God Almighty? A man to admire and respect and emulate. Michael might not know better, but the Charley ought to have known what kind of man Bram Rafferty was!

Yet he had placed Michael O'Malley in Bram's care with every appearance of relief, as if Michael could not have been in better hands! Bram Rafferty was not the man to raise Michael O'Malley. Not a boy who held the promise of a fine, honest man. Michael would be better on the streets of New Orleans than at Seven Pines where his *hero* would disillusion him and ruin that sense of honor and integrity.

* * *

Bram stood at the window ignoring the street below to stare at a sky filled with clean, cotton-boll clouds that appeared to sit inert on the hot humid air rising above the City. He drank his coffee and waited for Michael to return with a copy of the *Picayune* and thought about his wife.

She had not listened to anything he said. *If,* he had said, *if.* She chose to ignore that and pick out every ugly, frightening thing that followed and come to her own conclusions.

He shifted his weight, distributing it squarely over both feet, as though to brace himself against his own thoughts. Anger had driven him to that kiss, and desire. A desire that grew with every glimpse of her, that invaded body and mind whether he was awake or asleep. A desire that no longer cared whether she came to him willingly or unwillingly—only that she came.

Why this woman and no other? It was more than her beauty. It was her pride: a pride that matched his own. It was her strength: the mettle that held her family together and ran Seven Pines and supported her brother. It was her heart: loving and gentle and tenaciously loyal.

Loyal—even where it was not warranted. Jesus! That Wade Downing, so little deserving it, should have that loyalty! That he, who loved nothing and no one but himself, should have that deep, abiding, forgiving love!

He was her brother. She would believe in him until Wade Downing himself disillusioned her.

Bram raised the cup to his lips, grimaced, and lowered it to the sill. He knew about love betrayed. He knew about disillusionment. Whenever it would happen, he would not be the cause.

A door opened behind him and Bram turned. "Mi—" Damask stood in the doorway of her room, cheeks glowing with color. She wore a simple frock in a shade of raw honey that heightened the taffy shadows and gold highlights in her hair, but it was the firm resolution in the tilt of her chin that held his attention. She swept through, crinoline swaying, and pulled the door closed behind her. Folding her hands neatly at her waist, she pointed her small straight nose at him. "I want to speak with you."

He leisurely perused the agitated rise and fall of her breasts, then sought the safer territory of her cheeks, which were shading to a deep, dusky rose. Cheeks as soft as velvet, as smooth as a baby's skin . . .

Bram mentally shook himself and nodded for her to continue.

"I do not want Michael to return to Seven Pines with us."

Bram's expression of polite interest congealed.

"He is a—a—"

"You object to sharing Seven Pines with another of the leavings of the New Orleans gutters?" His disappointment sliced deep. A loving and gentle heart, he raged with cynical despair, but no room in it for a boy who had nothing and belonged to no one, whose pride would be strained to its limits if he was left to grow up alone on the streets of the City.

"No, I—"

"It's a fine Christian lady you are, Mrs. Rafferty," Bram sneered. "You wouldn't know about a place like the House of Refuge, and it would curl your silken hair to hear what could happen there!" He leaned toward her, every syllable clicked off. "It's a reformatory where honest orphans like Michael O'Malley are incarcerated with the dregs of the gutters. Hardened criminals who would descend on him like vultures tearing at a carcass. It's his pride they cannot abide. If they could not destroy it, they would slit his throat with no more remorse than you would feel to swat a fly!"

Huge liquid brown pools glazed with shock stared up at him. "Bram, I—"

"Don't say another word!" he threatened and sucked in a shaky breath. "Michael O'Malley comes with us! He, at least, has a man's pride and will earn his way, unlike that sniveling excuse for a man you call a brother. And you, my dear loving wife, will treat Michael with the respect he deserves or, I promise you, you'll regret it!"

Bram's blood throbbed with a maddened ferocity that made him giddy, and the scar on his temple ached as though it were freshly made. He moved, stiff-gaited at first, then faster and smoother, knowing only that he had to escape that room and her and the corrosive acid of yet another disillusionment. One more in a long line. Why did he cling to hope? Frail, futile hope.

Michael, the *Picayune* folded beneath his arm, was reaching for the knob when the door flew open. The Mister tore through with the black, thunderous countenance betokening a man who would welcome trouble if it came to him. Michael, staring after him, sensed another presence. The Lady hovered in the door as though she wanted to call the Mister back, but was afraid.

Damning all women and their ability to invoke murderous rages in otherwise rational men, Michael thrust the newspaper into her hand and rushed down the stairs.

He discreetly trailed Bram on a rambling tour of every bar in the vicinity. They said the way to tell a gentleman was by the way he held his liquor, and after a full day's consumption, the Mister's walk was just as sure and straight as always. Begad! Michael swelled with pride. He's as fine as a blooded gent!

It was late when Michael leaned against the wrought iron fence enclosing Lafayette Square. The moon crowded the stars in the night sky, and he was tired. His thoughts wandered to the heavenly comfort of the trundle bed in the Mister's room. He could almost hear the whoosh of air as he sank deep into the feather tick, and feel and smell the fresh clean sheets.

He ran his hands along the buttons of his waistcoat and smoothed the lapel of his frock coat, wriggling his sock-clad toes, encased in shiny black boots. His thin chest puffed with pride.

When they had returned the Lady to the hotel the night before, the Mister raked his hand through his curly black hair until it was as rumpled as an unmade bed, then looked up and said, "Come along, Michael." Their first stop, to his horror, was the bathing room in the hotel basement. There he had been forced to scrub his skin raw before it met the Mister's standards of cleanliness. He didn't like having his ears and neck inspected or his hands turned about and his toes pulled apart, but when informed he would not be taken to the tailor and cobbler in his present grimy condition, he decided it was not too high a price to pay.

A roar from the throng jamming the square woke Michael from his reverie. He ignored the raving speaker and cursed the fact that tomorrow was Election Day in the City, and that the crowded streets were making the task of tailing the Mister doubly hard.

He stepped onto the raised brick footing that supported the fence. His searching gaze came to an uneasy halt. Those men. He had seen them more than once during the day. They were an evil sort, unlikely to be interested in the political speeches shouted into the torch-lit night.

Michael fixed their faces in his mind, but it was the fourth man that held him. He had a thick matted beard laying atop a filthy flannel shirt, and his eyes pierced the crowd with a vicious, insane look of hate. Michael followed the line of the man's stare. Gooseflesh crept over his skin. It was the Mister he was looking at!

As he watched, the Mister moved off in the opposite direction, toward the St. Charles Avenue exit of the square. Michael's attention jerked back to the four men. They craned their necks to follow their quarry's progress while shoving a path through the crowd. At that moment the speaker made some statement that brought wild cheers and hats thrown into the air.

Michael started forward. The men surged back like breakers on a seashore, and he was jammed against the fence. He cursed luridly. His sharp elbow sank into a groin. His teeth clamped over a hand. A cuff caught him across the ear and it rang with the tinny sound of a steamboat whistle. He looked around wildly, knowing he would never cross the square in time. Damn all women! The Mister would be home, safe in the depths of his feather tick, his wits as keen as ever, but for the Lady!

Following the fence and battering paths where none existed, Michael reached the gate onto Camp Street, opposite St. Charles Avenue. Shoving his way through an assembled group, he tore down the street, rounded the corner, and dodged the men standing on the sidewalk. The roar of the crowd was a buzz in his ears as he flew into the intersection.

Ham-fisted hands closed around his arms. "Slow down, boy!"

It was useless to fight the strength in those hands. Michael went still and stared up at the Charley. "Spring yer rattles, sir! Me Mister be trailed by divilish beasties and I fear for his life!"

"Boy, if you're fooling with me . . ."

"Noo, sir! Let me go! They be after himself, to be sure!"

The constable reached for the rattles hanging from his belt, *springing* them to summon aid from any constables in the area. His hold loosened. Michael was off down the street in the direction of the hotel like a small tornado.

The impossible had happened to Michael O'Malley. There was a promise of a roof over his head, and a soft bed to sleep in every night. He would never be hungry again, and he would live with a real family, earning his way as he should. It was a dream he had never dared to dream, and now it was threatened.

"Saint Patrick," he prayed, "watch over yer sons. Give me strength . . ."

Ahead, the Mister halted in the glow of a streetlight. A match flared and disappeared behind his cupped hands. Behind him, the four men moved out of the shadows in a rush.

"Beware, sir! Behind . . ."

They were on him! Energy surged through Michael, but he felt as if he were caught in a slow-motion nightmare. Fog rolled in from the river, misty tentacles wrapping around the light post, reaching a tentative finger toward a man who tumbled to the paving stones. A bellow of anger charged through the night. Light flashed from the silvered blade of an upraised knife. Another man fell. The swirling fog lifted.

The rasping breathing of the grappling men grew louder. The knife made its inevitable descent.

Michael tucked low, diving at the knife-wielder's knees. The man fell backward, stumbling over him, and Michael grunted with pain. A fist caught him square on the last button of his waistcoat and sent him skidding bottom first into the street. He struggled to rise as the first Charley slapped the flat of his spontoon up beside the head of the heavy-bearded man. The Charleys swarmed, quickly subduing the attacking trio. Suddenly, Michael felt himself being lifted in strong arms and crushed against his Mister's chest.

"You little fool! Have you no more sense than to be charging full-bore into a fray of armed men? You need your backside blistered, Michael O'Malley!"

He was thumped onto his feet with tooth-jarring speed and the Mister's hands began running over his arms and chest. Michael pulled away and drew himself up. "I'll be thanking ye, sir, to be keeping yer hands to yerself!"

Bram braced on one knee, grinning broadly. "I see you're no worse for your tussle with those skulking cowards. It looks like I should be thanking you for coming to my rescue. How was it that you were out here?"

"Taking a walk in the fresh air, sir. If it's any of yer business," Michael added belligerently.

"Ah, Michael, you'll have to do better than that."

Michael squirmed. Begad! Could the man be reading what was written on his soul? "Ye were looking for trouble when ye left the Lady." He thrust out a pugnacious jaw. "I followed ye."

"All day?" Bram rolled with a wide smile of amusement. "I've found my own Irish leprechaun to be keeping me from harm." Bram grimaced as he clasped his upper arm.

"Do you know these scoundrels, sir?" one of the Charleys asked.

Bram's eyes slid from man to man with a flare of surprise. "Yes, the Caswell brothers. The last time I saw them they were slave patrollers in De Soto Parish. We had a—a difference of opinion when they beat one of my people."

Jethro Caswell lunged for Bram, but was caught and held back. "Yeah. It was your lady that had us fired, but it's you we ain't forgetting, *Mister* Bram Rafferty. You just keep watching over your shoulder 'cause one day we'll be coming!"

"Not soon, you sorry rogue!" the Charley said roughly.

As the brothers were led away, the youngest one giggled. "Hey, Jethro, maybe the one what hired us'll get him 'fore then. Hehehe."

Frost-fettered shock caught Bram in the act of turning to speak to the constable. He swiveled around, a fleeting expression of pain marring the symmetry of his features.

"Shut up, you dimwitted fool!" Jethro Caswell hissed.

"Why, I ain't said nothing," the boy whined.

"Constable," Bram said, his voice devoid of the emotion that ripped through his gut like redhot pincers, "keep the boy here. Send the others on."

The constable leading the Lafayette Square watch signaled for the elder brothers to be taken on to the City Hall jail, then stood to one side, slapping the handle of his spontoon in the palm of his hand.

The boy, mouth slack and eyes agog, flinched with each soft sound and shrank back toward the Charley, holding his arms as though the man might protect him.

"What's your name, boy?" Bram asked, his voice deceptively, cruelly gentle.

"They . . . they calls me Dodger," the boy choked out, wild eyes rolling toward the spontoon.

"Well, Dodger," Bram murmured, clamping a firm hold over the nausea churning in his stomach, "why don't you tell us who hired you?"

"D-D-Don't know nothing!"

"Dodger, Dodger . . ." Bram shook his head pityingly.

"Aint' funning! Don't know nothing! Never seen whoever sent that paper! It was wrapped around a twenty-dollar gold piece and it wasn't signed! Just said we could do us and a lot of other folks a favor by making sure Rafferty didn't go back to . . . to . . ."

He wanted to know, had to know. But, God, how he hoped it wasn't true! Blood ran warm through the icy fingers clamped around his upper arm, and Bram licked lips that had gone as dry as sawdust. "Seven Pines," he said and almost started with surprise that the words came out so evenly from his aching throat.

"Yessir! Yessir! That's it! Seven Pines! Jethro was mighty het up, but we couldn't find out nothing 'cepting it was a nigger what brung it. Skinny as a rail we was told."

The ache spread in Bram's throat like a fetid bog while he watched the boy being hauled away.

"If they didn't discover who it was, I doubt we'll be able to," the constable said. "I'm sure they were thorough. A little blackmail when the deed was done, you know. Do you have any idea who it might have been, sir?"

Did he have any idea? Who else, but his soft, sweet, beautiful wife? His Damask with her liquid cinnamon eyes and playful dimple and loving, loyal heart.

"Sir?"

He shifted as if waking from a nightmare. "I'll press charges against the Caswells, but I want no attempt made to find whoever hired them. Is that clear?"

"Yes, sir, but you should expect another attempt. Anyone who has gone this far won't stop because of one failure."

"Good night, constable."

The man touched the tip of his spontoon to the leather brim of his hat. "Good night, sir, and . . . good luck."

Good luck, Bram thought bitterly and stood as still as a statue while blood puddled across the brick walk.

The last of the stairs sapped his strength, but Michael gripped him securely around the waist and took the brunt of his weight. "Here, sir, lean against the door while I open it and light a lamp to show the way."

Clutching the sill, Bram slid himself forward. The combination of a full day's hard drinking, loss of blood, and shock made icy sweat bead across his forehead. His breath was shallow and quick, and when he lifted his heavy lids, he discovered he could not focus. "Michael?" he questioned thickly.

"Over here, sir. Hang on, sir." Light bloomed through the clear glass chimney and Michael ran back to the door. "Here, sir. I be strong. Lean on me, sir. That's right. I got ye this far, didn't I? Another step and ye can rest on the sofa."

Bram fell onto the plush covered seat, groaning when he jarred his arm. The fires of hell had centered themselves in his sliced flesh, but he welcomed the physical pain that held his tormented thoughts at bay.

"Water, Michael. Bring me water."

Damask slid from the recessed window seat where she had been staring into the night, mulling over all the things she intended to tell one Bram Rafferty on his return.

"Water!!" A day and night of distilling her venom added a decidedly shrewish sharpness to her mockery. "Are you sure it isn't more of that fine Irish Whiskey you're wanting, Bram Rafferty? A fine example you're proving to be for Michael!"

Bram paled. She was waiting up for him. He closed his eyes against a pain that ravaged the outer reaches of his soul. She was waiting, and there could only be one reason.

"The water, Michael," he said quietly, his eyes sliding away from the surprise and rapid conclusion mirrored on the boy's intelligent face.

Bram gathered his strength and forced an ice-rimed smile to his mouth. "Damask, me darling," he said in a derisive mockery of the Irish brogue, "it does me heart good to know ye do so long for the sight of yer beloved husband that ye'd be missing yer dreams. Or could it have been ye were expecting word of a different sort this night?"

The words pinged off the shell of armor Damask had constructed against him. She assumed her battle position, head high and arms folded across her chest, and marched around the end of the sofa in a double-time step that sent the skirt of her dressing gown sailing out behind her. "Drunk! You are the most disgusting—"

"Excuse me, Lady! Ye're in me way and the Mister needs his water." Michael pushed by her and knelt to hand Bram the glass. "Sir, ye be needing a doctor bad."

"Doctor?" Damask faltered, her folded arms loosening their grip on her seething anger.

"Mrs. Rafferty!" Bram cut across her hesitant question. "You have my permission to seek your bed. If I must make it plainer—you are not wanted! Good night!" He should have spoken sooner, before Michael returned, but he was getting light-headed and slow-witted. He shivered violently, sloshing water over the side of the glass. Michael hopped up to steady his hand and guide the glass to his lips.

Confusion held Damask immobile while the lamplight flickered across Bram's gray-tinged face. The fumes of liquor were unmistakable, but . . . but there was more to this than drunkenness.

"Michael, why does he need a doctor?"

"The Mister was—"

"Goddammit, woman!" Bram shied the glass at the wall, its splintering crash drowned by his roar. "Leave me in peace!"

"Michael"—Damask's voice climbed on a note of urgency—"why does he need a doctor?"

Caught between his Mister's anger and the Lady's determination, Michael gave Bram the rueful look of one man to another. "Sir, I haven't seen the woman yet who knows when to quit, and she can outlast ye on this one."

Despite the impotent rage that rolled along his veins like molten iron, Bram grinned. "Michael, you're wise beyond your years. We'll be getting on well together." He ruffled the boy's carroty curls with his good hand and lifted a shuttered gaze to Damask. "I've received a slight scratch in a scuffle with the Caswell brothers."

"The Caswells? But, how . . . You're hurt! They've hurt you! Oh! Those wretched beasts! Is nothing too despicable for them?" Damask flew for the lamp, returning to hold it close to Bram. A stream of red glistened on the limp hand resting across his thigh. "A scratch!" she breathed in horror. "I shudder to think what you call a real wound! Lean forward! Michael, help me remove his coat!" It was off in a flash, revealing Bram's blood-dyed sleeve. Damask gasped in dismay and knelt between his knees. Trembling fingers hastened down the row of buttons lining his waistcoat and up the row on his shirt. "Michael, go to the lobby. Tell them to send up hot water and blankets. Get Nero from the servants' quarters. Then find the nearest doctor."

Michael hesitated and Bram nodded to him. "Go, Michael. I will be fine."

Damask, unaware of the secretive current of knowledge that passed between man and boy, looked up. "Fine!" she sighed in disbelief. "It's a wonder you haven't bled to death while you sat here!"

The morning sunlight streamed into Bram's room on moted beams that slid through the mosquito netting to dance across his closed eyes. He swam up through a fog of laudanum-induced sleep with a growing awareness of a dull pounding in his head and a raging thirst. Something else hovered at the rim of his awareness. A coolness pressing against the throbbing hot flesh of his arm. He threw his good arm across his brow, peering from the shadow through slitted lashes.

"I'm sorry. Did I wake you?" Damask whispered while she pressed gently along his injured arm and lifted his swollen hand to knead the calloused palm and fingers.

He croaked hoarsely, and Damask poured a glass of water. Lifting his head with one arm, she held the glass to his lips so he could drink. He sank back, surprised that his strength flagged after so little exertion.

"Make a fist," she urged.

"What are—"

"Sh, you'll wake Michael and I've just gotten him to bed. You've found a guardian angel in Michael O'Malley. He wouldn't leave your side for a moment during the night. He watched everything we did as if he suspected us of doing you some harm."

Bram let the opportunity to comment on that pass. He was too tired to sift the truth from her words or expression. "Have you been up all night?"

"Yes. Make a fist." He complied and Damask gave him a tired smile. "Good. The doctor was afraid you might have lost the use of your hand from that"—one delicate brow arched—"scratch." She perched on the edge of the bed, lifting his hand to knead the fingers, and paused, staring down into the calloused, scarred surface of his palm. "I never knew a deck of cards could be so hard on a man's hands."

Bram declined to rise to that gentle baiting. "Where's Nero? Shouldn't he be here?"

"We may be very glad Wade insisted you have Nero on this trip. I know you weren't pleased by it, but he was a great help last night. I sent him to bed a few minutes ago. He'll be back after a few hours of sleep."

"And you?"

"I can rest this afternoon. I preferred to stay while the danger was greatest. Your hand needs to be checked periodically and you . . ." Damask's eyes fell before his penetrating stare. "You are my husband. I have certain . . . duties."

"Duty," Bram grunted. It was what he wanted. A wife as bound by duty as he would be, sharing no more than their dedication to the land and the son that would be their legacy to that land. But that prim, resolute word, *duties*, twanged a dissonant chord within him. He didn't want Damask tied to him by duty.

A full-blown scowl sprang to his face. How did he want her? Jesus! He must have been crazy to imagine there could ever be anything else between them. And crazier still to think he wanted anything else! He must never forget that Damask was bound by a prior loyalty, and she was not a woman who did things in a halfhearted way. What was she capable of doing if she thought Seven Pines or her precious brother were threatened? It was she who had seen that the Caswells were dismissed. Did she know they would come to the City? Had she hired them? Who else had so much to gain from his death?

"Tell me," he asked softly, "did you, just once during the night, think how fortune would have smiled on you if the Caswells had succeeded?"

Damask dropped his hand as though it had turned to a live coal in her grasp. "That is a beastly thing to ask!"

"Think of it, colleen," he pressed in a silky tone. "You would be free of a man you despise. Seven Pines would be yours, its debts cleared and money left for improvements. Think of it." He brushed his fingers insinuatingly along her forearm.

She snatched her arm away, scrubbing the spot he had touched. She riveted him with a cool, contemptuous gaze. "I know this . . . arrangement was not of your choosing, as it was not of mine. However, I am not so eager for its end that I would stoop to wishing you dead! Each of us is trapped by circumstance and our own stupidity. We can do no more than attempt to make the best of this—this situation. I ask only that we bring to it some dignity. After all, we do have certain duties."

His face blackened with rage, arched brows sweeping together thunderously while he struggled up on his good elbow, his swollen arm dragging uselessly along his side. "The only *duty* I require of you is to be left in peace," he shouted hoarsely.

"I gladly give you the peace you crave. Lulu will take care of you until Nero awakes."

She spun around, making rapidly for the door, and Bram sank back with a frustration more keen than he had ever experienced. She had appeared truly shocked at his suggstion, appalled that he would think she could *stoop to wishing him dead*, genuinely outraged by what he said.

Was she a would-be murderess acting a part or an innocent caught in the crossfire of another enemy? Who then? Her brother? But Wade wasn't in the City. He was to have

remained at Seven Pines. He had a motive, but she had
motive and opportunity. Hell, were they in it together?

"Nero, you're supposed to be resting!"

The surprise in Damask's voice pulled Bram upright.

"Couldn't sleep," he mumbled, ducking his skull-like
head. "I brung these fresh wrappings for Master Bram's
arm. That doctor said to change 'em ever so often."

"Very well. He's awake now."

The door closed behind her with a careful snick that spoke
of a suppressed longing to slam it. Bram's eyes met the
blank expression in Nero's. For an instant, he thought, he
saw an infinitesimal light of antagonism flickering deep in
those dank brown eyes. He felt a chill trickle down his spine
with a cold corpselike finger. He shook himself and lay
back.

"Let's get it over with."

It was the fever, he thought, as he watched Nero bend
over his arm. The fever was giving him fancies.

Chapter 10

BRAM *downed the cognac in a single gulp. Thumping the lead* crystal tumbler down onto the marble mantle, he shot a restless look around the sitting room, then stared blindly into the hearth. His left arm hung useless at his side, a steady throbbing centered in the wound. Sporadic radiating darts of pain filmed his face with a light sheen of sweat. He had managed to dress with Nero's disquietingly unobtrusive help, but the sleeve of his frock coat secured his swollen arm in a vise. There was no help for it. The plans for the dinner and opera tonight were made. He had never given in to the weakness of pain or injury, and he saw no reason to start now.

Behind him, Damask entered quietly. She was dressed for the evening in a beruffled gown of white-worked muslin that should have made her feel exquisite and dainty and all of those wonderful things a woman likes to feel. Instead, she felt . . . besmirched. Smeared by the filth of his accusation that she could wish him dead. It was a cruel thing to say. However much she longed to be rid of him, she had never wished for or thought such a heartless thing, and she resented him thinking she could.

"Mr. Rafferty."

"You went out yesterday, alone!"

A gaze of feigned disinterest lingered on him, and drifted away. "Yes, since I could do nothing for you, I saw no reason to sit in these rooms. I spent the afternoon with my cousin, Madame Cambre."

"New Orleans is a powder keg waiting to explode on Election Day," he said heavily, not turning to look at her. "I would have forbidden it had I known."

"I was perfectly safe. Elize sent her carriage." Damask stared at the unyielding line of Bram's back, her lip curling with distaste. "You should not have taken your anger out on Lulu and Nero and Michael. They were not responsible for my going, nor could they have prevented it."

Bram glared down at the spray of dahlias filling a squat brown vase on the cold hearth. It had been ridiculous to think she had run away from him. Run away from him, and run to . . .

No, as long as he had Seven Pines, she would stick to him like a cocklebur. So why had he lain upon his bed, wide-eyed and sweating through the hot afternoon, unable to rest or sleep or relax until he heard the closing of the hall door and the soft murmur of her voice?

Bram looked around, a steely light in his cold stare. "Be glad my anger was exhausted on them. It was a dangerous thing for you to do."

"Perhaps," she said casually, though the cold light in her eyes was a match for his, "but I came back, safe and sound."

"From your cousin's, so you say. I thought it more likely you had gone to visit your . . . Mr. Marlowe."

Hearing Hunt's name gave rise to a vexing quiver of alarm, and Damask looked up from the soft kid glove she was smoothing over her fingers. "How do you know about Hun . . . Mr. Marlowe?"

"Do you think Wade could resist the pleasure of informing me about that *alternative* your grandfather mentioned?"

"Wade?" Damask raised a bewildered gaze to Bram. "But, why? He . . ."

She broke off and moved to the mirror hanging on the wall, as though to check her hair, but her downcast eyes saw nothing except a sunny morning past and Wade patting her arm, awkwardly as always, before she was driven away from Seven Pines by her despised husband.

Wade told her it was all for the best. That was what Mama always said, wasn't it? he insisted. Everything happens for the best. She had a husband now to take care of her and Seven Pines. She should be glad, Wade had pressed. After all, it was unlikely Hunt could have been brought to the altar. A man didn't like his wife to be more accustomed to field hands and breeding lines than she was to ladies and gentlemen and afternoon calling cards. Besides, she would have felt uncomfortable and out of place in New Orleans society. With the gambler such things wouldn't matter. Of course, Wade had said and paused and looked away, it might be better not to mention Hunt Marlowe to Rafferty. There was no telling what he might do, he had added, the suggestion of ominous results appearing in his narrowed blue eyes.

Why would he have told Bram? It made no sense.

"Did you?"

The hard question brought her head up to meet the icy censure in her husband's eyes. "Did I what?"

"Meet your Mr. Marlowe!" Irritation filed the resonance from his voice.

"Meet . . ." Her eyes widened and color rushed into her cheeks. "No, and I find your insinuation insulting! You have been given no cause . . ."

"Haven't I?" Bram rushed on, damning himself, but unable to stop. "You vanished without a word! How do I know you weren't spending the afternoon with Marlowe while your *husband* was so *conveniently* out of the way?"

"Husband!" Damask whisked around, driven by anger or tension or some demon of self-destruction. She could no more have stopped herself than Bram could have. "You have been no husband to me!"

The distance between them vanished with lightning speed. Bram's contorted face lowered to hers, his eyes blazing a hot fiery blue. "That can be remedied!"

"Can it?" she asked, a hollow ache of haunting sadness

hovering in her eyes. "We have made a contract, not a marriage. Where is the affection, the caring, the sharing, the respect a husband and wife should have for each other? You want a son. But how can we teach him those things when his parents are hostile strangers and love is a word whose meaning they will never know?"

Bram paled, the feverish blotches of red stark against his sallow cheekbones. "Love!" he spit with revulsion. "He will be a man! Not a mincing fop sighing for love! He will have the land and his honor! What more will he need? There's a savage world beyond the fence of Seven Pines, Damask. A world of suffering and hardship, a world of thievery and murder. A world where a man's pride can be eaten away until he is an empty husk of what he once was. Do you know what happens to a man when he can find no work? When his children go to sleep crying over an empty belly night after night? Do you know there are places in this city where children wake in the night to find rats chewing on their fingers and toes? Love! How long do you think love lasts when a man is forced to stand by and watch his wife and children waste away and die from hunger and disease? How long before he begins to hate himself for his failure? How long before he begins to hate them for being the proof of that failure? Love fades quickly enough!"

Bram's chest heaved; his eyes were dark with pain. His hand came up as though he brushed away some vision and he staggered to the window, where he stood with one hand braced high on the sill, his head bowed.

Damask stared after him. Even if she could have thought of something to say, she knew he would not welcome it. A gambler he was, but, perhaps . . . more than that?

Rock-hard muscles strapped the broad back that shut her from his sight. Rock-hard muscles roped the length of that arm resting against the sill. Callouses, thick and old and laced with scars, hid in the coil of his fist. What had his life been before he came to Seven Pines? Dear God, what horrors had he seen—even endured?—to give that ring of truth to his every word?

A sentiment, born of her loving heart, fretted the corners of her self-righteous anger. At this moment she did not see Lulu's *devil gambling man*, only a man who suffered like any other. A man who may have suffered more than most.

He straightened, his back inching into a rigid line. Pausing, as though he gathered his courage for some ordeal, he turned to face her. His every feature was stone-hard, but his eyes—his eyes were fathomless pits that vanished into some distant hell.

"If . . ." His voice faded and he cleared his throat. "If you are ready, the carriage is waiting."

The relative cool of the twilight hour drew throngs of shoppers to the streets of the Vieux Carré. Damask hugged her side of the carriage, listlessly noting the lamplighter climbing the ladder to light the gas street lamps. If they were at Seven Pines, she thought with a pang of homesickness, Jims would be lighting the lamps in the dining room and checking the table settings. An occasional firefly would flit through the window to decorate the room with his greenish-yellow glow. The fragrance of pines would perfume the air.

She flicked a darting glance at Bram. His cloak of solitude was a tangible barrier she could cross. Why did she want to? Why did she have to fight against the need—why need?—to lay her hand atop the white-gloved fist pressing into the sculptured length of his thigh? It looked lonely somehow, sitting in the shadow above a patch of light that highlighted his knee. As lonely and bereft of comfort as he was.

The carriage slowed to a halt. She should have been excited, but she dreaded the long hours they would spend dining alone in the private supper room before the performance began.

The door was jerked open by the cabbie. Bram descended with a sharp indrawn breath when his arm brushed against the door. He helped her alight, his skin pale in spite of his dark tan, his left arm hanging limp at his side.

She was whisked into the dusk of the colonnade before she could look at tht exterior of the Theatre d'Orleans, and was rushed through the lobby and up a set of stairs with a curt, "We are late."

Damask hurried to catch up to his brisk stride as they started down a long door-lined hall. "How can we be late if we are dining alone?" He did not answer. "Please! You forget I do not have your length of limb."

His pace became more sedate in response and finally he stopped at a door, which he opened, nodding for her to enter. Damask stepped through, her eyes sweeping the room curiously. She had a vivid impression of brocaded opulence before she came to a stunned halt.

Cousin Elize was sitting on a wide sofa. Beside her was *Tante* Alzina Downing. Uncle James was ensconced in a high wing-back chair and Cousin Andy was standing beside a man who could only be Elize's husband, Andre Cambre.

"I see that Mr. Rafferty was able to keep this a surprise," Elize said laughing as she set her glass of champagne on a small *papier mâché* table. She came to Damask and hugged her lightly, kissing her cheek. "Can't you say anything?"

"I'm so surprised!" she answered breathlessly, drawing a laugh from the gathering. She looked back at Bram, who stood in the doorway watching her, his dark face impassive. He had arranged this wonderful surprise. Why? To wriggle his way into the affections of her family? Or simply to please her? Whatever the reason, she was happy. Her smile trembled, radiant with joy, and his expression lightened, a hint of a smile relaxing the taut line of his lips.

"Come here, child." Uncle James held out his one arm. The other had been lost on a cold, foggy December night in 1814 when he marched into battle to save New Orleans from the British.

Damask was clasped over his rotund belly, and she pressed a kiss into the wiry brush of graying muttonchop whiskers.

"Stand back now, so I can have a look at you," he said gruffly. "Alzina, m'dear, she looks just like her mother, doesn't she? A vision of an angel."

Tante Alzina gave her a shy smile. "Papa is right. It

seems only yesterday you were a little girl with long plaits my Andy could not resist pulling.''

"And for good reason, *Maman!* She followed Wade and me like a coonhound on the scent! What else could I do to discourage her?'' Andy gave Damask a roguish wink and scooped her off her feet for a robust hug. Setting her back down, he wrapped his arm around her waist, his wide candid smile turned somber. "How is it with you now? Are you happy?''

Her gaze fell. "Of course, I am. You must meet my husband,'' she said with a tinny brightness that changed to confusion when she felt Andy's arm tense while his eyes lifted over her shoulder and stared with a hard glassy sheen.

"But your husband and I are acquaintances of old. Isn't that right, Mr. Rafferty?''

There was a promise of reckoning underlying his pleasantly modulated tone, and Damask felt the same skin-crawling tension as when she'd heard Bram's silk-over-steel comments to the Caswells. "You . . . you know Mis . . . my husband, Andy?''

"We have met.''

Damask darted a quick look around. No one else had caught that hidden message. They were all looking at Bram with pleasant welcoming smiles. As she wondered what had caused that spark of antagonism, her uncle crossed to shake Bram's hand in the firm grip of men who met often, and in friendship. But Damask had no time to speculate about it before her uncle spoke.

"Mr. Rafferty''—her uncle's voice held an unmistakable note of respect, even admiration—"who would have thought when you and I first met that you would become my nephew?''

He pulled Bram into the room and rested a hand on his shoulder. "He marched into the bank when he was hardly big enough to see over my desk and, bold as brass, demanded to see the president. Had business to discuss, and no one else would do. Put that twit of a clerk, Marchand, in a dither, I can tell you. There he was, looking like something out of a rag picker's bag. Strutted right up to my desk, slapped down a picayune, and told me he wanted to invest it! By God! I'll never forget it!''

The waiter appeared with a silver tray reflecting delicate stemware filled with bubbling champagne, and Uncle James hefted his glass.

"A toast! To our Damask and her husband: May your lives be long; may your days be happy; may your union be blessed with many sons and daughters."

None realized that the color that flooded Damask's cheeks was due less to maidenly modesty then to the grim humor in her husband's smile.

Damask woke with the rising sun. Yawning widely, she looked around her room. Lulu had been at work early. The room was bare of the clothing and accessories she had scattered in the moonlit night.

It had been a wonderful evening, she mused, while curling on her side and tucking her hand beneath her cheek. The conversation had ebbed and flowed through course after course. Through the broiled pompano and baked turkey and tenderloin of beef in mushroom sauce, the tangled skein of family memories, part fact, part fiction, of the Downings, the Tureauds, and the Scarboroughs, were woven into a tapestry of welcome for Bram.

Elize began it when she suddenly remembered that Damask was named for their great-grandmother, Damask Tureaud Scarborough. Andre gave a good-natured groan when Elize set her fork aside and leaned forward to trace the family tree, relishing the tale of that first Damask and her rakehell pirate, Kinloch Scarborough. Then began the laborious task of tracing branches that suddenly looped back to entwine with others. When even *Tante* Alzina became confused, they gave it up with a laugh.

A mellow smile grew. Families. Uncles, aunts, cousins. How small the world seemed when a stranger was a cousin of a cousin. No longer a stranger but family. A thread in an intricate, ever-spreading web. What had it been like for

Bram to grow to manhood alone, with no one to care whether he was tired or hungry; no one to encourage him when his spirits flagged; no father to lead him into the world of men; no mother to gentle him for the world of women?

Damask rolled onto her back, kicking the sticky covers away to let the breath of a breeze that swayed the gauze netting cool her. He seemed to enjoy the talk that swirled around the table like the eddying smoke from the candles. As always the talk drifted from family to cotton and sugar cane to politics. Was it her imagination, or were those discussions growing more vehement and less tolerant?

They had all agreed that nothing short of a constitutional amendment to protect slavery would halt the growing aggression of the abolitionists; that the North was trying to dominate the South economically; that they would make every effort to contain slavery if they could not end it. They all agreed that slavery was a positive good; that tampering with this time-proven system would result in economic and social upheaval.

From those common stands, they diverged sharply. Andre Cambre was opposed to any compromise and felt the only course left was secession from a Union that threatened the very existence of the South. Uncle James's bushy brows drooped across his eyes when Andre declared his support of those fire-eating secessionist agitators—William Lowndes Yancey of Alabama and Robert Barnwell Rhett of South Carolina. The idea of secession was repugnant to him. Almost any compromise, short of emancipation, was better than disunion. Andy's stance was somewhere between the two. He didn't shrink from the idea of secession as his father did, nor did he find it the only solution as Andre did. When Uncle James looked to Bram, seeking support, Bram made only one terse statement: "We have rounded the corner of compromise, gentlemen. There will be war."

The words settled into the hushed silence like sediment from Mississippi River water settling in a jar. A shiver of alarm sped around the table. Uncle James had lowered his chin to his chest and stared at Bram through the wiry brush of his brows. Surely he would deny what had been said, Damask thought. After all, who was Bram Rafferty? A gambler, a liar, and a cheat! Why should a man of rectitude like her uncle listen to him, or listening, believe?

"It will be a sad day for us all," Uncle James said, heaving a sigh. "A sad day."

He listened, respected his opinion, and believed! Damask was stunned. Why would he accept the views of a man who was a notorious gambler, as Wade had claimed? The man of mystery followed by the worst of rumors, as Elize had said? Was it possible Uncle James didn't know what Bram Rafferty was?

No, he knew everything that went on in New Orleans. She had often heard her papa say that his brother made it his business to find out everything he could about the people that used his bank. It was a point of pride with him. He knew Bram Rafferty and, knowing him, liked him—even admired him.

Was it possible that Wade . . .

The ringing of the bells from St. Patrick's Church, fronting Lafayette Square a few blocks down the street, alerted Damask to the growing lateness of the hour. Leaving the disconcerting thoughts of her Uncle James's reaction to her husband, she turned to a problem of more immediacy.

What was there between Andy and Bram? Why had Andy so urgently insisted that she lunch with him today? It was more than a desire to extend their visit. She had not missed the hard look that rested on Bram when Andy tugged her off to one side, saying they must have a chance to talk privately. Whatever it was, she would know in a few hours.

The Mister was gone, Michael told her. It didn't seem possible that he could have been up and about this morning. Not when he had been flushed with fever and so obviously at the end of his strength when they returned to the suite in the wee hours of the morning. He had curtly refused her offer to look at the wound and swiveled away, reeling once, steadying himself, and planting one foot in front of the other with careful deliberation.

Andy arrived and thoughts of Bram scattered while her cousin's appreciative look swept from the red ribbons atop her bonnet to the hem of her white voile skirt. After a few floridly teasing compliments, Andy cocked his top hat at a jaunty angle and escorted her from the hotel with a speed she found breathtaking.

He lifted her onto the high seat of his phaeton, a graceful four-wheeler in black lacquer with red trim. Rushing around to the opposite side, he climbed up, thumping down next to her with an engaging grin.

"Hold on to your bonnet," he warned.

He slapped the reins across the rump of a shining black mare and off they went, dodging a lumbering omnibus that was slowing for its stop before the hotel. A curse trailed after them, and a dog ran from their path with a disgruntled yelp just before they shot the closing gap between two heavy-laden drays. The wind whipped at Damask's skirts and tugged at the brim of her bonnet, and she hung on for dear life while they recklessly sped through the broad sycamore-lined intersection of Canal Street. After a skidding full-speed swerve around a corner, she vowed she would walk back to the hotel before she rode with him again.

A moment later they came to a stop and Andy nudged her. "You can open your eyes now." She complied and discovered him grinning broadly. "I swore I'd have my revenge for that wild ponycart ride through the woods at Seven Pines. Remember?"

"You should have suspected something when Wade wouldn't ride with us," she said, laughing.

The restaurant, located at No. 50 Rue St. Louis, was a simple place with wood floors and bare walls, but Andy explained that the proprietor-chef, Antoine Alciatore, served the best food in the City. Madame Alciatore met them at the door, conducting them through the small room of white-clothed tables to a back corner where there was some degree of privacy. Moments later the chef hurried into the dining room.

Damask had a smattering of school-girl French, but not enough to follow the voluble discourse between Antoine and Andy about wines and sauces. Relaxing against the back of the bentwood chair, she looked around the room. Every table was in use. There was an old man, sitting alone and sipping a glass of wine; a French family with a stiffly correct Papa and well-behaved children; business men with the *Price Current* spread on the table before them.

The chef returned to his kitchen, and Andy complained goodnaturedly that he had yet to win an argument with Antoine—and how glad he was when he was served! As though by mutual consent, they did not mention Bram Rafferty through the long leisurely meal. The conversation revolved around the family, the City, and Andy's work at the bank with his father. After the dishes were cleared away, and he poured another glass of wine for her, Andy finally mentioned the subject that brought them together.

"I was surprised to hear you married Mr. Rafferty."

Damask's eyes dropped to the full-bodied burgundy sparkling along the curving sides of her glass. "It was rather . . . sudden."

"I can imagine," Andy said drily. "I want you to tell me why you did it."

The well-behaved children trotting to the door like a row of downy goslings were a safer subject for her attention than her cousin. "I don't know what you mean."

"Don't fence with me, Damask. I was there when Wade lost Seven Pines."

She should have known! Wade spent much of his time in the City with Andy. He had delighted in spoiling her illusions about her adored cousin by telling her of the little house tucked away on the fringes of Rampart Street where a beautiful octoroon mistress awaited Andy's pleasure.

Her eyes flew to him. "You know?"

"Yes."

"Then," she said, her expression hardening, "you know that he cheated Wade."

"Cheated? Bram Rafferty?" he burst out, rocking back in his chair. "Damask, where did you get an idea like that?"

"From Wade. He said he didn't know how—"

"No doubt," Andy interjected astringently.

Damask frowned. "He said he didn't know exactly how, but he was cheated."

Andy raked his hand through his shock of bronze hair and leveled a puzzled look on her. "If you thought he cheated Wade, why in hell did you marry him?"

"I . . . I didn't know it when we married."

"I see." Andy fiddled with the snowy edge of his napkin. "How did you learn that he, ah, cheated?"

"Wade told me. He wanted to protect me."

"Did he?" Andy asked with a sneer that brought the sting of hot color to her cheeks.

"Andy, Bram Rafferty is in the wrong here! Not Wade!"

"Is he? Would you like to hear how your brother lost your home and sold you into marriage with a stranger?"

"No! What possible good could it do?"

He leaned forward, elbows plunked onto the table, gold-tipped brows shadowing his eyes. "You're going to hear it anyway, because it might do you untold good. It couldn't be pleasant being married to a man you think cheated you of your home."

"Think! I know—"

"Listen! There were five men in the game: Wade, Rafferty, myself, and two planters from upriver. The stakes climbed out of my league. Wade's and Rafferty's, too, for that matter. I dropped out, but Wade was riding a streak of luck. It ran out, as it always does. I tried to get him to stop, but . . ." Andy shrugged. "Gambling is a sickness with Wade."

"A sickness!" Damask bent toward him. "Andy, I don't know why you are saying these things against Wade, but he himself has told me he dislikes gambling and only goes when pressured by his friends!"

A frown of concentration gathered in his eyes. "You don't know, do you? You really don't know." Seconds ticked by while his expression wavered on indecision. "Damask, what do you think Wade has been doing with his money?"

"Investments that went bad and some horses that went lame. A house that he has rented here with servants. But you should know all of that! Wade told me that you and Uncle James had advised him."

"Bad investments? Papa advising him on bad investments? And you believed it?"

"Of course I believed him," Damask cried. "Why shouldn't I?"

He covered her shaking hand with his. "Because, Damask," he said gently, "Wade is a gambler. Not for fun, not even for profit. With him it's a . . . disease. There have been no investments, no horses, no house."

Damask closed her eyes and sank back in her chair. It wasn't possible, yet why should Andy lie? He gained nothing from it. But, if he were telling the truth . . .

"Wade wouldn't lie to me, Andy. Not about this. Bram cheated him."

"Damask, Bram Rafferty did not cheat. He has a reputation all over New Orleans for honesty and integrity. He is respected and welcomed in every reputable gambling house in the City because he has never taken unfair advantage of his opponents."

"But Elize said"—she swallowed tension and nausea—"that he is followed by the worst kind of rumors."

"Rumors aplenty, and some vicious. Most started by men like . . ." He stopped and frowned. "Men who have lost large sums of money to him. Andre Cambre, for one."

"I see." Damask turned her hand beneath his to grip it as though it would brace her for what was to come. "Tell me about the game."

Andy's hand squeezed around hers, a grasp that was comforting and, somehow, an omen. "The planters dropped out and Rafferty stood also, but Wade insisted on continuing. His money dwindled. He grew desperate. The time came when he could not match a bet and Rafferty threw down the cards to quit the table. Wade grabbed his arm and told him they would play one hand. Seven Pines against everything Rafferty had. It was a ridiculous bet. Rafferty's holdings were not half the value of Seven Pines. He refused. Wade grew insistent. Rafferty lost patience and told him he was not a man who would steal the pennies from a dead man's eyes, nor the kind that would steal a man's home and livelihood. Wade was furious. He jumped up, slinging his chair across the room, and screamed that Rafferty was a coward. Every game in the room came to a halt. Every eye was riveted upon Rafferty while he sat down and picked up the cards.''

Damask raised her dull muddy gaze to the simple chandelier that looped overhead. ''Bram didn't cheat?''

''No.''

Chapter 11

DAMASK *watched Andy's phaeton pull into the avenue below at* a breakneck pace. Emotions in turmoil, she rested her cheek against the cool wood.

Could she believe that Wade had lost their livelihood in an insatiable quest for the "Big Win," as Andy called it? Could she believe that Wade had lied about everything, even Bram, with the certain knowledge that she would never accept a man without honor for a husband? No, she could not.

Wade loved her and tried to protect her, in his own way. He had warned her she wouldn't like New Orleans and wouldn't be comfortable here. Wasn't he right? He had told her not to expect too much, that men prefer their women sweet-tempered and pliant, not bold and forward. Hadn't he been proven true? Bram accepted her edict not to touch her with every evidence of outright relief.

Was she so plain, so unappealing, so undesirable? She wasn't as pretty as Mama, whatever Uncle James said. Wade had always told her it was a shame that Mama had been so beautiful and her daughters so . . . so . . .

He never finished it and left her with the nagging guilt that she had failed Mama and Papa in yet another way.

She sighed and moved and saw Michael trudging dispiritedly into the sitting room. When he saw her, he frowned and did an about face.

"Michael, is something wrong?" Grudgingly, he stared

across the gulf that separated them with an accusing glare and she frowned. "Come, sit by me on the sofa."

"I can hear what ye got to say."

"Very well," she said, curious about the anger radiating from him. "If you are going to work for Mr. Rafferty, you should know that he has the manners of a gentleman, and will expect you to have the same."

"Ain't gonna be working for him."

"Of course you are!" she burst out, and was shocked at her own vehemence. Had she had so completely accepted Michael's being raised under the tutelage of her husband? Was it possible she really believed Andy?

"Ain't gonna be working for him," Michael said implacably. "He's gonna die in that bed and ye, fine lady that ye are, niver setting a hand to save him!"

"What are you saying?" Damask's voice climbed on a shaft of fear. "You told me he went out this morning!"

Michael jammed his fists into his pockets and hunched his shoulders. "The Mister told me what to be saying. Humph! Out? When he hadn't a wink of sleep in the night? Out? When the doctor'd jist been telling him he'd have to cut off his arm before he died from the poison of it?"

"Cut off . . ." Damask swallowed a surge of nausea. Cut off his arm! That long arm roped with muscles. Those long fingers that had wafted across her flesh so gently, so very gently she still felt them in the lonely hours of the night. "I must see him!"

Michael took a step toward the door, as though to bar her way. "The fever's took him so's he don't hardly know he's in the world." The sneering challenge came hard and fast. "His arm be twice its size and his hand so swollen he can't bend a finger. And the cut be filled with yeller bile whose stench 'ud be making a fine lady such as yerself run scream- ing from him."

The boy's attitude toward her was obviously venomous, but Damask had no time to wonder about it. She sailed by him. "Hurry along, Michael. You wouldn't want to miss the sight of a fine lady such as myself running from her sick husband in horror.''

She took a deep breath and pushed the door open. Fetid air, the heat of the room, and the smell of sickness struck her in an odorous wave. She hurried into the cryptlike gloom, a film of sweat beading across her face.

Nero was napping in a chair, sleeves rolled high on his bony arms. His eyes popped open, revealing a startled quiver of fear as he jumped to attention. ''Miss Damask! Ain't no need . . . he be . . . Miss Damask!'' Nero tried to block her approach.

''Nero, open the windows!'' Damask pushed aside the netting and gaped at Bram's arm in horror. The swelling had stretched the skin drum tight. His fingers were spread like sausages, the crease of the elbow no more than a faint mark. He lay as still as a corpse, but heat radiated from his burning skin.

''Dear God! Why wasn't I told sooner?'' Not waiting for an answer, she loosened the bandage that bound his swollen arm. ''Michael, go downstairs. I want a bucket of ice sent up here every hour, and buckets of water now. On your way out get Lulu. Run, child! Nero, stay here until I change.''

Jesus! Michael wailed to himself. What have I done? He literally hopped from foot to foot in indecision. He knew the Mister needed to have the fever brought down, but . . .

''Michael! What are you doing here? Go!''

He took off with the despairing thought that the Mister was dead either way. As he flew down the stairs, Michael swore to himself that he would not rest until he had delivered to justice the man or woman who had hired the Caswells.

When Damask returned, Lulu was waiting beside the bed. Michael was right. The stench rising from the putrid cut was enough to make her run screaming. She swallowed her gorge. ''I don't know what to do for this, Lulu. Tell me?''

''Child''—Lulu shook her head helplessly—''I don't know.

If we was to home I could go to the woods and find herbs to make a poultice, but—''

"Michael will know where we can find what you need."

"Ain't never seen nothing like this." Lulu studied the oozing pus with a practiced eye. "That doctor, he done clean this up good, do everything that oughta be done. Shoulda healed up."

"Lady! Here's a bucket of water. They be sending up the ice."

"Michael, Lulu needs herbs to treat this. Where can she find them?"

"Closest place 'ud be the Poydras Market. If they ain't there, the French Market has most everything."

"Good. Take money from Mr. Rafferty's pocket, hire a cab, and take Lulu wherever she wants to go. I want fresh beef for broth and oranges and lemons. Tell them at the desk that I need a fire and pots for cooking."

The ice arrived and Damask began bathing Bram in the cool water. There was no time for thought, no time for anything but battling the raging fever.

Some time later, Bram's lashes fluttered up and his fever-bright eyes began watching her. She thought he was unaware of what was happening, until she heard a scratchy whisper, "Duty, Mrs. Rafferty?"

She lifted the sweaty strands of black hair from his brow with a slender finger. "Save your strength. You have a stronger foe than I to fight just now."

His lashes furled down to rest on his flushed cheeks and she reached for the bowl of water.

"I will never have a stronger foe than you, Damask," he murmured and was silent again.

Whether he slipped back into his feverish dreams or simply chose to ignore her, Damask didn't know. But his eyes never opened again. Sultry afternoon became sweltering evening while she tirelessly bathed him and pondered that curious statement.

Lulu and Michael returned with meat and fruit and herbs in twists of paper.

"Child," Lulu said after looking at his arm, "we got to take out them stitches that no 'count doctor sewed him up with. Then we gotta spread that cut and clean out the bile and pour this turpentine on it."

Damask's face blanched. A trembling centered in her knees and she sank into a chair breathing heavily. "Lulu, there must be something else!"

"I fetched herbs for poultices, but I ain't expecting nothing from that. Got too bad. You know I ain't got no use for that man, but I wouldn't be making him hurt for the fun of it. Gotta be done. If it ain't . . ."

Damask closed her eyes. "I'll wake him to explain. Get everything ready."

She went to his bed on legs whose muscles twitched with tension, and stared down into his sleeping face. His countenance was smooth, the brows forming a perfect arch, unspoiled by the mocking tilt of his waking hours. His lashes fanned across his fever-flushed cheeks, the tips curling up with the innocence of a child's. His lips were soft and wide and perfectly formed.

Her slender finger touched Bram's hot skin, tracing the white-ridged curve of the scar from brow to cheekbone. How had he gotten it? What forces shaped his baffling mixture of cynicism and compassion? He could look so hard yet now he was so vulnerable.

She had a sudden vision of him as a boy. Masses of black curls, grimy cheeks, elbows poking through holes in his sleeves—slapping his picayune on her uncle's desk. Could that proud little boy have grown into the man who cheated her brother? Was Andy right and Wade wrong? Why had Bram refused to defend himself?

"Miss Damask, a man what say he a constable wants to speak with you."

Damask left Lulu with Bram and hurried into the sitting room. "I'm Mrs. Rafferty. May I help you?"

"Excuse me, ma'am. I wanted to speak with Mr. Rafferty."

"My husband is desperately ill, sir."

"Ah." The man shuffled a leather-billed hat from hand to beefy hand, then crushed the cloth crown in a fist. "Desperately ill? Uh, we were needing him to, uh, we have the Caswells, we . . . if anything should, if he should . . ."

His kindly, coarse featured face screwed up in a pained expression. Damask could almost hear him wondering how he could ask her to inform them in the event of her husband's death. Though Michael had given her the doctor's opinion, she had not considered it possible. There was too much latent strength in that manly muscular frame. But there was, too, his fever ridden body soaking the linen sheets with sweat and the poison that had begun radiating from the festering wound in red streaks.

"If anything should . . . should happen," she faltered, "I will send word that those beasts are to be charged with murder and, hopefully, hanged."

"Yes, ma'am. Thank you." The man heaved a sigh of relief and turned to leave.

Michael, stirring the simmering broth over the hearth fire, his every sense alert to the danger of the constable talking to the Lady, breathed his own sigh of relief. It was short-lived.

"Uh, ma'am?" the constable said. "If anything happens, we'll try to find whoever sent that note. He's just as guilty as the Caswells."

"Note?"

"Yes, ma'am. The note hiring them to, uh, kill Mr. Rafferty before he went back to, uh, Seven Pines."

Shock shattered her hard-won poise. Her hand groped for the back of the sofa, and her mind reeled like a wooden top, skimming past the words before meaning could be grasped.

"Sorry, ma'am! Sure thought you knew!"

Michael squatted at the hearth, indigo eyes solemn and unblinking. He knew, she thought, and could not tear her eyes from his. "Please, I want to know about the note."

"Not much to tell," the constable said. "It was wrapped around a twenty-dollar gold piece and sent to the Caswells. Said Mr. Rafferty was here and they could do themselves and some other people a favor if they killed him before he got back to Seven Pines. It was unsigned. That's it. Mr. Rafferty told us not to look for whoever sent it, but, uh, well, if anything happens to him, it will be murder and we'll do our best to find out who hired them."

"I see. Thank you, constable. I'll let you know." The man left. Still, Damask's eyes were locked with those knowing, accusing man's eyes in the face of a child.

"Michael, you were with Mr. Rafferty when those men attacked him." He nodded. "You knew about this note?" He nodded again and her chin trembled. "Mr. Rafferty believes I hired those men to kill him, doesn't he?"

"He didn't say."

"Michael, you are avoiding my question. I believe you and Bram Rafferty are so much alike that neither of you needs words to know what the other is thinking. He believes I hired those men, doesn't he?"

"Yes."

Despair blurred Damask's vision, breaking the magnetic attraction of Michael's reproachful eyes. What was it Bram had asked her? *Did you, just once during the night, think how fortune would have smiled on you if the Caswells had succeeded?* And before that, his voice thick with sarcasm: *Could it have been you were expecting word of a different sort this night?*

She thought he was accusing her of *wishing* him dead, and all the time he was accusing her of paying and conspiring with the Caswells!

What had she done to make him believe her capable of that? The fact he did believe it was a cruel blow, almost impossible to think about when he was lying in the next room so close to death with so little recourse to save him.

Damask meshed her icy fingers to still their trembling, but she could do nothing about the slow, sorrowful thudding of her heart. "Michael, Mr. Rafferty will die if something isn't done. He might die anyway. What we must do will be extremely painful, but it must be done. Lulu will explain. I want you to be there to see what we do. And Michael?"

"Yes."

"If we can save him, I will have a favor to ask of you."
She turned to go, but stopped to look back. "I'm glad you'll
be going home with us, Michael. Mr. Rafferty will need a
friend there."

A misty rainbow arched high into the clouds over emerald
velvet hills. The freshening wind carried the smells of a peat
fire and bubbling mutton stew. Padraic Rafferty's fair face
crinkled with laughter. His children gathered round to listen
to the tale of leprechauns guarding a pot of gold. His wife's
worshipful gaze clung to his face. Their eyes met with pride,
with love, with infinite trust . . .

Bram groaned and forced his heavy lids up, trying to
shake the dream. So much happiness. There was never a
moment when love failed to enfold the Raffertys like a warm
wool blanket. But that had changed. Changed! He didn't
want to remember!

His eyes closed reluctantly on the sight of that glorious
spring day when Padraic Rafferty cast aside his spade in
their small potato patch.

"Mary, me darling, 'tis to America we be going!"

"Holy St. Patrick, save us! Ye mad creature, 'tis the
drink ye've been at again for sure!"

Padraic Rafferty laughed, his raw farmer's hands closing
around his wife's tiny waist to catapult her into the air. "Mary
Rafferty, ye desarve more than this patch of land 'ull be
bringing. Think on it, love! America! The divil take me if I
don't make of ye a princess in that grand land!"

So it had begun. A chilly crossing of the channel to Liverpool and a short wait in a wretched tenement. The first ship
leaving port was on its way to New Orleans, and Padraic
swore it was a sign that St. Patrick was watching over them
for the news had traveled to Ireland that a man could earn the
glorious wage of a dollar a day in that bustling port city!
Padraic's excitement was undimmed by the hardships of the
voyage in steerage, but Bram still suffered a small boy's fear
of the dark because of it. Burned into his mind were haunting memories: the smells of sweat, urine, vomit; the sounds

of coughing, laughter, tears; the screaming death of a woman whose child would not be born; the pinched faces of Paddy and Mary as they all gathered around their mother for comfort while she nursed Baby Annie at her breast; the rolling pitching ship tossing them thither and yon as it soared high on a storm-tossed wave and lurched into a deep trough; his mother crooning a lullaby; his father's promises of a land where hard work earned its just reward.

They arrived at last, more lucky than most, for the family survived the voyage intact. The sun was blinding, the August heat stifling, and Padraic Rafferty undaunted by the strangeness of the new land.

The family huddled at the ship's railing, and Bram's father lifted him and flung out an arm to encompass the teeming odorous docks. "D'ye see, me boy? 'Tis ours, to be sure! We need only reach out and grab hold! Do ye hear me, America!" Padraic shouted exuberantly. "The Raffertys have arrived!"

Arrived to be sure! To be fleeced by a smooth-talking Irish lad claiming they must buy a permit to disembark. Ignorant of the ways of the new land, Padraic gladly paid and asked the baby-faced boy for directions to a respectable boarding house. Mrs. O'Grady's it was, and a friendly smile she had for the weary travelers—until their money ran out. Then, a seedy, rat infested tenement near the docks was their next home while Padraic scoured the City for work.

There were slaves for farm labor. Slaves and freemen-of-color for waiting tables, for draymen and carpenters. What else could he do? At length he found work with a gang of Irish laborers draining a swamp for an upriver plantation. It was short-lived. Within weeks he was back with a vicious case of quartan fever. Between alternating chills and fever, Padraic Rafferty cursed the land where an Irishman's life was cheap enough to waste on those dangerous tasks a planter would not risk his valuable slaves to do.

The bottle became Padraic's solace and shield. Before two years passed, the loving Raffertys were scattered or dead—leaving ten-year-old Bram with a guilt he would carry to his grave.

Bram's face twisted. Silently, he cursed the weakness that allowed the invasion of those memories. His good arm rose to rest across his eyes while the long fingers—so graceful and well cared for, until one looked into the calloused, scarred palm—balled into an impotent fist. His father's face hung before him, the fair features bloated and bleary, and Bram heard again the question filled with surprised wonder: "What have ye done, me boy? What have ye done?"

Pain streaked from the blazing inferno that was his arm. Bram embraced it, sinking into the red-tinged dark. A pressure on the bed and the touch of a cool hand on his brow brought him reluctantly back to consciousness.

"Bram, can you hear me?"

He moved his arm to reveal his eyes, metallic bright and mocking. "It is only my arm that is useless, colleen." His gaze roamed the melancholy expression that marred the sweet line of her lips and muddied the cinnamon hue of her eyes. What had happened? She looked lost, heartsore. "Come up here," he urged, concern warming his voice. She balked and he smiled. "Don't you know that a sick man needs to be humored? Come up." She crawled up to sit beside him and Bram's big hand cupped her cheek, his eyes searching hers. "What has hurt you, colleen?"

The caressing endearment insinuated itself into Damask's heart with a tiny thrill of pleasure. Her hand came up to cover his while she solemnly studied his dark features. This was the man Uncle James respected. The man Andy, once he knew Bram had not coerced her into marriage, admitted to admiring. The man Wade called a liar and a cheat. The man who thought she . . .

She pulled his hand from her cheek and stared down into the palm while the tips of her fingers brushed it with a featherlike caress. "This is not the soft, perfumed hand of a gambler, but the scarred hand of a laborer. I know so little about you, Bram. Not even your favorite food." Her eyes raised to meet his and she made a poor attempt at a smile.

''What good wife does not know what to set upon the table to please her husband?''

Bram traced the pure curve of her mouth, vainly seeking the dimple that her deepest amusement or pleasure exposed. ''Ah, colleen,'' he teased, forcing a chuckle. ''You have to be asking an Irishman what his favorite food is?''

His venture into humor failed miserably. Damask settled her grave stare around the region of his collarbone. ''Michael told me you saw the doctor this morning.''

''It's nothing to concern yourself about,'' he said, his tone carefully neutral.

Flaming color climbed the deep vee of Damask's dressing gown, washing across her cheeks, bright and hot. As hot as the glare of molten gold that sent confusion swirling through the fevered passages of Bram's mind.

''You are the master of Seven Pines! Everything to do with you is of concern to me! Do you think I will sit idly by and watch you die from the poison in this arm? *No!* Seven Pines needs you! Her people need you! I . . .''

She jerked back, hand flying to her mouth. She did not need Bram Rafferty. She had managed perfectly well without him before. She could do so again! She worked to save him as she would any sick human being. She wanted to save him because she would not allow him to die thinking her a would-be murderess!

Scrambling from the bed, Damask avoided the hand Bram stretched out to her, and rapidly recounted what Lulu said needed to be done. ''It will be very painful, but this is the only hope of saving your arm. If you do not trust . . .'' She closed her eyes. She hadn't meant to say that. It would be unbearable if Bram learned she knew. ''If you would prefer another doctor, I'll have Michael try to find the best one in the City.''

Trust. Bram's dull gaze moved across the room, his teeth clenching. That was the question, wasn't it? Conflict raged. His heart cried that Damask could not be capable of murder, but reason asked who else had so much to gain. Wade was not in the City, but Marlowe was. The man Wade said Da-

mask would have married. They could be fellow conspira-
tors, Damask and her Hunt Marlowe.

Jesus! She was every man's dream of gentle, loving
beauty. But her face was marked with tension. Why? Was it
concern for him, or concern that she might not have the
chance to finish what she had started? Bitterness bloomed
like a splatter of blood. Concern for the master of Seven
Pines, perhaps. For him? Not likely.

Bram's eyes cleared and he stared across the room where
a misty cloud was framed in the open window. He knew
what he was going to do, but for the life of him, he didn't
know why. A wry twist of his lips accompanied the thought
that he must be losing the knack for survival.

Hot water. Scissors. Cotton cloths. Turpentine. Needle
and thread soaking in whiskey. All on the small table drawn
up beside the bed. The knife with its red-hot blade was in the
sitting room fireplace. Michael sat at the head of the bed, his
thin fingers splayed across Bram's shoulder. Nero's bony
hands with nails bitten to the quick pressed Bram's wrist into
the feather tick. A thick padding of linen towels lay beneath
his arm.

Damask swallowed hard. If only Bram and Michael would
not watch her every move. Even when she looked away,
she could see those eyes, indigo and ice, alert, measuring,
distrusting. A trickle of sweat slipped into the cleavage between her breasts and beads gathered on her forehead.

It was no more than an effort to delay her distasteful task,
but she leaned across him. "Bram, please, whiskey will dull
the edge of the pain."

"I don't need it."

"But you will!"

Bram reached up, his hand sliding around her neck to
draw her down. His lips were hot and dry, a searing brand
slanting desperately over her mouth. Then his eyes were
probing hers, searching their depths with an angry question.
"Do what you must," he said hoarsely.

Do what you must. Did he think she would take the scissors and plunge them into his chest? She told him that Seven Pines needed him. Didn't he realize what that meant to her? How could he go on believing the worst about her?

She pulled back with a sudden thought. She believed the worst about him. She hadn't done anything to earn his trust or his respect. Could she really blame him for what he thought?

She couldn't ask Lulu for the scissors. Not yet. Not until her hands stopped trembling and the knot in her stomach eased. She drew a breath, and her nose and throat were ravished by the pungent, tarry odor of turpentine.

"Lulu, the scissors."

They lay cold and awkward in her palm, those scissors she used so casually to snip threads. But these threads held together the straining lips of a pus-filled wound. One slip could mean agony for Bram.

She rested her hand on his hot, bloated arm and felt him go rigid.

"Lady, 'tis after midnight. Come away with ye now."

Damask blinked, took a deep breath, and nearly gagged at the smell of turpentine and scorched flesh.

The light of the single oil lamp pulsed across Bram's sleeping face and she laid her hand on his brow. "Michael, I'm afraid of this fever."

" 'Tis burning off the poison, Lady."

"He was so brave, Michael. Never to utter a word or a sound. And I hurt him. I hurt him terribly."

"Ye should have left the doing of it to Lulu. 'Tis no easy thing to cut into a man's flesh with his blood running warm over yer hands. Ye can be proud, Lady. Niver did ye falter or tremble. Steady as a rock ye were when the Mister were needing ye."

"Is that how I looked?" Damask laughed shakily. "I assure you it wasn't how I felt."

"Och, sure now. That's the courage of it. To be steady when yer insides are as trembly as calve's-foot jelly." Michael scowled and ducked his head as if embarrassed.

"Take yerself to yer bed, Lady. We'll be seeing to the Mister."

"I'd rather see you get some rest."

"I'm used to taking me sleep whenever and wherever I can be getting it. And the Mister 'ull be needing ye when he wakes."

Damask was so tired she fell into her bed exhausted, without expending the effort required to remove her bloodspattered dressing gown. Sleep came quickly, and was as quickly broken. A question stalked the recesses of her mind like a sinister ghost, but when she reached for it, it faded away. It was important. She knew it. But she couldn't force it into conscious thought.

The sun had not risen when she gave up the fruitless effort to sleep. A long bath in tepid water cooled her before she dressed hurriedly and rushed into Bram's room.

One look at Michael's white face with bluish circles of weariness ringing his eyes sent her flying to his side. "Michael, you look ready to drop!"

He gave her a tired smile. "Ye look as fresh as spring, Lady."

Damask put her arm around his drooping shoulders and took the wet cloth from his hand. "Come, you'll sleep in my room where no one will disturb you."

He stumbled along at her side. "What if the Mister needs me?"

"You won't be any good to him if you make yourself sick. You need your rest." She stopped and tipped his chin up, meeting those steady indigo eyes with an even gaze of her own. "I promise to take very good care of Bram while you sleep."

She waited while his eyes searched hers, and she wondered why the opinion of one small boy could be so important to her. At last, his hand came up, thin knobby fingers wrapping around hers. "I know ye will, Lady."

Shortly, he was all tucked in and sound asleep. Damask kissed his forehead, a familiarity she knew he would never have permitted were he awake. He was such a serious little boy, so proud and so alone. Seven Pines would be good for him.

She sent Nero off to rest and approached Bram's bed on tiptoe, only to find there was no need. He was awake and watching her.

"You are gentle with the boy."

"It's easy to be gentle with Michael. I'm glad he will be returning home with us."

"You did not always think so."

"No, I didn't." She tested his brow and found it somewhat cooler.

"Have you decided a child from the gutters of this City might be worthy of Seven Pines after all?"

"I never thought Michael was unworthy of Seven Pines. I would have welcomed him if . . ."

"If?" he prompted.

"If he were going to be raised by anyone other than you."

"And you've changed your mind about that?"

"Yes."

Bram found he could not hold her unwavering gaze. His eyes wandered to the streak of pink-tinged light pouring through the window. He had been a fool to jump to the conclusion she did not want Michael. There was evidence in everything she did that she had an infinite capacity for love. He had no doubt that Michael would know that love. She would fold him to her heart and give him as much or as little as he was willing to accept.

And for himself? Would there be forgiveness? Her cousin Andy must have told her the truth. Would she accept it? Or would she cling to Wade's lie?

The lethargy of incipient sleep claimed him, and his thoughts began to drift. Would he ever know what it meant to bask in the warm glow of Damask's love? To share her life, to . . .

He wakened with a jerk that sent an agony of pain through his wound. Jesus! he thought with scathing disgust. He must be weaker than he thought! Love! Did he forget so quickly that love was for babes and old men and women? So she saved his life and his arm. It didn't mean she didn't save it for a quicker end later!

"You must rest, Bram," Damask whispered and pressed a soft kiss to his brow, her hand lingering on his whiskered cheek.

He tried to hold on to his suspicions. He tried, but they evaporated like shredding mist.

Chapter 12

DAMASK *found a seat in a small sitting area of the lobby* clustered with chairs and tables strewn with the *Price Current* and a variety New Orleans newspapers. Lulu's scolding voice echoed faintly through the cavernous spaces. Damask's smile sparkled in her eyes. No doubt the porters would be relieved to see the baggage loaded and the Rafferty party on its way.

Bram, Michael at his side, was paying the bill and arranging for another night's lodging later in the month. He shouldn't be out of bed. The raw angry color of the wound was fading and the swelling in his arm had subsided for the most part, but the fever lingered. Was there ever such a stubborn man? The only thing approaching cross words between them during the last three days had come when he told her of his intention to leave today. He needed to go to his plantation, Dublin, he insisted. And she wanted to visit her great-uncle and cousins at Bonne Volonte, didn't she?

She did. She had wonderful memories of Papa Kinloch, and her cousin Petite's letters through the years had made her feel she was a part of the family at Bonne Volonte, but . . .

She sighed, toying restlessly with her gloves. She hated to leave. Caring for Bram had been both peaceful and pleasant, the bond between them much like that achieved in those few weeks before their marriage—and Wade's return.

Wade. What was she to think of her brother? Every mo-

167

ment in Bram Rafferty's company served to strengthen her growing conviction that he was incapable of a dishonorable act. He thought she had hired the Caswells, yet he had been kind, almost . . .

Another wistful sigh escaped her. As sick as he had been, he had joined Michael's conspiracy. Each of them had tried to keep her entertained through the long hot days they were sequestered in his sickroom. Could someone like that have cheated her brother?

It was possible Wade had convinced himself, despite every fact to the contrary, that he had been cheated. Wade did have a way of persuading himself that what he wanted to believe was true. It was a trait she considered an endearing little quirk of his personality, even amusing, because she recognized that everyone had those blind spots, even herself.

But this was too serious. He had accused Bram of a heinous act, and Bram had not denied it. She felt the familiar spurt of agitation. It always came back to that. He had not denied it. Out of pride or out of guilt? She could not ask how. It would raise the specter of distrust that she had worked so hard to dispell by devoting herself to his care. Still, sorrow weighed heavily upon her.

Because she had always been loved and cherished by her family and friends, she was baffled and a little frightened to discover she could be judged so harshly by Bram. It colored her every thought, killing the natural curiosity that should have asked: If not me, who? The question stalked the recesses of her mind in an incessant quest for release, but when she tried to remember it, she was left in distraught suspense.

Footsteps clicked an uncertain rhythm across the marble floor. Damask, glad of any interruption of her thoughts, looked toward them.

Hunt? Hunt Marlowe? What was . . .

He stumbled and righted himself in a posturing effort at dignity, and closed the space between them with the careful steps of a man who doesn't know where the floor might be with his next footfall.

"Mizz . . . Mizz," he began, lips puckered beneath the flamboyant, if somewhat ragged, sweep of his moustache, "Mizz Raff-ff-erty."

The rank scent of a musky perfume drifted about him, blending with the stale smells of cigar smoke and whiskey. The gray irises of his heavy-lidded eyes were bedded in red-veined whites, and he had a wrinkled, dissipated look that brought a fiery blush to Damask's cheeks.

Unsure quite how to respond, she relied on the crutch of courtesy and extended her gloved hand. Hunt pulled it up to his lips as though he dared not attempt bending over it.

"I jus' heard you were in . . . in the City," he muttered, his bleary gaze drifting across the froth of lace atop the brim of her bonnet. He blinked and found the region of her eyes with an effort. "Why, Damask? Why did you do this to me?"

Damask flashed a harried look around the lobby. Lulu had passed through with the porters and had not yet returned. Bram and Michael were still at the desk. She caught Hunt's arm and led him to the rotunda, where a broad column blocked them from view.

"Hunt," she began in the soft and soothing voice she would use with a unhappy child, "you know you didn't want to marry me. You should be relieved that—"

"Didn't want . . ." He raked a shaking hand through his sandy hair and stared at her as though she had lost her wits. "Where did you get an idea like that?"

"Why . . ." Damask faltered. "Hunt, you know you accepted every delay of our marriage . . ."

"Because I'm trying to esh—establish my practish here in the City!" he said indignantly. "I wanted to give you everything you deserve and haven't had!"

"But Wade said—"

"Wade!" he ejaculated, suddenly cold sober. He rolled his red-rimmed eyes to the single chandelier hanging from the center of the dome overhead. "Wade!" His eyes dropped to meet hers with the hard, implacable look of a man who has decided that nothing but bitter truth will do. "Wade would tell you anything to keep you working at Seven Pines and earning the money he gambles away here!"

"Gam—" She couldn't finish. The word stuck in her throat like a lump of raw dough.

"Of course! Gambles! My God, Damask," he groaned wretchedly, "you must be the only person in the state who doesn't know!"

"Why . . ." She licked her lips and tried to control the quiver in her voice. "Why didn't you tell me?"

"Tell you?" His silvered eyes held the bright shine of newly minted coins. "Would you have believed me or anyone else over your precious Wade?"

No, she wouldn't have. She hadn't quite believed Andy; she just couldn't accept it deep down. She kept hoping . . .

"What do you think Wade is doing in New Orleans now?" Hunt said, his hard tone relentless. "Trying to get another loan—that he won't pay back—from your uncle or your cousin Andy or me."

She had to believe it now. Both Andy and Hunt confirmed it, and neither had a reason to lie. Wade was a gambler. It was a sickness as Andy had said. He had siphoned the wealth of Seven Pines and borrowed money he had no intention of paying back. Her pride cringed. While she was working so hard and forcing everyone at Seven Pines to do without because she could not bear the thought of going to any of the family, Wade was . . .

If only Papa were here! He would have known what to do! And he would be, if it hadn't been for her.

"Oh, hell! I shouldn't have told you that! There's nothing you can do about it anyhow." The angry frustration faded into lines of poignant wistfulness. "Damask, why did you marry Rafferty? Why didn't you wait for me?"

* * *

"Michael, go out and see if Lulu and Nero need help. We'll join you in a few minutes."

Michael's eyes traveled from the dark hand protruding from the white cotton sling to Bram's face. "I'll fetch the Lady for ye, sir. Ye can take yerself to the carriage and rest a bit."

"You would coddle me like an old woman?" Bram grinned.

"The Lady says ye're from yer bed too soon. She says we're to be seeing ye consarve yer strength, sir."

Bram looked down into the small earnest face and reached out to caress Michael's angular cheek. Thinking better of it halfway, he clapped him companionably on the shoulder. "I have enough strength to escort the Lady to the carriage. Run along now."

As the boy hurried out, Bram's keen blue eyes swept the lobby, coming to a halt on the betraying folds of Damask's yellow muslin skirt. She must be taking a last fascinated look at the dome rising above the rotunda.

The fever had tired him more than he liked to admit and there was a dull ache in his arm. Damask had given him three days of near perfect serenity, marred only by the lingering sadness that dwelt deep in her eyes.

She needed a change, and a trip to Dublin was perfect. It would set them on the first leg of the journey to visit her great-uncle at Bonne Volonte on Bayou Teche, and it would give them a few more days of each other's company with a minimum of intrusion from others. But there was something else, and Bram smiled a slow smile while he thought of it. He wanted to show off Dublin. Like a small boy with his favorite toy, he wanted her to see it, to approve of it, and love it as he did.

Lost in a pleasant reverie, Bram crossed the lobby with a jaunty step, walked into the rotunda—and the blood congealed in his veins.

Damask nestled against Hunt Marlowe, her hands clutching his forearm. Their eyes were riveted on each other with an intensity that isolated them from any world beyond the circle of that near embrace.

"Hunt—" Her soft whisper reached Bram, and the sudden surge of sickness deafened him to all else.

He swallowed the acid that burned his throat. What a fool he had been to succumb to that seductive sham of innocence! He found his voice, and the words he uttered with deceptive lightness froze her heart and sent a tremor of fear through her.

"And here I was afraid you might have been lonely during your wait, colleen."

Damask released Marlowe's arm. Her face was white to the lips, her eyes huge burnished brown bruises that stared up at him. Distractedly, she pressed her fingers to her temple, and nausea churned in his belly.

"Bram . . ." Words failed her; she surmised what he was thinking. She rushed on in a despairing voice, "Bram, I'd like you to meet Hunt Marlowe. Hunt is—"

"We've met," he spit out, not bothering to explain.

"At your uncle's bank." Hunt glazed each word with ice. "Rafferty."

Silence fell. Antagonism crackled in the air.

"If you will excuse us, Marlowe, my wife"—Bram emphasized the word—"and I have to cross the river to catch the train at Algiers."

Damask stepped to his side, slipping her hand through his arm, and Bram fought the compulsion to fling her off like some loathsome insect that crawled across his skin.

The only conveyance to be found at La Fourche Crossing, where they left the train, was a sturdy farm wagon. Nero, Lulu, and Michael found seats on the wagon bed in the midst of the luggage. Damask and Bram shared the seat with the driver, a wiry Acadian with the swarthy leathered complexion of a man who lived outdoors. If he had expected pleasant company on his long ride, he was sadly mistaken. No one spoke a single word during the jolting two-hour ride along the dirt road hugging the natural embankment of sinuous Bayou Lafourche.

Only Michael was alive to their surroundings, chin propped on his fist, bright indigo eyes peering over the sides of the wagon. The Acadian cottages crowded one after the other like beads on the black ribbon of the bayou. They followed a common pattern: front porch; steep-pitched roof; gray, weathered exteriors; and yards cluttered with children and flowers. There were the sounds of clucking chickens and squealing pigs, of dogs barking and cows lowing. Behind the cottages were gardens and crops, and beyond them was the twilight mystery of the swamp. A place of moss-hung cypress and tupelo gum trees, of murky shadows and eerie piercing bird calls screaming above the roar of alligators.

It seemed to Michael they had been traveling forever when they rounded a bend and came upon Dublin. It claimed a straight stretch of the torturous bayou. A neatly pruned Cherokee rose hedge lined the road. Beyond a carefully clipped emerald lawn dappled by the shade of spreading live oaks and towering sycamores, was a circular shell drive flanked by twin rows of crepe myrtles in frilly pink bloom. Two houses hugged the rim of the drive, separated from each other by a triple row of oleanders the size of small trees and draped with bouquets of fuschia flowers. Beyond was a small quarter street, a barn and stable and outbuildings of varying sizes. A glimpse of a garden could be seen against the backdrop of Indian corn fields. Above the tasseling corn rose the ghostly gray-bearded cypress of the swamp.

The two houses along the drive were shaded by oaks, cottonwoods, and magnolias, and skirted by deep beds of flowers. The larger one rested on brick pilings about four feet from the ground. It was a simple dwelling, square, with a deep encircling porch and steep roof broken by dormers all around. The smaller house was a cottage, much like the

Acadian ones; it sparkled in the bright sun from a fresh coat of whitewash.

Serenity drifted on the air like the perfume of the flowers and Michael sat up alertly, thinking he had never seen a more beautiful place. *Someday, someday,* he thought, unaware that the word was a ghostly echo of his Mister's own lonely youth.

The wagon came to a jarring halt before the steps of the large house. From its door tumbled a stair-step assortment of café-au-lait children, followed by a tall spare octoroon wiping her floury hands on a snowy apron.

Bram climbed down and the children clattered down the steps to beseige him with the careless abandon of those sure of their welcome. The smallest of the boys climbed Bram's leg with the agility of a tiny monkey, grinning down at his brothers and sisters from his superior position on Bram's hip.

Rising above the shouts of "Mister Bram! Mister Bram!" was a keening wail. Bram squatted to the tiny girl who howled her disappointment.

"Gussie, what's this?" he asked sympathetically.

That was all she needed. Her small face turned inside out and she began squalling in earnest. The boy slipped off Bram's knee, awkwardly patting her shoulder. "Gussie, Gussie, don't cry. Ain't no need for you to cry," he said. "You can have my place."

As if by magic the squalling stopped. Gussie gave a little sniff, jumped on Bram's knee, and wrapped her arms around his neck. "Gussie love Mister Bram," she giggled.

"Have you been a good girl?" he asked in the manner of a long played game. Her head nodded vigorously. "Have you helped your mama?" She nodded vigorously again. "Did you give Nightwind a carrot everyday like I asked you to do?" She started to nod. Uncertainty crept into her widening eyes. "Augie help me," she said with a bright grin.

"Good. Now what do you think you should have as a reward?"

Gussie leaned close, whispering in his ear, her eyes sparkling hopefully. Bram put his lips to her ear and whispered back. She let out a happy squeal and began clapping her hands. A moment later she slipped off his knee, turning to lean over it while she dug into the bulging pocket of his coat, to withdraw the bag of candy Bram had bought when the train stopped at Des Allemands Station.

The woman waded into the group of children. "Ya'll git! Plenty time to talk with Mister Bram later. Shoo! And I don't want to hear no hollering! Little Karl, blow that conch shell for your papa then divy up that candy fair to all." The children dashed up the steps to the porch while she leveled a wide rueful smile on Bram. "I go down on my knees every night to thank the Lord you ain't around here all the time. If you was, these young'uns would be so spoiled we wouldn't be able to do nothing with 'em." Her eyes dropped to the sling. "What you done to yourself?"

"Nothing, Liza."

"Humph! If I know you—and I do," she said, shaking a skinny finger, "it ain't even been took care of proper."

"My wife has seen to it." Bram turned to the wagon, holding up his hand to help Damask down, and told the driver to go on to the little house where they would be staying.

"Damask, this is Liza von Hessemann. Her husband, Karl, is my overseer, and they are both long-time friends."

His voice hardened slightly at the end with a warning he need not have given. Damask colored, her gaze falling. "Mrs. von Hessemann—"

"Honey, you call me Liza. Ain't that just like a man! Here you are tired out from that long trip and he keeps you talking in the yard. You come on in. Just made fresh coffee." She put her arm around Damask's shoulders and led her up the steps, throwing an admonitory glance at Bram. "I expect it'll be taking Mister Bram a while to be figgering out a little thing like you can't be drove like no mule. And here he didn't even tell me he was coming! I'll have to send some of the girls over to the house for a quick cleaning. Mister Bram,'' she threw over her shoulder, ''bring yourself right up them steps. I got vinegar pie hot from the oven.''

Dusk came late to Bayou Lafourche. The lengthening shadows, stretched far across the lawn while the vivid hues of tropical greenery darkened to blend with the fading light. A single star twinkled.

Damask was alone on the small cottage front porch. The rocker was still. The night smothered her in a heavy blanket of unfamiliar sweetish scents and rank odors.

She had to accept the fact that, no matter how it tore at her heart, Wade had lied to her for years. He had drained Seven Pines dry, lost it, and sold her into marriage with a man he then unjustly accused of cheating him. She had to believe all the ugly and hurtful things now.

Wade was . . . weak. How strange that she hadn't realized it before. He had clung so to Mama as a boy. She always protected him against everything, even Papa's anger and aggravation. Then he relied on her. And now . . .

Who else would help him and protect him, if not her? Who else would care for him as Mama and Papa would have done?

''Lady, why are ye sitting here in the dark? Ye've had a long day. Ye should be taking yer rest.''

''Michael!'' Damask jerked up. ''You frightened me!''

''Sorry, Lady. I thought for sure ye heard me clumping up them steps. Ye should be going in now, Lady. Ye're sure to be tired after these last days and the long trip today.''

''Oh, Michael—'' Damask shook her head. ''What are we going to do with you? You're worse than a hen with two chicks.''

''I've got to be earning me way.''

''So you do. Come over here, please. Give me your hand.'' His face was a blur of white against the dark night, his expression unreadable. ''Do you remember that I said I would be asking a favor of you?''

"Yes."

"Michael, I don't want Mr. Rafferty to know that I have learned about that note. I'm not asking you to lie to him, but I am asking that you not volunteer the information."

"Why?"

"You are too intelligent not to have noticed that things between Mr. Rafferty and myself are not what they should be. It would make them so much worse if he learned that I know of his suspicions. I swear to you that I had nothing to do with it, and no harm will come to him because I know now."

"I believe ye had nothing to do with it, Lády. And I think the Mister would be knowing it, too, were he thinking straight." Michael snorted. "Neither of ye can see to the end of yer nose! Can ye be telling me why 'tis so hard for ye to be telling the Mister the truth? If ye've no feeling for him, how could it be making things so awkward for ye? Ye're wanting him to be believing in ye, to be trusting ye, without ye having to proclaim yer innocence. 'Tis the truth of it, isn't it?"

"Yes, Michael. It is."

"I'm thinking there was a time when the Mister was needing ye to be believing in him, and ye failed him."

"Yes, Michael, there was," Damask said softly.

He patted her shoulder, a strangely adult and patronizing pat that forced a smile to her mouth. "Ye should be talking it out with the Mister. For all he's acting the fool, he isn't one. Ye should be taking a man's good advice, but if ye're not I'll be keeping yer secret for as long as I can. 'Tis getting late. I'll light the lamp to be showing the way to yer bed."

Damask was undressed down to pantalettes, camisole, and corset, her hair freed from its snood. She balanced precariously on a three-legged stool, brushing her shining mass of pale gold hair before the small mirror atop a shaving stand. The door creaked open behind her.

"Michael, is that you? I'm so glad! I was afraid I'd have

to wake Lulu to prize me out of this corset. Would you mind untying it for me?'' She gathered her hair at her nape, pulling it forward over her shoulder.

Steps moved across the floor and fingers tugged at the bow at her waist. ''Be glad you are a boy, Michael. I've often thought it must be wonderful to have the freedom of trousers.'' She fell silent while fingers worked at the strings. The corset fell away. Damask caught a glimpse of a large dark hand.

''Pantalettes become you much more than trousers would, colleen,'' Bram breathed against her shoulder.

The brush went flying. The stool wobbled and shot out from under her, and she shrieked in earnest. Bram saved her from a fall at the cost of a painful wrench to his bad arm, and Damask pulled away from him, wrapping her arms across her chest.

Her eyes were enormous pools of darkness in her ashen face. ''Wha . . . What are you doing here?''

''This is my house, and that,'' he nodded toward it, ''is my bed.''

''Oh!'' Damask jerked up as though she had been pricked by a pin. ''I didn't know. Of course, I'll leave.'' She edged toward the chair where her clothes lay. How stupid of her not to notice there was only the one bed in the cottage! How humiliating it was to have him find her here—as if waiting for . . .

A heated blush sped from the lace-trimmed neckline of her camisole.

Bram had spent a long frustrating day. His arm ached abominably. He was feverish, and his patience was worn to the width of a hair. His blood boiled and his temper flared. ''Goddammit! Where do you think you are going to sleep?''

Damask clutched her petticoat to her breast like a shield. Nero was sharing a bed with Little Karl. Pallets were laid in the other room for Lulu and Michael, but no arrangements had been made for her. She assumed the bed was hers, and gave no thought to where Bram would sleep. If he took the bed, she had nowhere to go.

Was this wretched day never to end? she wondered wildly as she stumbled toward the door.

"Where in hell do you think you're going?"

The lash of his voice stopped her in her tracks. She swung back and raised luminous eyes aswim with uncertainty. Soft black curls tumbled across his forehead in abandon, but they could not soften the stony countenance that measured her and found her lacking. She had failed him and herself and her responsibility to her family and home.

Her defenseless posture made an ache of longing constrict Bram's chest and an emotion buried long years ago sprang to life. He gave it no name but there rose in him the unrecognized need to protect Damask, to shield her from the harsh cruelties of life. It was a soft emotion, a gentle yearning—a weakness!

Ruthlessly thrusting that feeling aside, Bram's brows formed a solid line over the chips of ice that were his eyes. "You will sleep in that bed with me while we are here," he grated, every word torn from his throat. "But don't worry, Mrs. Rafferty," he added with a sneering smile, "I wouldn't dream of putting my *filthy* hands on you."

The color that washed her cheeks was so hot she wondered that she could not hear her skin sizzling. Hotter words sprang to her lips but were extinguished by a cold dousing of reason. She wouldn't be able to deny she meant those words once flung at him in the heat of anger. And she couldn't abandon her brother, who needed her more than ever now. Nor could she cast aside her own pride and tell Bram Rafferty that she wanted to be a wife to him—in every way. She didn't dare take the risk he might spurn her and kill whatever chance they had to salvage their marriage.

Whether it was caution or cowardice, Damask didn't know. But it was a gamble she refused to take.

Chapter 13

THE *moon had long since begun its descent in the western sky* when Damask's eyes snapped open. *Wade was in New Orleans!* Hunt Marlowe's statement sang in atonal harmony to the question: *Who had hired the Caswells?*

She lay rigid, nails cutting into her palms, a scream burbling up inside her. The cold sweat of fear trickled across her temples and trailed around the curve of her neck.

It must have been someone else! An old enemy, perhaps. But none of them would know the Caswells! Was it possible that the brother she loved would pay to have a man murdered?

It had to be someone else!

She lay awake through the night, taking comfort in Bram's soft even breathing. It had taken him so long to fall asleep. They had spent hours side by side in stiff discomfort because of the forced intimacy of sharing his bed. And when the first signs of morning crept through the sky on gray streamers, he woke and stole from the bed while she feigned a deep and peaceful sleep.

She was alone—but for the terrifying company of her own thoughts. Her eyes were gritty from lack of sleep. Her every muscle ached from bow-strung tension. Her mind dipped into the rutted path: Only two people could gain anything by Bram Rafferty's death, and she had not hired the Caswells.

An eternity later, humming sounded in the next room. Eager for any interruption, Damask sat up. "Lulu?"

The door creaked open. A bright yellow *tignon* popped through. "She ain't here, ma'am. I'se Polly. Lulu gone to git your washing water. I'se cleaning for Master Bram. Polly always do the cleaning for him. You want I should tell 'em to bring your breakfast?"

"No, Polly. I'll wait until after my bath. Has Mr. Rafferty gone out this morning?"

"Yessum." Polly pushed the door wide, entering with an odd hobbling walk. No more than sixteen, she had the soft unformed features of a child and the large, innocent brown eyes of a doe. Damask's gaze moved from Polly's face down to the clubfoot she dragged. "Master Bram take the Little Master down the bayou to M'sieu Chardonnay's. They gitten a pony for him. Oughta be back any time. They something Polly can do for you, ma'am?"

"No, you can go back to your work."

"Yessum." Polly's smile was bright with pride. "I got to git this place shining the way Master Bram like it. Them gals what clean yesterday, they just give it a lick and a promise. Cain't do nothing right. Master Bram, he say cain't nobody make this house shine the way Polly can."

"Have you been with Mr. Rafferty for long, Polly?"

"No, ma'am. It was just 'fore cane harvest two seasons ago that Master Bram take up with my missy," Polly answered in her soft lisping voice. "She like a wild 'simmon. All purty on the outside and hard seeds on the inside. Seem like I couldn't do nothing the way she like it. One day he come when she giving me a good whipping with a cane switch. Ain't never seen a man so hoppin' mad! He snatch up that switch and break it in so many pieces they wasn't a inch anywhere a-straggling together. And his eyes! They gits all cold and clear like that ice Missy git for her rum punch, then he say to her, 'How much you want for this gal?' And Missy gits her squinch-eyed look and say, 'A thousand dollars!' And Master Bram, he say, 'Done!' Now they both knows I ain't worth no thousand dollars! Ain't nothing but a quarter-hand, and I tries to tell Master Bram that when he hustle me outa there. But he say to me, 'Polly, you is worth more than a thousand dollars to me.' ''

Polly took a step closer to the bed, her foot dragging. ''Miss Damask, I know Master Bram ain't a-coming back to Dublin like he useta, and, well, I ask him this morning if he'd be taking me with him when he leave, but he say . . . he say I has to ask you. Miss Damask, Polly ain't never been worth nothing to nobody but Master Bram, and I sure does want to be where I can do for him 'cause they ain't no better man in this whole country.''

They ain't no better man in this whole country. Damask was beginning to believe it herself. Bram seemed to have no fault she could use to justify her loyalty to Wade.

Even if Wade hired the Caswells—and who else could it have been?—he was still her brother. Their ties were the strong cords of kinship, lives spent together, laughter and sorrow shared. Whatever he was, she could never escape the fact that she had wronged him. That he might have grown into a different man had their parents lived. If he was weak, she had made him that way. He needed her, and she could no more abandon him in this, his mistake, than he had abandoned her when she made hers long ago.

She could not choose between Wade and Bram! But her silence might well be construed as a choice of sacrificing Bram to Wade.

''Miss Damask?''

Damask reached out to touch her arm. ''I would be very glad to have you return with us.''

''You won't be sorry, Miss Damask.'' The girl beamed. ''I ain't so fast, but they ain't much I cain't do once I sets my mind to it.''

The morning passed quickly. As Damask slipped her breakfast to the hound that curled around her feet, she heard the sound of hooves clattering up the shell drive.

''Lady! Lady! Come see!''

She hurried onto the porch. Michael sat atop a chestnut pony with a crinkly coat and a long waving tail that nearly brushed the ground. His grin split his thin face from ear to ear and his dark indigo eyes seemed to have captured two falling stars.

"He's a fine hoorse, Lady! Look at him! D'you know what they were calling him?" His face mirrored disgust. *"Fantaisie!* Such a name for a hoorse! I'm going to call him Prince! Now that's a fine name for a grand hoorse!"

"Indeed it is." Damask's gaze strayed to Bram, who was dismounting his own sleek black stallion. She descended the steps to stroke Prince's velvety nose. "He's beautiful, Michael."

"That he is, Lady. He's got spirit! Me very own hoorse! Ooh, there's so much I need to be learning! The Mister says he'll be teaching me how to curry and care for him. There won't be nothing too good for me Prince."

"Won't you come down, Michael? There's breakfast . . ."

"Ooh, noo, Lady." He straightened his spine in an obvious imitation of Bram. "The Mister says I'm to lead his Nightwind to the stables for him." Michael took the reins from Bram and threw Damask one last happy grin.

She watched him ride away. "If we allowed it, I suspect Michael would begin sleeping in the stables." She turned to Bram and found his eyes on her, his thoughts hidden by a studiously blank expression. The hot breeze blew soft tendrils of champagne-colored curls into her eyes and she pushed them back. The silence grew awkward and she rushed into the breach. "Polly spoke to me about coming back to Seven Pines with us. I told her we would be glad to have her there. I hope that was agreeable to you."

"It was. You'll find Polly to be a hard worker."

"I gather she was mistreated before you bought her. I'll try to be especially careful with her."

"If I had not known you would, I would never have given my permission for her to come with us." Bram touched the brim of his hat. "If you'll excuse me."

He was so cold. Cold and indifferent. It hurt, she realized with a flare of surprise. Why should it hurt?

A week of sweltering summer days blended as one. Light morning showers turned the bayou country into a steamy cauldron. The air was redolent of the cloying sweetish perfume of cape jessamine and magnolia, tainted by the smell of death and decay that rode the miasmic breezes blowing out of the swamp. A sprinkling of freckles popped on Michael's pug nose, and a moustache of beaded sweat adorned his upper lip. He spent his days brushing and exercising Prince, tramping the fields, and talking to anyone who would feed his voracious appetite for learning. Like a sponge, Michael absorbed the information he prized from everyone with his earnest questions and solemn face. Nothing was too dull or farfetched that he would not listen with that look of total concentration that made even the reticent garrulous. The days at Dublin were some of his happiest, but they were blemished by worry about his Mister and the Lady.

Bram worked from sunup to sundown. As his father had used the bottle as a solace and a shield, so Bram used his work. It left him too tired to think and calmed the unwelcome emotions simmering within him. True to his word, he taught Michael how to care for Prince and took him on tours of the fields and outbuildings, answering the unending flow of questions with patience. But it was obvious to Michael that his unhappy thoughts were far away.

It was even more obvious to Damask that he was avoiding her by coming to their bed long after she was supposed to be sleeping. Bram could sink into his work, exhausting both mind and body, but Damask had no such relief. Liza kept household chores running like clockwork, and Damask hesitated to intrude on the routine. She felt like a guest at Dublin, and by the day it looked more and more like she was an unwelcome guest.

She floated through the days, a silent, somber wraith. Michael brought her wildflowers and sat with her on the bank of the bayou for hours while she stared at the sluggish water as though it held endless fascination for her. He knew she visited with the old ones in the quarters every day and spent time in Liza's kitchen, but no one seemed able to spark any life in her.

Time, though it seemed to stand still, did pass. The morning of Damask's last day at Dublin began like all the rest. In the gray light of false dawn Bram woke her as he eased from the bed. She lay perfectly still, listening to the rustling sounds as he dressed, smelling the aroma of his cigar drifting in through the window from the porch.

It was a sticky morning. Not the faintest sigh of a breeze moved the mosquito netting that hung from a hook on the ceiling and draped across the four tall cornerposts to form a tent over the bed. Damask threw herself on her back.

One more night of imprisonment on a soft feather tick within night-shadowed prison walls of sheer gauze. One more night of screaming tension while she waited for the even cadence of sleep to claim him. Surely they could have separate rooms at Bonne Volonte. She could not bear being so near a man who detested the very sight of her.

Damask heaved herself out of bed. Everything at Dublin had conspired to show her the worth of Bram Rafferty. Here was all she wanted for Seven Pines, and Bram's guiding hand had shaped it. His praises were sung everywhere. By Polly, who fairly worshipped him. By the old ones rocking in the cool shade of the chinaberry tree, who were more than happy to tell her how their lives had eased since the new master's coming. By Karl. By Liza. More cautiously, by Michael.

The curiosity, born in Bram's first weeks at Seven Pines, returned to haunt her. He was an engima she was desperate to solve. A gambler, but no gambler had scarred, calloused palms or a swollen musculature whose rippling definition spoke of heavy labor. He was driven by ambition, yet the money that could have helped to make that ambition a real-

ity was spent paying five times or more the worth of a crippled slave girl. What was Bram Rafferty?

There was someone who could tell her. She wouldn't
leave Dublin without one last visit with Liza.

Bram folded his arms and leaned against the paddock
fence. Beside him, Michael aped his position by drawing
one booted foot up to brace his heel on the lower rail.
Nightwind and Prince lipped the sparse grass in the pen,
snuffling and snorting with contentment. Bram looked down
at the fiery red head of tight drawn curls, darkened by sweat
from their morning tour of the cane fields.

"I haven't seen much of you the last couple of days, Michael."

"I been learning what I could, sir. Won't be no good to ye
if I don't. Little Karl and me been watching the hands
hoeing in the cane. He's been telling me how ye plant the
cane every third year and how ye've got to get it in before
the first frost or it's ruint. Yes, sir, there's a powerful lot I
need to be learning."

"Don't spend all of your time in work. Take some time to
enjoy yourself."

"Enjoy meself!" Michael's voice climbed to a falsetto,
the look in his dark eyes incredulous. "I've no time for such
nonsense! Ye're taking me to yer plantation, and me not
knowing which end of a plow to be sticking in the dirt! No,
sir! I've no time for such nonsense! I've got to be learning
so's I can be of some use to ye. If I can't be earning me way,
I'll not be staying, and that's a fact!"

"Jesus, Michael! Do you think I'm an ogre? Take some
time for yourself. Go fishing with the von Hessemann
boys."

"Fishing!" Michael's indigo eyes rounded in amazement. "Fishing? You mean set on the bank waiting for a
dumb fish to swim by and hook himself? No, sir! That's not
for Michael O'Malley!" The tight crop of curls stretched
and popped back like springs. "I'd rather spend me time lis-

tening about the planting of the cane. That'll be doing me some good!''

Bram cleared his throat raucously. "Michael, it isn't good for a man to spend all of his time working."

"To be sure ye're saying that now, sir. Ye've got what ye were wanting. But all these years ye been working, how much time were ye wasting on yer own pleasure?"

Bram sobered with chilling rapidity. "Not enough, Michael, and I wouldn't want to see you pattern your life after mine. You should want more for yourself."

Michael's wide, unsettled eyes pleaded with the hero of his small boy's heart. "The land, sir. The land makes it all worthwhile."

Ice-blue eyes moved, following the row of crepe myrtles to the bayou, and beyond where a breeze fluttered the ribbonlike leaves of the cane like slender pennants. Was a lifetime of self-denial in the pursuit of a dream worth it? The reality had become a nightmare, but that was not for Michael to know.

"Sir?"

"Yes, Michael," Bram said heavily. "The land makes it all worthwhile. The land, son. The land is all a man can ever trust."

But Michael had a horrible suspicion he didn't believe it. There was a hollow ring to his words, and the Mister would not meet his eyes. His big hands clenched together, and his fingers rubbed across the curving scar on the back of his left hand, a sure sign he was upset. Michael wanted to pull him away from the thoughts that gave him that cold, set expression, and there was one subject . . .

"Sir, I'm worried about the Lady." Bram's eyes latched onto him with an intensity that made Michael shiver. "Haven't ye looked at her, sir? I'd say she's niver been much for weight, but a breeze 'ud be blowing her over now. And she's so pale. Remember that first day when I carried yer packages? Jesus, sir! I thought an angel'd been sent to us for sure. Such a smile she had and her cheeks blooming. Ye come so late to yer bed, sir. Ye can't be knowing how she wanders along the bayou at night like a lost spirit. Sir, she took awful good care of ye. Couldn't nobody have done more! I know ye be thinking she be the one, but it ain't true, sir!''

Bram found he could not hold Michael's earnest gaze. He looked away and felt the nervous ticking of a muscle in his jaw.

"Can't ye do something for her, sir? She needs ye!''

"Michael, there is too much here that you don't understand.''

"Oh, to be sure!'' Michael scoffed, his jaw assuming a pugnacious jut. "I know what I be seeing! 'Tis a stubborn man ye are, Bram Rafferty! And 'tis the Lady what's suffering for it!'' With that Michael stomped off, taking a cutting swing at a tall milkweed that crossed his path.

The latest result of Liza von Hessemann's fertile womb slapped a tiny honey-brown hand across Damask's mouth and gave a toothless, gurgling laugh. Miniature fingers wrapped tightly around her thumb and she drew it to her lips for a petal soft kiss.

"None of my babies took to cuddling the way that Bess does.'' Liza reached for a glass to cut the biscuit dough. "Long as a body's holding her, she's happier than a crawfish in his hole.''

"She's such a good baby, Liza.'' A note of wistfulness filled her voice. Surely it was only human to envy Liza her noisey brood and loving husband. Her own situation had never appeared so bleak as it did here on the hearth of a family bound by ties of affection and love and trust.

Bess's soft breath fluttered against her neck, and she rubbed the baby's back while rocking in the oversize rocker flanked by a cradle and a crockery butter churn. Her eyes roved along the plaited strings of garlic and onions hanging from the exposed rafters beside strings of hot peppers and hemp sacks of potatoes. Steeling her courage, Damask drew breath to launch into the topic that had brought her to Liza's kitchen.

"You've known Mr. Rafferty for a long time, haven't you, Liza?"

"Sure, honey. Karl and me have known him since . . ." Her expressive brown eyes, the only thing that kept her from being unbearably homely, took on a faraway look.

"Yes, it was eighteen and forty-nine. Karl's papa died that year and the old man's son didn't want Karl around to remind folks he had a brother born of a freedwoman. Karl tried to find work as an overseer, 'cause that was all he knew, but . . ." She shrugged. "Just wasn't no work anywhere. So we up and go to the City. Karl found work on the docks. Out in the boiling sun all day, toting bales. He'd come in at night so wore out he couldn't eat. Just wanted to hit that bed and sleep. And his hands! Lordy! What that work done to his hands! Rope burns and splinters and cuts! I was plumb sick with worrying about him."

She popped the biscuits into the oven built into the side of the fireplace. "That's when he met Mister Bram. They worked in gangs. If you got a good'un, where everybody pulled his weight, it was easier. But Karl got in a bad'un. When Mister Bram's gang lost one of their men, he asked Karl to take his place."

"He worked on the docks!" Damask was stunned. "But . . . but I thought he was a gambler!"

"Hasn't that man told you nothing?" Liza grinned. "That's a fool question! Never seen a man so little given to talking about himself." She poured a cup of coffee and came to sit near Damask, settling her knobby elbows on the table. "He done both. Docks in the day and gambling at night. Started that dockwork when he was thirteen. Worked there plumb up to the day 'fore he left for Mansfield."

Liza set her coffee aside and laced her fingers. "I remember the first time I seen Mister Bram. Karl talked for weeks about his friend at the docks. He taught Karl the easiest ways to roll a barrel and lift the bales, tricks to make the work easier on a man. So I up and tell Karl to ask him to Sunday dinner." Liza's wide smile slipped across her face. "Karl says it was the only time he ever saw me speechless.

There I was expecting a big black buck, and what comes strolling in? A white man with the bluest eyes I ever saw! Had a box of candy under one arm and a bunch of camellias in his hand and the solemnest face a man ever wore. Thought he didn't know how to smile 'til he got down in the middle of my floor to play with Little Karl. I watched him playing with that baby, and I thought to myself, 'Liza, that man needs a powerful lotta loving, but he'd rather be dead than admit it to a soul!' "

Love? Bram Rafferty? Damask was too ladylike to snort—out loud. She had never seen a man more self-contained, more arrogantly sure of himself. He had made it painfully obvious that he had no need of anything more than "companionable arrangements."

"About a year later he bought Dublin and hired Karl as overseer," Liza added. "It was a dream come true for us."

"When did he start gambling, Liza?"

"Long 'fore we knew him. In the last six years or so, he'd quit the dockwork in the winter season to ride them riverboats. Long about March or April, he'd come to Dublin for a couple of weeks. Child, he'd be so low and wrung out, it would break your heart to see him. But in a few days, he'd be fine. It was like the land give him the strength to go on. I do believe that man thinks the dirt got a soul! Karl, now, he loves the land, but his way is different."

Liza fell silent, sipping her coffee and thinking. "I never could figger that Mister Bram. He works so hard, scrimping and saving. But he won't allow the niggers to be worked near as hard as some rich folks do. Even pays 'em for working on Saturdays and Sundays! Karl thought he was plumb crazy! But it's worked good. Chores around here git done in half the time. We've had two boys buy their freedom! Mister Bram took 'em up-river to free territory to sign their papers, since they made that law disallowing emancipation. Even give 'em the money to make their way east! Guess he'll be doing that for the others, too."

"What kind of a man is he, Liza?" Damask questioned softly.

"Honey, he's a good man what knowed nothing but trouble his whole life. I expect he's had so much he's still looking for it when it ain't there. It's gonna take a lot of patience living with him."

Damask took her leave of Liza soon after. She wanted to think, to try to fit together the growing pieces of the puzzle that was Bram Rafferty. But all she could see was the pitiless sun beating down on the sweating, straining stevedores on the New Orleans docks. And Bram's hands. His beautiful hands. Long fingered, powerful, graceful. A gentleman's hands—until the scarred calloused palms were turned uppermost.

The white oyster shell drive crunched beneath Bram's boots. His hands were jammed into his pockets, his shoulders hunched. An angry muscle worked along the ridged line of his jaw.

He had planned his life, step by careful step. Now those careful steps were finding ground more treacherous than the marshes of South Louisiana, so aptly called the *Prairie Tremblante* by the Acadians. No sooner did he find solid earth in the form of a strong determination to remain untouched by the emotions Damask aroused than the next step found him mired deep, his resolutions lost in the quicksand of those emotions. He had always known who he was, where he was going and why, but a few short months had changed him. Now he was consumed by the feeling that his dream had lacked substance.

The hot sun glittered in rainbow sparkles across the black surface of the bayou. Bram sank to the grassy bank in the shade of a willow, resting his folded arms on his drawn-up knees.

He was right to tell Michael the land made it all worthwhile. Only a fool would place his future in the doubtful hands of another human being! If the strong secure love of his parents could crumble to dust like aged bricks, it could happen to him, to anyone . . .

But the land was always there! The land returned the

worth of a man's efforts a hundredfold. The land asked nothing of a man he could not give.

He stretched out full length, cushioning his head in his hands to stare at the cotton-puff clouds scattered across the pale sky. It was peaceful there in the shade. The whirring flight of mosquito hawks was a soothing sound. There was a smell of the sea rising from the bayou. But neither smell nor sound nor peace calmed the restlessness that scraped at Bram's nerves.

There came a furtive crackling of the dry grass at the edge of the road. His every muscle jerked taut, his eyes sliding to watch from slitted corners. Slow scuffing steps approached. He caught the subtle suggestion of violet scent. Inexplicably, his taut muscles relaxed. Damask entered his line of vision, her head down. She wandered to the reed-choked water's edge, apparently unaware he was nearby. Minutes dragged while she stared at the opaque surface of the bayou, then moved farther away to sit in the shade of a blooming elderberry.

Bram watched her idly plucking at the grass. He wondered if she knew how she cuddled against him in the deepest reaches of the night, and how she rested her head on his shoulder and turned her face up to his. Her lips were so close, so frustratingly close. She was all woman then, with delicious curves melting into his, and a small hand resting on his chest like a hot coal. The dainty scent of violets would fill his nostrils, and the headier scent of woman urged the hot blood through his veins until his skin prickled with the heat of his need.

He told himself she was not to be trusted. He tried to summon a vision of her in Hunt Marlowe's arms, but it was blurred and indistinct. No matter how he tried, he could not summon any force to the conviction that Damask was guilty.

The bed had become a battlefield where Bram Rafferty waged a war against himself. A war whose purposes he did not recognize. He had never suffered the lack of women when his need was great, nor had he been forced to purchase relief. But the women were never more than brief, quickly forgotten interludes, arousing no more than a transistory physical interest. Flighty, frivolous women, chosen because they would never affect him beyond his will. For Bram Rafferty there had never been a wondrous first love to waken his dormant need to possess and protect. He was a man grown, and innocent of the hunger that could give birth to the most conflicting emotions a man might ever suffer. So he lay there night after night, listening to the humming of the mosquitoes beyond those prison walls of gauze, and felt Damask trustfully sleeping in his arms, and fought the hot waves of desire that he both hated and feared.

The cynical arch of Bram's brows flattened, his eyes moving away from her. Another night like the last and he would not have the strength to deny the urgings of his loins. It was because he had been so long without a woman.

A spark of interest flared in his eyes. There was a buxom redhaired widow in Thibodaux, who had a talent for laughter. The Widow East was what he needed. A woman unashamed of the urgings of her body. A woman who would meet his eager need with an eagerness of her own. The Widow East. His thoughts lingered on generous hips and full breasts and a red-lipped smile.

But the memory of her laughter had a coarse quality, and the heavy musk scent of her perfume was slightly repellent as he remembered it. The lush curves were becoming a trifle too generous, he thought with dwindling interest while a faceless vision formed. Chiming laughter accompanied the slight, trim form with its narrow hips belling from a tiny waist. Bram luxuriated in the feel of soft satin skin. He imagined burying his face in shining waves of champagne-colored hair. He imagined staring deep into cinnamon eyes and seeing the light of . . .

"Goddammit!" Bram cursed aloud, levering himself to his feet and startling a cry from Damask. She rose to her knees, eyes starting with shock, and Bram knew a frustration so keen he clenched his teeth and balled his hands into fists in an attempt to calm his trembling rage. "Goddammit, woman!! Am I never to be rid of you!" he spit viciously and swiveled on his heel.

Damask was still there when Nightwind thundered up the bayou road toward Thibodaux.

Chapter 14

HE *wanted to be rid of her*! Damask's first shocked surprise turned to anger. She hadn't asked Bram Rafferty to come riding into her life to turn it topsy-turvy! If he didn't want a wife, why didn't he throw them all off Seven Pines? How dare he ruin *her* life and act as though she had ruined *his!*

Dusk gathered in deepening shadows that pulled the darkening rim of night over the bayou. Bram didn't return and Damask tossed on her bed, carried along on a whirlwind of emotions that passed through indignation, anger, and self-pity until she was emotionally drained and drifted into a light sleep.

Nightwind's familiar neigh yanked her upright. A sound like a hoof pawing the steps followed and she swept aside the mosquito netting as light bloomed in the next room. Moment's later, she, Lulu, and Michael tumbled through the back door.

"It's the Mister!" Michael scurried down the steps. "Sir! We been so worried! Ye took off without a . . . ooh!" he breathed. "Whisht, Lady, the Mister's had a wee drop."

"I suspect it's more than that. See if he can walk in, Michael."

"Sir! Sir! Wake up!"

Bram, hanging limp across Nightwind's withers, groaned and licked his dry lips, squinting against the light. "It's a fine horse that can be bringing you to your steps, eh, Michael O'Malley?"

"To be sure, sir. Can ye be walking?"

"Of course!" Bram reared up and wobbled, struggling for an indignant frown. "I've had but a wee drop!"

Michael grinned. "Come down, sir. I'm thinking ye'll be finding yer bed a blessed place this night."

Bram's unsteady walk resembled that of a sailor treading the pitching deck of a ship, but he made it to the bedroom unaided. While Michael took Nightwind to the stable, Damask sent a reluctant Lulu back to her bed and prepared to give her equally reluctant husband what aid he needed.

Bram slumped on the edge of the bed, the light playing across the unkempt snarl of blue-black hair. Disaster! It had been a disaster! How could he have whispered Damask's name into the Widow East's ear? Jesus! The woman's screeching still rang in his ears!

There had been only one thing to do after that, but he found neither solace nor oblivion in the sparkling amber promise of Irish whiskey. What he did find was a bleak vision of emptiness and futility.

The whiskey had lowered his defenses. On the morrow they would rise up anew. The walls were too old and too strong for it to be otherwise. Tomorrow the land, that shining beacon of his ambition, would be enough. But tonight he knew that the land did not care who its master was. It could not cheer him, comfort him, laugh with him.

He ached to stretch his hand through the crumbled wall of pride, to feel the warmth of a human touch, to mingle soul and thought with another human being. But how, when his hands clenched into rejecting fists? How when teeth and lips clamped over the words that screamed his need in the recesses of his mind? He had been alone too long, he thought wearily. The habits of a lifetime could not be shed because of a single night's weakness.

He studied Damask with a brooding look. Light silvered the halo of curls feathering around her face, but that was all that remained of the girl who had stood on the porch at Seven Pines. She seemed a ghost of herself with wan hollowed cheeks and sad guarded eyes. Guarded. He recalled his brutal leavetaking and a ruddy flush heated his face.

"Damask, I shouldn't have said . . ." His throat closed over the apology. Could saying he was sorry ever erase his cruelty? Face twisted with regret, he leaned down, elbows braced on his knees, left fist pressed into his right palm. His fingers traced the puckered scar and his breath came in shallow gasps while memories sucked him back to the past.

The fires of Damask's wrath spluttered uncertainly. She edged closer, listening to the rasp of his breathing.

"Bram, what's wrong?" she whispered.

If he heard, he did not respond. She wavered. He had made it clear her very presence was a burden, yet she edged closer, unable to turn away. She saw nothing but the tangled curls spilling across his drooping head and his hands, squeezing and twisting while the fingers traced the curving scar. The tension that possessed him reached out to her, and she knelt before him. The handsome lines of his face were contorted with grief, his eyes blind and staring and black with the pain of a soul racked beyond bearing.

She sat back on her heels. He was always so confident, so arrogantly sure of himself that she had never noticed the vulnerability in the curve of his lips or in his eyes, liquid with a sorrow that tugged at her heart.

Her small hands wrapped around his. "Bram, everything will be fine. You will see. I'm here. I'm here."

She had no idea what she was saying. They were only words. Words to pull him back from whatever vision of horror held him.

Bram drew a long uneven breath and blinked. Suddenly, Damask found herself pulled onto his lap, his arms crushing her, his face buried in the curve of her shoulder.

"Don't say anything! For God's sake, Damask! Don't say anything!"

Shudders rippled through him and her arms crept around his neck. His need was a living presence with a force and will of its own, a presence her compassionate heart could not deny. His day's growth of beard scraped the tender skin at the hollow of her neck and the ragged breathing he fought to control fanned moist and warm across her throat.

She could smell bay rum and whiskey and something else. A heavy musky perfume. It did not repulse her. Obviously, Bram had looked elsewhere for solace. But he had not found it. He had returned to her to bare his need. The hurt he had dealt her melted away with that knowledge, and Damask bowed her head over his.

She thought of Michael, so much like Bram that boy and man seemed one to her. Each had that awesome strength and courage; each had that sterling integrity, setting them apart from ordinary men. And each also had a rigid pride that made her quake with fear. There was a brittle quality to the arrogant assumption they needed no one. Michael was young. With care, his need might be nurtured. But what would happen when Bram was confronted by a need for love he could no longer deny?

Gently stroking his neck, she rested her cheek against his hair, damp from the night air. The wall Bram had erected to hide behind was beginning to crumble. Tonight he admitted his need, but tomorrow, she feared, he would regret it. Her hands moved across his back to clasp him to her in a fiercely protective gesture.

She was wrong. Regret was not waiting. The vision of horror was fading rapidly under the assault on his senses. Damask was life and woman, the hope of heaven, the promise of hell. The familiar scent of violets ravished his mind, dissolving the vision, but leaving in its wake a need so acute he dared do nothing but deny it.

It was the whiskey, he assured himself. The whiskey made him weak. Tomorrow he would be himself again. Deep inside, Bram knew it was not the whiskey.

He wanted Damask. More than land. More than life. Not only the slender womanly form that had become his essence of desire, but her thoughts, her heart, her gentle looks, her soft words. He wanted her and he was afraid. Afraid that desire had become need.

He raised his head and loosened his hold, but she did not move. Instead, she lay back against his arm, staring up at him with an expression of tender concern that winnowed its way into his heart and hardened his resolve.

"Tomorrow," he said flatly, "I will take you back to Seven Pines. We can begin divorce proceedings there."

Damask's eyes widened. He would run rather than admit his need! Liza was right. He needed love, desperately, and he would rather be dead than admit to it.

Instinctively, she knew that this was Bram's last, perhaps only, chance. He would never again allow anyone to get close to him. He would be alone, his life a plodding emptiness of wasted days. A good man. The kind of man she could respect, and there were so few of those. She was stunned that she was plotting to save him, when such a short time ago her most heartfelt wish was to be rid of him. Or was it something else? She didn't know and had no time to sift her reasons. She only knew that she was going to protect Bram Rafferty—even from himself.

Her chin climbed and her eyes met his unflinchingly. "There will be no divorce."

He stared for a moment and blinked as though distrusting what he had heard.

"No divorce," she repeated distinctly.

Frustration, rage, and suspicion mingled in his contorting features as he caught her arms, fingers biting to the bone. "Why? We both know it is the only way to rectify a disastrous mistake!"

"But we don't both know that."

The fearless honesty in her steady gaze shook Bram's resolve. He wanted to shake her into submission to his will. He wanted to throw her across the bed and take what he had so long yearned for. He wanted to demand the truth from her. Yet, he could do none of those things.

"I will sign Seven Pines over to you," he promised in a gutteral whisper. "It will be yours. You will be free."

"I know you will," she said simply.

"Get up!" He nearly threw her off his lap. Pacing across the room, hands raking through his hair, he swiveled around and leveled an icy stare. "You would hold a man who does not want you!"

Flayed pride brought a searing blush, but Damask held his brilliant stare. "You won Seven pines and accepted responsibility for her and her people. I will not allow you to shirk that commitment."

"No matter what price you have to pay?" he asked with an ominous hiss.

"Perhaps," she said so softly he leaned closer to hear, "I do not find the price too high."

Bram looked as though he had been struck to stone. The brilliant color of his eyes faded to a dull slate-blue. The clock on the mantel ticked away the seconds. A screech owl screamed in the night, and Bram Rafferty knew he was defeated. He could not force a divorce on her. He could not humiliate her by deserting her. But he knew he couldn't resist much longer the desire that fed upon itself with every passing day. Even now he wanted to . . .

"Damask," he whispered raggedly. Catching himself in that weakness, he whirled away, sucking air into his burning lungs. There was a reason. There had to be a reason for her not to release him, but whatever it was he didn't want to know. His excesses were catching up with him. "Go to bed," he said tiredly. "There will be no divorce, but we must rise early to return to Seven Pines."

"No!"

Bram jerked around, his every doubt brought to screaming life by that cry.

Damask knew it was a mistake. She should have used calm reason, but the cry had burst from her on a flooding torrent of fear. If Wade were at Seven Pines, if Wade had hired the Caswells, if, if . . .

She could not be forced into choosing between them!

Struggling for composure, she knew her next proposal only delayed the inevitable. "Papa Kinloch is expecting us, Bram. Please, we can't go back to Seven Pines, yet."

This time she did not look into his eyes with fearless honesty. She could not meet them at all. Sickness clogged Bram's throat. "I would give much to know . . ." He could not finish. Should he be glad he had been given this warning? Whatever awaited him at Bonne Volonte, he would be ready.

Bayou Teche. The sugar paradise. Overhead, oak and cypress limbs tangled in a vaulted ceiling. Below, in the black water, floating logs resolved themselves into toothy yawning alligators. On the west bank, higher, less prone to flooding, were manor houses in the old French and Spanish styles or the relatively new Greek Revival. Behind them were small villages that supported the nearly self-sufficient life of the plantations. Beyond was the undulating green sea of the Attakapas Prairie, named for a local Indian tribe long gone from the region. There sturdy mustangs roamed wild and planters kept massive herds of cattle on *vacheries*, or ranches. On the east bank were huge red brick sugar houses, bright rubies bedded in endless fields of sugar cane that yearly claimed more of the bordering swamps.

The sternwheeler back-paddled to a halt in the center opening of the floating bridge that joined the two halves of Bonne Volonte, as similar bridges linked plantations up and down the bayou. A gangplank was laid. Damask eyed it warily, none too anxious to begin her passage across so flimsy a contraption. Nero and the porter had no problem carrying the luggage down, but the sight of them bobbing and swaying made her dizzy.

"Is something wrong?" Bram asked with the cool disinterested tone he had used since their predawn rising.

"I'm putting off the inevitable," Damask answered lightly.

His lips thinned. "You make a habit of that." He signaled Nero to take the last trunk, nodding for Lulu to follow. "I'll wait for you at the bottom." He descended with sure-footed ease. Damask tested the plank with a ginger toe. "Hop on and run. Momentum will carry you down. Don't look at the water! Look at me!"

Run! He must be mad! Damask stepped on to the slanting plank and wobbled, caught herself and took a skimming step, then another, and another. Below, the water rippled, a log floated to the top and—winked at her.

"Bram!" she wailed and lifted her skirts, flying down the gangplank and launching herself into his waiting arms. "An—an alligator!" She hugged his neck in a death grip and shuddered violently.

"It's all right, Damask," Bram murmured. "He's gone now."

"Are you sure?" She threw a look over her shoulder and saw the reptile gliding through the water at the edge of the bank. Sighing in relief, she loosened her hold on Bram's neck. Their eyes met . . . clashed . . . meshed . . . and anticipation scudded through her.

A frown moved across his face like the shadow of a summer cloud, and Damask felt the almost infinitesimal shift of his arms as though he meant to release her, followed by a possessive tightening that set her pulse skittering.

His eyes moved across her face with an absorbed look, as though he were memorizing every nuance of color and contour. The pale ice-blue shaded to a smoky hue and Damask waited, unwilling to do anything that might destroy the tenuous thread of intimacy spinning between them.

This, she realized with a burst of self-awareness, was why she wanted to come to Bonne Volonte. At Seven Pines Bram could avoid her with his work, and Wade would be there. But here Bram could not escape her. Here, she would be gentle and biddable, but she would never let him forget that she was a woman and he was a man.

And such a man, she sighed as she melted into the kiss

that claimed her mouth at long last. By the very cruelty of his rejection of her, Bram had told Damask far more than he suspected. Deliberate cruelty was foreign to his nature. If he had no feeling for her, it would not have been necessary, and that realization gave her the tiny hope she hoarded in her heart.

There was hunger in the crushing grip of his arms and the flaming slant of his mouth across hers. Bram's lips moved across hers like a man starved, and Damask yielded eagerly, sweet breath sighing through when the firm tip of his tongue roamed her sensitive upper lip and flicked tantalizingly against the tiny indentation where her dimple hid.

The sternwheeler chugged away and footsteps swayed the bridge, but Damask was happily oblivious. Three sharp raps on the wooden planks and a roughly cleared throat startled her from her total absorption in Bram. Two sets of eyes flew open, smoky blue and fuzzy liquid brown, and for the space of a heartbeat Damask was in complete frustrated accord with her husband.

He lowered her to the deck, his color high and hers flaming, and they turned to Damask's uncle like mischievous children caught in the act of pilfering from the cookie jar.

Papa Kinloch, in his early seventies, had the lean, vigorous look of a younger man. He tossed his mane of iron gray hair, his snapping black eyes peering down his hawk's beak of a nose. Damask felt her blush deepening until her skin burned.

"Well, girl, I see you found yourself a man who knows how to treat a woman. By thunder, sir!" A broad grin tilted the brushy ends of his moustache up. "It is an honor to meet you. I had almost given up hope on this younger generation! Faugh! Dandies begging to kiss the tips of a lady's dainty fingers! Grab them up and give them a good buss, I say! That's the way to treat a woman! Kinloch Scarborough here. Welcome to Bonne Volonte."

"Sir." Bram extended his hand and found it taken in a

powerful grip that proved the infirmities of age had failed to touch Kinloch Scarborough.

"I must thank you for bringing Damask to visit us. The last time I saw her she was hardly more than a babe to be dandled on the knee. Now look at her! A woman! By Gad! A beauty!" A long finger tapped Bram's shoulder. "Might I suggest you tell her that often? Women love to hear it, and you'll be surprised at how it smooths the running of your household."

Damask suppressed a strong urge to kick Papa Kinloch in the shins, and was glad when she flicked a glance at Bram and found him grinning, perfectly at ease. She was so happy she flung her arms around her uncle.

"Faugh! These cursed women!" He cast a wry glance at Bram. "Forever hugging and kissing a man! Have sons, my boy! I have a house full of granddaughters! A cursed nuisance!" For all his protests, he hugged Damask tightly and kissed her cheek, keeping his arm around her waist as they left the bridge.

Hurrying down the brick-paved walk was the rest of the family, fifteen-year-old Titia in the lead. Unconcerned with presenting a laydlike appearance, she lifted her skirts to her knees and sprinted, thick black hair straggling from a haphazard bun. Following at a more sedate pace came *Tante* Euphemie, her small chubby features blurred with the abstracted air of a dreamer. With her was Petite, at nineteen the oldest of the Scarborough girls at home. Bringing up the rear was seventeen-year-old Chatte, a small voluptuous girl with a mass of midnight hair, sultry black eyes, and pouting lips. Damask recognized them all from Petite's voluminously detailed letters.

After the confusion of introductions and welcoming hugs, they sorted themselves into a short procession following the brick walk to the house. Titia hurried ahead, Bram was flanked by Chatte and *Tante* Euphemie while Petite, Papa Kinloch, and Damask followed.

The manor house at the top of the landscaped lawn

showed the West Indian influence of that first Kinloch Scarborough's day. It faced the bayou, two stories high with a tall hipped roof. There were no windows, only wide French doors leading onto the deep surrounding veranda supported by turned cypress columns. Flanking the main house, adjoining the veranda, were two wings of similar construction. Further back, on either side were *garconnieres,* built for the bachelors of the household and guests.

They climbed the exterior stairs on the side and entered the first parlor. "We have two guests," Papa Kinlich was saying. "Ah! Mr. Buckner, here you are. I'd like for you to meet my great-niece and her husband, the Raffertys. Damask, Mr. Rafferty, this is Kaiser Clay Buckner of Boston, Massachusetts. I met Mr. Buckner in the City a few weeks ago. He told me he had come South to study our *peculiar institution* for himself. And what better place could he do that than at Bonne Volonte?"

Kaiser Buckner was tall and trim with flaxen hair and beautiful cornflower blue eyes that were eclipsed by a dazzling smile. "It is an honor to meet you, Mrs. Rafferty," he said in those careful, clipped syllables of the North.

"Mr. Buckner"—Damask watched him bend over her hand—"please forgive me for staring, but you are the first Yankee I've met. I am quite astonished to find you do not have horns and a tail."

He threw back his head and laughed. It was the joyful sound of a man who had a great zest for life, and reminded Damask sadly of how few times she had heard Bram's laughter.

Kaiser retained her hand in his and smiled down at her. "And I am quite astonished to find a Southern Lady honest enough to admit to what many must think." He extended his hand to Bram. "Sir, you are most fortunate in your wife."

Bram gave a noncommittal nod. "Mr. Buckner, I hope we will have a chance to talk during this visit. I'm very interested in what is happening in the North. I believe it very likely that you and I may meet on a battlefield in the near future."

The residual sheen of amusement vanished from Buckner's eyes, his expression turning to one of somber surprise and agreement. "So, you think that, too, Mr. Rafferty. That is why I have come South. If I fight, I want to know what I am fighting for, and what I'm fighting against."

"If more men thought as you do, sir, there might be no need for war."

"We live in an imperfect world, Mr. Rafferty. I will be very glad to exchange views with you."

Damask moved closer to Bram's side. Hearing his conviction that they were heading for war confirmed by a Yankee was frightening. "Mr. Buckner, surely you do not share my husband's pessimism about our country's future."

"I am afraid I do, I—"

"So here you are, young man," Papa Kinoch interrupted. "Damask, my dear, we have a surprise for you."

She turned around, noting Petite's expectant smile, and saw . . .

"Wade!"

"Damask, really," Wade sighed as he leaned back against the crack of the twin doors separating the two parlors. "What will Papa Kinloch and Mr. Buckner and the girls think about you dragging me off? This kind of behavior may be acceptable at a backwater like Seven Pines, but you are in politer company now. There are certain rules."

"I am sure they will all understand that a brother and sister might have things to say after a separation."

"They might have. Your Mr. Rafferty didn't. He was quite alarmingly flushed." Wade fastidiously tinkered with his cuffs, slanting an oblique look Damask's way. "Something wrong there? He hardly looks the indulgent bridegroom."

"How did you expect him to look, Wade? This is not the usual marriage."

"Oh, I thought you'd have brought him around by now. After all"—his head raised, shallow blue eyes sharpened by some emotion—"you always were able to wrap Papa around your little finger. You don't really think it was anything *I* said that convinced him to take Mama away that day, do you?"

Guilt and grief stabbed into her heart. "Wade, you were Papa's son. He loved you."

"But you were his beautiful, fair-haired little girl," he said with a ring of ancient bitterness.

Damask stared at him, aghast. He was jealous! And he had always been jealous of her closeness to Papa!

"Wade, I'm sorry, I—"

"Forget it, Damask," he said softly, worry puckering across his brow beneath the lank blonde hair. "It wasn't your fault that Papa preferred you to me."

"But . . ." She wheeled away, walking to the open French doors to stare out over the lawn. Was this another reason piled atop all the others that Wade had become a . . . what?

She turned back. "I had dinner with Andy while we were in the City."

There was a spark of discomfort in the eyes that flashed toward Damask. "What could possibly interest me about your dinner with Andy? He's something of a bore, you know. Were it not for that tasty piece he has tucked away on Rampart Street, I'd say he was as dull a fellow as Uncle James."

"Wade, he told me," she said softly. "Everything. Why, Wade? Why didn't you tell me about the gambling? How could you do it? You know how Papa felt . . ."

"How?" he flared. "Do you know how hard it is to live on that pittance you allowed me the first year I went to the City? If I had been given enough money to survive, I never would have started gambling in the first place. But, no," he sneered, "there wasn't any money for me. *You* had to buy that sawmill!"

"Oh, Wade." Helplessly, Damask pressed her fingers to her burning eyes. Was it her fault? Her fingers inched down her cheeks, muddied eyes staring at him. "I'm sorry. I've tried to do what was best for us all."

"I know," Wade said, his shoulders slumping. "Papa would have been proud of you. He always was. It was only Mama that . . ."

He heaved a sigh that ate its way into Damask's smarting conscience. He was her brother. No one else knew how tender and sensitive he was. He might gamble, but she would never believe he was capable of murder and she would not hurt him more than she already had by asking him about the Caswells. There was another explanation. There had to be.

Bram slid a chary look from Wade to her and back again when they rejoined the family. Had he taken a dagger and thrust into her breast it could not have hurt more.

The pain of it blossomed deep within her and with it a single question: Why? Why should what he thought hurt her?

The answer burst upon her with the shattered, splintered brilliance of an exploding star. She loved him. Heart and soul. Hopelessly. Helplessly. Irrevocably.

Chapter 15

"THEY *should have been back by now*! *How long can it take to* ride through the cane fields?" Damask pushed her embroidery into the basket and stood, her restless steps muffled to silence by the Aubusson carpet.

"Damask, you've been here a week and you've hardly let poor Mr. Rafferty out of your sight!"

"Chatte! For shame. Such a thing to say!" Petite chided her sister.

Damask heard neither of them. She stood at the French doors staring at the cane fields beyond the bridge. It was madness, this terror that held her enthralled whenever Bram was out of her sight! Nothing could happen when Papa Kinloch, Titia, and Mr. Buckner were with him. And Wade. Wade wouldn't hurt him; he couldn't. Yet, she never saw Wade and Bram together when her insides didn't twist like a sodden sheet being wrung dry.

It was almost as if . . . as if she didn't trust Wade! Perhaps his lying about the gambling had shaken her faith in him a little. But gambling and murder were two very different things.

It had to be her. Her new feelings for Bram were making her too cautious. She knew how vulnerable he was. It was proved to her every night when she changed the bandage on his healing scar.

She rubbed the Brussels lace curtain between forefinger and thumb, her lips tugging down. At least he was letting her do that for him now. At Dublin he had taken it to Liza. If only they had brought Michael with them.

Was there ever a man more stubborn than Bram Rafferty? Ignoring her would raise both eyebrows and questions, so he was trying a different tack, the shield of a light teasing attitude. So close she could come, and not a step further. He would not humiliate her by requesting separate rooms. No. He simply slept on the cot in the dressing room, and treated her like a pesky littly sister when he was unable to avoid her. Still, there was a not so subtle difference. His eyes followed her when he thought she was unaware of him. Sometimes, when she rested her hand on his arm, a tremor stirred beneath the layers of coat and sleeve. If she brushed against him, he would carefully move away. Perhaps his withdrawal to the dressing room was a better sign than she thought. If he trusted himself, he could . . .

She saw them, Wade trailing along behind as they headed for the bridge. "They're back. I see Bram!" she shouted over her shoulder as she rushed for the side stairs. She flew down the walk, the deep rose-colored skirt of her simple day dress lifted high to reveal layers of petticoats beneath. The pins holding her snood worked loose and her hair spilled down her back, a glorious flood of pale gold. Bram was in the lead and he slowed his mount as she approached and reached up to rest her hand on the saddle.

"You were gone so long," she complained softly. "Did you have a nice ride?"

Before he could answer, Wade pulled up beside her, shallow blue eyes sharp with malice as he stared down his pinched nose. "You are not on a backwoods plantation now, Damask. Here women are expected to act like ladies! You looked like a hoyden, racing down the drive with your hair straggling!" Sharp spurs roweled his horse's flanks mercilessly. The animal leapt ahead.

Hot color burned Damask's cheeks, and her hands moved to her hair, pulling it forward over her shoulder, her shaking fingers digging for the pins. Bram's long arm coiled around her waist and the earth shifted. She gasped with surprise as she was gently hauled up and settled in the saddle. Bram's eyes, glinting cold fury, followed Wade's progress around the corner of the house.

"Bram, don't be angry with him. He's only trying to help me. I've never—"

"Do you really believe that?" he asked, his eyes dropping to hers with a skeptical expression.

"Yes," she said softly. "I do. I know that tact is not one of Wade's strengths, but . . . it is for my own good."

"Damask, Wade is a . . ." he began hotly and broke off, his eyes darkening with conflict. Apparently he decided his opinion of her brother was better left unsaid, though his eyes did not clear as they frowned down into hers. "Pay no attention to Wade, colleen. There are men who prefer their ladies to act like women."

"And you, Bram?" Her voice dipped into its lowest register with breathy urgency. "Which do you prefer?"

The arm behind her back jerked taut and his lashes swept over the blue eyes that took on a sapphire glow. His chest rose and fell rapidly against her shoulder as if he labored against some emotion that savaged his better intentions. His jaw worked and he looked away and closed his eyes for the space of a heartbeat. When he looked back, she knew she had lost again. The wall was up.

A crooked grin creased his cheeks beneath his remote gaze. "Do you think I would complain because you are so eager to see me?"

There was nothing to do but follow his lead and take what comfort she could in the fact that his arm was still tense at her back. It wasn't easy for him, and that gave her a forlorn hope. Her smile trembled at the corners as she raised her eyes to his. "Perhaps I was just bored with sewing and women's chatter."

"I give you fair warning." A brow climbed over his shuttered gaze. "I'm a dangerous man to tease. 'Fess up, colleen."

If only he were, Damask thought as her look lingered on the smile that didn't reach his eyes. He was never going to allow her to get close to him. And yet, his heart thumped furiously against her arm. There was some hope after all.

"The only thing I will confess, Bram Rafferty, is that you are too puffed up with masculine pride as it is." A smile took the sting from her words. "You've turned Papa Kinloch's household upside down, and left poor Mr. Buckner pining for attention."

"Pining, is he?" A cool note crept into the husky timbre of Bram's voice. "I thought you kept him well entertained."

Damask flashed a glance at him. "What else can we do, left out as we are?"

He grunted, a sound somewhere between irritation and aggravation. "You know perfectly well that he has received the lion's share of your cousin's attention, but he seems especially interested in long chats with you. Why is that, I wonder?"

Something warned Damask that the time for teasing had passed. She raised her hand to touch his chest, and felt his thumping heart sprint against her palm. "Bram, Mr. Buckner is interested in everything about the South. Do you know that he thinks all slaves are as viciously whipped as in that . . . outrageous book of Mrs. Stowe's? When I told him we don't allow whipping at Dublin and Seven Pines, I'm not sure he believed me! And when I told him about you buying Polly for a thousand dollars to get her away from . . . from your . . ."

"Who told you about that?" He tipped her chin up to his lowering frown.

"Don't be angry. Polly wanted me to know why she wanted to come with us. She just said that you had . . . taken up with her mistress."

"She shouldn't have told you."

Damask pressed her palm to his cheek, her eyes soft, searching. "It was long before I met you, but . . ." Her voice dropped to a whisper. "I would like to think there will be no more women like her, that we—"

"Damask!" Titia rode up beside them. "Mr. Buckner and I are going to ride over the prairie. Why don't you and Mr. Rafferty join us? We'll take a picnic lunch."

It had meant very little to Damask when she was told that Bram had sent Nero back to New Orleans to get hers and Michael's wardrobes from the tailor and seamstress while they were at Dublin. Now, she was glad. Very glad. Even in that confection of frilly, flounced, white-worked muslin worn to the *Theatre d'Orleans,* she had not felt so delightfully feminine as she did in her tailored riding habit. It was made of a rich brown *cachmerette,* a fabric light enough for summer wear, and the cut was severe. The basque bodice with its short skirt flaring from the waist had tight-fitted sleeves. The skirt was full over a rustling quilted taffeta petticoat. Her habit shirt was a pale yellow linen with dainty ruffles spilling down the deep vee of her coat. She wore brown kid boots and a brown silk top hat with a trailing scarf in pale yellow silk that matched her gloves.

Perhaps it wasn't what she was wearing that made her feel all woman today, she thought with a wary glance at the tall figure of her husband. He was dressed all in white with a wide-brimmed straw hat, and looked deliciously dark and wicked. It was sinful for a man to be so handsome! And more sinful for a man to look at a woman the way he had looked at her from the time she ran up to him at the stable. Butterfly wings played havoc with her breathing, and Damask looked away across the rolling swells of green prairie.

Bram's leg brushed hers and she looked around. "You seem pleased with yourself today, colleen," he rumbled softly. "Tell me, what thoughts hide behind the golden glow of your eyes?"

"Oh," she said lightly, and tried to smile, but found her lips beyond any command. "I was just thinking that now I know how Aunt Sarah's blackberry tarts feel when they are eyed so voraciously.''

Bram's black brows knitted in a puzzled frown, then shot up, curling lashes spreading wide. Damask waited for no further reaction. Flicking her light quirt against her mare's flanks, she urged her mount ahead.

''Do you see the trees lining the *coulee* ahead?'' Titia asked as Damask pulled up beside her. ''We'll stop there. I must do something, but a picnic basket will keep you entertained while you wait. Just moor your mounts.''

''I will never get used to that,'' Buckner said with a shake of his head.

''What is that, Mr. Buckner?'' Damask asked.

''Moor your mount! In Boston we only moor boats and ships!''

''I must admit it is new to me, too.''

Titia laughed. ''Mr. Rafferty, you are familiar with the Acadians and their peculiarities of language. Perhaps you will explain.'' She waved her hand and galloped off.

Damask looked at Bram. ''It does sound odd.''

''I suppose it does. Mr. Buckner, look at the prairie. What does it remind you of?''

''The sea, of course. An easy, gentle sea. There, where the clouds cast a shadow, it has the blue-green color of the sea.''

''Yes, it looked the same to the first Acadians who settled here, and their language reflects it. When they set out to cross it, they say they *mettre la voile*, or set sail. Do you see the tongue of trees leaving the *coulee* and jutting into the prairie? That is called a *pointe*. And to the north, that circular patch of trees surrounded by light grasses. That is called an *ile*, or island. We do not ride to that spot; we *navigate* to it.''

They *navigated* to the *anse*, or bay, formed by two tongues of trees licking into the prairie from the *coulee*. Dismounting, they partook of a light repaste of wine and cheese and bread, talking desultorily of inconsequential things until

Damask saw the horse threading its way through the stunted oaks.

"Titia, here you . . ."

Gone was the sidesaddle and the elegant black habit with its frothy wisp of a hat. Titia swung out of her western saddle and strode toward them, wearing . . . *trousers!*

She struck a mannish pose, her golden cat's eyes glistening with amusement. "Well, what do you think?"

"What will Papa Kinlich say?"

Titia sat cross-legged on the ground and reached for a piece of cheese. "What do you think? His roar would be heard clear to the City! That is why Julian met me here with my saddle and clothes. We'll have to come back this way so I can change. A cursed nuisance!" She echoed her grandfather, and her wide red lips curled into a grin. "Come now, Damask, admit it. This is much more convenient and comfortable than those tons of skirts men keep us swaddled in! And to ride across the prairie astride—there is nothing like it! I feel as free and wild as the wind!"

There was not a single concession to femininity in Titia's costume: a crisp linen shirt with turned-down collar and cravat; a gold silk waistcoat and black frockcoat; and those black trousers that hugged Titia's endless legs. Damask sighed wistfully and Bram's brow quirked into a disapproving arch.

"I've often thought the freedom of trousers must be wonderful. Where did you have them made?"

"A tailor, of course."

"A tailor! Titia . . ."

"Titia," her cousin mimicked, "how immodest! Just what Petite said. But what seamstress knows how to fit trousers? Besides, Julian went with me." Her eyes strayed to the young slave who served them and she grinned. "He frowned the tailor into such a fit of trembling, he could hardly take his measurements. Even though he disagrees just as heartily as Papa Kinloch would. Don't you, Julian?"

The young man's lips twitched briefly before the mask

settled back into place, but his bright black eyes staring down an unmistakable hawk's beak of a nose gleamed with amusement. "You will have your way, Miss Titia."

She laughed and stood. "Come, if you are to see the prairie, we should be going."

Bram walked Damask to her horse, cupping his hands to help her mount. When she was settled, her knee around the horn and her foot tucked into the stirrup, she felt his hand slide beneath her pantalettes to caress her calf. His eyes were hot as they stared into hers, but a smile hovered around his mouth. "If I ever find these encased in trousers, colleen," he warned lightly, "I will take great pleasure in ripping them off you—and paddling your delightful little rump."

Damask leaned down, holding his eyes in an embrace that promised much, then brushed her lips across his. "Surely, husband, you could think of something better to do than that."

His hand tightened around her calf. "I gave you fair warning . . ."

"Of course. You are a dangerous man to tease." Damask sat up, her eyes wide with deliberate innocence. "Empty threats. How can I take them seriously when I have seen no evidence of danger?" She wheeled her horse around and galloped after Titia and Kaiser, leaving Bram standing in the shade of a stunted oak with a growing smile.

He joined them quickly, the smile still in place. They crossed the rolling prairie flushing rabbits from their lairs, circling the dangerous boggy wetlands alive with cranes and herons and ducks, crossing tiny bayous and dried up *coulees*. On the horizon, a dark ribbon of trees separated the grassy sedge of the prairie from the cloudless azure sky. In the distance was a dark patch of brown. As they drew nearer, Damask saw that it was a huddling herd of cattle, thousands, milling and lowing and cropping grass.

At first she thought she imagined the faint squealing squeaking noise. "Titia, what is that sound?"

"That awful screeching? The ox cart. What perfect timing! We'll have our lunch in the *ile* on the other side of the herd. They are bringing it from Bonne Volonte. Hurry! I cannot abide this sedate pace."

Titia's horse leaped ahead, Buckner following, but Bram reached out, his hand closing over Damask's reins. "You haven't ridden in a long time, colleen. We'll take it slower."

The herd parted as Titia and Kaiser thundered through. Damask turned to Bram, a definite pout to her rosy lips. "You are treating me like an old woman! I can ride every bit as well as Titia, even if it has been a long time!"

"I'm sure you can, but then . . . we would not have time for this." His arm snaked out and swept Damask from her saddle, leaving her feet dangling and the top hat swaying at the end of the scarf caught beneath his arm.

His mouth swooped upon hers in a ravenous bruising kiss that spoke of desire too long denied. Her lips parted for his questing tongue and she felt its delicate searching touch in sensations that shimmied along her nerves to swelling nipples and aching loins.

Bram raised his head, eyes glowing down at her. "I warned you, colleen," he said, his breath ragged. "You've earned your punishment by toying with me all day. Come, you are too far away to suit me."

He settled her in front of him, reached across to tie the scarf of her hat around her saddle horn, and caught the reins to lead her horse.

Damask sighed and snuggled against his chest, one finger exploring the gap between two buttons of his waistcoat, then slipping beneath his shirt to rub his chest and tease a coil of hair. A mellow gaze traveled up to the strong line of Bram's jaw. "Such punishment, husband. Do you think I deserve to be so horribly chastised?"

"Sorceress," Bram said roughly and lowered his head. The horses clopped an aimless, winding path through the lowing cattle, drawn by the smell of water. They reached the *ile* of cottonwood trees surrounding a clear pond at the same time the squeaking ox cart did, though neither Bram nor Damask was aware of it.

"Really, Damask!" came Wade's nasal whine. "You are worse than a painted harlot panting after a well-paying customer!"

Damask was never sure how she ended up on the ground clinging to the stirrup to still her reeling world while Bram crossed the clearing in the blink of an eye. His big hands wrapped around Wade's lapels, jerking him from his horse and shaking him viciously.

"You sniveling little cur! If I ever hear you talk about her like that again, I will kill you!"

Wade gave a frightened squeak, his head lolling as Bram shook him like a great sleek cat with a rat. Damask rushed to them, tugging at Bram's arm. "Please, put him down. Bram! Put him down!"

Slowly, his hands unclenched and Wade slid to the ground, sagging before he stumbled away to drape himself across the wheel of the ox cart he had followed out.

"Bram," she soothed, and his eyes, void of all expression, moved to her, "you must not get so angry. It's Wade's way. He doesn't mean to be cruel."

"No one speaks to you that way," he said in an uninflected drone.

"Come. We'll take a walk around the pond. Come." She slipped her arm around his waist and led him away.

Wade straightened, raking his lank blonde hair back and tugging at his lapels. They disappeared into the trees at the far side of the pond, and he sniffed. "I suppose we can't expect any better of him. It's unfortunate that Damask is so plain and has had so few men in her life. I should have expected her to fall for the first thing that passes for a man to come along."

Titia's eyes narrowed, breath scratching from her throat. "You . . ."

Kaiser Buckner's fingers dug into her arm. "Mr. Downing, if you will excuse us. Miss Scarborough has promised to tell me about the *vacherie.*'' He offered his arm to Titia and they strolled away.

''Why didn't you let me tell that pompous goat what I thought of him?'' she hissed furiously.

''Because his skin is just as thick as a goat's. It would have accomplished nothing.''

''It would make me feel better!''

''And me,'' he admitted, ''but I assure you, your cousin will want this smoothed over. Whatever he is, she loves him. It is a kindness to her to ignore it.''

They soon returned to the cool shade beneath the cotton-woods, where a cloth had been spread and piled with baskets and bowls of food and bottles of wine. Bram and Damask emerged from the trees, arm in arm, his tense anger replaced with a smile.

Wade ostentatiously claimed the far corner of the broad white cloth, opposite Bram, but the initial awkwardness was eased by their hunger. Talk was at a minimum as they dug into the basket of fried chicken and ladled up bowls of gumbo.

Wade's shallow blue eyes settled on Bram with a malignant stare. Damask sighed and looked away, unconsciously overlaying Bram's strong self-assured features with her brother's. The wealth of tumbling black curls opposed to lank, indeterminate blonde; steady ice-blue eyes opposed to vacillating blue; rugged beard-shadowed skin opposed to baby smooth cheeks affecting sparse muttonchop whiskers. Startled by the realization of what she was doing, she looked back at Wade, noting the short, sharp nose above thin, discontented lips. What was wrong with Wade that he could never be satisfied? His life had always been one of ease, yet he faced it with a perpetual sneer.

''You aren't eating?''

Bram's husky voice whispered in her ear, and Damask found real concern clouding his eyes. ''I'm not hungry.''

"You haven't been hungry for weeks." He toyed with a feathery curl, tracing the lobe of her ear. "You are far too thin, colleen," he whispered. "Now, Chatte . . .".

He let it hang and Damask narrowed her eyes.

Bram's teeth flashed white in a broad grin. "You're jealous. I think I like that." Laughter welled up from the warming core that was his heart. "Shall I warn Chatte not to ogle me on pain of a she-cat clawing her eyes?" The teasing laughter in his eyes died as he raked Damask with a saddened look. He lay back, cushioning his head in his hands. "Eat."

Damask grabbed up a chicken leg and bit into it with a vengeance but it turned to sand in her mouth when she saw the malevolent look that Wade stabbed at Bram.

The afternoon passed slowly, the shadows of the cotton-woods stretching far beyond the *ile*. It was inevitable that talk would turn to the differences between the North and South.

"Abolitionist! Certainly not, Miss Scarborough," Kaiser replied to Titia's heated question. "I'm an antislavery man."

"I fail to see the difference."

"But there is one. The abolitionists want slavery abolished throughout the Union. A few are willing to offer compensation for the loss of your, ah, your property, but the majority feel that slavery is a moral evil and the owners do not deserve compensation. I must admit that the intransigence of the South has led to the yearly growth of that majority. However, there are men, antislavery men, who do not believe in slavery, but are willing to allow its existence as long as it does not extend to more territory."

"Allow!" Titia shrilled. "We do not wait for the North to *allow* us to do anything! We are sovereign states bound by a common federal law . . ."

"Exactly, Miss Scarborough. Bound by a common federal law. What happens when the majority of the people in this country oppose slavery? When the congressional stranglehold of Southern politicians is broken? When laws are passed by the majority to abolish slavery?"

"Secession!" Titia's eyes shot gold sparks.

"If you are allowed," he answered flatly.

"Mr. Buckner," Damask, hoping to cool their rising anger, joined the conversation, "have you never considered what would happen to our people if they were suddenly freed? You must see what suffering freedom would bring them. Papa taught me that our people are the children of our family. They must be loved and praised and as gently chastised as a child. We cannot take away the protection we have offered, leaving them helpless."

"Mrs. Rafferty, you call them children, but they are men and women with hopes and dreams, people, like you and me. You've told me how your Harford has, in effect, been your overseer for years. Don't you think he could work his own land, feed and clothe his family, make his way without your help?"

Damask's eyes darkened. "I suppose he could, but Harford has everything he needs at Seven Pines. Why would he want anything else?"

"Because he is a man, Mrs. Rafferty. And everytime you treat him like a child, you strip him of a part of his pride."

"What you don't understand, Mr. Buckner, is that our people love us as we love them. I cannot think of one that would leave if he were given the chance."

"Damask coddles our people beyond all reason, Mr. Buckner," Wade injected, his eyes sliding to Bram. "It is no wonder they refuse to accept any guiding hand, except hers. Take my body servant, Nero. A lazier, more shiftless—"

"I find that strange, Downing." Bram interrupted, his icy stare boring into Wade. "I've found Nero to be bright, hardworking, and quick to please. Perhaps it is his treatment that makes the difference."

Blue eyes met and held until the dry wind from the prairie vibrated with tension. Wade's thin nostrils flared, and unhealthy color blotched his face while his lip curled into a snarl.

"What would *you* know about the treatment of slaves? You're nothing but a—"

"Wade!" Damask bent toward him with the hot, feral eyes of a tigress protecting her cub. "You will *not* insult my husband!"

Wade reared back as though she had set her hands to his shoulders and pushed. Eyes rounded with shock slowly narrowed, inching toward Bram with an expression that combined a malicious hatred with the smug look of one who holds a well-loved secret. He climbed to his feet, fastidiously straightening his sleeves as he slid a glowering look at Damask.

"I am only your brother. I suppose it was to be expected you would forget your loyalty to your family when you have managed to entrap a man—at long last."

He stalked off, mounted up, and rode away, leaving Damask staring blindly at her clenched fists. What had that look meant?

"Entrap a man," Titia echoed indignantly. "Damask, I never heard such nonsense. Why, everyone can see the way Mr. Rafferty watches you with his heart in his eyes. I only hope that someday I will have a man who loves me half as much as he loves you."

Damask's face whitened to the color of bleached linen. "How . . . how kind of you to say so, Titia," she managed to scrape out past the constriction in her throat. "If you will excuse me, I must walk off this meal." She stood with jerky movements, turned to the trees with her head high and her back stiff.

The brown *cachmerette* of her riding habit blended with the shadows, and Bram stood. "Excuse me," he said, and without further explanation walked off in the opposite direction onto the prairie.

It was a subdued quartet that mounted for the return trip to Bonne Volonte beneath a prairie sky awash with rose-edged clouds and lavender twilight.

Chapter 16

HIS *heart in his eyes*! *If only* Titia *hadn't said it*! All *the good she* had accomplished was wiped out! Damask twisted on the stool, agitated fingers spinning the bottle of violet scent on the marble-topped dressing table. The days since their ride had seen a return of the aloof stranger. He was as courteous and correct as any bridegroom should be, but when his expressive eyes rested on her they were as bland as *blanc mange*. Even his voice was cautiously neutral. Damn! she cursed to herself, her head jerking emphatically.

"Ouch!"

Lulu gripped a hank of her hair. "You as squirmy as a worm in hot ashes! How I s'posed to git this done if you ain't still?"

Damask subsided. "Hurry, Lulu! I want to be all done when Bram comes out!"

"Humph! Ain't no need to git all gussied up for that man to see you put all them ladies in the shade! You think he ain't got no eyes?"

"Oh, no, Lulu, he—"

"Humph! I seen him git all stiff and proper when you's looking, but you ain't seen the look he give you when you ain't! That devil got a powerful hunger, and if you ain't careful, you gonna be the meat on his table!"

"Lulu, do you really think so?" Damask breathed.

"Child, you sound like you looking forward to it!" Bootbutton eyes rolled to the heavens then came back to trap Damask's hopeful gaze in the mirror, the jabbing comb punctuating her words. "You listen to Lulu! I seen you gitten all soft and moony-eyed! Now, I know that man's done some good things—wasn't nobody at that Dublin what had a bad word to say about him. But that don't make him right for you! That devil's had a powerful hurt one time or t'other, and all the loving in the world ain't gonna heal him! Give him your heart and he gonna break it up in little pieces and stomp on it! Watch your step with that devil, 'cause just about the time you think you done caught him, he's gonna be turning on you like a cornered wildcat!"

Lulu sniffed and nodded her head, returning to the task of plaiting Damask's hair.

A powerful hurt, Damask repeated to herself. She had seen his agony and his vulnerability, and he had turned to her in his need. He could be healed. She knew it. She was going to do everything in her power to teach him that love was not to be feared.

A high-pitched giggle sounded from the adjoining bedroom, rising above the murmur of voices and the muted practicing beat of a waltz. Through the slats in the French doors seeped the aromas of roasting beef and pork, and the cloyingly sweet perfumes of cape jessamine and magnolia. Bonne Volonte had been in a dither for days, with tonight's ball occupying everyone's mind.

Damask had been kept running thither and yon, a welcome extra pair of hands and feet that Petite put to good use. She smiled a secret smile. Bram would not find it so easy to ignore her when he held her in his arms to waltz her around the dance floor.

A deep-seated glow bloomed brightly. "Hurry, Lulu, hurry!"

Damask's trembling haste was well worth the effort. Even Lulu's prim, disapproving lips widened to a grin when Bram strolled from the dressing room tugging at the ends of his cravat, and stumbled to a halt with his jaw agape.

Damask wore the ballgown that had been folded in paper at the bottom of her treasure chest. Since he had chosen both fabric and style, the gown was nothing new to him, but the way it looked on her was. The fragile apricot-colored tissue silk complemented the honey tones of her skin. Ten yards of skirt were covered with the popular flounces, the fabric so light they floated with every movement. The bodice was simple and unadorned, hugging her tiny waist, curving low to expose a shadow of cleavage and baring the honeyed gleam of her shoulders with dainty puffed sleeves that cupped her arms. Her hair was worn in a regal coronet fronted by the tiara of honey topaze from the parure that should have been her wedding present, but had, instead, been left on her dressing table earlier in the evening.

Her hand came up to touch the necklace at her throat. "Thank you, Bram," she said softly. "It's beautiful."

He nodded absently, eyes sweeping her from top to toe, then rising to linger on the shadow at the low curve of her bodice. He stirred restlessly, his brows drawing together. "Must you wear that dress, Damask?"

The gold lace fan snapped together. "You don't like it? But it is the one you chose for me."

He dragged his eyes from her in a supreme effort of will, and busied himself with his cravat. "Yes, I did, and you look quite . . . delectable . . ." Lulu's loud sniff drew a sharp look. "However, it is a little, um, revealing. I would prefer that you not bare so much of your, um, your bosom."

The fan jerked up to her breast and Damask blushed to the roots of her hair. "It is daring . . . but you chose it, Bram."

The cravat was yanked into a hasty, hopeless knot. Bram's dark face grew thunderous, the scar ticking wildly at his temple. "Must you keep reminding me? That was before—" He stopped and threw her a stormy look. "Wear what you like! Nero! I need another cravat!"

Well pleased with this anger, Damask went to him, gently pushing his hands away. "If it is your wish, I will change," she said compliantly as she worked the knot from the silk. "I dressed only to please you. No one else."

Her sweet loving look went to Bram's head like the heady

fumes of a good Irish whiskey. All foreknowledge of danger was burned away, his anger evaporating like a frail morning mist touched by the hot sun. A reluctant smile relaxed the grim line of his mouth and his hand curved around her neck, the rough pad of his thumb brushing her cheek. "Then I will not deny myself the pleasure of seeing you in it—even if I will have to rise with the sun to duel every man who enjoys it as much as I do."

The above-ground basement of the main house was cleared and converted into a ballroom, the cypress flooring polished to a mirror sheen that reflected a rainbow of crinolines. Chairs and *papier mâché* tables topped by lush bouquets of flowers lined the walls. Sconces with dripping candles shed a flattering light over the guests, some of whom were casting covetous, curious glances at the dark, brooding figure of Bram Rafferty. Damask smoothed a wisp of hair at her nape with a nervous gesture, wishing heartily that every woman there was as ugly as sin. The thought drew a faint smile. She was jealous. The smiled dwindled, her eyes drifting to her husband, who stood a few feet away talking to Papa Kinloch.

"Mrs. Rafferty, it isn't fair, you know," Kaiser Buckner said, a disconsolate droop to his mouth and a merry twinkle in his eyes.

"What isn't fair, Mr. Buckner?"

"That Louisiana should have so many beautiful ladies. I've traveled all over Europe and never have I met so many with such grace and charm and beauty."

"Fie on you, sir," Damask rejoined lightly. "You know you are perfectly safe lavishing compliments on a settled matron like myself. Will you take your courage in your hands and risk it on one of our young and beautiful belles?"

"Perhaps I've been caught by a Yankee harridan."

Damask cocked her head to one side, studying him thoughtfully. "No, I don't think so. There is too much mischief in you yet, sir."

He threw back his head, laughing joyously. "Mrs. Rafferty, you are a treasure beyond price." At the head of the room, the orchestra swung into the opening bars of a waltz. "I hope you don't mind, but your husband promised your first waltz to me."

"He did?" Damask flung an anxious look at Bram, who was deep in conversation with her uncle and ex-Governor Mouton. So he had found a way to avoid her. She had hoped for so much from tonight. Closeness, communion, anything that would make it easier for her to say what must be said. She could not delay it any longer. It was time that he knew she no longer believed he had cheated Wade. But he made everything so difficult!

Kaiser was a marvelous dancer with a natural rhythm. Damask drifted about the dance floor like a down feather wafted on a tender breeze. However correct he was, the admiration that shone in Kaiser Buckner's cornflower blue eyes was balm for Damask's soul. It made her feel almost . . . beautiful.

The waltz's end brought her to Bram's side in a last exhilarating whirl. There Kaiser lavished her with outrageous compliments—until he was impaled by twin chips of deadly ice-blue. An irrepressible grin quirked high and one lid dropped in a teasing wink. "I feel a distinctly dangerous chill, Mrs. Rafferty. Later, when I've gathered my flagging courage, I hope you will give me another dance."

"It would be my pleasure." He walked away, and Damask raised a brittle gaze to Bram. "He said you promised him my first dance."

"I did," he said repressively.

"I had hoped to dance it with you."

Bram frowned, his hands clasping, the long fingers rubbing across the glove that covered his scar. "Dancing is one of the social graces I never acquired." His eyes lifted to a flickering candle. "This is the only time I've ever regretted it."

She could hear the strain in his voice as he made that confession and the tight knot of exasperated, angry frustration dissolved. Her gaze was liquid, tender, and loving, as she brushed his lapel with wifely intimacy. "Then I shall enjoy watching the dancing with you."

Bram caught her hand, rubbing his thumb across the palm before drawing it to his lips. "You will dance, colleen," he said huskily, "because I will not be denied the pleasure of watching the most beautiful woman on the dance floor."

The words were sweet, and her ebbing hope surged, full and flowing again. Color touched the high curve of Damask's cheekbones and her smile grew radiant. "Then I will dance," she promised, "but there will not be a moment when I do not regret that my partner is not you."

Bram was oblivious to the looks of curiosity and amusement that followed him as the hours drifted by on the lilting strains of waltzes and the vigorous tempos of mazurkas and polkas. Damask was the magnet, his eyes the metal, bright blue steel that warmed and burned and blazed hot. A film of sweat covered his brow and soaked his palms. Strain pulled his lips taut and corded his square jaw.

Papa Kinloch introduced him to the guests. While one half of his mind attended those conversations, the other half followed Damask around the dance floor, hot eyes straying to catch a glimpse of apricot tissue silk or the honeyed gleam of her shoulders or the angelic radiance of her face.

No conversation was so interesting or important that it couldn't be broken off with the last fading bars. Bram would make his way to the edge of the dance floor, waiting there for Damask. He visibly swelled with pride that this stunning creature, a dream of honey and apricot and sweet dimpled smile, was his. And he also cursed the fact she was too eagerly petitioned as a partner by young men and old.

But no matter how handsome or attentive her partners were, her bright cinnamon eyes seemed to see nothing but him. It became increasingly difficult not to snatch her into his arms in a jealous rage each time she was returned, and it became impossible not to touch her. His lips tingled and grew full, his skin prickled hot, and all he could do was cup his itching hand possessively around her waist.

Breathless from a fast-paced polka, Damask declined another invitation to dance. Fanning her flushed cheeks, she gave Bram a brilliant smile that sent a lightning-swift bolt of desire streaking through his loins. His eyes squeezed shut and he swallowed hard. Scooping up two glasses of champagne, he handed one to her and drained his in a single gulp. Jesus! He had to get away from her for a few minutes! Maybe he could cool his hot blood in the night air.

"Here you are, Damask." Titia breezed up. "I've hardly had a chance to speak to you. How I envy you that lovely gown! Look at this!" She wadded her skirt in her hands, yanking it by inches. "White! My worst color! Papa Kinloch is so old-fashioned!"

"Titia, white becomes you . . ." Damask began.

"Sir, you offend me!" A feminine voice, deliberately loud and cutting, brought all conversations in the area to a halt. "I do not dance or speak with Yankee abolitionists!"

Kaiser Buckner stood just beyond Titia, frozen in a polite bow before a young woman in blue. Damask thrust her glass into Titia's hand and stepped around her.

"Mr. Buckner, I fear you will think me terribly bold, but you did ask for another waltz. The music is so lovely—shall we make it this one?"

"Could I refuse so pretty—and timely—a request? I would be honored, Mrs. Rafferty."

They swung onto the dance floor. Damask saw Bram's approving nod and something else that startled a chirrup of laughter from her. "You have been avenged, Mr. Buckner. Might I suggest you look over your shoulder?" He glanced back, then gave Damask an inquiring look. "We women have our own methods of dealing with rudeness, and they can be just as effective, if not more so, than a meeting on the field of honor. Titia's dainty foot has done enough damage to that girl's ballgown to send her upstairs for the rest of the evening. She'll dance with no one else tonight."

He smiled, that dazzling smile that brought lights of amusement leaping into his cornflower blue eyes. "And I thought ladies were shy, delicate creatures who could not survive without a man's protection.''

He swung her into a series of graceful turns that sent her apricot skirt sailing and her laughter chiming with delight, and Bram wheeled away, striding rapidly into the cool night. The music ended and Damask lifted the fan from its loop around her wrist, plying it vigorously. She longed for a turn around the grounds, away from the stifling perfumed atmosphere of the ballroom. But Bram was nowhere to be seen.

Buckner escorted her out beneath the veranda, so she could breathe the cool night air. A nearby column was covered with the twining vine and heartshaped leaves of the night-blooming moonflower. The large blossoms, emanating a fragile sweet perfume, glowed white in the semi-darkness. Down the lawn, spreading oaks rose in black shadows against the velvet night, silvered columns of moonlight piercing the canopy of leaves. Here and there lanterns twinkled from low limbs.

"Isn't it beautiful?" she asked wistfully. "Would you mind walking through the grounds with me, Mr. Buckner? I dread returning to the heat of that room."

"It would be my pleasure."

They strolled down the brick path, until Damask sank onto a bench with a grateful sigh, eyeing the proferred glass of champagne with amusement. "Do you know that I never had so much as a sip of wine before I met my husband?"

"I suspect that is the same for all well-brought-up young ladies, North and South."

"I should imagine it is."

"Damask?" Bram's dark shadow moved near and a tremulous happiness warmed Damask's heart. He had come for her. He didn't want to, but he had.

"Mr. Rafferty, now that you have come I will see if I can't find Miss Scarborough to thank her for that little . . . service she performed for me."

"There is no need for you to leave," Bram said stiffly.

"Mr. Rafferty!" Kaiser exclaimed in horror. "Moonlight! Champagne! A beautiful woman! You Southerners can't be that different from us Yankees!'' He took Damask's hand. ''Thank you for rescuing me from that embarrassing situation, dear lady.''

Bram neither moved nor spoke as Kaiser's steps faded into the night, and Damask waited with bated breath.

He could fight his need no longer. The fact had been forced on him when Damask laughed up at Buckner and an urge to murder possessed him. It did not matter that he approved of her reason for the dance, or that neither had exchanged so much as an improper glance, or that he admired Kaiser Buckner as a man. It mattered only that Damask was in Buckner's arms, that she was freer and more open with Buckner than she had ever been with him. The sharp cat's claws of jealousy shredded his resistance. And it was the memory of those feral yellow lights glittering a protective rage when Damask told Wade that he would not insult her *husband* that slew the struggling remains of his resistance.

She was his. Whatever hell might come, for now, she was his. His arm moved, his hand extended. ''Come to me, Damask.''

She stood. Two hesitant steps and her hand rested in his. There was something different about Bram. She could feel it in the humming tension. She could hear it in the compelling command.

Bram's arms embraced her and his mouth molded itself to hers with searching sweet hunger. The famine had been long, Bram's resolve tested to its outermost limits. Now he had a ravenous appetite only Damask could sate.

His lips were fire and ice sending alternating rivers of heat and icy chills rippling along her nerves. His bruising kiss burned down her throat, down and down to the enticing shadow at the low curve of her bodice.

''I haven't heard a word that has been said to me all evening. All I could see or think or feel was you. I am bewitched,'' he muttered thickly, his hot breath slipping beneath her camisole to spread its moist heat.

Damask tried to say his name, but her tingling lips could

not form a single word. Her hands tangled in his hair, pressing him closer. His shaven cheek prickled lightly across the mound of her breast, rolling the apricot silk away from that honey-tinted globe, his lips following. His tongue circled the peak of her breast and enervating waves of pleasure streaked out, lighting the embers of her passion and draining the strength from her legs.

Bram retraced his fiery path to her lips, his hand cupping her cheek as he stared down into her eyes. "Come with me, colleen. It is time."

Arm in arm they strolled to the foot of the steps, where Bram pulled her to him for one wild, sweet kiss fraught with yearning before they climbed to the veranda and entered their room. Lulu and Nero were sent to their quarters and Damask leaned against the door, watching Bram light a single candle. Her eyes traced the bronzed contours of his face and studied the dark gaze that lifted to her. She could see avid hunger, and deeper, the shadow of doubt.

An ache of sorrow sprang to life. Sorrow that he was driven, not by his love and trust of her, but by the desire he could no longer command.

She pushed away from the door. Silently turning, she tilted her head. He fumbled uncertainly with the catch of her necklace, and a curse hissed beneath his breath. The eagerness betrayed by his clumsy fingers and the curse eased her sadness. He desired her.

The necklace dropped to the nightstand with a metallic rattle. Bram's lips seared her shoulder and left a trail of fire to her ear.

The muted sounds of voices and laughter, of music and merriment accompanied his reverent wooing. He undressed her slowly, stopping often to savor the essence of her lips and shoulders, to nibble her fingers and kiss her palms. The jessamine-scented night was made for love, and the long wait had made this celebration of life all the sweeter. Finally she stood before him, dressed only in silk stockings and frilly garters, the tiara decorating the coronet of her hair.

There was a languid trancelike quality in the air as her

eyes locked with his and her fingers moved to the top button of his waistcoat. Surprise flickered in his eyes and a soft tattered breath escaped him.

After the buttons were undone, Damask removed the silk cravat. As it floated gently to the polished floor, Bram drew a deep shaky breath. His face somber and absorbed, he removed the tiara and scattered the pins until her long satiny braid uncoiled. Brown fingers raked through the thick mass of her hair until it tumbled around her in wild abandon, glittering a soft, muted gold in the candlelight.

Glowing, smoky blue eyes moved across her face, touching the spots of rosy color marking her cheekbones, tracing her small straight nose, lingering on the curve of her lips before rising to probe her cinnamon eyes with the hot flame of his passion. Damask waited, breath, thought, feeling suspended. His knuckles caressed cheek and jaw and arching neck, and nestled in the hollow at the base of her throat.

As if he were unable to prolong the slow arousal of the senses, he swept her high in his arms and gently laid her on the bed. She watched, her eyes dark with mingled wonder and trembling passion, as he stripped off frock coat, waistcoat, and shirt to reveal his broad furred chest and powerful arms.

He sat on the side of the bed to remove his boots and she sat up, greedy fingers exploring the rippling play of muscles across his back. One boot thudded to the floor, and a tremor raced across his flesh. The muscles ridged and tightened, his neck cording. Flickers of excitement burst like fiery suns at the tips of Damask's exploring fingers, spreading heat up through her arms into her mind. The shallowness of Bram's breathing matched her own, and she flattened her hands, smoothing the palms over the molded contours of his back.

He caught her hand and pulled it around to his lips. "I want to be patient, but you aren't making it easy."

Damask, dormant desire raised to a fever pitch, nibbled the lobe of his ear and made a sound between a growl and a purr. Her lips touched the pebbling chills scampering across his shoulder. "Where would the pleasure be if it were easy, Bram Rafferty?"

The second boot thumped to the floor in a trice and Bram carried her down to the pillows, holding her in a quivering, painful grip, his head bowed against the ivory curve of her breast as though he fought for the few shreds of control that remained.

Touching, tasting, exploring, Bram began working his gentle magic and swept Damask into those spiraling passages of passion. It was a melody of love, more telling than words could ever be. What he could not say, or even allow himself to feel, he told her with every reverent caress. With his eyes, his hands, he worshipped, and transported her to quivering ecstasy.

There was only Bram, his deep voice rumbling in her ear, his furred chest prickling her sensitive nipples, his full shaft hot and throbbing his need within her. Slowly, so slowly, he pumped in and out, long liquid strokes, and soon she was sailing with him along tumultuous heights to that blinding peak where the mind splinters into scintillating fragments of pure sensation.

They clung together, gasping breath gradually calming. Bram eased himself away and pulled Damask into the crook of his arm. She snuggled there, her breasts pressed to his side, her knee drawn up over his thighs. The brilliance of Bram's eyes dulled, a frown knitting stark lines between his brows. For all his experience, he had never before been driven to such euphoric heights of passion. It had always been a physical thing, pleasant, even exciting, but his heart and mind were untouched.

His stomach knotted. He didn't want or need this violent soul-shattering emotion that propelled all hope of control from its path. Control, restraint, self-discipline; those were the parameters bounding his life. He could not exist with this flawed, fractured feeling, as though his life, his dreams, his feelings were careening wildly toward some disastrous end.

While he rejected, Damask accepted and gloried in what

they had shared. He couldn't be so tender and giving if his feelings were not strong. He would accept it, too. Perhaps not now, but soon. Perhaps he held back because he thought she still accused him of . . .

If he did, she owed him that truth, at least. She squirmed up, raising herself on one elbow to look down at him.

"Bram, you've never asked about my luncheon with Andy. Haven't you wondered what we discussed?"

His eyes moved away from her to stare into the heart of the guttering candle. "I thought you would tell me when you were ready, if there was anything of importance to tell."

"I know that you did not cheat Wade. Andy told me—"

"Did he?" Bram's head whipped around. "I've been a gambler for a long time, Damask. There isn't a trick I don't know. Your cousin, for all his competence, is an innocent whan it comes to the tools of the gambler's trade. He, no more than you, can know that I did not cheat Wade!"

Damask pressed her fingers to his lips to still the spate of harsh words. "I know you did not cheat Wade. I know that you have never cheated anyone in your life. I know it because I know you. You've had my family and myself completely within your power for months, yet I've never seen you do a dishonorable thing. You've been a more kind and loving brother to Tessa than Wade has ever been. You've given my grandfather the respect he deserves. You—" Her eyes dropped. "You've accepted Wade after he wronged you cruelly. You are doing for Seven Pines and her people everything I could ever want done. You've shown me more patience and generosity than I deserve. Bram, don't you see how much you've given us?" Her small hand rested on his chest, her voice low and earnest. "I owe you a debt I can never fully repay."

In those last spasmodic pulses of light before the candle guttered out, plunging the room into inky night, Damask saw Bram's face grow frigid, the scar writhing to life while his lip lifted in a sneer.

"A debt!" The words stabbed through the darkness and

the feather tick heaved beneath Damask as Bram rolled away and began hauling on his clothes. "I'd almost forgotten how you sold yourself to buy security for your family. I suppose I should be glad that you, like any good whore, wants to give value for value! You were very good, Mrs. Rafferty! So good you can consider your *debt* paid in full. I've never been forced to buy the women that warmed my bed, and I don't intend to start with you! We will consider Michael the heir to Seven Pines! I don't think I could force myself to touch you again!"

The French doors were jerked wide, and Damask saw Bram's threatening black silhouette framed against the lighter velvet of the night. The jessamine-scented breeze coiled around the edges of the doors and struck her with a perfumed *whoosh* when they slammed shut.

Bram reeled down the stairs, his arm snaking out to catch the uniformed sleeve of a waiter passing at the bottom. "Four bottles of Irish whiskey! Here! Two minutes!"

Two minutes later, bottles tucked securely under his arms, Bram circled the rim of the lawn, avoiding the couples that strolled in the moonlight. His boots thumped a dull sound to the end of the bridge where he finally sat, legs dangling over the edge. Liquid fire poured down his throat and spread scalding heat around the walls of his stomach.

The air rising from the bayou was cool and damp, the water a viscous black where it was not streaked with the frail glare of moonlight. The sugar house across the bayou was a tall Stygian shadow, and Bram stared at it, his eyes focused on a time long ago when his world was shattering into ever smaller, ever more devastating fragments.

His sister. His beautiful sister with her gentle, serene smile. How he loved her, looked up to her. The only beautiful thing left in the horror of his life.

How many Sundays in that first year had he and Baby Annie played in the squalid street near the docks, waiting for their first sight of Mary, bobbing along with packages of food and presents? Even his father, sunk deep in self-pitying lethargy, would laugh when she capered and mimicked the eccentric old dowager that treated her more like a daughter of the house than hired help. She spun them such tales. Such lying tales!

They had been alone when one of her *patrons* approached her, and Bram discovered there was no eccentric old dowager. Only an endless procession of men buying the use of her body. She tried to explain. She wept and pleaded but he could neither listen nor understand. All he could see was that paunchy weasel-faced scum and his sweet beautiful sister. How he hated her! He nearly choked on every bite of food his mother forced on him. His skin crawled beneath the brush of the clothes bought with Mary's earnings. But he never breathed a word. His mother died believing his sister was safe in the employ of a generous old woman.

His sister, last seen on that night nineteen years ago when they were all that were left of the Raffertys. And the last words he had hurled at her in an excess of pride and disgust were all he had left of her: *I will never go with you! I'd rather be dead than be raised by a whore!*

Where was she? What happened to her? Had she forgiven him? Bram kneaded his neck and stared at the silver disk of the moon. Had he forgiven her?

Air hissed through his clenched teeth. Jesus! He swore he would never buy a woman! That he would never coerce a woman into giving him the use of her body! He swore he would take only that which was freely offered!

The bottle tipped high, pointing to the flaming star that arced through the heavens trailing a sparkling wake before it winked into nothingness. Damask and his sister. No sacrifice was too great for the people they loved.

Damask. Soft, sweet, gentle. How would he deny himself the tender rapture he had found only with her? His lips thinned to a grim line, the muscles of his forearm cording as he squeezed the neck of the bottle. After the way he left her, he wouldn't have to worry. She would hate the very sight of him.

He turned the bottle up and drained it dry. Hours passed.

The music stopped. Lanterns sputtered out one by one. The roar of alligators quieted as dawn neared.

Bram made his none-too-steady way to his door. Hands ·clenched around the wrought iron handles, he bowed his head. He was a coward! What could one wisp of a girl do to a man his size? She wouldn't rage or shriek or scream. That wasn't Damask's way. No, she would just raise those soft cinnamon eyes, and deep within them would be the wound he had dealt her. Jesus, why had it hurt so much when she spoke of a *debt* after . . .

His shoulders began to shake with laughter. It was funny, the mighty and powerful Black Irish Rafferty, known to make brave men quake in their boots, was shrinking from the look in a woman's eyes!

A scuffing sound stilled his amusement. Bram listened, but heard nothing more. The door handles squeaked when he released them and turned away. At the head of the stairs he paused, digging in his vest pocket for a cigar, but his cigar case was in his coat—inside that room—and he didn't need anything bad enough to chance a meeting with Damask.

His booted foot lifted, swinging out over the first step. He felt the pressure of hands in his back, a hard rapid push that sent him tumbling and sliding. Sprawled across the brick sidewalk, he fought for breath, fingers digging at the bricks in an attempt to push himself up. He rested on one elbow, testing arms and legs to see if anything was broken, feeling his bruised ribs and trying to shake the fog from his head. Had he imagined that push? His eyes climbed the stairs, step by step, to the ruffle of taffeta that draped over the edge, and up to Damask's face.

Suddenly, Bram Rafferty was stone-cold sober.

SEVEN PINES PLANTATION
Mansfield, Louisiana

July 1859

Chapter 17

IT *was as if he viewed her through frost-rimmed glass. Those eyes,* pools of quiet caution, watched her until Damask thought she would go mad. The bitter rage that vibrated from him before he flung himself out of their room at Bonne Volonte was gone. Now he was withdrawn, polite, cautious.

Damask rocked with the jolting sway of the clattering buggy. Nightwind's and Prince's clopping hooves followed. He watched her. She could feel it as though he had reached out to trail a finger across her nape.

She closed her eyes, trying to piece together the scattered puzzle. *A debt!* The word stabbed into her consciousness now as it had then. Did he believe those ugly, hurtful, hateful things he shouted into the inky darkness? Was that how he saw her? A whore hawking her wares to pay her debt?

Too stunned for tears, she had sat through the endless hours of that night in the same position he had left her, staring at the French doors. It made no sense. She could only believe he meant every word, and that gave her the skin-crawling sensation of being soiled. Damask thought nothing could be worse, but it could.

Gray light striped the slatted doors. Footsteps approached, heavy and uncertain. The doorknob rattled, and her heart tapped drumrolls against her ribs. A shadow fell across the slats. She waited, a scream clawing at the back of her throat. The knob rattled once more, a step shuffled, and the shadow vanished.

He was leaving, without talking to her, without giving her

a chance to defend herself! Rage propelled her from the bed. Her numbed legs collapsed and she rubbed them frantically, groaning at the stinging needles of returning feeling. Scaling a chair, she whipped on her dressing gown and stumbled to the door. A wild rush carried her to the top of the stairs— only to stop and stare, anger smothered by concern. Bram was sprawled across the brick walk, his eyes climbing slowly to meet hers.

She flew down to kneel at his side, to touch him and to find out if he was hurt. No, he said in a slow careful voice while those eyes, dark with caution, watched—as he had watched her ever since.

Damask sighed and threaded her fingers and raised her haunted gaze. Home. She was going home. Nothing would seem so bad there.

The road to Seven Pines was narrow and lonely, a dim tunnel cooled by lanky pines and crowded by the tangled growth of honeysuckle and brambles. Squirrels frolicked overhead, rabbits hopped away into the depths of the forest, and once, the sharp little nose of a fox peered from the shadows of a thicket before he streaked away. They had not passed a house for miles, or seen a living soul, when the familiar landmarks of Seven Pines came into view.

"Dread! Stop the buggy! Lulu, we're home! Michael?" She called out, waiting while he pulled Prince to a halt by the tall spindly wheel. "What do you think of it?"

Her shining eyes danced from the white-washed snake-rail fence to the sun-dappled yard and the Big House; then west to the stable and the fields ringed by woodlands; then east to the huge barn with its maze of fences formed into lots, where cows and mules grazed on hay; and beyond, to the fields of cotton and corn and peas. Home.

"Ye haven't a neighbor, Lady?" Michael asked doubtfully.

"Of course. A few miles up the road. Isn't it wonderful, Michael?"

"Yes, Lady. Wonderful, to be sure."

"Hurry, Dread! Hurry!" she cried impatiently and the buggy jolted forward.

A quarter child, posted as a lookout atop the fence, scrambled down and raced toward the house shouting, "Miss Damask's home! Miss Damask's home!"

The buggy wheeled up the drive to the sound of the ringing plantation bell and the sight of the people of Seven Pines gathering to greet her. Damask thought her heart would burst with joy as she tumbled out into Harford's waiting arms. She sped through the growing crowd with a word for everyone, claiming the children had all grown a foot while she was gone.

"Ya'll git outa my way, young'uns!"

"Aunt Sarah!"

Damask was pulled into the soft cushion of her bosom, then held away while Aunt Sarah looked her up and down with a frown. "Master Bram, what you been doing to this child? She done got porely!"

Bram dismounted, making his way to her side. "She was homesick for your good cooking, Aunt Sarah. I'll expect you to see that she eats from now on."

"Sure enough will! Looks like a stringbean! But I'll get that fixed in two shakes of a rabbit's tail. You's looking porely yourself, Master Bram. Amarintha!" she hollered. "Back to the cookhouse, gal! Got to get some good eats for the table!"

Damask felt a tug on her skirt and looked down. "Sim!" She swept the toddler into her arms and whirled around and around in a swirl of skirts. Coming to a stop before Bram, she raised a bright, unshadowed smile. "Look! Look how he's grown! Isn't it wonderful? We're home!"

"Miss Damask!"

Regretfully, she turned away, wondering what they might have said to each other had they been alone.

"Child, child, you don't know how empty this old house can be."

"Jims!" Sim was passed to Johnson and she flew into Jims's arms.

He hugged her tightly, then held her away. "You's looking mighty peaked."

"Nothing that being home won't cure. How's Gramps?"

Jims's face clouded. "He ain't doing so good. I'm afraid he done took to his bed. Doc say he just gitten old and wore out."

Gramps. Her friend and teacher and mainstay. He couldn't be . . . not now when she needed his wisdom more than ever.

The smell of old age, compounded of decaying flesh and discarded dreams, brought Damask to a faltering halt inside the door. She searched the single room for some sign that the scent was false. "Gramps?"

The patchwork coverlet on the bed rippled and her name was murmured in a cracked and fading voice. Damask rushed to him, flinging herself down at his side. He had aged immeasurably in the short space of weeks, and seemed withered and ancient, lost beneath layers of quilts that obscured his shrunken outline. She leaned down to kiss his forehead and found the translucent flesh cold against her lips.

"Gramps? It's Damask. Can you hear me? I'm home."

"Damask?" Sunken eyes moved in the protuberant sockets, and a thin wrinkled hand struggled off his chest. Damask caught it, and pressed the frightfully frail and cold skin to her cheek. "You've come home, dear child. How are you?"

"Fine, Gramps. Fine." She kissed the flesh-covered claw that his hand had become. "I missed you. I promise, I won't ever leave you again."

"No," he said in a parched rattle. "No, you won't have to." He listened alertly to the sound of a step. "Who is here? Damask? Who is with you? That step . . ."

Damask glanced up through a haze of tears. "It's Bram, Gramps. He has come to say hello."

"Bram? Yes, Bram. A fine man. Damask?" His hand wrapped around her wrist with surprising strength. "Do you

remember what I told you? Look to your heart and you will
see him. Have you looked to your heart, child? Have you?''
She bowed her head, the brimming tears spilling down her
cheeks. ''Damask?''

''Yes, Gramps. Yes,'' she said thickly. ''I've looked to
my heart.''

He sighed and sank back onto the pillow, worried folds of
skin rearranging into lines of contentment. ''You are happy
then. I can go in peace. You are happy, child.''

Damask's eyes lifted slowly to Bram's tall, broad frame
at the opposite side of the bed. She found the eyes shaded to
dark sapphire and emptied of all expression.

''Yes, Gramps,'' she murmured brokenly. ''I'm happy.''
The fan of dark lashes sagged over her tear-scalded eyes,
and her head dropped onto the bed.

Cursing the weakness that led him to it, Bram knelt beside
her. ''Damask, leave him to Bif. This is not good for either
of you. Come, let him rest.''

Her fingers arched and dug into the quilts, and her head
shook. ''I need to stay!''

''He's tired, colleen. Let him rest.''

She would stay, and it wouldn't be good for either of
them. Bram, heart aching for the old man he had come to respect, caught her and swept her against his chest. One muffled protest sounded, and her arms wrapped around his neck
while he carried her to the Big House.

''Master Bram, that ain't Miss Damask's room no more.
We done fix up Old Master John and Miss Anna's room for
ya'll. At the back, 'cross the hall from your old room.''

''Get Lulu.''

He laid her on the intricate crocheted coverlet of the bed
her parents had shared, and hardened himself against the
memory of the last bed he had shared with her. She curled
up, rolling away from him.

Bram frowned and hovered, unable to make the decision
to leave her. He sank down beside her. ''Damask, if you
want me to go, I will. But I would like to help you if I can.''

She rolled onto her back, bonnet askew and the ribbon beneath her chin straggling. Swimming cinnamon eyes touched him and fled. "It isn't necessary. I know . . ." Her voice quaked out of control and she stopped and swallowed and Bram felt his own throat convulse. "I know how it . . . it disgusts you to be near me."

The soft words ripped through him. Oh, God, he thought weakly. Was that what she thought?

He pressed the heels of his hands to his forehead. "My disgust is not with you, Damask, but with myself. I've discovered it is no easy thing to use a woman like you to gain my own ends." He stood jerkily, half turned back to her, then strode toward the door. "I sent for Lulu."

"Bram!" He paused at the door, turning back with slow reluctance. "You . . . you do not think of me as a . . . a . . ."

"No!" He couldn't. In spite of everything, he couldn't.

"Thank God!" She breathed and sat up and, incredibly, stretched out her arms to him. "I need you, Bram."

Did she? Was this another trick to lull him? Did he care? No, not if he could hold her, just hold her close one more time.

Eager steps carried him to the bed, eager hands caught her and pulled her onto his lap, eager lips buried themselves beneath the brim of her bonnet knocking it aside to press against the coiling tendrils at her temple while she trembled against him.

Had he been so drunk he imagined that sharp shove? It was possible whoever did it slipped around the veranda before Damask came out of her room. She was not capable of the duplicity required to kill him the same night she responded to him with such passion.

And there had been passion. A soaring escape into ecstasy that he smirched with the filth of his accusation. Why had he done it? It was more than that sudden stunning parallel between Damask and his sister. It was almost as though he had been waiting for something he could use to spurn her!

He was terrified of that loss of control, and terrified that he had grown to need this woman as he had never needed another human being.

Her trembling stilled and she rolled her head along his arm, her brown eyes liquid with a fearful question. "He's going to die, isn't he, Bram?"

He stared down at her, wondering that she could look to him for comfort. His calloused thumb caressed her flushed cheek while he tried to formulate an answer that would give her no false hopes, yet would ease the pain of the inevitable.

"Your grandfather once told me that your grandmother's passing was a torment that would end only when he joined her. Think about it, Damask. For him death is not to be feared. Instead, it is a gateway to the loved ones he has lost."

"I'll miss him," she said tremulously.

"He will always be with you, colleen. Those we love live on in our hearts and thoughts. Close your eyes and you will see him. Listen to your memories and you will hear him. He will never be lost to you."

"How beautiful, Bram. I'll remember it." Her eyes were soft, her hand gentle on his cheek as she raised up to press a petal-soft kiss to his lips. "Thank you."

Every doubt, every thought fled. Bram crushed her to him with desperate longing, his lips slanting across hers to taste the tempting, teasing dimple.

"My, my, what have we here?"

Bram's head snapped up and Damask gasped.

Wade leaned an angular shoulder against the sill, giving them an arch look. "You look like you've seen a ghost, sister. Who else did you expect to find waiting for your return? I did leave Bonne Volonte before you, and arrived yesterday—without that hearty welcome you were accorded." His nostrils flared away from his thin nose. "I wondered what sent Lulu scurrying out of here. Couldn't you have the decency to wait for night? I would think you would have gotten more than enough of each other already."

Bram felt the slow slide of Damask's hand falling away

from his nape and coming to a rest on his chest. She had gone rigid in his arms, as rigid as he.

"Do I call you Brother now?" Wade asked snidely.

"Bram will do if you think Mr. Rafferty too formal."

"I believe sharper or cheat would be more appropriate."

"Wade! Get out of here! Get out!" Damask lurched off of Bram's lap screaming, and Wade backed away, hurrying down the hall without another word. She tugged off her bonnet, holding it by the ribbons, while her shoulders sank in defeat. "I will speak to him," she said dispiritedly.

"You should rest. The trip was long . . ."

"No!" She whirled around, eyes huge, and made a nervous, negative gesture, as though she would take back the vehemence with which she had shouted. "I'm sorry. You must be tired, too." Her gaze drifted to the bed, then swept the room. "Why did you bring me here?"

He stood. "Our things have been moved in here. Jims thought it would be what we wanted since this was the room your parents shared."

"I see." Her eyes searched his face.

Seconds ticked away to minutes, while his eyes remained riveted on hers. Useless pride locked his tongue against any expression of desire and need. The frail bond linking them together had been shattered by Wade, and Bram had neither the courage nor the confidence in her or himself to weave it anew.

He wrenched his eyes from her, pushed his hands in his pockets, and strolled to the door. There he stopped, staring into the room opposite. "I will have Jims move my things back to my old room."

Behind him, Damask blanched. His steps echoed away down the hall and she lurched to the window to see a scene she had envisioned often in the weeks she was away. Amarintha snapping beans in the shade outside the cookhouse. The quarter children playing beneath the pines. Harford descending the red ocher path. A curl of smoke from the cookhouse chimney pointing a lazy finger at the sky.

She viewed it all with numbed detachment, heart and

mind frozen by the terrible conviction that Bram had lied to her. Out of kindness, perhaps, but he had lied nonetheless. He did believe those hideous things he had shouted at her in the inky night with the musky smell of their lovemaking hanging in the warm air. And she had had so little pride she flung herself at him, forcing him to lie to her!

She must find a way to hide her love. It was not fair to Bram to inflict her weaknesses upon him. She must never touch him, never intrude her presence upon him, never follow him with her eyes. Her heart twisted. Where would she find the courage? Never to watch him, to see the fluid ripple of those strong muscles across his shoulders or the bulging power of his arms. Never to study his beautiful hands. Never again to know the ecstasy they shared. Even now she could feel the feathery touch of his palms smoothing down her shoulder, the ravishing tenderness of his lips, the surging tempest that wooed her soul from her body.

Damask pressed her fists to her lips. There was nothing left to her but pride. Her pride and Seven Pines. It would be her lover, her companion, her strong shield against the emptiness of her days.

A restless urgency impelled her into the hall, where she found Nero exiting Wade's room, his arms filled with clothes. "Nero, that can wait for a day or two. It's been a long, tiring trip for us all."

His dark, hooded eyes dropped. "Master Wade say that body servant Mister Scarborough lend him didn't do nothing what he like. He want them all cleaned today."

He began to turn away and Damask saw the deep gouge, seeping blood along his jaw. "Nero, how did you do that? Let me see it."

"Ain't nothing! Ain't nothing!" he said agitatedly, gripping the clothes and pulling away from her.

"It is something, Nero. It needs to be seen to."

"Please, Miss Damask. Please! Master Wade, he—"

Damask caught his arm, and his eyes darted about wildly. "Nero, did Wade do this to you?"

"Don't say nothing, Miss Damask. Please, don't say nothing. He kill me for sure!"

"No, he won't. Go have Lulu look at that, and put those clothes back. You need a rest and you'll have it."

She hurried down the stairs. What manner of man was her brother? He had been raised with everything he could need; Bram had grown up with nothing. If Bram were bitter or cruel or heartless, it could be understood. But Wade?

"Miss Damask—" Jims caught her at the bottom. "I hates to bother you with this, but I got to know what to tell Master Bram."

"Jims, could it wait? I've got to find Wade."

"But this about Master Wade. Master Bram left a whole wad of money with me to pay for the shingles when they come from Shreveport. They come, but I ain't had no money to pay for 'em. Miss Damask, Master Wade took that money for his trip down-river, and I don't know what to tell Master Bram. He bound to be asking when he see the roof ain't shingled yet."

Cruelty. Thievery. What else? Damask wondered. Did she know as little about the brother she had lived with all of her life as she had about Bram Rafferty on his arrival at Seven Pines?

"Tell Wade I want to see him in the parlor. Now."

Damask took a seat in the wingback chair, arranging the folds of her muslin skirt and resting her hands in her lap, as if outward appearances of calm could ease the tension that quivered inside her.

"I have been summoned to the august presence?"

Wade stood before her, thumbs hooked into his pockets as he rocked back and forth on his heels. "Sit down, Wade. There are things we must discuss."

"Oh?" He slumped onto the sofa, thin legs stretched out before him. "I understand your husband will not be sharing your room. Has he grown tired of you already? I shouldn't be surprised. You threw yourself at him like a shameless wanton at Bonne Volonte."

Tactless. She always thought Wade was tactless, but he wasn't. He was . . . cruel, deliberately, maliciously cruel. She flinched away from a battering barrage of images. Wade slapping America when she was too slow in serving him. Wade taunting Tessa. Wade lashing out at a playful kitten that had scratched him. And later—Oh, God!— later, that same kitten found limping and mewling and bleeding, its claws jerked out. How could she have forgotten those things?

"I have not asked you here to discuss my marriage." Damask studied him as she would have a stranger for whom she developed an inexplicable antipathy. "You have harmed Nero."

Wade sat up, something ugly and threatening in his hunched shoulders. "Did he tell you that?"

"He didn't have to. I saw him."

"Then you saw wrong, and if he told you I hit him, he was lying! Who will you believe? A slave or your own brother!"

Who will you believe? How often had Wade hurled that question at her? How often had he been lying, as he was now? She felt as if she was really seeing him for the first time. Had he always used her love and trust to have his way?

"Neither Bram nor I will permit any abuse of the people here, Wade. You will remember that in the future or the doors of Seven Pines will be closed to you." His eyes widened with shock, and for the first time, Damask spared him no pity. "I understand you have stolen the money Bram left with Jims."

He jerked up, his face blotching with streaks of red. "Stolen! I merely took what was rightfully mine! Have you forgotten what he did? Cheating us of Seven Pines!"

"No, Wade," Damask said with a calm that surprised her, "Bram did not cheat you."

"Pah! You know nothing!" Wade leapt up, glaring down at her. "I tell you he cheated me! I am your brother, after all! You owe me your loyalty!"

"Yes, you are my brother, and I do owe you loyalty. But

not the blind, thoughtless loyalty I've given you in the past. I am nothing if I'm not honest with myself and those around me. My husband is an honorable, decent man who would never stoop to thievery—as you have done.''

"How can you speak to me like this?" he lashed out. "Have you become so cold and heartless, so enamored of that gambler that you have forgotten your family obligations?''

"It won't work, Wade. I know what my obligations are, and where my loyalties lie.''

"He owed me that money, Damask!''

"He owes nothing to a single member of this family, least of all you.''

"Owes me nothing!" Wade shouted. "This should all be mine! *Mine!* And it will be again! You wait and see!''

It was there in his eyes, the same look she had seen at the picnic in the *ile.* The expression combined malicious hatred with the smug look of one who holds a well-loved secret. An expression that was almost . . . almost evil.

A thought occurred to her. A thought that held the same nose-wrinkling stench as the pus oozing from Bram's wounded arm. Chills clambered across her skin and sank deep into bone and marrow.

She groped for a memory that wavered indistinctly in the back of her mind. A sound. When she had rushed from her room, she had heard a sound like leaves brushing across the roof, but there had been no hint of a breeze. It couldn't have been leaves. It was a furtive sound, like muffled, hurried footsteps!

Bram Rafferty, no matter how drunk, would not fall down a flight of stairs unaided. She had seen him far drunker at Dublin, yet he had dismounted his horse and walked to their bedroom unaided. There was only one explanation. He had been pushed.

An algid finger of horror prodded her upright. After she had flown down those stairs to kneel at his side, his voice had been slow and careful, his eyes dark with caution—because he thought she had done it! That was why he had watched her ever since! He thought she was capable of giving herself to him in one moment and trying to murder him the next!

There was only one person at Bonne Volonte who could benefit from Bram's death or injury. Only one person who could have hired the Caswells.

Damask's eyes, dark and hopeless, clung to Wade as if she could peel aside the veneer of civilization to see the soul beyond. His lip crested in a sneer, and she shrank back against the chair, nausea churning in her stomach. She knew she was right.

Wade was her brother. What touched him must touch her. The evil in him reflected on her. But was he evil? He was so much like a child pummeled by uncontrollable emotions; and like a child, he yielded to those impulses, never thinking before he acted. He always regretted the hurt he caused. He told her so, weeping and pleading for forgiveness, moaning, "If only Mama were here . . ."

Tangled in her own emotions of grief and guilt, her anger and indignation had always melted away. But murder! That could not be explained away in a torrent of weeping remorse!

She had to face the fact that Wade was capable of murder, but what could she do? How could she choose between the man she loved, who neither needed nor wanted her, and the brother she had wronged, who needed her now more than ever?

Her trust in him was gone, but the love was still there, feeble, but alive, a pitiful tenacious remnant that struggled to hold on to her old perception of Wade, despite everything to the contrary. He was her brother. Her blood. She could not abandon him entirely. Neither could she stand aside while he harmed her husband.

She stood, slowly, stiffly. Bracing her fingers across the arm of the chair, she met his eyes unflinchingly. "If you harm Bram in any way, I will see that you never receive another penny from Seven Pines for as long as you live! You are my brother, and you can stay here—on sufferance! If anything—*anything!*—endangers Bram, I will see that you leave here and never return. If he should be—'' Her eyes dropped briefly, then climbed once again to meet his, the color hard and polished with resolve. ''If he should be killed, I will see you hang.''

Wade's face paled to a pasty white, his eyes huge and disbelieving. ''You chose that gambler over your own brother? Is there no room in your heart for your family, for me?''

''Wade, love is not like a measure of sugar, so much and no more. Neither is it to be spent frivolously. Love is respect, and respect is earned. Bram Rafferty has earned my respect, and I will stop at nothing to protect him—from anyone!''

Something slimy coiled deep in Wade's eyes. ''Are you accusing me of trying to murder your husband?''

''Yes. I'm not interested in your denials. I'm warning you that it had better not happen again.''

He smiled, a smile that sent a *frisson* of fear scrabbling down Damask's spine. ''I assure you I will do nothing to harm the gambler you love so much. A pity he doesn't love you, isn't it?''

With that parting shot he strolled from the room whistling a merry tune, and Damask sank into the chair and dropped her head into her hands.

''He's wrong, Lady.''

Damask looked up into Michael's steady indigo eyes. ''You heard?''

''He's wrong about the Mister, Lady. Ye've had yer family around ye all yer years. 'Tis hard for ye to be understanding what it is for a man to be alone. When ye have no one to call yer own, ye get to thinking ye don't really need no one. Then, when someone does come along, ye can't be letting go of the notion. Ye think it won't last because it never lasted before. D'ye see, Lady?''

''Yes, Michael, I do see. But things are not quite that simple with Mr. Rafferty and myself.''

''But they are, Lady! The Mister's a stubborn man, but he

loves ye! He loves ye so much he daren't do nothing but deny it! If ye'll just be having some patience with him, he'll be admitting to it. I know he will!''

"Oh, Michael," Damask sighed. She didn't believe him about Bram. Love was trust and respect, and Bram Rafferty neither trusted nor respected her. But her heart was torn by pity for what she had learned about Michael himself.

"Are ye going to tell the Mister about yer brother?''

"No, I don't think it would serve any useful purpose. Mr. Rafferty knows to be careful. But I do have an idea that I'm sure will work. Would you like to walk with me to the quarters? You can meet our people there, and hear what I'm doing. You might be able to help.''

Chapter 18

CHORES *were done and breakfast was over when the slaves of* Seven Pines began converging on the grassy expanse in back of the Big House. It was an obviously puzzled group that gathered on the orders of the new master, and there was much shuffling and whispering as Damask stepped onto the porch.

Dressed in a gold-checked gingham that was simple and cool for a day that promised to turn blazing hot, she made her way to the nearest rocker and sank down onto the cowhide seat. Harford's inquiring look drew a smile and a lift of her brows that said she knew no more about this than he did.

Michael came to stand at her left, his freshly scrubbed face flushing beneath the curious scrutiny of that sea of other faces.

And then Bram, tall and dark, his face molded in lines of solemnity, took a place behind and to the right of the rocker, one strong hand resting on the uppermost slat, the other thrust into his pocket.

His ice blue eyes moved slowly, touching one face, then another with a look of cool assessment. He hesitated a moment, his eyes dropping to the soft waves of Damask's hair, pulled back into a dark brown snood.

"Today is the Fourth of July, 1859. Independence Day," Bram began. "I've called you here to tell you that I will be making some changes at Seven Pines that will affect all of you. First, you will no longer work on the gang system. Your work will be divided into tasks according to your ability. When your task is done for the day, your time will be your own. Second, I am setting aside one acre for every man and woman over the age of seventeen. This will be your land, to be worked singly or as a group effort as you wish. You may plant whatever you choose, and I will furnish the seed for this first year. For those of you who plant corn, I'll buy it from you unless you can get a better price elsewhere. If you plant cotton, I'll sell it for you through my factor in the City. The time spent working this land will be your free time, after your tasks are completed for the day. If I find anyone shirking my work, his or her acre will be returned to me for a period of two seasons. Third, if any of you wish to hire yourselves out on the weekends to neighboring planters, you have my permission to do so. If any of you are interested in learning a trade, discuss it with Harford first, then both of you come to me.

"Now, you will have several methods of earning money of your own. If you wish to keep it yourselves, that is up to you. If you wish to place it in our safekeeping, I will ask Miss Damask to keep a ledger book with a page for each of you. At any time, she will be able to tell you how much you have accumulated and give you any or all of it as you wish."

Bram fell silent, his hand gripping the slat with white-knuckled tension. Once again his eyes fell to Damask's hair, shimmering with gold and taffy lights. A frown touched his face and was gone. His eyes lifted once more to the gathered crowd and he drew a breath.

"There may be some among you who want to buy your freedom. If you wish to do so, come to me. I will tell you how much you are worth and help you in any way I can to achieve that end."

He caught a movement from the corner of his eye and looked down. Damask stared up at him. Her face was still, her eyes wide with that expression of perfect tranquility that he was beginning to feel would drive him to madness. Was there no life, no anger, no hope left within her?

Her lips moved. Whether it was a smile of approval or a grimace of anger, Bram could not tell. Her dark lashes swooped down over her eyes, and her head dipped before she turned back to face her people. Did she agree with what he was doing, he wondered, or did she simply accept what she had no control over?

He should have consulted her or, at the very least, informed her about his plans. But how could he when she had withdrawn from him so completely? Wherever he was, she wasn't.

"The Downings from Blackberry Hill and their people will be joining us for the celebration today. Enjoy your holiday."

They began drifting away, whispering among themselves, the air crackling with the tension of suppressed excitement. Bram waited while Damask stood, her back to him as she watched the dispersing crowd. She turned slowly. He saw the outline of her cheek, then her profile, then her full face tilted up to him, her eyes glowing with approval.

Relief rushed through him, coursing with such power it left him feeling weak and giddy.

"You do everything for their good," she said, her voice soft and warm, and wafting against him like a loving, tender caress. "Thank you."

He wanted to speak, to say something, anything. But longing pressed in a solid lump at the back of his throat and stilled his tongue.

She moved to step around him, and the subtle suggestion of violets traveled a current of air and snapped the shackle of restraint. "Damask," he said, surprised at the husky throb of his own voice.

She paused, a shadow hovering in her eyes, a shadow so near fear it made his heart ache. He reached up and put his hand on her shoulder and felt her go rigid. His forefinger lifted and drifted to the arch of her neck. It touched and trembled and moved down the warm honey-toned flesh to the lace collar. Her lashes fluttered over her eyes and she swayed and a ragged breath shuddered between her parted lips.

"Damask, I—"

"Don't touch me, Bram," she whispered, a tortured gaze raised to his. "Don't touch me. I cannot bear your touch."

Longing was gone. There was nothing left but shock and a sick feeling and his hand lingering on her shoulder as though it refused to move. Then she was gone, fleet steps growing quieter, and he was alone with Michael staring up at him with sad, wise eyes.

"Sir, she—"

"Not now, Michael. Not now."

The steps squeaked beneath his feet, and the clipped grass gave off the aroma of watermelons as he strode toward the nearby field with its tall green cotton. A shaking hand pulled the chased silver cigar case from his pocket. Soon, he sucked in a bracing curl of smoke and turned to look back at the house.

His eyes lifted to the second floor porch, where Nero hung over the railing staring down toward the quarters. His usual expression of passivity was gone, and his teeth were bared in a grimace of commingled pain and rage, his hooded eyes starting from the sunken sockets in his skull-like face. Nero, Bram thought with regret, the only Downing slave who would not be given his chance for freedom.

A white hand suddenly hooked over Nero's upper arm and he was jerked around. A cold chill of apprehension tingled up Bram's spine when he saw Nero flare like a vulture preparing to tear into his prey. The impression was gone as soon as it came. Nero's rage subsided, his body shrinking into its sparse lines, thick lids dropping to shield his expression. But the impression of docility implied in his meekly bowed head was belied by the relentless severity of the lines in his spare stick of a body as he turned his back on the yard and stepped into the house.

Behind him, Wade propped his hands on the horizontal railing, eyes sweeping from the quarters to Bram. He smiled, a wolfish smile of such rapacity and hate it brought a cold sweat to Bram's brow. The icy trickles dropped stinging salt into his eyes, yet he could not blink, nor look away until Wade straightened and strolled into the house, leaving the merry notes of his whistling floating on the hot still air.

Wade Downing. Bram had classified him as weak, and had promptly ignored him. Only Damask, he had thought, possessed both the reason and the strength of will to see him murdered. But she didn't have the heart for it. He knew that now.

However, Downing did. The weak could have a formidable strength. He threatened Wade Downing's comfortable existence; Downing would need no more reason than that.

It had been a mistake, ignoring him. He had all but accused Damask. Thank God, he hadn't gone so far as to actually do it. But he had done worse. He had shut her out. He had distrusted her. And now he reaped the bitter reward of his own actions.

The sound of a wagon rattling up the drive pulled Damask down the hall. She burst onto the porch and rushed down the steps, her arms outstretched.

"Tessa!"

Before the wagon could pull to a complete stop, Tessa jumped off the wagon bed shrieking Damask's name. They met in a flurry of skirts that lifted a small dust cloud. Question cut across question; answers were muffled by hugs.

Damask, flushed with happiness, saw Bram coming down the steps. Her smile quivered and vanished. "Tessa's home," she said softly.

Tessa tore out of Damask's arms and flung herself at Bram's chest, nearly bowling him over. His grave, almost sad expression was obliterated by a pleased smile as he swung her into the air.

Wishing that she dared to be as free with her affection as Tessa, Damask turned to greet her cousins.

"I'll be picking straw from my hair and gown the whole day!" Jane Downing complained with a merry twinkle. "But I could not resist the idea of a moonlight hayride back to Blackberry Hill tonight. Much more appropriate for you newlyweds."

Damask hugged her. "I have a nice fruit punch cooling in the spring house."

"Wonderful! I'm parched!"

Michael stood on the porch, looking uncertain and a little lost, and Damask hurried to him. "Do come. I want you to meet everyone." Taking his hand, she led him to her sister. "This is Michael O'Malley, Tessa. He has come to live with us. Michael, this is my sister, Tessa."

Tessa's round brown eyes widened. "Are you my new brother that Damask wrote about?"

Michael's eyes moved to Damask and she nodded. "Yes, he is."

Tessa's sweet smile lit her face, and her pale gold ringlets bobbed merrily as she leaned over to kiss Michael's cheek, leaving his face almost as red as his carroty curls. "I'm glad. Damask and me always wanted lots of brothers."

Damask introduced Michael to her cousins, John Robert and Jane Downing, and Garnett Lee Downing. "I'm going to let you and the girls introduce yourselves. Would you mind taking them around to see the tables we've set up?" Michael flung her such a look of horror she had to chew her lip to keep from laughing.

Her dancing eyes met Bram's in a brief moment of communion. The corners of his lips trembled and he coughed behind his hand, then leaned down to Michael. "A gentleman always sees that the ladies are entertained. You can take them to see Prince if you like, and ask Aunt Sarah for some cookies and milk."

Michael's indigo eyes silently pleaded, but Bram gave a short shake of his head. Thin shoulders reared back in the attitude of an onerous duty that he would perform to the best of his ability. Michael bowed politely in the direction of the five Downing girls, and swept his arm toward the side of the house. "Ladies, if ye please."

They disappeared around the corner and Jane Downing hooked her arm through Damask's. "I do believe he would rather have cut off his arm! That look was priceless! He's a handsome child. A relative of yours, Mr. Rafferty?"

"No, Michael is an orphan. We found him in the City, or"—his eyes, laden with memories, moved to Damask—"I should say he found us."

Memories. There were so few, Damask thought. So few to last a lifetime. She urged Jane into the house with a promise of cool fruit punch, the men following. While Jims served them, she tried not to watch Bram, but found it impossible. Why had he touched her? She could still feel that caress feathering down the side of her neck. It had aroused such a fire for love she had been afraid she would lose all pride and throw herself into his arms begging him to believe her.

"Damask? Damask!"

"Yes, Jane," she said with a start of surprise.

"I asked if you've told Samson."

"Samson? I don't understand."

"Why, that Mr. Rafferty has bought Patience and Affy! They are bringing their things with them today." Damask gaped blankly and Jane laughed, her harum-scarum curls bobbing drunkenly. "I see he wanted to surprise you, too. He made the arrangements with John the day you were married."

Why, when she had lost him forever, did she realize how much she loved him, how worthy he was of that love? Her sorrow grew, a painful throbbing in her breast, filling her to the exclusion of all else.

Bram looked up and her eyes dropped to her lap. Soon, soon it would be easier. When she had more practice at hiding her feelings, at submerging the torrent of longing for him beneath a more practical exterior. It had to get easier. The conversation buzzed around her incomprehensibly, until—"War! Garnett Lee Downing! Whatever are you talking about?"

"Now, now, Jane." A rattling cough punctuated the breathless murmur. "Garnet Lee is right, my dear. The abolitionists will not rest until they've pushed us into defending our rights."

"John, I know that ridiculous book by that Stowe woman

has the Yankees stirred up against us, but . . . war? The very idea is incredible!'' Her warm rich laugh trilled out. ''You men!'' she scoffed in the way of women everywhere.

Bram believed war would come, Damask thought. And if it did, she would exchange the torment of being near him for the terror of fearing for his life.

''It's nothing to laugh about, Jane.'' Garnett Lee paced across the room, puffing his cigar to light it and tossing the match into the fireplace. ''I met a Yankee in the City last summer. He thought it amusing when I assured him the South would not hesitate to secede were we pushed further. He said we have threatened secession once too often. There are few left who believe it is more than an idle threat we use to have our own way. I don't mind telling you, it frightened me.''

Bram would leave, perhaps be killed, and the promise born in the depths of a feather tick at Bonne Volonte would never be realized.

''Really,'' came Wade's sharp voice. ''War? Nonsense! Those Yankee merchants would not stand for a halt to their profitable trade.''

She prayed he was right so that Bram would remain at Seven Pines for her to love from afar, and Michael would grow to manhood, the child of her heart, the heir to her home.

''I'm not so sure of that, they—''

Damask shot to her feet. ''Don't you think we should go outside? I'm sure the tables are ready now.'' Garnett Lee, interrupted so abruptly, stared, and Damask went to him, linking her arm through his. ''Aunt Sarah says no one likes a young hog the way you do, so she's having an extra shoat roasted. Your very own.''

Garnett Lee's thick hand covered hers, a grin splitting his kindly face. ''Well, let's get out there. I'm starving!''

Damask looked around the room, carefully avoiding Bram. ''Do come. It's too nice a day to stay cooped up inside like setting hens.''

* * *

A cool breeze stirred sluggishly beneath the pines. Tables covered with checkered cloths groaned beneath the weight of platters of steaming biscuits and fresh baked bread; crockery bowls of snap beans, fried corn, butterbeans, and field peas; jars of apple jelly, persimmon jelly, and blackberry jam; cakes and cobblers and pies. There seemed to be no end to the food, and room still had to be made for rashers of roast beef and pork. And in the spring, watermelons and canteloupes were cooling. Master rubbed elbows with slave, black child with white child, and the good-natured wrangling that accompanied those initial frantic minutes of piling plates high gave way to the sounds of clinking forks, groans of pleasure, and sighs of contentment.

The afternoon drifted by lazily. Most of the children hurried away from the table to play, Tessa and the Downing girls joining them. But Michael stayed at Damask's side, listening to her talking to her cousin while Bram talked to the men. He had been up early, wild with excitement about his first holiday at Seven Pines. He had eaten until he was stuffed, and the longer he sat the drowsier he got. Soon he was leaning against Damask.

She hooked her arm around him when he fell asleep and began to slide. Smoothing the fiery curls away from his forehead, she pressed a kiss to his warm brow.

"Bram," she murmured, reaching out to pluck his sleeve.

He turned to look at her, and his eyes dropped to Michael. "He's had a long day."

"Yes. Could we carry him inside and put him to bed?"

Bram lifted Michael, and Damask hurried ahead, up the path and into the house, rushing up the stairs to fold back the cover on Michael's bed. He was as limp as unstarched linen while they undressed him and pulled off his boots. Their hands touched just once, and Damask gasped, jerking away.

After that Bram was careful to avoid any contact with her. This renewed evidence that she could not bear his touch festered within him, and the companionable silence turned grim.

Outside Michael's door, Bram stopped to watch her. Michael stirred, half waking, and she leaned down to hum a soothing lullaby. There was such a tender, loving look on her face, Bram had to look away and swallow the lump that came to his throat.

What had happened? he wondered. She could not look at him. She could not bear his touch. If he came in to a room, she left it as quickly as she decently could. The only time she would sit still, and that not easily, was when they shared their meals. Then she smeared her food all over her plate, taking a bite only when Jims or Michael urged it on her. If he asked her a question, she answered—but in a voice that rustled like dead leaves scraping across a winter field. If she was forced, through politeness, to smile, it was an empty thing void of the essence that was her.

It seemed she now hated the idea of being married to him so much she was killing herself by inches. Jesus! He wanted her. She was seared into his mind, taste, touch, smell. A burning brand that blazed through the long nights of tossing on his lonely bed—and knowing she was close, so close, yet so far.

I need you, Bram. She had really said it. Had she meant it? Could he take any hope from it? No, she had just learned her grandfather was dying. He could not use that weakness to bind her to him. What could he use?

The thought that sprang to his mind was so startling he jerked up with a surprised grunt. Love! Love? He must be crazy! He loved no woman, nor did he want any woman to love him! He wanted . . . he wanted . . . what?

He wanted to see her smile, from her heart. He wanted to see her with that radiant glow that was so uniquely hers. He wanted . . .

Hell! He didn't know what he wanted!

Damask came to the door.

He shouldn't do it. He knew it, but the compulsion was irresistible. He reached out too touch her arm. She shied away, eyes clinging stubbornly to the floor, and he was left, his outstretched hand slowly clenching into a fist.

Chapter 19

IT *was mid-August. The sun-seared earth slapped hot against the* soles of Damask's bare feet. The hem of her oldest dress swished around her ankles, and her sunbonnet lay limp against her back, the calico bow pulling across the base of her neck. She wandered from the shade of the pines to the first row of cotton in the Gin Field.

The bright green, deep-toothed leaves were dusted with the reddish tint of the soil. She fingered a fragile bloom with the delicate appearance of a hibiscus. The rich, cream-colored petals had unfurled in the cool of the morning before the sun rose. By tomorrow morning the color would be shaded to a delicate pink that would gradually darken throughout the day. By sundown, it would be a rich red and the petals would fall off, leaving the tiny green form that would develop into a hard wood-textured boll.

Beside the bloom was a dark boll beginning to split. Damask tugged at the stem to peek through the spreading points where the hint of the white cotton lint showed. The field had been picked late in the past week, but it was already beginning to look like a carpet of green scattered with white fleece.

"Swing low, sweet chariot, coming for to carry me . . ."

Damask watched Dread swinging down the rows, head and shoulders above the cotton. His voice, deep and melodic, vibrated across the hot field. It was a sad song, usually, sung slowly with every drop of sorrow wrung from every note. But not the way he sang it, with that wide smile and joyous timbre. Dread, whom Damask had never heard sing, and had seldom seen smile.

Bram. Everything came full circle to Bram. Damask thought back to her days at Dublin. No sad, chanting refrains drifted across the humid air there. Only lighthearted songs of cheer, the slaves attending their work with squared shoulders and springy steps. Now, she was seeing that at Seven Pines.

Her people had never been sullen or sad, but there was a difference now. It was pride, the same pride she had seen in those dark faces at Dublin. The men stood straighter. The women held their heads higher. Their eyes were brighter, livelier, perhaps because of the promise of freedom, however distant.

Whatever it was, the words *Master Bram* were endowed with magic. The shabby gentility that had defaced Seven Pines was gone. It was obviously a working plantation, and every corner showed evidence of his meticulous care. He conferred often with Jims and Harford, listening respectfully to all they had to say.

And Tessa. Bram's name was a talisman against tantrums and willfulness. A frown puckered Damask's forehead. Did her own eyes betray that same worshipful adoration that Tessa's did?

If only Wade would drop his sneering attitude and those constant, wearing, sniping attacks on everyone. As if the oppressive summer heat was not enough, they all had to contend with Wade. Everyone had become edgy and jumpy in his presence. Tessa occasionally burst into tears over nothing. And Michael grew quieter by the day. Even Bram was not unaffected, though he visibly clenched his teeth over what he might have said, and spent as much time away from the house, day and night, as he could.

There were things to be thankful for. There had been no further attempts to harm Bram, raising the hope that Wade had accepted Bram's new position. Just as satisfying was the fact that she had not betrayed herself. She kept Bram's house clean, had his favorite foods served, mended his clothes herself—the only sewing she could settle to. It was the only time she felt close to him, holding the fabric that had touched his skin. The tiniest rip took hours because she drifted away so often to those few happy times they shared.

She never intruded her presence on him, and only saw him at mealtimes or those few occasions when he sought her out to discuss the business of the plantation or to see if she wanted to go to town with him.

Hungry for the work she loved, she drank in his every word and offered what advice he asked for, then returned to the duties she adhered to with a regimen that pronounced them just that—duties. The satisfaction to be gained from keeping the house clean, overseeing the harvest and storage of vegetables and fruits, planning meals and tending the sick in the quarters was minimal. But to involve herself in the work of the crops would put her into direct and painful contact with Bram, and that she could not do.

Though it was her dearest wish to go with him into Mansfield for a day of shopping, she always refused, assuring herself he was only being polite.

It was easier during the week when they were going their separate ways, but her resolve was sorely tested every Sunday when they were thrown together for long hours. Riding to church in the buggy, sitting through the long sermon, and going to Blackberry Hill for a picnic with her cousins or having them return to Seven Pines were exquisite torture. Sometimes, she had to clench her hands to resist the impulse to touch him. She ached to brush her fingers along his broadcloth sleeve, no more than that. When he helped her out of the buggy, the touch of his hand on hers siphoned both energy and will, leaving her light-headed and breathless.

At least she had Tessa and Michael. Tessa with her incessant chatter and her eagerness to sit beside Bram. Michael with those wise indigo eyes. Sometimes she could not hold that solemn gaze, and his small hand would pat hers in that strangely adult way he had.

Damask sighed and raked her toe through the dirt. She

should be proud that she was molding herself into the kind of wife Bram wanted. He told her once that they would share nothing but Seven Pines and the son that would be its heir. The son had turned out to be Michael, whom she could not love more had he been born of her body. He had become child and brother and friend. Somehow, somewhere, she had lost that urgent need to pass Seven Pines on to a child of her own. Was it because Michael was the son her father could have loved? So much different from . . .

Her eyes lifted to the bright sky, agitated fingers mangling the frail petals of the cotton bloom.

"Miss Damask! Miss Damask!"

"Joe, what's wrong?"

The child hopped up and down with excitement, his thin arm pointing toward the band of trees beyond the snake-rail fence. "Christabelle done got her horns caught in a forked tree again! Grandpappy say they in so tight they ain't nothing to do but cut down one side of that tree!"

"That's dangerous!"

"Yessum, that's why he say for you to come see."

He took off at a run and Damask lifted her skirts to follow. The shrieking voices of the children reached her before she turned the arch of a long curve and saw them peeping through the slats and hanging over the top rail, their shrill voices offering bits of giggling advice. Damask climbed the fence and Moses plucked her off the top rail, but her skirt caught on a splinter and he held her until it was loosened for her. She looked back.

Bram held the hem of her skirt pinched between his fingers. She squelched the oh so familiar bubble of joy she experienced at the sight of him. Calmly nodding her thanks, she turned away.

Christabelle lowed mournfully, her gold tail with its brush of dark hair at the tip swishing back and forth while she moved from side to side like a stick on a swivel. Damask knelt and rubbed her brown nose.

"Christabelle, you naughty girl. Why does everything you see through the fork of a tree look so good to you?"

"I tell you, Miss Damask"—Harford squatted beside her—"me and Moses done everything we know. Tried lard. Didn't work. Tried to prize 'em outa there. Wedged in too tight. I done sent to the New Clearing for the crosscut saw. I know it's dangerous but we can tie a rope around the trunk and pull when it start to fall."

"Good. Do you think we should cut off her horns after this? That cross stick we tied around her neck hasn't done any good. This is the third time she's managed this trick since she started wearing it."

"Well, I expect so," he grinned, " 'less you want to cut down every forked tree—"

"Pappy! Grandpappy!" The voices of the children blended as one. "Run! Run! Here come Plumb Mean!"

Bram, instantly alert, followed the line of the pointing hands to a rustling thicket of brambles. A long wicked-looking horn tossed up and through, followed by its twin. The cantankerous bull burst through the thicket with an exasperated bellow and Bram sprinted for Damask, swept her into his arms, and raced to a nearby pine. Throwing her onto a low-growing limb, he vaulted up beside her a split second before the bull thundered past below them.

"Harford! Moses!" Damask called out, as she clung to the trunk with her dusty bare feet dangling.

"I'm over here on the fence, Miss Damask," Moses answered. "But it look like Plumb Mean done treed Pappy like a possum—again!"

There was a burst of laughter from Moses, and Damask smiled, raising sparkling eyes to Bram. "Poor Harford, his boys have teased him unmercifully since Plumb Mean treed him last fall."

"That dadgum bull!" Harford raged from a sweet gum close by. "I'll git him this year for sure! And that's a promise! You hear me, you mangy varmint! Come slaughtering time, I'll git you for true!"

Below them Plumb Mean trotted around his newly secured domain with an arrogant swagger. His great horns, festooned with a webbing of briars, swung from side to side and he snorted with a cocky belligerence.

"Moses!" Bram shouted. "Bring three ropes from the stable!"

"Yes, sir! Hang on tight! Young uns! Stay away from this fence if ya'll don't want that bull coming through it."

Damask, eyes brimming with merriment, watched the restless bull. Her cheeks were flushed, and a smudge of dirt covered the tip of her nose. She was a mess with straggling hair and ripped seams. She had never looked more beautiful or more desirable to Bram.

Her cinnamon eyes met his and his heart lurched in his chest. "You won't let Harford slaughter him, will you?"

"No," he muttered thickly, wishing she were an ugly, ill-tempered shrew he could actively dislike.

"Master Bram, ya'll sit tight," Moses called out, as Johnson clambered onto the fence. "We'll rope that critter and tie him to a tree."

"Throw one to me," Bram shouted back.

"They can do it." Damask clutched at his arm, her eyes dark with concern. "They have experience with Plumb Mean."

Her hand was small and fair against his dark arm peppered thickly with black hair. Bram stared at it, unable to raise his eyes to meet hers.

"You ready, sir?"

"Throw it!" Bram caught the coiled rope, dexterously fashioning a sliding loop. "Harford, keep him busy for a few minutes."

"Sure enough! Hey, you mangy critter! Just wait for slaughtering time! Stringy meat for my table!" Harford threw a stick, and Plumb Mean snorted, pawed the ground, and let out an earth-shaking bellow, then charged the tree, sending down a sharp-pointed rain of the tiny macelike gumballs.

"Come on over!" Bram swung down from the limb and stepped around the trunk, nodding toward Moses and Johnson to fan out in a semicircle. Johnson dodged through a stand of young pines while Bram cautiously skirted a patch of briars. A stick snapped beneath his boot, and Plumb Mean wheeled around. "Now!" Bram whirled the loop over his head and threw with unerring aim, jerking it tight around the base of the flaring horns just as Moses' loop slid across the bull's black nose.

"Got him!" Johnson shouted. "But not for long! Just caught one horn and—"

The bull's great black head swung around, red-tinged eyes glaring at Moses. His nostrils flared and his horns lowered to a menacing angle. One hoof raked a slash in the earth, then the other. He charged. Johnson's rope slid off the horn. Moses jumped behind a tree, leaning out to throw his loop just as the maddened bull swerved to charge Bram.

Backed into an empty cove surrounded by tangled blackberry vines that reached far above his head, Bram could only wait and hope he could avoid those dangerous horns. Johnson threw his rope seconds before the bull reached Bram, the perfect loop falling easily into place just as Damask's scream sliced through the air. The vicious pointed horns jerked, the tip sliding along Bram's shrinking ribs.

Moses and Johnson set their weight to the rope while Bram pulled free of the briars and eased past the snorting bull. Wrapping his rope around the trunk of a nearby tree, he secured it with a strong knot.

Damask, goaded by terror, lost sight of him around the tree. "Bram!" she called out, her voice cracking. He came from behind her, ducking under the limb, and she breathed a sigh of relief that was short-lived. "You're hurt." His shirt was in shreds, and a seeping scrape across his ribs lured her trembling hand.

Bram shrank from that touch, both mentally and physically afraid, not of her, but of himself. The words that came were blurted out, thoughtlessly, recklessly.

"A few inches over and your Plumb Mean could have saved you from a distasteful marriage."

Damask froze, hand outstretched, the pain that clutched at mind and heart showing stark in her eyes. He still believed that she wanted him dead! What more did she have to do to disprove it? She had done everything for him, everything she knew to do!

Pain was burned away in the eyes that turned to cauldrons of molten gold. "Don't you ever say that to me again!"

"Why not?" Bram's voice was soft as he clapped his hands across the branch on either side of her hips. "It's true, isn't it?"

"No!" she shouted and stopped, her mouth rounding in a softly breathed, "Oh." The back of her fingers pressed against her lips, her dirt-smudged nose peeking over the curl of her fingers with an appealing vulnerability.

"No?" he questioned inexorably.

"No, Bram," she answered with quiet finality, "because what we have isn't a marriage. It never has been. It's an arrangement, the arrangement you wanted."

"Damask, I—"

"Please, no more now. Just let me down."

He didn't want to let her go, not like that. He felt he had been so close to discovering an answer. But he could not hold her there when she gazed at him as though her eyes held all the sadness in the world.

He caught her around the waist and lowered her by reluctant inches, senses swimming at her nearness. His arms ached with the effort required not to drag her close as her feet settled to the ground, the hem of her skirt folded over the top of his boots. She swayed there a moment, and reached out, her palm resting against his ribs above the seeping scrape. Flesh to warm flesh, her hand quivered against him, and her eyes raised to his with a soft yearning.

"I'll tell Lulu. This should be—"

She whirled away without finishing, skirts hiked to her knees as she ran nimbly into the surrounding woods, and Bram knew he could not let her go. Not this time.

Damask wound through pine thickets and circled bushes. Gasping for breath, she came to a stop, leaning against the trunk of a pin oak. Then she heard the running steps that followed, and she caught a glimpse of white through the trees.

He was following. Oh, God! She had almost given herself away! If he pressed her again, pride would be gone, along with everything else!

She darted away, running through patches of green brightened by shards of sunlight piercing the treetops. He was getting closer . . . closer . . .

She stumbled over a clump of fern, and Bram caught her as they both went tumbling. He rolled to take the brunt of the fall.

Suddenly, Damask was flat on her back, Bram's long length pressing her into the soft matting of leaves and pine needles. His arms were rigid with tension and his eyes bored into hers with an angry question, their color darkening to sapphire.

"Where did she go, Damask?" he asked, his voice hoarse and ragged as though the perplexing question had been dragged from him against his will. "Is she there, hiding beneath the shell of a wooden doll that now inhabits Seven Pines? Will I ever see her again?"

His mouth lowered to hers, moving, searching with infinite tenderness while Damask lay inert, unresponsive. Her mind floated in numbed detachment. This could not be happening. She was dreaming it out of the depth of her own need.

Bram pulled back, frowning down at her. Why had he thought she might respond? Why should she be any different after all these weeks of shying away from him, of hurrying away from any room he entered? Jesus, why couldn't he forget? Why did he wake night after night, his loins afire with the dream of satiny limbs twining around him, delicate nipples quivering beneath his lips? What happened to the eagerness she displayed that night?

He could not believe it had only been to pay her *debt!* She wanted him then, just as much as he wanted her now. A painful tightness drew across his loins, spreading an ache down his thighs. He rolled away from her, drawing up his knees and resting his forehead on his folded arms while he tried to calm the surge of desire that savaged his good intentions.

He felt the fleeting touch of her hand on his shoulder and flinched away, afraid the least encouragement would have him throwing her to the ground and taking her whether she willed it or not. He heard the sharp hiss of her breath, the scattering rustle of leaves, and the pounding of her bare feet across the earth, growing fainter and fainter until it vanished altogether.

His bitter laughter rang through the woods, a hideous mockery of humor. Overhead a squirrel peered over a branch, his bushy tail twitching before he disappeared into the safety of his nest. A blue jay chattered angrily, his dark tail pointing to the sky.

Bram pressed the heels of his hands to his eyes. It was funny. He had come to Seven Pines so cocky and self-assured, certain he could use her to beget his sons, then forget her as easily as he had all those other faceless women. Now that dreamed-of dynasty of Raffertys was as empty and meaningless as his life.

"Master Bram! Master Bram!" Johnson's basso voice rumbled through the trees.

"Goddammit!" Bram breathed. He could not take a step without a dusky shadow! Devotion was one thing; this was something else altogether! "If you come one step closer, I'll wring your neck!" he shouted.

"You know you ain't gonna do no such thing! Where else you get a nigger to push that plow like me?" Johnson, wearing a broad grin, stepped into the clearing.

Bram pushed himself up, leveling a black frown. "Don't you have work to do? If not, I'll speak to Harford and have something assigned to you!"

"Done my work. Ain't nothing else 'til chores. What you got to do today, Master Bram?"

"Oh, no! I don't intend to make it easy for you. Dammit! If I didn't know better, I'd think you had been *sicced* on me like a hound after a coon!"

"Now what you think that for?" Johnson asked easily.

"Ain't so many places to go around here that one don't fetch up against t'other."

"Yes, but if it's not you following me, then it's Dread. And if it's not him, it's Moses . . ." Bram stopped, thinking about what he said. It was true! Since the day after his return, he had been trailed relentlessly, and had never had a moment alone unless he rode Nightwind or sent one of them away in a raging temper—which only meant that another one appeared within minutes of the last. "Who put you up to this?" he asked, a pitiless determination in his pale eyes.

"Put me up to what, Master Bram?" Johnson shifted uncomfortably.

"To trailing me! Never leaving me alone!"

"Master Bram, you sure got funny notions. Ain't nobody been trailing you." Johnson's face brightened. "I plumb forgot! Pappy ask me to take that saw back to the clearing where the boys is working."

"Oh, no!" Bram's hand closed around the massive black forearm. "I want an answer, and I want it now! You make a poor liar! The truth, or I'll know it."

Johnson's face screwed up in a pained expression. "Master Bram, I can't tell you. I done give my word I wouldn't say nothing!"

Bram made no reply, waiting with an implacable look that said he would stand there all day. Johnson heaved a dolorous sigh.

"It was Miss Damask. Her and Master Michael, they come to the quarters and git me and Pappy and Moses and Dread. She say you ain't never to git outa the sight of one of us, not for one little minute. She say you ain't never to git on your hoss without one of us done check the cinch. She say you ain't never to do nothing without we done check it over to make sure it's safe."

Bram's fingers peeled away from Johnson's arm to rake through his hair. "Did—" Breath failed him. "Did she say why?"

"Well, that was a puzzlement. She say Master Wade, he done got tetched in the head and she afraid he might try to hurt you. And sure enough! We done found your cinch sawed near clean through once. 'Nother time we find a rattler in the feed bin just 'fore you come out to give Nightwind that handful of oats like you do every night. And this morning, when Joseph saddle up Nightwind, that hoss put up such a ruckus we like to never git that saddle off him. You know that thorn tree what grows down to Persimmon Bayou? Somebody done shave them thorns and weave 'em through that hoss blanket. Master Bram, if you mounted up that hoss, he woulda kill you for sure.''

''I see. And you told Miss Damask about these incidents?''

''No, sir. Master Michael say they ain't no need to be worrying her. Say she got enough worries, and we just 'sposed to watch all the harder.''

She had been protecting him! Protecting him against her brother!

''Master Bram''—Johnson's heavy brows joined at the bridge of his nose—''I done told you somebody trying to kill you dead, and here you is looking like I done give you the best news you ever had!''

''Damn, if you haven't!'' Bram swiveled on his heel and hurried off in the direction of the house, Johnson trailing along behind. As they neared the quarters, Bram heard Tessa screaming his name. He sprinted forward and saw her running down the path. She stumbled and fell, leaping up with Miss Pettigrew clutched tightly in her arms.

''Bram!'' She lurched into him, her arms sliding around his waist as she pressed her face into his chest.

''Tessa''—he tugged her chin up, looking into her terror-stricken eyes—''what's wrong?''

''Wade!'' she wailed. ''He's mad at Damask! He's saying such mean things to her!''

Bram calmed the feverish impatience that urged him to fling Tessa away and hurry to Damask. ''Tessa, you want me to go to her, don't you?''

She nodded and Bram extricated himself from her clinging arms as gently as he could, then raced up the path.

Wade's shrill tirade had drawn Aunt Sarah and Amarintha to the open door of the cookhouse, and Bram heard Aunt Sarah's heartfelt "Thank the Lord" as he rushed by.

"What do you mean?" came Wade's cutting sarcasm. "You won't allow me to talk to Michael that way? A gutter rat from the City brought here and set up as the son of the house! I tell you I won't stand for it any longer! Look at him! An Irishman!" The words were an epithet. "Little better than a nigger! Haven't you read all of those advertisements in the *Picayune? No Irishmen need apply.* Why do you think they say that? Because no decent, self-respecting person will have anything to do with them! And you! Married to one! Oh, I've seen the way you look at him. Like he was God Almighty! But he doesn't give a tinker's damn about you, does he? I always told you no man would want a woman with nothing in her head but an accountant's column of figures!"

The shrill voice drilled on as Bram took the steps two at the time. Wade spilled his venom in a piercing scream of resentment and invective. Bram burst in on a scene that sent the hair prickling along the back of his neck and raised a bloody haze of murderous fury.

Damask had pulled Michael to her, her arms shielding the head of flame red curls pressed against her breast. While Michael tried to escape that maternal, protective embrace, Wade stalked them, his hand raised, the sharp lines of his face twisted into a grotesque mottled mask. Before Bram could shout or reach them, Damask backed into a table and Wade's open palm cracked across her face, sending her reeling and crashing to the floor.

Bram's roar of outrage jerked Wade around, his mottled coloring fading to dead white. One squeal of panic erupted before Bram's hands closed around his throat, dark fingers digging into the stringy lines of Wade's neck. His shallow blue eyes were sharp with terror as they bulged from the frame of sparse lashes, and his hands clawed at the relentless bands of death shackling his throat.

"Sir, let him go! Whatever he is, he's the Lady's brother! She'll not want ye murdering him, sir!" Michael pounded on Bram's arm, desperate to make him release that grip. "Sir, let him go! Ye're killing him!"

Bram's lips curled with disgust, his eyes blazing.

"Sir, let him go! The Lady, sir! Ye must see to the Lady! She hasn't stirred, sir! Ye must see to the Lady!"

Those words penetrated the pounding blood that deafened Bram to all else. His fingers loosened, curling away from the livid marks that flamed against Wade's pale skin.

"That's good, sir," Michael soothed. "That's good. Now, ye must see to the Lady."

Breath sobbed into Bram's lungs. His eyes blinked, the thatch of black lashes blinking as he tried to rid himself of the red haze that blurred his vision.

"Damask? My God, Damask!" He stumbled to her, falling to his knees. A tremor of fear raced across the well-defined muscles straining against his shirt, and his hand shook against the cool, pale skin of her brow. Her lashes fluttered against her cheeks, then opened to reveal the confusion in her eyes. She sat up abruptly.

"Michael!"

"I'm all right, Lady."

Her eyes moved past him to Wade, resting on his elbow, his fingers rubbing his neck. His thin lips lifted into a sneer and his eyes promised revenge, but he said nothing as he hauled himself to his feet and straightened his clothes.

"What happened?" she asked softly.

"Your husband tried to kill me!"

"Bram?"

His eyes flickered with fury, but his voice was calm. "He hit you. No one hits you and gets away with it."

"Oh, Bram, he's . . . he's a child . . ."

His hand shot out, imprisoning her wrist. "No one hurts you, Damask! No one!" She flinched away from his powerful grip and Bram's hand pulled away from her arm, his face twisting with regret. "Michael, leave us. And take that piece of offal with you."

They were alone with their fears and misunderstandings, and the misconceptions that raised a wall between them.

Bram's fists pressed into his thighs, the muscles cording to his shoulder. Was he wrong? Did her protection mean no more than she would not see him hurt, no matter who or what he was? The conviction that she might care for him dwindled to nothing. He could feel her watching him, feel those soft cinnamon eyes moving across his face. He wondered what she was thinking, but when he looked at her she looked away, blushing lightly as she nervously smoothed at her skirt. "Are you hurt?" he asked, his voice distant and cold.

"No, I was only stunned," she whispered.

"Look at me, dammit!" Her eyes jerked around to him, wide with sudden fear, and Bram laughed shakily, fingers raking his hair awry. "I didn't mean for that to be so . . ." He frowned, deadly serious of a sudden. "Damask, I don't think either of us can go on as we have. It isn't good for you or Tessa, and Wade and I can no longer live in the same house. I made a mistake coming here and marrying you. We can still correct it. I can go away and take Michael with me . . ."

"Michael? You will take Michael? But he is all I have of . . ." Damask looked away. Could she tell him Michael was all she had of him?

"Damask, Wade will never accept the boy. He will make his life a hell. Michael will be better off with me. Later, you can think about a divorce."

"Of course," she murmured dejectedly. "You must be free."

Rage flared in Bram and he caught her, pulling her around to face him. "It is not I who needs—"

"Miss Damask! Miss Damask!" Jims came running in. "Better come. I'm afraid your grandpappy's taking his last breath."

Chapter 20

BRAM *held the reins firmly in one hand, the other propped on his* thigh. He rode through the speckled light and shadow beneath the canopy of pines bridging the Mansfield-Logansport Road. Thunder rumbled in the distance, and a freshening wind whispered through the treetops. There was a sharp taste to the air, reminding him mercilessly of the first day he came up this road, before he met Damask. Before his life was turned inside out.

Behind him, Michael rode Prince beside the wagon and talked to Johnson and Samson, their voices murmurous background to Bram's heavy thoughts.

The old man clung tenaciously to a frail wisp of life. It had been days since he opened his eyes. Still, Damask would not leave his side. There was a translucent pallor to her face, the fragile veining marked in hollow cheeks beneath prominent cheekbones, and her eyes were sunk in dark hollows of weariness and grief.

Lulu was frantic with worry, and had set aside her distrust long enough to beg Bram to force Damask from her grandfather's bedside. He tried gentle reason. It failed miserably. In anger, spurred by fear for her health, he lifted her without further argument and carried her to the Big House. Damask put up no more than a weak protest and was asleep before he climbed the stairs. But the following morning she had risen, her eyes bright with accusation when she brushed by him in the hall, not speaking as she hurried back to her grandfather's side.

There had been no further discussion about his leaving, but Bram was determined to go as soon as possible. It did neither of them any good to prolong the torture of their marriage. He had brought Damask nothing but grief and heartache. A divorce would be easy with his consent. She could claim desertion.

And then she would be free to marry her Hunt. It would reassure him to know there was someone with her— someone besides Wade. Bram pinched the bridge of his nose and rubbed his burning eyes. The scar began an angry ticking beat in his temple. He would just as soon not know what Damask did, however. He would cut her cleanly out of his life.

Forget her! Bram warned himself. It did no good to keep thinking about her or to curse himself for ever believing she could be involved in an attempt to murder him. It did no good to regret the cruelly barbed accusations he had flung at her. He recognized that he had willfully destroyed any feeling she might have had for him.

It would be easier to forget, once he was away and did not have to look at her face across the table or listen to that soft, sweet voice that sent waves of longing swelling through him.

At least Wade had been quiet. There had been no outbursts, no snide remarks, no *accidents*. The man slipped around the house with the stealth of a cat, taking out his wrath on his bodyservant, Nero. Since Damask had begun spending both her days and nights in the Old House caring for her grandfather, the Big House echoed with increasing frequency from Wade's screaming tirades against Nero for infractions of his orders.

Nightwind snorted, rising on his hindlegs and coming down with a jolt. "Easy boy, easy," Bram said rubbing the sleek black neck.

Nero had begun sliding around the house like a malignant shadow, spreading ripples of uneasiness wherever he went.

Bram's regret for giving Nero to Wade grew by day, and the worst of it was, there wasn't one thing he could do about it. The transfer of the property deed was legal and binding. Unless Wade agreed to sell Nero back to him, his hands were tied. Downing always needed money. He would approach him when . . .

An explosion shattered the peace of the pine forest, sending animals scurrying beneath bushes and birds flying through the trees. Bram felt a sting. Nightwind gave a neighing scream, rearing to paw the air before he plunged ahead. His great hooves dug clods of dirt from the rutted road, his black mane whipped out behind him, and his tail flew straight out as he fled pain and fear caused by that sound. Bram leaned over his neck, his knees hugging the stallion's sides, his voice low and soothing. Nightwind gradually slowed, calmed by Bram's voice. The mad gallop became a canter, then a trot, finally a blowing walk with foamy sweat stringing from the stallion's lips and nostrils, and sliding down his sides.

Bram dismounted, coming around to Nightwind's great head. There were two neat holes in one twitching black ear and a bloody streak gouged across the tender flesh of his nose. The stallion's hide quivered beneath Bram's hands, but slowly the blowing breaths eased. Michael came pounding up on Prince, the wagon following.

"Sir! Are ye hurt, sir?" Michael threw himself from the saddle. "A shotgun it was, sir! We should have gone looking, but all we could think about was seeing if ye were hurt!"

The wagon came to a halt with a screaming of the brake burning against the wheel. Samson and Johnson jumped down. "Lord, Master Bram," Johnson shouted, "I thought you was done for!"

"I'm fine, Johnson. Nightwind took a few pellets, but he's unharmed."

"Sir, yer coat is ripped here. Were ye hit?"

Bram lifted the lapel away and saw a streak of blood where a pellet had plowed across his chest. "It's nothing. I'll not have the Lady bothered with this, Michael. Samson, Johnson, not a word."

There was a flinty hardness to Bram's face as he swung into the saddle and took off at a gallop. The sky was growing gray, thunder growling as lightning flashed on the dark horizon. Bram trotted up the drive, heading for the stable. There, Bram massaged a stinging ointment into the furrow that streaked red across Nightwind's black nose. Giving the stallion an extra portion of oats, Bram left the barn and started for the house. The sight of Damask slumped on the steps of the Old House with Jims and Aunt Sarah and Lulu clustered around brought him running.

"Master Bram!" Aunt Sarah wailed, her chubby cheeks wet with the tears she dabbed away with the corner of her gingham apron. "Old Mister Barton done breathed his last!"

"Jims, send someone to Blackberry Hill. Tell Mrs. Downing she is needed here." Bram sat beside Damask, his hand moving to the bright wisps of hair at her temple. "Damask, your grandfather was old and tired. He was ready to go. Remember what I told you. He will always be with you."

Her head raised, her eyes hollow and dark with grief. "I didn't want him to go," she quavered. "Everyone has left me. Everyone. Even—" Her eyes widened, as a rage of grief and loss twisted within her. "Why haven't you gone? You promised you would!" she struck out blindly, her words more devastating than any blow. "You've brought nothing but misery with you, turning us against one another! Why do you stay? What more will have to happen before you leave us in peace!" She jumped up, knuckles pressing against her lips, tear-flooded eyes dark with horror before she whirled away to run for the Big House.

From the mill just beyond the quarters came the whining sound of sawing and the pounding of a hammer as Samson fashioned a pine coffin. The word had been passed to the fields, where the cotton picking would continue until it was time for the funeral service late in the afternoon. Spirituals, lamenting sorrow and loss, wailed through field and forest.

At the Big House, Jane Downing arrived, abustle with sympathy and common sense. She soothed Damask's and Tessa's grief with gentle concern and glasses of warm milk dosed with a light dollop of laudanum. They slept peacefully, insensible to the pall that had settled over the house.

Bram and John Robert escaped the gloom for the relative peace of the back porch. They sat in silence, each lost in his own thoughts, and casting uneasy glances at the threatening skies. Black clouds rolled in from the horizon, pushing before them a fresh damp wind.

Rain for the funeral would be bad, but too much rain for the cotton could be a disaster. A heavy rain for a day or two would not be too harmful, though some blooms and bolls would be lost, but anything longer than that would adversely affect the yield.

Wade came swinging around the side of the house with a merry whistle. There was a shotgun slung over his shoulder and two rabbits in his hands.

"Good hunting," he said with a sidelong glance at Bram. Hefting the rabbits for their inspection, he looked at his cousin. "I thought that was your buggy out front, John. Didn't know you were coming out today."

"Your grandfather died this morning, Wade."

"Oh? Well, it was to be expected, wasn't it? Have to get these to Aunt Sarah." He sauntered toward the cookhouse.

John Robert shrugged. "Wade has been a strange one from the cradle." He frowned thoughtfully, staring at Wade's back. "There was an awful lot of blood on him for those two small rabbits."

There was too much blood. The rabbits were stiff with rigor, but the blood streaked across Wade's shirt was bright and fresh. An ugly thought pulled Bram from his chair. He excused himself and found Jims, telling him to look for Nero. But Nero was nowhere to be found, and was still missing when the funeral service began late in the afternoon.

The grave was dug next to a stand of pines topping a low hill near Persimmon Bayou. It was a desolate scene. The sun was blotted out by charcoal clouds edged in mourning black and illuminated by the fluorescence of lightning. The wind whipped through the pines, and tore at Damask's black skirt and bonnet, molding the black veiling to her face. John Robert stood at the head of the grave, his voice solemn as he intoned, ''Yea, though I walk through the valley of death . . .''

Damask sagged and felt Bram's strong arm slide around her waist. Her grandfather was gone. Soon, Bram would be gone. Thank God! Gone, and safe. There would be no one left but her and Tessa and Wade. Then she could try to help her willful, childish, petulant brother.

She stared down into the dark hole at the pine box.

''Damask,'' Bram murmured.

She woke from her reverie and heard the singing of her grandfather's favorite hymn, *Rock of Ages*. Her eyes sought Bram's through the veiling, and she leaned against his chest, weeping softly. He leaned down to lift a clump of the red earth of Seven Pines, and Damask heard the dull thud as it hit the pine boards. Then Bram led her away while the last notes of the hymn trailed into silence.

''My dear, you know we'll stay if you need us,'' Jane told Damask.

''No, there's no need. Truly, there isn't.''

''Very well, but you'll let us know if there is anything we can do?''

''Of course, and thank you.''

Damask watched Jane dash into the windswept night, where Bram waited to help her into the carriage. Her tongue flicked the sharp taste of the air from her lips and she shivered when a gust of damp wind lifted her skirt. It was a strange night, reminiscent of that other night long months ago. The memory gave her a chill of foreboding. There was something ominous hanging over all their heads. She wished Bram had left when he said he would.

The rattling of the buggy was lost in the booming roll of thunder that vibrated through the Big House. A jagged flash of lightning revealed to Damask the brooding look with which Bram regarded her as he came up the porch steps. She pulled her shawl tightly around her shoulders and turned to go into the house. He followed her, his steps slow and uncharacteristically heavy. Unable to seek the lonely privacy of her room, Damask went into the parlor and lifted the matches to light the lamp. Cheerful yellow-tinged light spread outward, and she moved away from it to take a seat on the sofa, watching Bram walk across the room and brace his arm on the mantel.

"I'll be leaving in the morning," he said quietly, his low-pitched voice inutterably weary and sad. "Jims can pack for Michael and me tonight. You should have no problem with the cotton. Harford is, as you know, able to do everything that needs to be done. I intend to sign Seven Pines over to you, but you will have to have a legal guardian. Have you anyone in mind?"

He never looked at her, and Damask bowed her head. "Bram, I'm so sorry for what I said this morning. None of it was true."

"It doesn't matter now, and there are more important things to discuss in the—" Bram's jaw clenched tight, a frown drawing across his brow. "—in the short time left us. I thought perhaps your . . . your Mr. Marlowe. He seems honest enough, and he would have your best interests at heart."

"Not Hunt," she said softly. "Anyone else. Anyone you think suitable."

His eyes touched her and slid away. "Very well. If you will excuse me, I have to meet Dread in the stable."

He left and Damask's head sagged against the back of the sofa. She must have imagined the defeated slump to his proud shoulders and the downward tug of his lips. Dear God, she prayed, give me the strength to let him go.

"Lady?" Michael joined her, perching on the edge of the sofa. "Is it true? The Mister says we're leaving tomorrow."

"Yes, Michael." She pulled him to her, her cheek pressed against the top of his head. "Promise me you will write often. Let me know how you are, what you are doing.''

"I promise, Lady. But why? Why?''

She cupped his face in her hands. "It's for the best, Michael. Mr. Rafferty is unhappy here. I don't need to tell you that. He needs you, Michael. Go to him now.''

A lantern hung from the post at the end of the stall. Bram leaned down to rub the skittish mule's foreleg, his hand traveling up to the shoulder. "Old Boy, I think your plowing days are over. You're entitled to a well-earned rest now.''

He moved out of the stall, shutting the gate behind him, and pausing to light a cigar. Thunder cracked overhead and Bram looked up, an arrested expression on his face. He thought he saw a shadow before the lightning died away.

He shook himself. It was this blasted day! The metallic taste in the air! The wind and clouds and no rain. He'd been jumpy all day.

Bram walked over to a stool made of a stump and sat, breathing deep of the earthy smell of the barn. He would go to Dublin from here. The cane harvest would keep him busy for a few months. Then what? He had Michael now. The boy needed more stability than his previous life offered. He needed a home . . . a mother. Jesus!

Another booming roll of thunder beat against the barn, sending a golden rain of hay sifting from the loft. A scintillating bolt of lightning blazed from the sky, and a malevolent shadow appeared in the open doors. Wild maniacal laughter raised the hair on Bram's body. He stood and the shadow moved into the lantern light, a bright golden ray flickering off the barrel of a revolver.

"You got more lives than a cat, Mister Bram Rafferty! But I got you this time! This time you won't git away!''

Nero shuffled forward and leaned against a stall, his skull-like face grayed and dripping sweat while his shirt stuck to his chest and arms in dark strips of dried blood.

"Sit! I want you to know why I'm doing this!''

The revolver never swayed from its target, the center of

his chest. Bram sank back onto the stump, his eyes narrowed and watchful. Nero! All this time it had been Nero!

"I would have served you faithfully! I swear I would! But you had to give me back to *him!* It was *you* what put me back in that hell!" Nero screamed. "Oh, it was a pure pleasure, it was, to watch you burn with that fever. Didn't you never wonder? That doctor, he was careful. He didn't know I was smearing horse droppings on those wrappings. Then Miss Damask had to take over and she wouldn't let me near you!" He shuddered, and his teeth began to chatter. "The snake . . . the cinch . . . they been watching you like . . . like a hawk. Couldn't do nothing to git next to you and . . . Master Wade, he been gitten plumb crazy mean!" The laughter came again, a low repellent grating. "He's a fool! Done miss you with that shot this morning! Didn't do no better'n I did! A cat! That's what you is. A cat with nine lives. But they all used up now." He shifted, pushing away from the stall door. "Master Wade say if you ain't dead by morning, I gonna be one dead nigger. Yeah, come morning they be burying you and I be one free nigger!" His arm straightened, the bony finger tightening around the trigger.

On the path leading to the barn doors, Michael bumped into Johnson. "What are ye doing out here?" he asked, trying to slow the rapid tattoo of his heart. "Ye nearly scared me out of me wits, coming out of the dark that way!"

"Got this funny feeling. Had it all day. Seen Master Bram heading this way, and decided to set here 'til he come out. But, I coulda swore I seen somebody else go in there a minute ago."

Rastus sped by, a red streak in the night.

"C'mon," Michael shouted and was off.

Rastus skidded to a stop in the broad open doors, a growl pouring through his bared teeth with a chilling resonance. The coarse red hair rose in hackles along his back and he crouched low to spring. Nero looked back, the gun wavering in his hand and Bram dove to one side.

Pandamonium broke loose. Dread entered through the

back door. Bram rolled across the dusty, hay-strewn floor. Rastus arched through the air, saliva dripping from his fangs. Nero uttered a frustrated scream and swiveled around, his frenzied eyes following Bram's rolling path. The barrel lifted. Dread lunged forward. Michael and Johnson burst in. Yellow flame spewed from the muzzle, and the crack of the gunshot broke with a deafening sound.

Inside the house, Damask jerked up from her doze on the sofa. The thunder had sounded so much like a—a shot! She rubbed at the throbbing pain above her temple. She was overwrought from the weather and Gramps's death.

Icy fingers squeezed her heart, freezing it in her chest. A gunshot? Her hands began to tremble, and soon those rattling tremors communicated themselves to her whole body.

She knew! She knew!

She leaped to her feet, fleeing the house. The wind struck her like a blow, and she struggled against it frantically. The night was an abyss of blackness with the kettledrum of thunder reverberating in between the eerie syncopations of phosphorescent light. The wind screamed and tore at her. Damask leaned into it, her arm folded across her face to protect it from the pinecones and sticks that flew through the air.

At the bridge crossing the swale, she stopped, turning her back to the wind to catch her breath, and her hair blew across her shoulder like a pale banner. Lightning sliced through the heart of a cloud.

Two figures stood midway down the long pasture that stretched from the barn to the road. Lifting her skirts, Damask crossed the bridge and began running toward them, fighting the wailing wind that was like a solid wall.

She fell against the trunk of a pine, hugging it, her fingers digging into the rough bark. Lightning illuminated Wade, with his back to her, and Nero, his hands raised in an attitude of pleading. The battering wind carried their words, sharp and clear, back to her.

"I shot him dead like you wanted! Now, you got to free me! You got to keep your promise!"

"Of course you'll have your freedom, Nero." Wade's voice slithered through the gusts swirling around them. "The freedom of the grave!"

A shot rang out and Damask watched, horrified, as Nero screamed and threw out his arms, falling backward. She left the protection of the tree and ran to him, falling down at his side. Blood poured from the gaping wound in the center of Nero's chest, and his eyes were wide and staring.

"He's dead, Wade! You killed him! Why?" she cried.

"I told you I would get Seven Pines back! I told you!" he shouted exultantly. "Now, there is only one person standing between me and what I want! Your Irishman is dead! Nero killed him! That leaves only you! *You,* Damask!"

Bram dead! Agony tore through her. Not Bram! Not Bram moldering to dust beside Gramps! She swayed with the pain of her grief.

Suddenly, her arm was caught and she was spun around. Wade's hand cracked across her face. Helplessly, she stared up at him, tasting the blood on her split lip.

"It's too bad, isn't it, Damask? Poor Nero! He went mad, and killed my sister and her husband! You have to die! I knew it the day you came back to Seven Pines and chose that gambler over me!"

She hadn't! She had tried to protect both and had failed to protect either one.

"Do you have any idea how I've hated you all these years?" Wade screamed above the wind and thunder. "It wasn't enough that you stole Papa's love, and he had no time for me after you were born! Oh, no! Then you had to murder them both, Papa and Mama!"

"Oh, Wade," Damask breathed, shrinking back with her head bowed.

"Do you know how I laughed to myself when I lost Seven Pines to that gambler? The saintly Damask had lost her beloved Seven Pines! A gambler would rule it and her!" He reached out, tangling his hand in her hair and jerking her head back. "He should have been grateful! And you should have, too! Where else would you have gotten a husband! I gave you that, and what did you give me? Nothing! You turned on me! You turned on me, your brother!"

He stepped back and the revolver bore down on Damask. She was numbed by grief and shock, and she felt no fear. She would be united with Bram in death as she had not been in life.

A dark shadow lunged out of the night. It locked with Wade in mortal combat, forming a single figure framed against the cracking light. Damask watched, unable to move, even when the shot sounded and they both went still. Like black statues, they stood, until the slighter figure began sliding, falling and clutching at the larger one until he stepped away.

"Miss Damask, you hurt?"

Yes, she was hurt, though the scars of it would remain unseen. Her brother had hated her. All these years while she was loving him and excusing him and blaming herself, he had hated her and used her. He had murdered his servant and her husband, the only man she would ever love. The pain and the sorrow would come, but now, she felt separate from it all, insulated by shock.

"No, Dread," she murmured, "I'm not hurt."

He knelt, his thick hand resting at Wade's throat. "Dead."

"How did you know to come out here?" she asked dully.

"Master Wade whip Nero something bad today, and Nero, he act real funny. Say he had something to do tonight. Had to be tonight. So, when Master Wade show up so soon after Nero done shoot Master Bram and then take him outa there, I think maybe I better go, too."

"Dread, he killed Nero. I don't want any of this to touch you. We'll tell the sheriff they killed each other. You remember that. They killed each other."

"Yessum. I remember. Now, you better come to see 'bout Master Bram."

"They said he was dead."

"Close to it, but he still breathing."

"Alive?" Her head snapped up, one forearm sweeping her wind-blown hair back from her face. "Bram is alive!" Joy, piercing, almost painful, jolted her upright.

The doctor had come and gone. Outside, the wind howled and thunder pulsed through the black night. Bram lay unconscious, his dark head swathed in a white cotton cloth, the gouge above his temple dressed and treated. Head wounds were strange things, the doctor assured Damask. It was possible he would wake with nothing more than a headache. It was also possible he would not wake at all. There was nothing to do but wait.

Damask sat beside his bed, the lamplight playing across her somber face, her hands idle in her lap. He was so still, like a little boy asleep. The lines of his face were mellowed and softened, the curve of his mouth vulnerable. He was alive and safe now.

Her thoughts drifted through the months since she had met him. Pictures of Bram formed in her mind: his face lit by laughter, tense with passion, tight with anger.

She sighed, a thread of sound. Above all, she desperately wanted another chance for them.

Bram moved and Damask leaned forward to watch him. The even tenor of his breathing changed, becoming harsh and strident. His dark hand dug at the sheets and his head moved on the pillow. His peaceful expression gave way to a grimace. Suddenly his eyes flew open and he struggled to sit up.

"Mary!" he called out hoarsely. "Don't leave me, Mary. I love you!"

THE LETTERS

Seven Pines Plantation, Mansfield, Louisiana
Wednesday, September 21, 1859

Dear Mr. Rafferty,

Having been assured that your health is a matter of time and rest, I feel it best that I leave. Too much has happened for me to remain here.

Michael insists on joining Tessa and me, though I know he would rather stay with you. He says we will need a man and, in truth, I will be glad to have him. I have grown to love Michael as the brother I always wanted, the son I would be proud to call my own.

I would ask one favor of you. On the night you were injured, Dread saved my life at some risk to his own. He will be in danger if rumor of it should spread. Therefore, I ask that you give him his freedom. Perhaps our mutual friend, Mr. Buckner, might offer Dread assistance in settling into his new life in the North.

Please, do not try to find us. I will not be contacting any of my family and you will only worry them. I will file for divorce as soon as possible. I am sorry for so much that has happened. Forgive me.

Let go of the past, Bram. Look to the future. I would like to think that someday the tall strong sons of Bram Rafferty will ride through the fields of Seven Pines.

God keep you,
Damask

Chapter 21

BRAM'S *face grayed. The letter slid from his nerveless fingers,* and the dull ache in the healing furrow that crossed his temple became a steady throb. His head sank into the pillow, black curls fanning across the snowy linen.

"Where did she go?" The words were dull, devoid of emotion.

"I don't know!" Lulu wailed and wrung her hands. "She ain't been herself! Not herself a-tall! All these weeks you been down, she ain't hardly left this room. Wouldn't let nobody else do for you. She stand here by the hour staring down at you. Ain't smiled. Ain't said nothing! When Doc say you git better, she heave the sigh like the weight of the world been took from her shoulders. Then she scratch that paper. Say when you wake up I's to give it to you with this." Lulu laid the purple velvet jeweler's box on the bed. "Then she make ready. Day fore yesterday they leave. Her and Miss Tessa and Master Michael. She say to me that you be needing Jims and me now, and we's to do for you like we always done for her. She say . . ."

Lulu broke down and covered her face with her hands. "She say you a good man what knowed nothing but trouble, and you deserve better'n what you found here. That's all. She ain't smiled, not onct! And her eyes was all dark and far away, like she done left us already. Oh, Master Bram, it done broke my heart to see her looking like they wasn't no hope left in her! She wouldn't tell me where she was going or what she would do. And Master Michael, he say she ain't told him nothing either. He say for me to tell you he sorry to go, but Miss Damask, she need him more.''

Lulu sniffed and drew a shuddering breath. ''Master Bram, you can't let her go! You gonna try to find her, ain't you? What my baby do all by herself?''

''Bring the lap desk, Lulu.''

She rushed out, and Bram pulled the velvet case toward him, flipping it open and lifting out the necklace. The gems dripped from his dark hand like droplets of honey. Light sparkled deep within each stone, with a false warmth. But they lay icy and lifeless across the rough surface of his palm.

He closed his eyes. A vision came, so strong his nostrils spread to catch the fragile scent of violets.

His hand trembled as it had when he fumbled with the clasp, with her skin like warm satin beneath his eager fingers. Bram's face twisted with grief. The necklace struck the far wall with a sharp metallic clatter and the velvet box followed with a dull thump. His blood pounded and his hands flew to his head, teeth clenched against the rhythmic cadence of pain in his wound.

''Master Bram, you oughtn't to git excited this way. It ain't good for you.'' Lulu pulled his hands away from the bandage that wound around his forehead.

''Get rid of it! I never want to see it again!''

Lulu's forehead puckered. ''If that's what you want. Drink this.'' She held a cup to his lips, ''You need sleep.''

''No! I have to write those letters!'' God! His head was splitting. ''I have to know where she went!''

''Drink! Can't do nothing if you make yourself sick.''

She gave him no choice. Bram drank, then lay back. Lulu waited for the laudanum to take effect. The clenched line of his jaw relaxed. His hand groped across the edge of the bed and Lulu frowned, reluctantly reaching for it and wincing when his fingers tightened painfully around her hand.

''She left me, Lulu,'' he whispered. ''She left me.''

Tears squeezed out, trickling from the corners of his eyes and Lulu gaped. ''You love her!'' she said in a cross between accusation and disbelief.

"No! No!" Bram shouted hoarsely, his eyes flying open.

She leaned down, bright black eyes like agates. "I seen mules less stubborn than you! Why you think you got that big empty hole where your heart is? You love my baby! Been loving her a long time! You just too mule-headed to admit it! What you think life is, boy? Think you can live all your days without nobody? When it's all over, what you got? Nothing! 'Cause you ain't lived! Say it!" The sharp fear was fading from Bram's eyes as sleep claimed him, and Lulu caught his shoulders, shaking him until his lashes fluttered up. "Don't you go to sleep on me now! Say it!"

"I . . . I love her." The black lashes swooped down to his cheeks once more. "God help me, I love her," he breathed and sank into sleep.

Lulu's work-roughened hand patted his cheek, her prim lips widening into a gentle smile. "Lord, was there ever such a fool stubborn man? I shoulda knowed he didn't have no chance onct he laid eyes on my baby. Lord, you just help him find her, she do the rest. This one wild hoss done fought the bit long as he can. He ain't got no strength for no more."

Bram slept the clock around. After a light meal, presided over by the once again prim and unsmiling Lulu, he commenced the awkward task of writing Damask's family.

He chewed the tip of his pen, eyes dark with indecision. The whole story was too long and complicated to commit to paper, and he wanted to retain their sympathy or he would never hear news of her whereabouts. At length, he decided to write of the death of her grandfather and of Wade's attempts on his life and subsequent murder by Nero. He explained that the shock of these events had been more than Damask could bear, and she had, though innocent, assumed a part of her brother's guilt and fled Seven Pines.

The letters were sent to Mansfield for posting that afternoon. Then there was nothing to do but wait. Dizziness and blinding headaches imprisoned Bram in his room with nothing but his memories.

He remembered the painful ache in the breast of a dirty, tattered urchin who stoutly declared it was nothing more than hunger and cold. To admit it was a burning need to love and be loved would have destroyed him. Thus, he denied it, and each year the denial grew stronger. Finally, there came a time when it was buried so deep he could not recognize the manifestations of that need when they appeared.

Slow days crawled while Bram recovered under Lulu's watchful eye. Gradually the dizziness that felled him when he tried to rise lessened. He lay abed, staring sightlessly at the far wall with his ever-changing kaleidoscope of memories.

Cleansing winds of change banished the dark shadows from the corners of his soul, and the mellowing of Bram Rafferty, begun the moment his vivid blue eyes locked with tender nut-brown cinnamon, was completed. He could think of his father without the gut-twisting agony that had scarred his life.

The day came when he could rise and sit in a chair. Then another day when he could walk downstairs. Finally, the day when he could bury himself in the work of harvest.

It was a different man that rose from his bed. There hovered about him an aura of peace that was new, but with it was a shadow of sadness lingering in the cool depths of his eyes. The beautiful lips that had so seldom widened to a smile never did so now.

Tempered by sorrow accepted at long last, he was stronger than he had ever been. The terrified little boy was gone. Bram Rafferty was a man: seasoned, ripened, matured by his harsh life. He could admit, without fear, that he loved Damask with an all-consuming passion that would end only with his last breath. He was whole of heart and mind.

His thoughts often dwelt on that night at Bonne Volonte when they shared a union so perfect, so incredibly beautiful and right, that its memory was enough to carry him through his days.

October 18th dawned cool and fair with the morning bell ringing its strident tones to awaken the quarters. Bram sat on the back steps, Rastus coiled around his feet, the smoke of his cigar swirling on the crisp air. The heart-shaped leaves of the redbud near the cookhouse had turned yellow and begun to fall, and the canvas of the woodlands was splashed with russet reds and autumn oranges. But Bram had little thought for the portents of coming winter.

It had been weeks since he had sent those letters, and not a reply yet. Worse, he had no idea which direction Damask had taken. Through the steamer, he had traced her to Baton Rouge, but from there she had vanished. He saw Michael's cunning hand in that. Damask would likely have gone straight to her destination, but the change of steamers in Baton Rouge meant she could have gone anywhere, up or down the river. He was almost certain she had gone to New Orleans. Michael knew the City, and it was large enough for them to lose themselves, but he had to wait at Seven Pines until he was certain she had not gone to any of her family.

Damn! He could not leave, even then. There was the cotton to be picked and baled and sent down-river, and no one in charge but he.

Bram threw the stub of his cigar into the yard and raked his hands through his hair, frowning down at Rastus until a sudden thought threw his head back. There was another letter to be written! No, two! If she had gone to the City, he had friends who could find her. And if they couldn't, Hunt Marlowe would!

A few hours later Bram rode through the dusty streets of Mansfield. A knot of men, gathered at the corner of Polk and Washington Streets, hailed him as he passed.

Dismounting before Buck and Thomas, the dry goods store and post office, Bram whipped Nightwind's reins around the hitching post. He posted his mail to New Orleans and found that two letters had arrived for him, one from Acadian Star, the other from Damask's cousin at Milliken's Bend. Bram tore into them, devouring their contents, only to find they knew nothing and he had succeeded in worrying them frantic.

"Mr. Rafferty, I almost forgot. This package came for you."

Bram took it, frowning down at the brown wrapping. He hadn't ordered anything. His eyes fell on the delicate script in Damask's hand. He yanked a penknife from his pocket to cut the string, and opened it with shaking hands. There was no letter, only the long rectangular copper stencil, carefully carved with *B. Rafferty, Mansfield, Louisiana*.

"A nice one, Mr. Rafferty," the postmaster said. "You'll be marking your cotton bales with that for a lifetime."

"Yes," Bram answered dully, "a lifetime."

His mind was consumed by Damask on the long ride home. The satin texture of her skin, the saucy dimple that trembled to life when she laughed, the cinnamon eyes that could sap the strength from his thews. Dear God, where was she?

He was met at the door by Lulu and shook his head as he handed her the stencil. "She sent this. No letter. Nothing to tell where or how she is."

The first frost came, spreading a blanket of white across the land. When Bram returned from the fields that morning he found the house in an uproar of preparations for the winter. Floors were being cleaned and carpets laid, the sheer summer drapes replaced by heavy winter ones.

In Damask's room he found Lulu sitting and rocking, hands slack on the wooden arms, tears rolling down her wrinkled cheeks. She had aged in the weeks since Damask had left. There was white in her hair now and an old, worn look in her eyes.

Bram went to her, kneeling at her feet and gathering her hands in his. No words were needed to express the grief they shared.

October became November. Sweet potatoes were dug and bedded in pine straw. Pumpkins were harvested and cotton bales were piled to the ceiling in the storehouse near the gin. The weather turned nippy, and in the fields, fires were lit for the pickers to warm their hands. Sweet potatoes and corn dodgers roasted in the ashes for the hungry.

The overcast sky was alive with ducks and geese. The rabbits that hopped through the fields had grown their thick winter coats. Samson, studying the thick, shaggy hair on the calves' necks and the thick, tight shucks on the corn, predicted a long cold winter.

And then it was December. In the tidal wave of hate that rolled across the nation, in the wake of John Brown's raid on Harper's Ferry, and his subsequent execution, Seven Pines was an isolated island of calm. Hogs fattened in the sties near the barn, several well on their way to becoming *set-down hogs*—so fat their hind legs would not support them and they could only *set down*. A cold wind whistled through the fields, and the fires burned brighter. Samson checked the paws of trapped rabbits and found them extra thickly furred, another sign that the coming winter would be hard and bitter cold. Collard greens and cabbage were harvested from the garden, and the last letter from Damask's family came.

She had not contacted anyone. No one had any idea where she might have gone.

In mid-December the last of the cotton was picked and baled. The following day, smoke curled out of the cookhouse chimney and mouth-watering aromas floated through the cracks at windows and door. A hog roasted in a pit lined with hot coals and bonfires warmed the quarter street, where preparations were underway for a feast and a frolic. The men gathered around the bonfires to drink from the jugs of whiskey Bram supplied. He joined them for a few minutes, sipping from a jug and listening to Harford play his gourd fiddle to the accompaniment of a cowhide drum and bone rattles. It was their celebration for a hard job well done.

Bram found Dread and asked him to return to the house with him. In the study he stoked the fire and told Dread to have a seat. Then he moved to the desk, leaning back against the edge, his arms folded across his chest.

"Miss Damask left a letter for me in which she said you

saved her life and you could be in some danger because of it. I would like you to tell me what happened."

Dread sat ramrod straight, obviously ill at ease. "Ain't so much to tell, Master Bram. That evening me and Polly find Nero down to the bayou, 'side the Bear Wallow Field. Master Wade done took a whip and skinned the hide off him. Polly, she want to tell you, but Nero, he wouldn't hear nothing 'bout that. Said he had something he had to do and it had to be done that night. So we help him back to the house. Well, that night when I walk in the barn, Nero shoot you. 'Fore you could blink an eye, in come Master Wade. Tell us to send for the sheriff, then he take that pistol and march Nero outside. At first I didn't think nothing about it, but the more I studied the curiouser I got. See, that evening, Nero say if he don't do whatever he had to do that night he gonna be one dead nigger. So, I decide maybe I just trail along to see what happen. The wind was up and it was dark as pitch 'tween them lightning strikes. By the time I find them he done shot Nero and got that hoss pistol bearing down on Miss Damask. He plumb wild crazy, screaming at her and saying he got to kill her dead. He say Seven Pines gonna be his and she the only one in his way. When he took to gitten serious I dove in there and wrestled him for that pistol. When it go off, he don't get up. And Miss Damask, she say we tell everbody that Nero and Master Wade done kill each other. That way I don't have no trouble for it."

Bram's hands were clenched around the edge of the desk so tightly, the tips of his fingers were dead white. A steady throbbing centered in the livid furrow that plowed into his hairline. He calmed himself with a deep breath.

"I see why she was troubled. Regardless of the reason for what you did, the fact that you killed a white man would go hard for you if it were discovered. She asked me to take you North and free you."

"Free!" Dread rocked back. "You mean I'm gonna be free! Up North free?"

"Yes, we'll leave after New Year's, but there are a few

things I need to know. Is there any place that you would like
to go?''

Dread shook his head. "Master Bram, I don't know nobody or no place, but I ain't so particular. Any place what's
free got to be good!''

"Last summer Miss Damask and I met a Yankee from
Boston, Massachusetts, an antislavery man. I believe he
would be willing to help you get a job and settle into your
life there. I'll give you the money you need to travel and live
on until you can find work, and I'll take you to St. Louis,
where I'll sign your emancipation papers. You'll also have a
letter of introduction from me.''

"Free! I'm gonna be free! You wouldn't josh me 'bout
this, Master Bram?''

"No, Dread. This is small enough payment for Damask's
life.'' He stood and stretched out his hand. As strong as he
was, he winced at the pressure of Dread's overjoyed
wringing. "In less than a month you will be a freedman.
Why don't you go out now and tell Moses and Rosetta? It
will take them a while to get used to the idea of losing you.''

It took nearly a week of trundling back and forth between
Seven Pines and Smithport Landing on Bayou St. Pierre, to
haul the cotton for shipping. The wagons were loaded with
five bales apiece, 187 bales in all, each marked with the
copper stencil Damask sent to Bram. The steamer wallowed
low in the icy water, nothing but the stack showing above
the wall of cotton bales that lined her sides. Bram listened to
the ringing of the wheelhouse bell and the sharp report of the
hissing steam and watched it chug down the bayou until he
could no longer read the marking, *B. Rafferty, Mansfield,
Louisiana.*

He remembered the pride he had expected to feel at this
sight. Though he dredged deep, he found only emptiness
and a vast relief that the job was done. He was free to follow
Damask, to find her, to bring her home, and then—to leave
her.

New Orleans, Lousana
Desember 20, 1859

Mi deer frend Bram,

I take pin n hand to writ yu we hav bin serchng the City
for yor missus, but hav cum up emty hand. Derry has
clumped nto evry seemster shop and frited the ladees nto fits
with his ugle fac. We hav spred the word but no won bi her
nam anywher we look. As for the boy, do yu kno how
manee redhead bloo eye Irish boys ther r heer? We r at our
wits end, mi frend.

I am sahry to say we hav had no mor suksess at findng
Mary.

Sinseerly,
Jerry Finn

Chapter 22

DREARY *clouds banked across the wintry sky, sinking lower and* lower until it seemed they hunted a perch on the towering masts of the sailing ships anchored at the docks. The damp wind wailed a bitter, mournful cry, and Bram raised the collar of his wool cloak to block its icy touch. He waited with ill-concealed impatience for the gangplank to be laid. His obligations to Seven Pines had been discharged. The cotton crop was in and he was free. Dread was well on his way to Massachusetts, proudly wearing the cambric shirt lovingly stitched by Polly. Harford had been given instructions for months to come. He had promised a weeping Lulu he would not return without Damask.

He still had no proof she was in the City, only one backhanded sign. He had never received a reply from Hunt Marlowe, and that made Bram suspicious.

Bram climbed into a waiting cab, and his bags were loaded. Memories of Damask moved across the backdrop of his thoughts. Pain sliced deep with a cutting edge of fear, and Bram buried his face in his hands. "Oh, God! Damask, where are you?"

"Did ye say something, sir?" The cabby poked his head in the window.'

"Yes," Bram said shortly. "I want to go to the law office of Mr. Huntington Marlowe. Do you know where it is?"

"Aye, sir. In the Vieux Carré. Royal Street."

"Quickly man! There will be something extra in it for you."

The cab wheeled through the muddy streets sending rainbow arcs of muddy water onto wet irate passersby. Bram clung to the hand flap, rocking with the motion, his face grim. In an amazingly short time he was making his way across the wet sidewalk, into a dim hallway leading to offices that opened onto a gallery. He paused before one, his teeth clenching as his hand wrapped around the brass knob and turned it.

Hunt Marlowe, seated behind a carved oak desk, stuck his pen into the inkholder and leaned back, lacing his fingers over his flat middle. His gray eyes went hard and cold, but he said nothing.

"Where is she?"

"I don't know."

"Dammit, man! I have no patience for games! Where is she?"

"By God, Rafferty!" Hunt shot out of his chair, leaning his fists on the desktop, his face contorted with anger. "What more can you do to her? You've taken her home and seen her brother turn against her! How much more do you think she can take?"

"So you do know where she is."

"No, damn your rotten soul to Hell! I do not! I've had communication with her, but I have not seen her! She is alone, out there"—a rigid arm with a shaking finger pointed—"trying to support herself and Tessa and that boy in God knows what fashion! They may be freezing or starving in some filthy hovel for all I know! *I cannot find her!*" Hunt jerked back, his jaw working, before he whirled around and braced his hands on the bookcase behind him.

"Jesus," Bram breathed. His knees suddenly weak, he sank into the leather chair before the desk, his hat sliding from fingers too weak to hold on to it. He had not, until that moment, realized how much he had counted on Marlowe knowing where she was and helping her if she needed it. A hollow, acid feeling clawed at the pit of his stomach. She has Michael, he told himself. She has Michael. He had to hold on to that or he would run through the streets like a screaming madman. Michael would never let anything happen to her. He would come to Marlowe or her family before then.

Late that night pellets of sleet rattled the window panes of the very same suite Bram had shared with Damask on their abortive honeymoon. He leaned against the mantel, arms folded over his chest, dull eyes staring blindly into the crackling fire. Why did he torture himself by insisting on these rooms? He saw her everywhere he looked.

Jerry and Derry Finn, sitting awkwardly on the fragile sofa in their thick flannel shirts, rough worsted trousers, and heavy brogans, exchanged puzzled looks. They had shared with Bram the dank dark hold of a ship for the crossing from Liverpool to New Orleans. As children, they had played in the odorous halls of tenements, and the filthy mud streets of the City. As young men, they had worked on the docks. If asked, they would have said they knew Bram Rafferty better than anyone—until now. The dark face that had greeted them was haggard and tired, the vivid blue eyes marked by suffering. And this over a *woman!* All their comfortable assumptions about Bram went reeling before that shockwave.

Bram braced his arm on the mantel, his face ruddied by the firelight. "She is here," he said softly. "I have proof of that, at least. I want someone to watch the office of a lawyer, Huntington Marlowe. Who can you recommend?"

"Horst be a good one for the task, Bram. He broke his arm and cannot find work. He'd do ye a fine job." Jerry slugged down his drink and set the glass aside. "I tell ye, Bram, we've combed the City 'til not a wee leprechaun could have escaped. Yer lady has hid herself well." He stood and went to Bram, a sandy freckled hand squeezing his shoulder. "Time is what we need, me friend. 'Tis sure we'll be finding her in time. The City is large. 'Tis easy for a wisp of a colleen to lose herself."

"That is what I fear, Jerry. She is an innocent lost in the wolf's lair."

January blew into February on a blast of icy air, and Bram still stalked the streets. Carefully, block by block, he canvassed the Vieux Carré, stopping in every shop that might hire a young woman. Again, again and yet again, he described the slight trim form, honey-toned skin, cinnamon eyes, and shimmering hair the effervescent color of champagne. No one recognized the description. No one recognized the names Damask Downing or Tureaud or Rafferty.

From the Vieux Carré, Bram moved downtown to the old Faubourg Marigny, then uptown to the Faubourg Ste. Marie, following the suburbs sprawling across the New Orleans and Carrollton Railroad to its terminus in the City of Carrollton.

March winds blew in, hot and dry, and Bram sank deep into a black depression that gnawed away the edges of his control. Weight melted from his tall frame, and his fever bright cheeks were hollow beneath piercing eyes that glittered fanatically. Sleep was snatched between dreams of Damask's face glowing with love and nightmares where she screamed her hate. He prowled the streets night and day, searching for the innocently seductive sway of skirts, a strand of shimmering hair fluttering beyond a bonnet brim, liquid cinnamon eyes.

And then one day he saw Michael. The boy was crossing Canal Street, walking through the median shaded by sycamores. Bram shouted and Michael looked up with a start of fear, indecision marking his features. Bram ran toward him and Michael raced across the street, plunging into a crowd of late shoppers in front of the D. H. Holmes store. He slipped around a corner, and Bram followed, but he was lost to sight.

He sank onto a brick stoop in the darkening shadows between two tall buildings, dropped his aching head into his hands, and cried in wrenching, hopeless sobs as he had not cried since the night he knew he was alone in a cruel world where love was a trap for the unwary.

April came with a shriveling heat more like midsummer, and with it came salvation for Bram Rafferty.

"We've found her!"

"Jerry!" Bram's face blazed with joy, his hands wrapping around his friend's brawny arms with a crushing grip. "Thank God! Thank God!" his voice quavered. "I've waited long to hear those words. Where?"

"Bram, me friend," Jerry's face twisted with regret. "I'm sorry, 'tis not yer lady. 'Tis Mary."

"Mary?" Bram turned away, rubbing his forehead to hide his bleak dejection. "Mary. Where is she?"

"I'll take ye to her now."

A short time later, a door opened at his knock and she stood there, looking not a day older than when he last had seen her.

Startled, she fell back a step. "Bram? Bram, is it you?"

"Yes. It took me a long time to grow up. Can you forgive me?"

"Forgive ye?" Her arms opened to him. "Ye always were a foolish boyeen, Bram Rafferty. Forgive ye, when it's me own self should be doing the asking!"

The cubicle was hot and airless, the single window high on the wall venting muted light that filtered beneath the second-floor gallery outside. The bare walls were adorned with swatches of cloth pinned in place, myriad patterns of pricks in the plaster giving evidence that this had long been a common practice. It was a monk's cell of a room with a single straight-backed chair and a small table, freezing in winter, stifling in summer. Here Anna Barton had worked since late September.

She sighed sadly, her slender hand moving to the small of her back to ease the ache there before her head lowered over the mint-green sheen of a fragile silk. In and out the needle wove while nimble fingers rolled the tiny hem on what had to be miles of flounces. A smile tugged at her mouth, the hint of a dimple appearing at one corner. She had developed a hearty dislike for this style of row upon row of flounces and repeated her vow never again to have such a dress.

The tinkling of the bell announcing customers in the shop drew her head up, a start of fear flaring bright gold in her cinnamon eyes. She listened with the alert tension of a wild creature. Hearing the murmur of feminine voices, she relaxed and shook her head with a wry smile. Bram could not possibly be in the City with the spring planting underway. He would have given up his foolish quest by now.

That near miss in February had affected her badly. If she had not happened to look up from the counter to see him through the window, he would have walked in and found her. As it was, she barely succeeded in yanking Molly from her cubicle and whisking the curtain closed behind her before he came in. Unable to resist the impulse to see him, she peeked through the slit in the curtains.

He seemed taller and broader. Perhaps it was the black wool cloak lined with glossy fur that gave his shoulders that breathtaking width. His step had been firm with a hint of impatience, and his cheeks were reddened by the blustery wind. Did she imagine that his face was thinner? The tip of his gloved finger had rubbed across his temple, and when his hand dropped, she saw the livid scar slashing just above the older curved scar. The warm rich depth of his voice weakened her knees. He was asking for her! Breath bated, she waited for Molly's reply. Truthfully, she told him she had never heard of anyone with those names he listed. Then he described her, and Molly's hands twisted together while she assured him she knew no one by that description.

It had taken every ounce of her strength not to fling the curtain wide and run to him. Only a firm reminder that he sought her through a misguided sense of duty kept her hidden.

A sound disturbed her memories and she looked up. A

boy of no more than five peeped in. He grinned and stepped through the curtain. Damask's eyes widened until a ring of white showed around the cinnamon brown. Inch by inch the color bleached from her face, a numbing shock freezing her.

He was a dark angel of a child with masses of soft blue-black curls and vivid ice-blue eyes outlined by a ring of dark sapphire.

"Hullo," he said with a smile.

"Hello." She fought to capture her fluttering breath. "What is your name?"

"Bram."

"And your mother's name?" She leaned forward. "What is your mother's name?"

"Mary," he grinned. "Mary O'Shea. What's yer name?"

"Damask," she choked out.

The curtain moved and she looked up. A tall slender woman stood behind the boy. Her features were pleasant, though unremarkable, except for the deep-seated serenity in her wide blue eyes.

"Bram, ye naughty boy." She lovingly caressed his cheek as she bent over him. "Ye slipped away for a look. He's a curious one, he is, miss. I hope he's given ye no trouble."

Damask shook her head dumbly and the woman gave her a curious look. At that moment a deep, masculine voice echoed through the sewing rooms. "Mary, love, hurry it along. I'm starving!" Bram Rafferty's voice!

The boy was hustled away and Damask heard his light voice. "I met a nice lady. It was a funny name she had, too." And the woman, soothing. "Not now, Bram, we must hurry."

Love! He called her his love! The mint-green silk slid from Damask's hands, trailing over the mourning black of her gown. Her hands lay slack, her mind dazed. Love. Love! *Love!* It echoed ever louder until her fists came up to press against her ears. Pain drove sharp splinters into her heart and she bent over, a low moan grating in her throat as

the tiny flickering light of hope that had burned
unwaveringly now weakened, diminished, and died.

Bram stood before the window staring into the night. A
letter from Blackberry Hill reported that drought had struck
northwestern Louisiana. Not a single drop of rain had fallen
since winter. The cotton was hardy, but the corn was struggling in the seared fields. He chafed to return to the land, but
knew he could accomplish as little there as here. He could
no more make it rain than he could find Damask. He rubbed
absently at the livid scar, a habit now when he thought of
her.

"Bram, the rascal will not go to sleep 'til he's had a word
with ye."

He turned from the window and touched Mary's cheek.
"I'm glad I found you. I don't know what would have happened to me without you and the boy these last weeks."

"Ye'll find her, Bram," she whispered.

He found the small Bram all tucked in, with only his eyes
peering out. He sat on the bed and pulled the sheet down below the boy's chin. "Are you giving your mother a hard
time?"

"No, sir. But ye wouldn't be listening to me and I've
something to tell ye. I met a lady today. She had a funny
name. Like that lady's name ye're looking for, sir. Da . . .
Damask. Is that right? Damask."

Bram stiffened. "What did she look like?"

"Oh, she was pretty, sir! Her hair was like gold and there
were funny little curls flying around her face. And her eyes
were brown, and her voice was soft. She was nice. I liked
her, sir."

"Where did you see her?" Bram asked urgently.

"In the shop where ye went to get me mother's dress,
sir."

Within minutes, a cab was barreling through the Vieux
Carré. The horses were pulled to a rearing halt, and Bram
leaped from the rocking vehicle. His heavy fist beat a rapid
tattoo on the shop door. "Open up!! Let me in!" He gave

the door a last bang that threatened to shatter the glass, and came out from under the overhead gallery to shout impatiently at the dark rooms over the shop. "I'm looking for Miss Pellier, the owner of the seamstress shop! By God, I'll find her if I have to wake up the whole City!"

A dim light appeared in the slits of the shutters as a Charley ran up the street, a lantern swinging from his hand. "Here, man, you can't wake the block with your shouting!"

"Miss Pellier! I'm not leaving until I've spoken with you!" Bram shook the Charley off like a bothersome gnat.

The man set his lantern on the brick sidewalk, sprang his rattles for assistance, and threw them aside, then made a dive for Bram, wrapping his mighty arms around his chest. "Sir, come along quietly," he grunted. "Miss Pellier is a respectable woman. You can't shout at her from the street!"

Bram broke the man's hold, and his face turned up to the rooms over the shop. "Miss Pellier." he yelled.

Up and down the street heads peeked cautiously through doors, but over the seamstress's shop nothing could be seen but a shadow hovering behind the shutters.

The Charleys' reinforcements arrived. A blow struck Bram from behind. He whirled to meet it with a snarl. It was a short, sharp tussle, three against one. Like the Charleys, Bram knew every dockside trick. Unlike them, he was fueled by frustration and rage.

At last he could do something! The first smile in months twisted across his mouth. Tension, held tightly in check for too long, was released in an explosive blow to a paunch, another that connected with a jaw. The third Charley circled him warily, ready to charge if he could find an opening. Bram crouched, fists ready, turning and turning to keep the man before him, a growl rumbling in his throat.

Lamplight spilled across his face, and the Charley came to an abrupt halt, his jaw dropping. "'Tis himself! Sir, why be ye causing this ruckus in the street?"

"Tim? Tim!" Bram jumped forward, grabbing his arm.

"Miss Pellier knows where my wife is! I've got to talk to the woman!"

"Ye been looking powerful long, sir. I ken yer impatience. A minute, if ye will." He cupped his hands over his mouth. "Miss Pellier, 'tis Timothy Maguire. There's a gentleman here has a question for ye. Come out now; he'll do ye no harm."

Minutes later, Bram threw himself into the waiting cab. "Rousseau Street!" he shouted. "And fly! Triple your fare!"

God! Oh, God, no! Bram fell back onto the cushions and clamped his trembling hands over his knees. Terror beaded icy sweat across his forehead. Rousseau Street! Rousseau Street, where a harvest moon once spilled through an open window touching a woman whose bloodless face mirrored a perfect tranquility, touching a man whose bleary features had found peace at last, and touching a boy with riotous black curls and blood-drenched hands and vivid blue eyes with a look as old as time.

The cab flew through the dark night with the driver's voice shouting encouragement, his whip cracking. Past the St. Charles Hotel and Lafayette Square, around the circle at Tivoli Place, into Nayades paralleling the New Orleans and Carrollton Railroad, then a skidding turn into St. Andrew Street toward the river and Rousseau Street. Memories sliced through Bram like a scalpel through a putrid boil.

He could smell them now, those rank odors that permeated the air of Rousseau Street: the stench of the docks; the smell of fish and tar and filth; the acrid ammonia smell of urine and manure from the cattle pens lining the river; the smell of death and rot and blood from the slaughterhouses. The Irishman's perfume.

The cab skidded to a halt before a scabrous three-story building. Bram climbed out, told the cabbie to wait, all night if he must, and carefully avoided looking at the hulking black shape of the building across the street.

He picked his way up the sagging steps and crossed the

landing into a hallway dimly lit by a single gas lamp. The musty smells of rats and mice mingled with urine and rotting garbage and stale cooking odors. Damask was here! In this! He stopped, closing his eyes to fight down the gorge that rose in his throat.

He climbed a rickety stairway and then another. This was her landing, lit by a low flaming gas lamp. His hand raised, knuckles rapping against the door. Instantly, the low murmur of voices beyond it ceased.

The door opened a crack. "Sir!" Michael's voice shrilled. He darted a glance back into the room, then slipped through the door, pulling it to behind him. "Sir, ye must go away!"

Bram knelt on one knee and pulled Michael into his arms. Holding him tightly, he cradled the small head in his hand. "I've missed you, son," he said roughly. "Have you been well?"

Michael pulled away, squaring his shoulders, but sniffing suspiciously. "I didn't want to leave ye, sir, but the Lady needed me. And now . . ." His voice wavered and he cleared his throat, earnest eyes searching Bram's face. "I have to ask ye to leave, sir. The Lady come home early to-day and went to her room. She hasn't stuck her nose out since."

"Michael, I have to see her."

The squared shoulders slumped. "Come in then, sir."

He walked in and Tessa gave a glad cry, launching herself into his arms. "I knew you'd come! Didn't I say so, Michael? Take us home now." Her eyes filled with tears, and her lips tugged down. "I miss Lulu and Jims! I want to go home, Bram. I want to go home!"

He held her, drawing his knuckle down her cheek gently. "Sh, Tessa, don't cry. I would gladly take you home, but I have to talk to Damask first. It will be up to her."

"She won't go!" Tessa wailed. "She said she never wanted to see Seven Pines again!"

Damask was asleep when Bram slipped into her room. He

spent the night in a chair beside her bed. She tossed often, rattling the cornshuck mattress, and Bram ached to hold her close and soothe her.

The night sky lightened to blue. Sunlight crept across the sill and inched over the floor. Rousseau Street awoke with familiar sounds, and Bram thought he recognized some of the voices he heard. The smell of frying bacon fought the odors in the air, and a whiff of roasting coffeebeans came in the window. In nineteen years, nothing had changed. Bram leaned forward, bracing his elbows on his knees, his hands rubbing his face.

Damask resisted waking up, hanging on tenaciously to blessed thoughtless oblivion. Bay rum and starch. The smells wafted about her, mercilessly reminding her of Bram.

Her lashes opened. Bram, so real, so close. How many times had she dreamed or imagined that she would wake one day and find him there? He looked different somehow, almost gaunt, and there were bluish circles beneath his eyes. He looked exhausted and almost as sad as she felt.

"Why did you leave me, Damask?"

"Because I could not stay with you after . . ."

Horror dawned. This was no dream! Bram was here! If she reached out her hand, she could touch him. Her fingers coiled into her palms, resisting the temptation.

"How did you find me?" she asked with quiet resignation.

"Does it matter? I'm here." He sat on the bed, bracing one hand on the mattress across her. Musing wonder filled his eyes as they caressed the tousled champagne curls, traced the pure curve of her mouth, and rose to search her eyes. "How can you be more beautiful than I remembered?"

Temptation. She had no strength to resist it. Her hand rose, hesitating before her slender, tapered fingers brushed lightly across the livid scar and trembled against the blue-black curls. "Are you recovered from this?"

"An occasional headache. That will go away in time." His fingers closed around her wrist and he pulled her palm to his lips, pressing a kiss to it, then nestling it against his chest. "Damask, I've had much time to think in these last months," he said, and she wondered at the rough rasp of his voice. "I know that we have begun wrong, but . . . is there no chance for us to begin anew? I swear, I would give you no cause for regret."

"What . . ." Her eyes widened. "What are you asking?"

"Come back to Seven Pines as my wife. Damask, I—"

"No!" Damask rolled away, pushing his arm aside, scrambling to her knees on the far side of the bed. "What kind of man are you? How can you ask such a thing of me? As your wife? Your wife?" A wild shriek of laughter shattered the stunned silence and as quickly turned to stony fury. "I have never been your wife, nor will I ever be! I have only one wish, and that is never—*never!*—to see your face again!"

Bram whitened, his eyes stunned and hurt. "I will grant your wish," he ground out, "but first, here is the deed to Seven Pines. I will not be returning there."

A high-flown rage consumed Damask. She snatched the paper from his hand, tore it to shreds, and threw it at him. "It is yours! I will never go back there!"

"Damn you!" Bram's fingers dug into her shoulders and shook her until her vision blurred. "I will not have you living in this hell hole, eking out a living by sewing. You will go home, if I have to drag you by the hair to get you there!!"

"That is the only way you will succeed! Don't you understand? There are too many memories for me there! Memories of you!" The rage drained away abruptly. "I can't live there. I can't," she whispered.

"Do you hate me so much?"

Damask drew away, fists pressing against her mouth.

"Good-bye, Damask," he said and was gone.

"Oh, Bram. I love you. I love you too much to live with my memories," she whispered. "And I love you too much to share you with yours."

St. Charles Hotel, New Orleans, Louisiana
April 20, 1860

Dear Mr. Scarborough,

I have found Damask. She is determined not to return to Seven Pines. I have informed her Uncle James, but have no hope that he will be able to influence her. For that, someone who is more forceful than she is needed, and I believe you to be the only one who can do it. She is living with Tessa and Michael in a filthy tenement at No. 50 Rousseau Street and is working for a seamstress, a Miss Pellier. I beg you to come to the City and use your influence with her. Take her to Bonne Volonte. Convince her to return to Seven Pines. I am enclosing the deed which has been signed over to her, a new one, as she tore the last one to shreds and threw it in my face—which should give you some idea of what opposition you will encounter.

I have been fortunate enough to find my sister, Mary, from whom I have been parted many years. With her son, Bram, we will be going to Dublin on the Lafourche south of Thibodaux. I will remain there in hopes of hearing word of the success of this mission I beg you to undertake.

Sincerely,
Bram Rafferty

Chapter 23

DAMASK *adjusted the flame of the oil lamp and bent over the* frayed cuff she was mending. Michael read, his light voice stumbling over an occasional unfamiliar word. Mr. Twiggs would then stop him, pronounce it, spell it, pronounce it again, and define it. Then Michael would repeat it back to him.

Her eyes lifted to watch them, lingering on Jedediah Twiggs's kindly features. He was a man of medium size with a round, apple-cheeked face topped by a high, broad forehead and soft, baby-fine blonde hair. Peaceful blue eyes framed by round-lensed spectacles glanced her way and Damask smiled and bent to her stitching.

It had been Michael who had found these rooms in Rousseau Street, all she could afford on her poor salary. Damask wondered how she would have managed without him. Alone, she would have been forced to throw herself on her family's mercy within a month. They would have been glad to take her and Tessa in, but her pride would not allow it.

Michael stayed with Tessa during the day, taking her for long walks before their daily trip to the Poydras Market. There he haggled mercilessly for bread and vegetables and meat, and Damask had a sneaking suspicion the vendors gave him lower prices just to be rid of him. If there was a bargain to be found, Michael O'Malley knew where to find it and how to get it, stretching her small wages to include a few small luxuries such as an occasional ribbon for Tessa's hair.

Michael taught her what little she knew about cooking—after suffering through a few days of charred meat, dried beans with the texture of wooden marbles, and gummy rice. Now she could make an Irish stew that even Michael praised—and he was brutally honest about her cooking.

And it was Michael who had drawn their neighbor, Mr. Twiggs, into their small family group.

A teacher in the City's public school system, Mr. Twiggs had no family and had lived simply in his room for many years. His every extra picayune was saved to indulge his one passion—books. His walls were lined floor to ceiling with book-laden shelves, and Michael, on first seeing that awesome sight, was thunderstruck. "Begorra! I never knew there could be so many books in the whole world!" he had said. Mr. Twiggs watched his small hand worshipfully touch a nearby leatherbound volume.

Soon there were nightly lessons in reading, writing, and arithmetic in the dreary, bare room they used as sitting room, kitchen, and dining room. A corner enclosed by a curtain hid Michael's bed. Damask and Tessa shared the single bedroom. When lessons were done, Mr. Twiggs would clean his spectacles with great care, hook the frames behind his ears, and lift whatever volume they were currently reading, one chapter per night. Then his gentle voice would assume a dramatic quality that transported them to lands and worlds far from the stench and hopeless resignation that infected the inhabitants of Rousseau Street.

This night, Jedediah Twiggs folded the book he held. "Michael, you are progressing so rapidly, I believe we can move on to the next reader."

"D'ye think so, sir?" Michael's eyes shone with pride. "Did ye hear that, Lady?"

Damask looked up with a smile. "I told you it wouldn't be long before you were reading to me."

"Indeed, Miss Barton," Mr. Twiggs said, beaming, "in all my years of teaching, I have had only one other student with a mind to match Michael's. Bram had the same quick, inquisitive nature. He peppered me with an endless list of questions I could not answer, just as this young scamp does."

Michael's head snapped up, his eyes moving rapidly between Damask and Mr. Twiggs.

"B-Bram?" Damask faltered.

"Yes. Bram Rafferty. He was in my class the first year I taught in the public school system here. I sometimes think I would have given up teaching had it not been for him. It was a roguish lot I had, little interested in learning. But every year there seemed to be one student whose interest would not allow a teacher to throw up his hands and quit in disgust and despair. That year it was Bram. I had dinner with him about a month ago." He shook his head sadly. "The lad has had a sorry life, and he deserved so much more." His eyes raised to Damask. "I could have sworn I saw him coming from this building this morning, but I must have been mistaken. He would never return to Rousseau Street, after what happened. Still, it did look like him."

"What happened here, Mr. Twiggs?" Damask asked, fingers crushing the cuff.

"Oh, it's long ago and best forgotten, Miss Barton."

"Please, I would like to know." He gave her an inquiring look, and Damask shot an anxious glance at Michael. "Did Bram tell you why he is in the City now?"

"Yes, he's looking for his wife."

"Mr. Twiggs. My name is not Anna Barton. It is Damask Downing Rafferty. He was here this morning to see me."

"I see." His peaceful blue eyes were marked by a curious disturbance.

"Please, Mr. Twiggs. I know only bits and pieces about Bram's life. I would very much like to know the whole of it."

"It isn't a pretty story, Mrs. Rafferty." He shot a warning glance toward Tessa, who was nodding off to sleep in the rocker.

"Tessa, love." Damask went to her. "It's time for bed. Come along now."

Tessa stretched and yawned. "But Mr. Twiggs hasn't read our story yet."

"He won't be reading to us tonight, sweet. Maybe we can talk him into reading two chapters tomorrow night."

"Wonderful idea," Mr. Twiggs chimed in heartily. "Two chapters tomorrow night, Miss Tessa. My word on it."

"In your months here on Rousseau Street," Mr. Twiggs began when Damask settled into her chair, "you've seen something of the problems of the Irish here. Except for those few who make their fortunes, they are unacceptable socially. They've gained a reputation as hard drinkers and troublemakers, and many business establishments refuse to hire them. This keeps them in menial jobs, chained by poor wages to sections of the City like this one. In many ways, it was worse when the Rafferty family came here in the summer of 1839, and it was some years before the barriers were broken to allow the Irish into such jobs as cabbies, draymen, stevedores, and the like.

"Bram, at his mother's insistence, entered my class that fall, and I came to know the family. They lived in the building just across the street here. Mr. Rafferty was a proud man with a laughing way about him. Mrs. Rafferty was a little bit of a woman with a sweet smile. The lad took after her with his black hair and blue eyes. The other children had the look of their father, fair coloring and blonde hair.

"You should have seen them all setting off for a walk into the City, Bram sitting on his father's shoulders and Mrs. Rafferty carrying Baby Annie and the two older children walking along beside them. Mr. Rafferty was a great one for tall tales, and they all hung on his every word.

"Theirs was a house of laughter. The lad loved his mother, but he worshipped his father. That was why it was so hard on him when things began to change.

"Try as he might, Mr. Rafferty could not find work. Winter came and their money ran out. The children went to bed hungry every night, and they had to accept charity to

survive. Then, the oldest girl found work as maid to a
wealthy dowager, so she told them. I don't know how they
would have survived without her. But that, too, was another
sorrow for the lad. In those days there were few ways a girl
could earn a living, and there was only one way that might
support an entire family. Bram was the only one to discover
what she was doing, and he never told his parents, but he
hated his sister from the day he learned she was a . . . a lady
of the evening.

"Late in the spring Mr. Rafferty found work, draining a
swamp on an up-river plantation. It lasted only a short while
before he came down with an awesome case of quartan fever
and returned to the City. He was never the same after. Bitter! Bitter, he was! You know how dangerous the work of
draining a swamp is. The fevers and snakes and alligators.
Planters don't like to risk their valuable slaves,and the Irish
are always hungry for work, so . . ." He waved his hand
and shrugged.

"Mr. Rafferty took to spirits. He became sullen and angry and, in his cups, vicious. Mrs. Rafferty found work as a
washwoman at one of the hotels. She and their daughter
were the sole support of the family, and Mr. Rafferty, quite
naturally, resented it. It's no easy thing for a man who loves
his family, and would work to support them, to have to accept the food and shelter provided by his wife and daughter.
His sober moments grew fewer. The older boy ran away and
was never heard from again. That summer, Baby Annie,
who was an angel of a child, died of yellow fever. It was a
hard blow for the lad.

"So there were none left but Bram and his parents and his
older sister, who visited once a week. His father's drinking
became worse and, with it, his temper. The lad missed many
a school day that fall because he had been beaten too badly
to attend. Mrs. Rafferty was often seen with her shawl
pulled forward to shield her battered face. Sad, it was.
Sad."

He removed his spectacles and began polishing the lenses
with his handkerchief, lips puckered, a frown drawing

across his high forehead. "I suppose we should have seen that something would happen. Bram had changed from a mischievous imp to a solemn, frowning child far older than his years. And he became fiercely protective of his mother."

Mr. Twiggs settled the spectacles on his snub nose, his gentle blue eyes assuming a faraway look. "I will remember that night to my dying day. A Charley came and summoned me to their rooms in hopes I could reason with the lad. There was a harvest moon low on the horizon, like a great coin embedded in velvet. Since then I cannot abide the sight of it, for it brings with it the memory of that chamber of horror.

"Bram's father had come in drunk. Nothing unusual in that. He began beating the lad's mother, and her great with child. Unfortunately, there was nothing unusual in that either. But I think something must have snapped in the boy. He would tell us nothing about what happened, no explanation for what we found. We could only assume that he fought his father, and a frightful battle it must have been. You've seen those curving scars on Bram's temple and the back of his hand? A broken bottle his father wielded. It's a wonder the lad wasn't killed, but somehow he managed to stab his father with a knife—and killed him. His mother died from—" Mr. Twiggs bow-shaped mouth grew taut. "—from the beating. I'll never forget how the lad looked. A child, so young, drenched in blood that poured across his cheek and dripped from his hand.

"His sister had been summoned, and she wanted the lad to come with her. She swore that now there were just the two of them she would give up her work as a—" He shifted uncomfortably. "—that they could live on her wages as a washwoman if she could find nothing else. It was heart-breaking the way she wept and begged him, but the lad just stared at her and said he would not live with a whore."

"Dear God," Damask breathed, propelled back to Bonne Volonte and angry words stabbing through the inky darkness.

"He refused to go to an orphanage. He said he could support himself. But that, we all thought, was impossible. He was only eleven years old. A child who had seen too much, had suffered too much.

"After running away from several orphanages and the House of Refuge, he found a saloon not far from here, where he could sleep in the storeroom and work for his keep. He contacted me soon after, though he has never set foot on this street again until this day. For years I met him at the school every Sunday afternoon to continue his lessons. He had an unquenchable thirst for learning, and I gave him books to read and study, and had more satisfaction from him than any student I ever had, until Michael here. But the lad was never the same after that night. He built a high wall around himself that no one was allowed to penetrate, and something died in him. The ability to love, I thought."

Mr. Twiggs leaned forward, his gentle eyes brightened by urgency. "I was wrong about that, Mrs. Rafferty. It was love I heard in his voice when he spoke of you. It is you who has made Bram Rafferty a whole man. Is there no way you can return to him?"

Damask sighed unsteadily, raising hot dry eyes to him. "No, Mr. Twiggs. It may have been love you heard, but it was not for me. For me there is only a sense of duty and obligation. His love is for another woman. She has given him a son. A—" She faltered. "A beautiful little boy, who is the image of Bram. I must divorce him to allow him to marry her."

Papa Kinloch blew through the small apartment on Rousseau Street like the tempestuous wind of a hurricane. It seemed to Damask she hardly had a chance to open her mouth before their bags were packed and they were all ensconced at Bonne Volonte. In truth, her protests were long, loud, and increasingly vociferous. But Papa Kinloch lacked her Uncle James's gently yielding nature. He stood in the center of the drab gray room, hands folded over the gold-headed knob of his ebony cane, glared down that hawk's beak of a nose, and declared adamantly that no niece of his would live in a hovel. Damask had met her master in stubborn determination and yielded with something less than graciousness. There was time only to write a quick resignation to Miss Pellier apologizing for the abruptness of her leave-taking and a sad good-bye for Mr. Twiggs.

Damask had enjoyed her independence in the City; it was reminiscent of the freedom she had known at Seven Pines before Bram had come. But it was heaven to rise late of a morning and find her bathwater waiting and a luscious breakfast ready. And no more miles of walking because she could not afford the fare for the omnibus; no endless hours of sewing in a tiny cubicle, staring at the blank walls and reliving every moment of her few months with Bram.

A week passed, then another before she realized Papa Kinloch had been biding his time.

"It was a man you had there, girl! Not a milksop! What happened that you would leave him—and don't give me that farradiddle he did about you assuming Wade's guilt! You have a head on those shoulders! A Scarborough would not be so daft!"

Damask chewed the side of her lip, but managed to raise a calm face to him, even though her eyes danced suspiciously. "But I am part Tureaud and Barton and Downing, Papa Kinloch."

He rounded on her with a jaundiced look, the tip of the cane rapping the floor. "I'll have no impertinence, miss! The Scarborough blood runs strong in you. Too strong! You're as stubborn as my Titia!"

Damask went to him, her hands resting on his sleeve. "Please, I don't want to worry you, and I don't mean to be stubborn, but it won't do any good to talk about it. I must divorce him."

Iron-gray brows lowered over bright black eyes that assumed a deadly expression. "Did the man mistreat you, girl?"

"No! Bram would never do that!" Her face flushed with anger. "You've met him! How dare you think such a thing of him!"

Acute frustration contorted his features. "Damned if I understand this younger generation! By thunder, girl, you leap to his defense like a bear with her cub!"

That was far from the last of their discussions, but each ended the same way. Papa Kinloch stomping off, shaking his head and mumbling about "this younger generation."

Though Michael quickly became a favorite of the Scarborough girls and was made to feel at home, he was not accustomed to such a leisurely life. Papa Kinloch gave him free use of the library, and Michael spent much time there, his snub nose thrust between the pages of a book, a small finger carefully following the lines.

But he felt at loose ends. The Lady had no need of him when she was protected by her family. And Papa Kinloch roared when he suggested there must be some way he could earn his keep. Finally, Michael screwed up his courage and approached the Lady, saying he thought it best that he return to the City. She turned as white as the lilies that burst through the soil each spring, and that was the end of his thoughts about leaving, but not the end of his dissatisfaction.

The Lady seemed to want him near, and they spent much time riding over the prairie with Titia, strolling around the grounds with Petite and picnicking in the lacy, airy summerhouse. Tessa, too, was unhappy, her homesickness for Seven Pines growing daily. Michael played games with her and read stories aloud, but it was no life for a man!

The last day of May was a scorcher, and Michael sought the cool shade of an oak near the bayou. Sinking down onto the thick grass, he plucked the swordlike stems and threw them into the water, watching them drift on the sluggish current. There was too much at Bonne Volonte, he thought with a glower. Rich foods and soft beds and plush carpets—and *women's chatter!* He missed the Mister and wondered how he was and whether he was happy with his son. A lump grew in his throat.

"Come here, young man. I would have a word with you."

Papa Kinloch sat on a wooden bench encircling the great trunk of an oak. Michael climbed to his feet and went to stand before the old man, bright black eyes and indigo blue locked with measuring looks.

"I've a notion, young man, that you are one who misses nothing. The girl is keeping her stubborn silence, so I want you to tell me what you know."

Michael squirmed. "Sir, the Lady—"

"The lady will thank you if we can straighten this out. And I would have that Rafferty as kin! Now, sit!" Michael folded his legs and sat. "The beginning!" the old man barked.

"It won't do ye no . . . any good, sir. The Lady's set on niver seeing the Mister again."

"Let me be the judge of that. The beginning!"

Since Michael had been confessor and friend to Damask during the lonely months in the City, he was able to begin at the true beginning, on the night Wade lost Seven Pines to Bram. He told of their marriage, the attack on Bram in the City, and his subsequent suspicion of Damask, the attempts on Bram's life and that stormy night when Bram was shot by Nero.

"Sir, the Lady loves him powerful hard."

"I've eyes in my head to see that! Why has she left him? Doesn't he love her?"

"I would have swore he did, sir! The Mister's eyes would light up like candles when the Lady came into a room, and he watched her like there wasn't nothing in the world he'd rather see. But the Lady says he loves another and has a son by her."

"A womanish fancy, I wager."

"No, sir! She's seen the woman and the boy. She says he's the spit of the Mister. He's even named for him."

Papa Kinloch straightened abruptly, alert black eyes latching onto Michael. "What's that, boy?"

"His son is named Bram, after the Mister, sir."

"Bram, is it? And the woman's name? Does she know that?"

"Yes, sir. She says it's Mary."

"Faugh! Two stubborn fools if ever I saw any! Mary, it is! Mary!" He threw back his head and roared with laughter.

Michael frowned. "Sir, ye cannot think their troubles are made for laughter?"

"Troubles? Their troubles are much of their own making!" He rapped the ebony tip of his cane on the grass and grinned down at Michael. "Boy, I've passed seventy-two winters and there are few surprises left for me, but I can still be amazed at the folly of a man and a woman in love."

Michael nodded his head sagely. "'Tis the truth ye've spoken, sir. 'Tis why this Irishman'll be spending his days a bachelor. I've no wish to be having me head tied in more knots than a sailor could be making."

This brought a renewed burst of laughter from Papa Kinloch. When he calmed, he reached over to ruffle Michael's hair. "A wise boy you are. It will save you much in the way of grief." He stood and flexed his shoulders, then winked in high good humor. "In a few days you will all be on your way back to Seven Pines—*with* your Mister."

Michael jumped up, his eyes shining. "D'ye think so, sir? How can ye know?"

Kinloch Scarborough put his arm across Michael's shoulders and began leading him toward the house. "Can you keep a secret, boy?"

"Tweedle-dum and tweedle-dee!"

Damask laid aside her fork and sent an inquiring look at Titia.

"Mr. Nixon of the New Orleans *Daily Crescent* said that was all the difference there was between an Abolitionist and a Republican. He was right," Titia added with a shake of her glossy black hair. "Think about it. What is their common aim? The destruction of slavery." She applied herself to slicing a forkful of succulent beef. "Tweedle-dum and tweedle-dee!"

Damask's appetite left her suddenly. She wished fervently that Papa Kinloch would not encourage Titia in her passion for politics. No twist or turn or speculation of the events of the winter and spring had been left unvoiced. There had been retiring Governor Wickliffe's message to the legislature in January, calling for a reorganization of the militia with a view to making Louisiana independent "should the hour of trial come." In his inaugural address, the new governor, Thomas Overton Moore, referred to John Brown's raid and the subsequent wave of Northern sympathy for him, saying it had "Deepened the distrust in the permanency of our Federal Government and awakened sentiments favorable to a separation of the states." And just weeks ago, on April 30th, the Southern delegations had withdrawn from the Democratic convention in Charleston. Now the Democrats were sorely divided and weakened while the Black Republicans gained strength by the day.

As unhappy as she was, it was impossible for her not to be affected by the fever that raged through the South. Politics was on every tongue, the word *secession* on too many. It was a chilling reminder of Bram's flat-out certainty there would be war.

And Bram would go! He was not a man to let another fight his battle. He would go, perhaps to be wounded or killed, and she would never know.

The ringing tap of a knife against a wine glass brought Damask back to the table, away from a bloodied battlefield with Bram lying helpless and alone.

"Ladies," Papa Kinloch said, "we are expecting a guest tomorrow. An important guest! Euphemie, I want you to talk to Cook tonight. A feast is to be prepared. Only the best. Titia, you are to see that the summerhouse is scrubbed spotless. This must be done very early! I expect him on the steamer just after noon. Chatté, Petite, you will set the gardeners to cutting flowers. I want flowers everywhere! And the summerhouse is to be strung with garlands. Set some of those potted things you like so much around in it, Petite."

"Papa Kinloch," Chatte sparkled, "who is our guest?"

"Papa Kinloch," *Tante* Euphemie asked, "how many will we be?"

"Our guest is a surprise, Chatte. And we will be, let's see, just two more, I think."

They adjourned to the parlor, Papa Kinloch surrounded by his women like an oriental potentate with his harem. He puffed on his cigar, grinned at Michael, and fended off their numerous queries as to who their guest might be. Finally, he stood and stretched, telling each one good night before he paused at Damask's side and tipped her chin up.

"I will expect you to get a good night's sleep, niece. No circles under those pretty eyes for our guest tomorrow."

Bonne Volonte, Bayou Teche, Louisiana
May 31, 1860

Nephew,

She is here. Come. Immediately!

Kinloch Scarborough

Chapter 24

MICHAEL *waited at the corner of the grounds near the bayou,* anxiously watching for the steamer. A slash of crushed grass marked his restless pacing. Delicious aromas floated on the hot air, tickling his nose and making his stomach growl with hunger. Chatte and Petite were at work in the summerhouse, bedecking it with garlands and flowers, their speculation about who their guest could be never coming near the truth.

Michael was grinning to himself when a faint rumbling sounded and the steamer poked its snub nose around the bend. Michael's hands drew into fists, his stomach knotting painfully. What if the Mister hadn't come?

Never had anything moved so slowly! Inch by inch it drew nearer. Michael's dark eyes squinted. He could make out people standing near the rail, one man taller than the rest. The man removed his hat and a shaft of sunlight struck a curling crown of blue-black hair. Michael whooped with joy and whirled, racing for the house, his small face beet red. He threw himself through the parlor doors, gasping, "He's coming!"

Papa Kinloch nodded. "You meet him, Michael. And remember! Not a word!"

"Yes, sir!"

Damask was bemused by her uncle's odd behavior. He had even gone to the extreme of overseeing her toilette, rejecting the simple gown in mourning black and rifling through her armoire with discontented grunts until he came across a tea-rose yellow voile with a deep square neckline

337

and pagoda sleeves. Her grandfather would forgive her for rejecting mourning, he informed her, then scowled mightily at the simple bun that rested on her nape. "It suits you," he had said, his face clearing, before he stalked from her room. Whirling back, he shook a threatening finger. "And no crinoline! Damned things! A man can't get close to a woman if he wants to!"

A worried frown knitted her dark brows now as she watched her uncle pace to and fro, his hands behind him, the cane held in one fist. Was it possible his mind was going? He seemed so vigorous and youthful. But, such strange behavior!

Suddenly his pacing came to a halt. He grunted and strode to the doors leading into the second parlor, pulled them shut, and then the French doors leading onto the front veranda, leaving only the ones at the side open. When that was done, he looked around, gave a satisfied nod, and resumed his pacing.

"Papa Kinloch," Damask asked softly, "have you been feeling well?"

"Never better, my girl! Never better!" He peered at her from beneath the bush of iron-gray brows, then threw back his head, shouting with laughter. "You think the old man is getting a bit barmy, eh?"

"Oh, no, sir!" Damask said, quite untruthfully.

The sound of steps climbing the stairs drew their attention to the doors. The pulse at Damask's throat quickened. Those footsteps had a familiar ring. Suspicion set her pulse thrumming. It can't be, she assured herself, but her fingers squeezed into white-knuckled fists.

He was there, standing in the doorway, broad-brimmed white straw hat held in his dark hands, his face lean and bronze beneath the tumbling mop of black curls, his brilliant eyes hanging on her with an expression that was at once wary and tender.

She could not move or speak or look away. He was so much thinner, she thought with a pang of fear. And there was something . . . a sadness deep in his eyes. Her heart lurched in her breast.

Papa Kinloch waited for them to drink in the sight of each other, then strode forward, hand outstretched. "Nephew, we've been waiting."

His voice shocked Damask from her hungry perusal of Bram's face, but still she could not find the strength to move. "Papa Kinloch, how could you do this?" she questioned faintly. "I told you. There is nothing we have to say to one another."

"If there is anything I have learned in my seventy-two years, girl," he informed her harshly, "it is that no disagreement can be settled without some communication between the two parties!"

"But this is no disagreement!" Damask cried out. "And talking will change nothing!"

"Sir! I will not have Damask badgered!" Bram added hotly. "It is obvious she cannot bear the sight of me." Papa Kinloch snorted with disgust, and Bram's eyes narrowed dangerously. "However good your intentions, sir, you have made a mistake in summoning me."

Bram turned to leave, but Papa Kinloch restrained him with a firm hand on his shoulder, and somehow maneuvered it so that Bram was inside the room and he was standing in the door. He reached for the handles and began drawing them closed. "Tell her about Mary," he said as the doors snapped shut.

Bram's black brows drew together in a puzzled frown that deepened when he saw the horror-stricken look Damask leveled on the spot where Papa Kinloch had disappeared from view.

"Damask, why would he ask me to tell you about my—"

"I don't want to hear it!" She turned away from him. "I won't listen to this, Bram," she said low and hard. "I want you to go. Now!"

Bram stared dully at the slender trembling line of her back. Slowly, the proud square line of his shoulders sank. Jesus, he had hoped for so much. It was cruel to give him that hope and snatch it away again. His strong hands shook as they closed around the wrought iron door handles, and he paused there to draw a deep, calming breath. Quickly, he stepped through and jerked the doors closed behind him.

At the foot of the stairs Papa Kinloch and Michael waited. Their faces turned up to him, expressions of happy anticipation falling into ludicrous lines of dismay.

"You told her?" Papa Kinloch questioned impatiently.

Bram shook his head. "She didn't want to hear anything from me. I know you meant well, sir—"

"By thunder! What did I tell you, Michael? Never have I failed to be amazed! Sir"—somehow he contrived to look up the stairs and down that hawk's beak of a nose—"are you so blind that you cannot see the girl is near mad for love of you? She thinks Mary is your light-o'-love and the boy, Bram, is your son!"

"What!"

"It's true, sir," Michael chimed in. "Her heart's nearly broke in two from thinking ye loved another."

Bram tried to shake the cobwebs from his head. "But, Michael, she could not have known about them when she left Seven Pines! Why did she leave?"

"Sir, ye were out of yer head after ye were shot. The Lady told me ye called out for Mary. Ye begged her not to leave ye; ye said ye loved her. That's why the Lady left, sir. She thought ye loved another and she couldn't stay with ye then. She wanted ye to be happy, sir, free to go to the one ye loved."

"Michael"—there was a haunted desperation in Bram's eyes—"are you sure?"

"Sir, the Lady loves ye. I would not lie to ye about it."

The doors slammed against the frame and Bram burst into the parlor. The crashing sound did not penetrate the fog of misery that enveloped Damask.

A strong hand beneath her chin forced her head up. Bram was there, kneeling before her, his face on a level with hers. Bram who had given her fleeting moments of happiness and months of sorrow.

"Damask, you must listen—"

"No." She forced his hand away, her nails biting into his wrist. How could he force this further humiliation on her? She could accept that he loved another, but she could not accept his feeling an obligation to her he didn't owe.

"Damask, please, Mary is—"

"Stop, Bram! Stop! I don't want—"

He hooked one hand behind her neck and clamped the other over her mouth. "Mary is my sister! Bram is her son! My sister and my nephew, Damask, nothing more!"

She gaped in blank astonishment over the trap of his hand. His sister. The sister he rejected.

Slowly, he moved his hands away while he watched her.

"Your sister?" she breathed in disbelief. Was it possible? His sister.

Bram gathered her hands in his, bowing his head over them, pressing the slender fingers to his forehead while he tried to gather his wits and calm the pounding of his heart.

He looked up, his eyes dark sapphires that burned into hers, and Damask perceived what she should always have known. Bram Rafferty would never desert a woman he loved or a child of his own.

"I'm so sorry for everything that has happened," he said softly. "If I could go back and change it, I would. But I cannot take back a single cruel word or thoughtless deed. I know you don't understand, but—"

"Bram," Damask yearned toward him, "there is no woman that you love?"

"Yes. Yes, there is," he said urgently. "I think I have loved her since my first sight of her at Seven Pines."

"Oh," Damask breathed mutely, the dark muddy color of her eyes brightening to glistening cinnamon.

"I love you, Damask. Is there any hope—"

His impassioned declaration was choked off, literally, when Damask snatched her hands from his and wrapped her arms around his neck. She leaned forward, laughing and crying. Bram, braced on one knee, was thrust back at a precarious angle. Then, he was falling, one arm clinging to his most precious prize, the other hand thrown out to break their fall. They settled on the muted blues and reds of the Aubusson carpet in a rustling flurry of starched petticoats, Damask's head resting on his forearm.

"I love you, Bram Rafferty," she whispered. "I love you."

His mouth lowered to hers, claiming the sweet curve of her lips with the soaring ecstasy of newfound love. The rough-textured palm of Bram's hand trembled against the downy blush of Damask's cheek. His lips moved slowly to the hidden hollow at the corner of her mouth, across her cheeks to her eyes. Gently, so gently, he kissed the fragile lavender-tinted lids before moving back to her lips. Drawing away, he sighed, a soft sound laced with regret.

"Beloved," he whispered unsteadily, "we must rise. Your uncle awaits us below."

Damask's hand moved to Bram's nape, sensitive fingers sliding up through the close-cropped curls. "Papa Kinloch won't expect us so soon, Bram. He has gone to so much trouble; it would be a shame to waste it."

Her lips moved perilously close, and a widening grin flashed white against Bram's sun-bronzed face. "A shame," he growled.

It was some time before they rose, torn between the sated contentment of love acknowledged and returned, and the frustration of passion inflamed and unfulfilled.

They wandered out to the lawn, where Papa Kinloch was surrounded by his women, a thorn in a brightly blooming bed of roses. He stood when he saw them coming, his face solemn, a perceptive gaze moving from one smiling face to the other. His lips pursed and his head nodded and he clapped a hand on Michael's shoulder. "I'd say it was a good day's work we did, eh, boy?" The ebony tip of his cane thumped silently on the grass. "Now, niece, for the wedding!"

"Wedding! Papa Kinloch, we are already married! In fact . . ." Damask's eyes sparkled up at Bram. "Do you know what today is?"

"Our first anniversary," Bram answered with a grin.

"Bah! You call that a wedding! It was a contract! To-day! Today, there will be a wedding!" Papa Kinloch said vociferously. "I've had your great-grandmother's wedding gown airing since Michael and I hatched our plot. There will be feasting and merriment tonight. Meanwhile, the parson is waiting in the summerhouse. So, off with you, girl! I want you to look your loveliest when I give you away."

"Papa Kinloch . . ." Damask flew into his arms. He hugged her tightly, a broad smile lifting the bushy ends of his moustache, dark eyes twinkling. "You are a humbug with the soul of a romantic," she said, "and I love you for it!"

Damask turned full circle before Papa Kinloch, then dipped low in a curtsy. Damask Tureaud Scarborough's wedding gown was a perfect fit. It was a simple gown in yellow silk gauze with a tight-fitting bodice and full gathered skirt. The three-quarter length sleeves had a single white ruffle, and a *fichu* of white silk edged with a self-ruffle was worn around the shoulders, crossing over the breast to give the pouter-pigeon shape so popular during the 1780s. The hat had a full puffed crown in yellow silk gauze and a wide curving brim in white trimmed with bright yellow feathers, a yellow bow, and streamers.

Kinloch Scarborough raised Damask to her feet, clearing his throat. "Lovely, my dear. Lovely. My mother wore this gown on every anniversary she shared with my father, and they repeated the vows they had sworn."

"I'm sure Bram is as honored as I that you permit me to wear her gown today."

He sniffed and the cane thumped. "Humph! You could come to that young man in a hempsack and he would swear there was none other to touch you for beauty! Come along," he said gruffly, "the parson is getting restless."

Settling his top hat over his mane of hair, he gave it a perky tap before bowing and extending his arm. They strolled through the crazy-quilt pattern of light decorating the red-brick walk, winding through the lawn between azaleas like huge fuschia cushions sprigged in green, and around tall camellias covered with pure white scentless blossoms.

The summerhouse was a marvel of lattice work and climbing roses, the interior festooned with garlands of ivy and decorated with potted ferns and violets, added hastily when Petite discovered what the occasion was to be. The shade of an oak cooled it, and the water lapping against the bank of the bayou nearby provided soothing music. *Tante* Euphemie wiped her eyes and blew her nose in a lace-trimmed handkerchief, and Tessa wriggled about on the cushioned seats lining the octagonal walls, craning her neck for the first sight of Damask. The parson, having overcome his initial surprise over being summoned to perform a wedding at the home of the Catholic Scarboroughs, held his well-thumbed Bible and waited with a look of seraphic patience. Michael attempted to look suitably serious, but found it to be a lost cause. The corners of his mouth kept pulling into a smile that inched wider and wider.

To all outward signs, Bram waited patiently. There were no betraying signs of nervousness. His gloved hands hung easily at his sides. His mouth was a firm pleasant line. He did not move about or fidget, but there was an air of quivering alertness about him, and the ice-blue eyes had assumed an incandescent color.

When he caught sight of Damask, his dark face betrayed a surprised wonder, as he raked her with a look compounded of love and sudden despair. She looked ethereal, a dream that might vanish, before he could reach out, grasp it, and call it his own.

The tips of their fingers touched, their hands clasped, and Damask felt the trembling in his hand and saw the steadily darkening color of his eyes. She knew the conflict that raged within him: the hope that he had truly come home and the fear that this new joy would be taken from him. She smiled with gentle reassurance and squeezed his hand lightly.

"Beloved, I'm here," she whispered, echoing the promise made at Dublin. "I'll always be here."

His eyes cleared and his arm went around her to draw her close. Damask's voice was calm and distinct as she promised to love, honor, and obey. Bram's voice, however, wavered on a tremor of emotion, his eyes suspiciously bright as he leaned down to seal their vows with a kiss of aching tenderness.

A shower of rice rained about them, and they turned with a laugh. Damask hugged Michael, and Bram shook hands with a grinning Papa Kinloch.

"I don't know how we can thank you, sir."

"By thunder, Kinloch Scarborough Rafferty has a nice ring to it, nephew."

"Done," Bram grinned. "The first boy shall be named for you."

"Humph! Make it the second. The first should carry his father's name, and I've a suspicion there'll be more than enough babies to go around."

Damask was alone in the chamber she had shared with Bram on their previous visit to Bonne Volonte. Another of Papa Kinloch's orders. Everything was to be as it should be for a first wedding. Her aunt and cousins and Tessa had accompanied her to this chamber, helping her to change, brushing her hair until the golden highlights shimmered to life. They had insisted she climb into bed, and each gave her a kiss before they left. Surprisingly, it was Titia, the one Damask would have thought least likely to have inherited Papa Kinloch's streak of romanticism, who had hugged her tightly and wept, saying she envied her the love of a man like Bram.

She was too nervous to remain in bed, and crawled out, her hand smoothing the peach-colored silk negligee over her hips. Steps sounded on the veranda and Bram stepped into the room, pulling the doors closed behind him and leaning back with an amused grin.

"Damn if I thought that meal would ever end. I could have eaten sawdust for all I tasted."

Apprehension vanished and Damask giggled. "Me, too."

His eyes moved from her face. The grin slipped a little, then vanished. He jerked up from his slouching stance at the door, a spark kindling in glowing pools of ice-blue. The gown was a peach-colored haze floating about Damask's delicate frame, molding itself to the round curve of her breast, dripping from rose-tipped peaks, clinging to the arch of her hips, casting mysterious shadows across the nest of gold at the joining of her thighs.

His breath left him on a long sigh and he took a single step forward, his arms raising. Damask ran to him, her arms looping around his neck, and Bram hooked an arm beneath her knees and swept her high against his chest. He searched her face, his eyes shading to smoky passion.

"If this is a dream, let me sleep forever," he said huskily.

"No dream, my love. No dream." Damask's fingers traced his lips and cupped his cheek, her lips molding themselves to his with rapt insistence.

She sank deep into the cushiony softness of the feather tick, the tiny dimple quivering flirtatiously. Bram leaned over her, arranging her hair in a fan of waves and curls high on the pillow. He nuzzled her ear, and she heard the deep breath he drew, then released with a sigh.

"Violets. I have had to avoid the flower vendors in the City all spring. I could bear neither the sight nor the scent," he rumbled with a hint of remembered pain. "Love, don't ever leave me again. I swear, the sun has not risen on a single day without you."

"Bram, I will never leave you. You are my life. Couldn't you see how much I loved you?"

He drew back, one brow quirked. "And how was I supposed to do that? You shied away if I touched you; you left any room I entered; you would not let me get near you."

Damask laughed. "I was afraid if you touched me I would throw myself into your arms, and beg you to love me as much as I loved you! And what about you? That day in the woods when I touched you, you flinched away as though I were something vile!''

"Vile! Never!'' Bram pulled the silk away from Damask's breast, his head lowering, his tongue teasing the rose-tipped peak until she gasped and tangled her fingers in his hair, drawing his head up to hers, her mouth clinging to his. He drew away, breath ragged. "I wanted you that day, Damask. I wanted you so much I was afraid your touch would drive me to rape. And I had hurt you enough. I would not have you hate me.''

"What fools we've been. I would have thanked you for it. Bram?'' She pulled his head down, her tongue flicking against his lips. "You don't intend to waste our night talking, do you?''

"Hmm. I don't suppose Papa Kinloch would approve of that, do you? And he has exerted himself to get us here. It would be a shame to disappoint him.''

"A shame,'' Damask intoned solemnly.

He rolled off the bed to shed his clothes. Damask curled up on her side, her hand beneath her cheek. The candlelight bronzed his lean, muscled torso, striking bluish lights in the thick furring that covered his chest, tapering to the thin line across the taut plane of his belly, widening . . .

Damask's cheek pinkened and her eyes climbed to the less awesome sight of his broad chest and swelling muscles. The candle was snuffed and Bram joined her, sliding into the bed and pulling her to him.

A cloud of peach silk drifted through a patch of moonlight, floating slowly to the floor where it settled without a whisper of sound. Slender satiny limbs entwined with darkly furred muscular limbs and the rhapsody of love began with the joining of lips and the tentative touching of tongues. Bram's strong hands roamed with gentle insistence, exploring the high curve of Damask's breasts, the indentation at her waist, and the bell of her hips.

She writhed beneath his touch, her mind swirling. His lips tugged at the swollen peaks his hands had made maddeningly sensitive, and she almost screamed aloud at the shaft of pleasure that streaked down to the persistent demand in the core of her feminine being. Her palms rubbed over the hard-muscled ridges of his back, across his shoulder and down his chest where the wiry hair prickled against her palm. Her knee rubbed along his thigh and she arched closer to him, pressing the length of her heated flesh to him. The throbbing ache became exquisite pain and still Bram explored, touching, tasting, loving. Her breath sobbed in her throat, all thought lost. Only feeling remained: the burning tip of his shaft brushing her leg, his hot moist breath searing her skin, his hands driving her beyond the realm of sanity into a world of passion that ravished the senses. When she thought she could stand no more, he moved over her, murmuring words of love hotly against her neck. Slowly, he filled her, hot, throbbing, rigid with his own need.

Damask moved with him, feeling the rough brush of his furred chest against her breasts. Faster and faster, the tension coiling tighter and tighter until she reached that blissful haven of surcease where the rhapsody of love flings its pulsing cadence to the stars.

Epilogue: November 6, 1860

"LULU, *you look tired. Why don't you go to bed*?"

The brush thumped onto the dresser top, and Lulu's thin brows climbed. "Humph! Ain't been tired a day since you done come home! Sides, that devil be feeling the cold when he git here. Got to keep the coffee hot to take the chill out."

Damask caught Lulu's hands and pressed them to her cheek. "Won't you ever admit you made a mistake about him? That devil, indeed!"

Something tender softened the expression in Lulu's boot-button eyes, but she sniffed disdainfully and lifted her nose. "A devil I call him and a devil he is. I just put up with him 'cause you ain't got no better sense than to think the sun don't shine for nobody but him! Guess it wouldn't do no good to tell you to git your rest. Be needing more of that now." Damask's gaze questioned and Lulu nodded sagely. "Yep. I'd say about spring we'll have us a little black-headed devil squalling his way into this world. When you gonna tell his pappy?"

"Tonight."

"Lord help us!" Lulu's eyes rolled to the heavens. "He'll be prouder than a rooster in a hen yard! As if he ain't struttin' proud already! Won't be no living with him!"

Lulu grumbled her way down the hall, and Damask turned out the lamp and sat on the rag rug before the hearth, a blanket drawn around her shoulders and cold toes wriggling near the red embers peeping through the ash. A son in Bram's image, she mused, though he would never have a son who looked more like him than his namesake.

Now there was a little black-headed devil if ever there was one! How one small boy could get into so much mischief in so short a time was a puzzle to Damask. In the two days they had spent at Dublin to allow her and Mary to become acquainted, the small Bram had been pulled out of the bayou three times, had fallen out of the hay loft once, had cut his leg with a machete, and had been chased out of the swamp by an alligator—all because of an insatiable curiosity. Dark angel and wicked imp all rolled into one, he was so disarmingly charming that even his mother could not correct him. Or his Uncle Bram!

Damask grinned to herself. That strong, manly spine was pure jelly! Her hand strayed to her flat abdomen. If there was to be any disciplining of the Rafferty brood—and she was determined to fill Bram's house with his children and the love and laughter that had been denied him—it was not going to come from their father who melted like hot wax at the first sign of anxiety in a child's small face.

The image of Wade hovered at the back of her thoughts as well. She had battered herself with guilt ever since her parents' deaths. She had taken the blame for being true to herself, and Wade had abetted her for his own reasons. He had used her love as he would have tried to use their parents' love had they lived. She could see that so clearly now. Her parents' deaths had been a horrible accident. But it was not her doing. Wade had become what he was through no fault of hers. The needle-sharp pangs of guilt eased somewhat. She accepted that neither of them could have changed their basic character.

The fire popped, sending a shower of sparks up the chimney. Damask jumped, then drew the blanket tighter around her. Her thoughts returned to those two days at Dublin with Mary. Since that fateful night of the harvest moon, Mary had worked as a washwoman at the St. Louis Hotel. She had met and married Patrick O'Shea, and had been widowed shortly after her son's birth. Yet there was no bitterness in her. Only a serene acceptance of life's vicissitudes. It was unfortunate that she refused to return home with them, for Damask would have loved to have had her near. But in her gently stubborn way, Mary was determined to support herself and her son, and returned to her job at the hotel.

Their arrival at Smithport Landing had been a shock. Hearing the news of the drought that had struck the northern portion of the state did not prepare them for the reality. The dry heat parched skin and lips and tongue. The green of the pines lining the road was dulled by layers of reddish dust that boiled in choking clouds from wheels and hooves. The sun-seared fields of corn were pitiful sights, hardy weeds providing the only greenery in acre after acre of immature stalks bleached white. Dried leaves rustling in the hot wind raised dusty swirls over the moribund land. The hardier cotton suffered less, though the sparsely leafed stalks were scrubby shadows of the tall lushly foliaged plants of the previous year.

At harvest time not a single ear of corn was to be had from vast acres planted, and the cotton was yielding half or less than normal. Papa Kinloch, on hearing of the total failure of the corn, had shipped enough to fill the cribs, along with fodder to see them through next year's crops.

Damask tucked her toasty toes beneath the folds of the blanket and reached for the poker to prod the log. A blast of heat struck her face as it rolled and settled. She set the poker aside, tucking her hands inside the blanket, shivering lightly as she listened to the moaning of the chill wind through the eaves.

The drought and its consequent devastating effects on all the planters would have been the overriding topic of conversation throughout the summer and fall, but this was a hotly contested presidential election year. Where men gathered, tempers flared. Northern sympathy for John Brown had hardened Southern opinion. The word *compromise* was an anathema. Rumors of abolitionist plots and slave revolts

raged like fire through dry timber. Many were patently ridiculous, but the credulous and fearful believed them im-
plicitly.

A little known backwoodsman by the name of Abraham
Lincoln had been nominated by the Republicans, but his
name appeared on no ballot anywhere in the staunchly
southern State of Louisiana.

The campaigning throughout the state, as it had been all
over the nation, was vociferous and energetic, with torch-
light parades and speeches, picnics and speeches, speeches
and more speeches. A mood of near hysteria had prevailed
in the last few wild weeks, and Bram had grown increasingly harried. He swore, until that very morning, that he
would not bother to vote. He had risen with a black scowl,
and when he rode away, the atmosphere inside the house
had been cooler than the one outside.

Part of it, Damask thought, was the letter they had received a few days before from Kaiser Buckner. He had
graphically portrayed the mood in the North. There, too, the
word *compromise* was not heard. The letter served to
deepen Bram's growing depression about the political situation.

Fortunately, the enclosed letter from Dread had given
them all a welcome smile. It was in his own awkward hand
with numerous misspellings. He had only praise for Buckner, who had apprenticed him with a carpenter and arranged
classes in reading and writing. He had seen the ocean and
was stunned by the size of it. He loved his work and was
happy in the North. Damask read it aloud for the whole of
the quarters, afterward placing it in the hands of his mother,
Rosetta. "My boy done learn to scratch the pen just like
white folks," she had said in an awed whisper as she
brushed it with trembling fingers.

Damask moved back from the heat a foot or so, then hearing a sound, half-turned, her head cocked to listen. It was
the door! The blanket crumpled to the floor and she jumped
up. Swaying dizzily for a few seconds, she smiled and reminded herself she would have to take more care now. But

when she heard the low tones of Bram's voice, she promptly ran down the hall. Bram was at the bottom of the stairs. He looked up and Damask stopped, uncertain of her reception after their cool parting that morning.

He smiled, and Damask laughed aloud and flew down the steps to launch herself into his arms. The low rumble of his laughter joined hers as he whirled her around and around.

"Sorceress," he murmured against her neck. "You've haunted my every thought all day! What a fool I've been in these last weeks! If the world goes up in flames tomorrow, we will still have each other. In the end, nothing else matters."

Damask pulled away. "Michael—"

"Is putting away the horses. He can see himself to bed."

Damask arched her neck to give his nuzzling lips freer access. "Lulu stayed up to keep coffee hot for you."

"Coffee! Ah, colleen," he murmured softly. His head lifted, one black brow quirked into a wicked arch, his eyes alight with amusement. "Lulu! Go to bed!" he shouted. "Your mistress has a better idea of what a man needs to warm him on a cold winter night."

"Bram!" Damask shrieked and buried her fiery cheeks in the curve of his neck.

Up the stairs they went, Lulu's deep throated voice following. "A devil I calls him and a devil he is."

Bram chuckled, a low amused rumble that startled her from her thoughts just before the strong support of his arms slipped away and she dropped onto the feather mattress with a whoosh of icy air. Drawing her knees high, she tucked the hem of her gown around her feet and propped her chin on her knees, cinnamon eyes glowing bright.

For a moment she pondered the idea of boxing his ears for his untimely playfulness, but he moved away and began shrugging out of his heavy overcoat. She damped the quivering expectation that tingled in her stomach and chewed away the smile that leaped to her mouth when Bram slanted a wicked gaze her way. He enjoyed the slow titillation of the senses, the interlude when dueling eyes spoke volumes and time stretched on the rack of anticipation, and he had taught her the delight of savoring that building tension. Pleasure feathered along her nerves with a winsome sweetness, and Damask cuddled her icy toes in the palms of her hands, raking him with a roguish look.

His long brown fingers worked at the buttons of his frock coat, slowly at first, but moving faster and faster until he reached the last one. The coat flew over one shoulder while his fingers tore at the buttons of his waistcoat. It flew off in another direction and he ripped the cravat from his throat.

Damask's lips twitched. She would have to rise early in the morning to gather the evidence of his haste from all corners of the room, or else try to ignore the knowing roll of Lulu's eyes and her dire mutterings about "that devil gambling man."

He watched her intently, with a hunger compounded of need, tenderness, and wonder, as though he could not quite believe she was real.

His scratchy woolen long johns sailed through the air, draping drunkenly over the spindle back of her rocking chair. He faced her in the magnificent glory of his bronzed nakedness. Damask's heart leapt into her throat, pulsing with excitement. She leaned back, her toes peeping from the ruffled hem of her gown, arms raised in welcome, her eyes glistening with the golden glow of her love. "Bram," she sighed, a gentle command, a sensuous invitation.

His blue eyes glittered, the muscles tightening across his high cheekbones in a look so intense it was almost like pain. He joined her, flinging the heavy layers of quilts up over them. "Damask," he murmured unsteadily, his hands cupping her cheeks, bright eyes darkening with emotion as they delved deep into hers, "each time, I must remind myself anew that you are mine, that this is real and not a dream."

His lips covered hers in a kiss of anguished tenderness. The powerful muscles of his back rippled warm and strong beneath Damask's caressing hands. She was his, body and soul. And soon there would be a child of their love. A son. The tall strong son of Bram Rafferty. The conscious world spun away on a dizzying swirl of pleasure. Forgotten was the child that floated in the protective cocoon of her womb. There was only Bram, his long muscled length pressing her gently into the feather mattress. His palms, roughened and scarred from his years of working in the blistering sun on the docks of the City, stroked the curve of her hip with exquisite care. His elegant fingers, sensitized by his delicate gambler's touch, explored the indentation of her waist with assiduous attention.

Soon the flimsy barrier of her flannel nightgown drifted to the foot of the bed. His lips etched a pattern of heat on her shoulder, moving to the mound of her breast, pausing to nuzzle the base of that swelling slope before rising with startling suddenness to capture the quivering peak. The moist warmth of his breath, the tickle of the matting of hair on his chest, the gentle insistence of his work-roughened hands drew that spring of tension, unbearably, painfully until her bare flesh strained toward his. Arching, clinging with grasping fingers to his hot, trembling thews, she hurtled toward the tantalizing threshold of ecstasy and found release with an explosion of light that shimmered across her eyelids, a rhapsody of sound that burst in her mind, rampant sensations of pleasure storming along her nerves.

Outside, the bitter winter wind whistled through the eaves, the mournful sound an eerie background to the cheerful snapping and crackling of the hearth fire.

Adrift on the wafting planes of blissful contentment, Damask could do no more than lightly rub Bram's back with a boneless hand before it slid across his heaving ribs. A smile, peaceful and serene, drifted across his lips as Bram caressed her face with the roughened tips of his shaking fingers. "I love you, Damask. Dear God, how I love you," he murmured against the fragile slope of her shoulder.

A smile of tender mischief tugged at the corners of Damask's mouth. "And we love you."

"Ah, lo . . . we?" He climbed on an elbow and rolled her flat on her back. "We?" he asked, his eyes intent on hers.

"A son, Bram. In the spring. A son for Seven Pines."

He stared a moment as though struck dumb, then his smile washed wide with the reckless abandonment to joy he had never allowed himself to feel.

Damask had banished the pain with her gift of love. A gift that betrayed his plans for a dynasty of Raffertys as the hollow dream of a man who dared hope for no more.

Now, he could hope for sons and daughters, not to fulfill his own ambitions or to follow in his footsteps at Seven Pines, but as the living embodiments of his love for their mother. Sons and daughters to cherish and teach. Sons and daughters upon whom he could, at last, lavish all the love that had ached in his heart through his long and lonely years.

This is the special design logo
that will call your attention
to Avon authors who
show exceptional
promise in

THE AVON ROMANCE

the romance
area. Each
month a new novel
will be featured

THE VELVET GLOVE

**An exciting series of contemporary novels
of love with a dangerous stranger.**

Catherine Lanigan
writing as

Joan Wilder

Romancing *The* STONE

87262-5/$2.95
Based on the Screenplay Written by
Diane Thomas

LOVING THE FANTASY

Lost in the steaming Colombian jungle with brutal killers
closing in, she felt like the heroine of one of her romance
novels. Except that romance was the last thing on her
mind...especially with Jack Colton, the bold American
adventurer on whom her life now depended.

But there are certain times, certain places, and nights that
may be the last, when a man and a woman can only be
meant for each other. And suddenly she knew that he was
the right man for her.